By Lee Pini

The Boyfriend Fix
Good at People
Strangers to Husbands
When We Finally Kiss Good Night

Published by DREAMSPINNER PRESS
www.dreamspinnerpress.com

Strangers to Husbands

LEE PINI

Published by

DREAMSPINNER PRESS

8219 Woodville Hwy #1245
Woodville, FL 32362 USA
www.dreamspinnerpress.com

This is a work of fiction. Names, characters, places, and incidents either are the product of author imagination or are used fictitiously, and any resemblance to actual persons, living or dead, business establishments, events, or locales is entirely coincidental.

Trade Paperback ISBN: 978-1-64108-761-2
Digital ISBN: 978-1-64108-760-5
Trade Paperback published July 2024
v. 1.0

To the hopeless romantics.

Chapter One

LEWIS IS drunk off his ass when he decides riding the mechanical bull is an awesome idea. After finding his pockets disappointingly empty of cash, he gets Stacy—also super fucking drunk—to spot him ten bucks.

When he gets back, some guy is handing over a ten to the operator. Lewis leans his elbows on the railing to wait his turn, and the guy looks over and meets his eyes.

Lewis's stomach swoops, and it's not just the six shots of tequila he chased the pitcher of beer with. The guy has this beautiful head of auburn hair, curly and thick, gorgeous cheekbones, longish, pointy nose, a sharp chin, and an even sharper smile. He's T-A-L-L, taller than Lewis, all legs in tight black skinny jeans. Jesus fuck it should be illegal for someone to walk around with a bulge like that.

The guy smiles slowly and says something to the operator, who shrugs and nods. "Wanna join me, cowboy?" Tall, Dark, and Gorgeous drawls to Lewis.

"Um," Lewis says. The guy unsteadily crosses the crash pad to the bull and puts one foot in the stirrup. Lewis's eyes go straight to his ass.

Damn. He is tooootally not a one-night stand kind of guy because he believes in LOVE, that's L-O-V-E Love. Or wait, no? He doesn't, not anymore. Love is dead! Love is dead, so he should blow this guy in the bathroom.

Hot Mystery Man's shimmery black tank pulls taut across his chest. Muscles in his forearm pop as he holds the pommel on the bull's saddle. The divots of his collarbone look like the perfect place for Lewis to put his tongue.

Does he want to join? Um, *yeah* he wants to join. He wants to join so bad he trips over his feet as he stumbles across the crash pad.

"How's that going to work, though?" Like he cares about anything except getting closer to this man.

The guy's gaze travels from Lewis's head to his feet and back up, lingering at his hips, his chest, his shoulders, and his mouth. Heat floods Lewis. His jeans tighten as his cock stirs.

"You'll know what to do once we start." The guy swings into the saddle and pats what little space is left beside him.

Yeah! He will, totally. He will, and—oh shit. Lewis knows he shouldn't ogle but he gets an eyeful of what's between the guy's legs, and. Nnnng. That is. He is. Okay they're in a western bar so the joke is *right there* but—

Okay. Fine. Yeah. The guy is well hung. And Lewis's mouth is literally watering.

If he was sober, he'd wait his turn. But he's not sober. He is not at allll sober. So he climbs on and finds himself basically in his new friend's lap, Lewis facing forward and the man facing backward. The heat of his legs pressing into Lewis's brings the stomach swooping back.

"Shouldn't we face the same way?" Lewis asks.

Up close, he can see Mystery Man's blue eyes and a thick scatter of freckles that start on his cheekbones and spill down his neck. How far down do they go?

The guy's smile gets wicked, and he leans forward. His lips brush Lewis's ear. And then it's all hot breath and gravel as the guy says in a low, dirty voice, "I like to look at men when they're giving me a good, hard ride."

"Fuck," Lewis breathes.

The guy draws back, looking ridiculously pleased with himself. And ridiculously drunk.

Lewis puts his hands on the guy's knees, and at his nod, slides his palms up his thighs to his waist. The man arches into his touch, and his body is warm and firm and Jesus—will Stacy be cool if he bails on the bachelorette party to take this gorgeous man back to his hotel room?

The mechanical bull starts rocking slowly, swinging in a gentle circle, and Lewis absolutely cannot tear his eyes away from the way the man moves. His hips roll, all fluid sex on legs, and one of his arms loops around Lewis's back as he shifts closer. He slides into Lewis's lap, and they're moving against each other, grinding their hips, and Lewis is so hard it hurts.

There's a rope overhead, and the guy pulls himself up with it. Lewis gets a view of his abs and treasure trail, and he wants to put his mouth there and lick and suck his way down, down, down—

His mouth waters. The guy's legs hook around his back, and he rubs his hard cock against Lewis's stomach.

Lewis can't breathe.

There's a shrill whistle and a couple catcalls. Without looking, Lewis knows it's the bachelorette party. A small, slightly more sober part of his mind informs him he's never going to hear the end of this—he's basically fornicating on a mechanical bull in the middle of a honky-tonk during his best friend's bachelorette party.

But as Lewis pushes the guy down to the bull's neck and ghosts his lips over the man's jaw with its prickle of stubble, it's pretty hard to care.

He smells like gin and rose; spice and wood; *sweat*, and Lewis has never wanted to take someone to bed so bad in his entire life.

The bull slows and stops. Lewis is still on top of the man. Their faces are inches apart. The man's freckles are like stars. Lewis's pulse pounds in his fingertips and in his crotch. His skin is on fire.

"Lew!" Stacy yells. "Who's your friend?"

The guy grins, and where before he was all sultry and sexy, now he looks a little shy, a little giddy, like maybe he can't believe he just did that. It's adorable.

Lewis grins back. "I think I should probably ask your name?"

"Tad," the man says, biting his lip and watching Lewis's mouth.

Lewis shifts off him as Stacy's friends keep whooping. "I'm Lewis. And I would really, *really* love to buy you a drink, Tad."

"I would really, really love if you bought me a drink," Tad replies. He slides to the ground and helps Lewis down, and the two of them stumble into each other's arms, crash pad undulating beneath their feet.

Lewis laughs and leans into him, Tad's arm goes around his waist, and before Lewis knows it, they're jammed together at the bar, doing shots. "Aren't you here with someone?" Lewis asks.

"My brother and his friends." Tad flaps a hand. "They're not *here*. I left them at some casino."

"You left them to come ride a mechanical bull?"

"I left them because they're boring."

"What about me? Am I boring?"

Tad's hair falls in curly wisps over his forehead. He has the clearest, prettiest blue eyes Lewis has ever seen. "I don't think you're boring. You're like, the least boring person I've ever met."

Leaning into him, Lewis says in his ear, "I don't think you're boring, either." He trails a finger along the line of freckles on Tad's neck, down to where they disappear under the neckline of his tank. "I like these," he adds, because it seems really important for Tad to know.

"Really?" Tad sounds awed.

"Mm hm." Lewis leans in. It's easy to dip his head to Tad's neck, because Tad is taller than him. He kisses the spot where the freckles spill onto Tad's collarbone and disappear under his clothes.

It's happening, isn't it? Finally. Love at first sight *is* real. Take that, Jonah! And Diego, and Liam, and Jayden, and every other ex-boyfriend who ground him down and made him doubt true love was out there waiting for him. The rom-coms and Disney movies he loves are right, after all! Because his stomach's fluttering and his heart's pounding and every inch of his skin has this buzz pulling him toward Tad.

Sure, Lewis is drunk right now—really, really drunk—but Tad is definitely a person Lewis falls in love-at-first-sight with.

Tequila seems like it will make him fall even more in love with Tad, so he gets another one of those. And so does Tad, and the night turns to a hazy blur of dancing and singing along to Garth Brooks and Dolly Parton and Carrie Underwood. Tad yells to Stacy at one point, "I'm sorry I didn't get you a gift!"

Stacy yells back, "I'm just really happy you're here, Chad!"

"It's Tad!"

Slinging an arm around Lewis's neck, Stacy pulls him in for a sloppy kiss on the cheek and shouts over the music, "Lewis looooooves you, I can tell! Maybe someday you guys will get married! Lewis, I really want us both to be married."

Goddddd Lewis wants to get married so bad. Ahhhh it would be *amazing*. Stace is getting married, which he is like, *so* happy about! They can both be married to the loves of their lives, which Lewis is now like 99 percent sure Tad is. Stacy will marry Alang, and Lewis will marry Tad, and everyone will live happily ever after.

Tad presses into his side. He laughs and nuzzles his face into Lewis's. "We'll have a long engagement."

Which is like the funniest thing Lewis has ever heard, and now he knows he's in love-at-first-sight with Tad.

They leave the bar, and—stuff happens? Stuff must happen, because Lewis is having a blast, he's having so much fun; his hand is in Tad's, he's kissing Tad, and there's champagne. It's the best night Lewis can remember having in forever, even if he already can't remember most of it.

DESERT SUN on his eyelids wakes Lewis. His mouth is gummy, his stomach is sour, and his eyes are sandy. Something is twisted around his legs. Hotel sheets? Hotel sheets. The air conditioner is blowing on him, which is when Lewis realizes he's super naked.

He rolls over, groaning—and discovers he's also super not alone.

But hey, if you're going to wake up in bed with a man you've only known for twelve hours, it might as well be the most beautiful man you've ever seen.

The most beautiful man Lewis has ever seen opens his eyes groggily. His hair is in curly snarls on the pillow. A flash of hot memory scorches through Lewis's body—his fingers twisted in that hair, a warm, wet mouth on his cock.

Mr. Beautiful, He-Of-The-Best-BJ-Lewis-Is-Pretty-Sure-He's-Ever-Had, stretches, and Lewis's eyes track down and back up his body. He's lean and gorgeous, rangy strength, legs for days, *very* nice cock currently providing a nice display of morning wood. The freckles are all over his body. Lewis vaguely remembers trying to kiss all of them before getting distracted by the aforementioned very nice cock.

Lewis hopes his breath isn't toxic. "Hey."

Looking sated and wrecked, Mr. Beautiful says, "Hi."

What are you supposed to say in the morning to the gorgeous guy you drunkenly hooked up with?

"It's Tad, right?"

Which isn't his best effort, but he's rewarded with a bright, beautiful smile. "Yeah. Lewis?"

Well, Lewis doesn't remember a whole lot else about last night, but at least they remember each other's names.

He extends a hand for a handshake. "Lewis Mancini-Sommer."

Tad's smile gets a little crooked and a lot mischievous, and Lewis's heart swoops. "You don't do this very often, do you, Lewis Mancini-Sommer?"

"Dry hump a stranger on a mechanical bull and then hook up with him? Not really."

Tad laughs. It's hoarse, but—it's such a nice laugh. Sounds out of practice. His hand slides into Lewis's and they shake, which is when Lewis realizes there's definitely cum caked in the creases of his palms. Like. Kind of a lot.

"I don't," Lewis says. "I mean, obviously not the mechanical bull stuff. But… yeah, the like, drunk hooking up."

There's a sad little twist to Tad's mouth for a second and he pulls the sheet up to his waist. Maybe Lewis is still drunk, but the sight of Tad being unhappy makes him want to fix it. "Hey, um. Is there, like. Anything you want to… do? Like breakfast? Or, I don't know, coffee?"

Or sex? Because Lewis is leaving Vegas today and obviously never going to see Tad again. So… sex?

Tad's eyes flick to Lewis's. "Can we do each other?" He bites his lip. "Sorry! God. I'm actually usually not like this, like, at all. Slutting it up isn't really my thing. I mean, it's fine if it *is* your thing, like, no slut-shaming! I'm just, like, not that way. Usually. I was last night I guess? Sorry, I just—I was here with my brother and his friends, and they make me feel invisible, and—wow, did I really just ask if you want to fuck and talk about my brother in the same breath…?"

That's a lot of words that Lewis's brain can't really process, not after the ones at the very beginning. "I think we should do each other." He slides a hand over Tad's stomach and up to his chest. His stomach is just defined enough, but still soft. His pecs, on the other hand, are hard and warm, and Lewis has a faint memory of sucking Tad's nipples and him really, *really* liking that.

So he brushes a thumb over one. Tad's eyes close and he breathes in hard, and Lewis rolls on top of him. Tad grabs his hand and brings it to his mouth, then stops. His eyes widen.

"You're married?" he demands.

"What?" Lewis laughs. "Um, no."

Tad jabs a finger at one of Lewis's. "You're wearing a wedding ring. Why would you be wearing a wedding ring if you weren't married?"

"I'm not—" But Lewis's eyes flick to his own hand, and—

He is. He *is* wearing a wedding ring. He's wearing a rose gold band (gay, wow) with a viney, scrolling pattern.

"What the fuck?" Lewis asks, looking at Tad, even though Tad's made it pretty clear the existence of the wedding ring was unknown to him until this moment.

"I don't sleep with married men," Tad says in the same tone you might say *I don't sleep with serial killers.*

"I'm not married!" Lewis repeats. Tad rakes a hand through his hair and starts to get out of bed, but Lewis grabs his wrist. "Um, hey, excuse me, Mr. I-Don't-Sleep-With-Married-Men? What's that on your hand?"

"What's *what* on my—" Tad looks at his left hand. There's a ring there.

Tad stares. "What the hell?"

"Fuck if I know," Lewis says. "I don't know where mine came from, either."

Their eyes meet. Lewis's mouth goes dry, and Tad scooches back into bed with him, holding out his hand until it bumps against Lewis's.

Tad's is also rose gold, with the same pattern of vines and flowers. The rings match.

The rings. Fucking. *Match.*

"Do you remember what we did last night?" Tad asks slowly.

"Well." Lewis looks at him meaningfully. "I remember doing a lot of things."

Tad's face colors. "Before that."

"Um." Lewis is saved from answering by his phone buzzing. He dives for it and opens the text from Stacy.

"Oh," he says. "Fuck."

I found this in my purse??? Stacy's text says. Beneath it is a photo of a marriage certificate. Lewis can only see four pertinent words on it: Lewis Mancini-Sommer… and Thaddeus Pierce.

Chapter Two

"SO... IS sex happening, or...?" is what Tad finally says.

Lewis is on his back, hands over his face. "I can't believe you're thinking about sex when we just found out we got married last night."

"Well," Tad says. And then, "Okay, I can see where it might feel a bit inappropriate."

"A bit?"

"In my defense, I like sex."

"That's not a defense, that's the human condition!"

"And I really liked sex with you," Tad adds.

That shuts Lewis up. He pushes himself upright. Tad looks embarrassed. "I don't do this very often, either," Tad says.

"Marry strangers?" Lewis asks, but his heart is slowing down and his lungs are filling easier. This isn't insurmountable. Divorce is a thing. And this is Vegas—it's probably just as easy to get divorced as it is to get married, right?

Tad wrinkles his nose, and it's very, very cute.

"I feel kind of funny about it," Lewis admits. He can't explain. It just... feels weird. Three minutes ago, this was still a hookup. Now they're going to have to do paperwork and legal stuff, and Lewis feels ill, even though doing legal stuff is his literal job, and he just—it just. Doesn't feel right. "I don't think we should," he says. After a second, he adds, "Sorry."

He rolls out of bed. "I'm going to shower. I'll just be like, five or ten minutes, and then we can figure out what we need to get divorced."

Something flickers across Tad's face, but Lewis refuses to consider that it might be hurt. You don't get hurt about a divorce following a drunken wedding that neither of you remembers.

"I'm guessing we'll have to start with the marriage certificate," Tad says dryly. Maybe Lewis imagined the hurt.

Lewis's head is pounding and standing up makes him feel sicker, but the shower helps. He'd like to stay in longer, but Tad probably wants to get ready. Or maybe they'll go back to his hotel on the way to city hall, or wherever they have to go for the divorce? Are there divorce courts on the strip?

When he steps out of the bathroom, a towel around his waist—he should have brought clothes in—Tad announces from the bed, "We can't get divorced in Nevada."

"Very funny."

"No, seriously!" Tad turns his phone toward Lewis, like he can read it from across the room. "Come here if you don't believe me. Look. 'In order to dissolve a marriage in Nevada, at least one of the spouses must have resided in the state for at least six weeks.'"

"Well, fuck that." Hopefully, Lewis adds, "Any chance you live in Nevada?"

"I'd rather die."

"Okay, well, it would help us out right now if you did."

"Die?"

"No! Live in Nevada!"

"I don't," Tad says, scooting over in bed to make room. Lewis slides in next to him. Their legs press together.

"So where do you live?" Lewis asks.

Tad tucks a piece of hair behind his ear. Lewis's eyes follow the movement. "Manhattan."

"Seriously?"

"Yeah."

"Me too!"

With an incredulous laugh, Tad says, "Really. That's... hm."

Nudging him, Lewis asks, "That's what?"

A smile flits across Tad's face. "Funny? A coincidence? Fate?"

"Not fate," Lewis says. He doesn't do fate anymore. If he keeps believing in fate, he has to acknowledge it has a hate boner for him.

"Fine. I guess we'll get divorced in New York?"

"I guess." Lewis thunks his head against the headboard. Pain ricochets through his skull. Fuck, he needs ibuprofen. "Wait, aren't annulments a thing?"

"I checked that too. We'd have to prove we were so intoxicated that we couldn't give meaningful consent." Tad hesitates. "It's just as easy to get a divorce, I think. Probably easier. Unless you have, uh, religious considerations?"

In another situation, Lewis might laugh about the idea of him being religious enough to care about having a marriage on his spiritual record. "No, that doesn't matter. I just want to do whatever's easiest. I can't believe I got *drunk married*. And I don't even remember it."

"I'm sure it was lovely," Tad says. "Maybe your friend Stacy took pictures?"

"I can't believe I came to Vegas for my best friend's bachelorette party and *I* got married."

"Hey. It's okay." Tad brushes Lewis's hair off his face, which feels intimate. And inappropriate. Because they might be married, and sure, they fucked last night, but they don't know each other.

Not that Lewis moves away. He likes the feel of Tad's fingers in his hair.

Tad stuffs his hand back along his side. "It's not the worst thing two people have ever done. I don't remember the wedding, but I remember the sex. It was good."

"It was," Lewis admits. Certain parts of him are regretting that he nixed a round two. Or possibly a much higher number.

If it weren't for the Dating Break....

Ugh. But no. In an alternate universe, this is the start of something. An alternate universe where Lewis hasn't spent the last ten years dating all the wrong men. An alternate universe where he isn't a sucker who got cheated on.

He scrubs a hand over his face. "Okay, let me think. First things first, we need the marriage certificate. I'll get that from Stace, if you wanna stay here and figure out what we need to do to get divorced."

Tad wrinkles his nose. "So I don't get to meet your friend? Even though we're married?"

"You met her last night," Lewis points out. "And we're not married for real."

"The state of Nevada disagrees."

Ugh.

Lewis drags himself up to get dressed. Tad grabs his phone. "You can use the shower," Lewis says.

Tad glances up. "Thanks."

Lewis doesn't move. It's hard to stop looking at Tad, sprawled on the bed. He really is beautiful. Beautiful and funny and *fun*.

But the Dating Break is in effect for good reason. Lewis has a decade of relationships that have ranged from meh to bad to prove that he sucks at choosing boyfriends. Getting so wasted that he can't remember marrying someone is just another tick in the Lewis Sucks At This column.

"Okay," Lewis says. "So, I'll see you soon."

"Mm hm."

Lewis wets his lips and opens his mouth to say something—he just doesn't know what. "Okay," he says again and lets himself out.

"THIS IS a look," Lewis says.

Stacy's blond hair is somehow both clumpy and frizzy, and it's also about three times the size of her head. She's still in her pajamas, and she also still smells like tequila. "I hate how put together you are right now," she says. Her voice sounds raw.

Lewis is only put together in comparison to her, but he's not arguing. "Can I have the thing?"

Putting her hands on her hips, Stacy says, "Lewis Stephen Mancini-Sommer, how dare you refer to your marriage certificate like that on the weekend of my bachelorette party?"

"First of all, it's just a piece of paper, second of all, it doesn't even count, and third of all, you can't go all rom-com with my life anymore." He peers around her into the room. "Where is it?"

Stace has that *look* on her face she gets when she's revving up to Full Romance Mode. "This is the best bachelorette party ever. My maid of honor found love!"

Trying to sidle past her, Lewis says, "Pretty sure hooking up doesn't count as finding love."

Not to be deterred—or pushed past—Stacy says, "It could. Plenty of people get married to a hookup. That's how Alang and I met."

"Alang and you are different," Lewis says. "You were both ready to give up on dating apps and swiped right one more time, and you both only did it because your BFFs told you to give this one last person a shot."

A disgustingly happy smile settles on Stacy's face. "I know. It's fate!"

That's the annoying part. Or it would be, if Lewis wasn't genuinely thrilled for his BFF. They used to go out and commiserate over how unlucky in love they both were. Then Stacy met Alang, and Lewis thought it meant he was finally going to find The One. Instead, he had more of the same shit relationships that peaked—or valleyed?—with Jonah, who stole his Pride Chucks after cheating on him with a guy from the gym.

"Tell me all about Thaddeus," Stacy says.

"He goes by Tad, and that's pretty much all I know about him."

"Lewwwwis," Stacy says. "Come onnnn. How was the sex?"

"None of your business."

She covers her mouth with a hand. "Oh my god, was it bad? Did you have whiskey dick? Did you come too fast?"

"Can you just let me in so I can get the thing?" Lewis demands.

"Did *he* come too fast?"

When he gives her The Look, she holds out her pinkie finger. "Remember the pact."

"We agreed the pact was nullified once you and Alang got serious."

She pouts. "Don't use lawyer words. Anyway, you're not serious about Tad."

"Can you just give me the piece of paper? We need it to get divorced."

Stacy's arm shoots out to block the door even more. Lewis isn't going to push past her—this isn't sixth grade and shoving each other to get to the good N64 controller first in Lewis's basement. "*Divorced?*"

"Um, yeah." Lewis gives her an incredulous look. "We don't know each other?"

"You could try to make it work!"

"Stace. You're clearly still drunk." Maybe he can duck under her arm? "You got your rom-com moment. It's not gonna happen for me. It's definitely not happening right now. Tad and I made a mistake. We're going to fix it."

Her eyes get big and honestly, he's too hungover to head her off. "Lewis, this is your fight against Fox Books. It's your working at the L fare token booth. It's your fake friendship with the prince of England."

"Do you have a point or are you just listing rom-com premises?" Lewis asks.

She purses her lips. "My point is that you're in your dark before the dawn, and you're going to meet the love of your life. And what if it's Tad?"

"I'll keep that in mind."

"You can meditate over it on your retreat," Stacy says triumphantly.

"Sure." Lewis folds his arms over his chest and stares her down.

Finally, she sighs and goes to retrieve the marriage certificate. It's creased but otherwise unscathed. Good. It would be just his luck if the thing was drenched with barbecue sauce and tequila, and no court would accept it because of that.

As she hands it over, she says, "I'd say congratulations, but you don't deserve it. Where's the Lewis who I cried with over *Love, Actually* and *How to Lose a Guy in 10 Days*?"

Lewis checks the marriage certificate again to make sure it's the authentic article, like it may have magically become a takeout menu in the last five seconds. "He realized life isn't a fairy tale when he got cheated on and his gayest shoes got stolen." He gives her a kiss on the forehead. "Limo will be here at eleven. See you then."

As he walks away, she lets out a squeal that echoes down the hallway. "Lewis!! What if this is your *What Happens in Vegas*?"

Chapter Three

TAD IS dressed when Lewis gets back. He's wearing the same spangly black tank and black jeans from last night—obviously—but his hair is damp, so he must have showered. In the morning light, there's more red in Tad's hair than Lewis realized—hints of burnished copper that catch the sun in a way Lewis has trouble looking away from.

Clearing his throat, Lewis holds up the marriage certificate. "I got it. What did you find out?"

Tad rubs his hair, and there's just enough length that it tousles, sticking together because it's still wet.

Somehow, he's even more attractive in the sober, hungover morning light than he was through a curtain of alcohol.

It's not a helpful thought.

"Technically we don't meet the requirements for a divorce in New York," Tad says. "The closest is the irreparable breakdown of the relationship."

"We could use that."

"For six months or more."

"Uggghh." Lewis sags onto the bed. Tad's expression is hard to read. "So we have to stay married for six months?"

His brain can't process this. His hangover has hit that point where it stops getting better, and you know you're just going to have to live with it until you can take more painkillers. And his chest is getting tighter and it's getting harder to breathe. And he doesn't want to have an anxiety attack right now, he really doesn't, but he doesn't think he can head it off.

"What a fucking mess," he says, squeezing his eyes shut.

The bed depresses as Tad sits. Lewis's body buzzes with the nearness.

"We don't have to act married," Tad says. "It's not a big deal. We'll just live our lives, and in six months, we'll do the paperwork."

His tone is so calm. Lewis's chest loosens.

There's a little smile on Tad's face, and it gives Lewis butterflies.

"We can even start the paperwork right away when we get back, if it would make you feel better," Tad says. He rubs his wet curls. There's a shyness to the gesture, which is funny, considering… well, everything. Drunk Tad wasn't shy, which Lewis liked. But Lewis likes this kind of shy version of Tad too. "I'm flying back in a couple days, so if you want to meet for coffee or something…."

"I'm actually not heading home for another week," Lewis says. "But yeah, once I'm back, let's do that. Sorry, it probably sounds stupid, but it really would make me feel better."

"It doesn't sound stupid." Tad tilts his head. "I wouldn't suggest it if I thought it was stupid."

Well, plenty of Lewis's exes thought his anxieties were stupid. He's been called a control freak more times than he can count. He's not a control freak, he just… he feels better if he knows how things are going to go. He doesn't like surprises.

Lewis clears his throat. "Well, yeah. If you give me your number, I'll text you when I'm back."

They exchange phones to enter their contact details. Once Tad's done, Lewis opens his contacts. It takes a second of scrolling—once all the way down to the Ts, once back up to the top, and then a slower trawl until he spots the new name.

Best Husband Ever

Lewis glances up. Tad looks unsure, but there's a twitch to one side of his lips and a spark of mischief in his eyes. For a second, Lewis gets caught up staring at Tad's eyelashes. They're brown and longish for a guy, and they make the blue of his eyes so intense that Lewis's breath catches.

"I just put my name into yours. You're making me look like a bad husband," Lewis says.

What is he doing? Is he flirting? Is he flirting with the guy with whom he's currently planning his divorce?

Tad laughs. Butterflies again.

They look at each other and things swing into awkward. "So… yeah." Lewis checks his phone. The limo won't be here for another hour, but he should round up the bachelorette party.

Tad's fingers fiddle with the seam of his jeans. They're so long and graceful. And strong. And Lewis gets a flash of memory—Tad's fingers gripping his cock, stroking him as the two of them made out against the wall—

Heat floods him. Is he embarrassed or turned on? Or—okay, both, but he's not sure what he's more of. Or if it matters. It's a thing in the past, a thing they did, that they aren't doing again.

He definitely needs to find something else to do before he finds a reason to get Tad's fingers on him again, because the longer they're in the same room together, the more Lewis wonders what the big deal about fucking one more time is, even though he was the one that said they couldn't in the first place.

"I have to go do maid-of-honor stuff," he says in a rush. "So, um. I guess I'll see you in New York. Or, we don't have to see each other. You can just email the paperwork. Or whatever."

Smooth.

"Oh!" Tad looks mortified. "Sorry, I didn't know you had stuff to do. Yeah, I'll...." He pauses. "You'll text me, right?"

There's not much choice, is there? "Yeah. Next week. As soon as I get back. I promise."

Tad nods and takes a step toward the door. He's biting his lip, not in a sexy way, but in this nervous way that Lewis, unfortunately, finds completely and utterly charming. What's wrong with him? He's been doing really good with not being tempted by cute guys since the Dating Break began. He's been doing so good that he wasn't even worried about being in Vegas, surrounded by temptation.

Alcohol and post-orgasm hormones, that's what's wrong with him. The alcohol made him disregard the Dating Break, and post-orgasm hormones are making him all moony over Tad, making him think he's adorable and beautiful and all that stuff.

"Are you going to be in Vegas for the next week?" Tad asks. "Because I'm here for a few more days, and if you wanted to hang out...?"

Lewis's heart lurches. He can't tell if it's because he wants to say no—or desperately wants to say yes. "I'm not," he says. "Going to be in Vegas, I mean. I have this thing planned. Stacy thinks I'm going on a chakra cleanse. Or a vortex detox. Whatever, I don't know. I just agreed I'd do it because she thinks it'll make me a better maid of honor."

At least she's her typical lovable self about it, but Stacy has definitely bought into the entire wedding-industrial complex. Her wedding is going to be P E R F E C T, and she has Ideas about how to make that happen.

When Tad stares at him blankly, Lewis can only shrug. "She read something on a wedding blog about how your wedding party has to bring the right energy to the event… I don't know. She's my best friend, so I'll do what she wants me to do."

"Except you said Stacy thinks you're going," Tad points out.

"Oh." Lewis rubs the back of his neck. "Yeah, I'm actually going backpacking in Humboldt-Toiyabe National Forest. I'm pretty sure she won't be able to tell the difference in my energy."

Tad laughs. "Unless you're giving off 'liar' energy."

"Her last dress fitting went three hours too long and she didn't notice that my energy was *I'm so hungry I'm about to eat the nearest A-line gown*, so I think I can sell it."

"So you're going backpacking with one of your friends from the party?" Tad asks.

Shaking his head, Lewis says, "No, I'm going alone."

His face lighting up, Tad says, "Oh! You must camp a lot!"

Excitement about his big adventure floods Lewis suddenly. City kid disconnects from the hustle and reconnects with what matters. Or something. Maybe he'll start a blog. "Nope, I've never camped before. Or done much hiking, but I always wanted to."

Tad looks at him like he's grown several extra heads. "You… what? You're not a hiker, you've never camped, and you're going backpacking in Humboldt-Toiyabe alone? Are you nuts?"

"Well, I can't go with Stace. Then she'll know I'm not flushing my chakra." He shrugs. "And I don't have anyone else to go with. Ava has to get back, and I'm not super close with the rest of the wedding party."

"I'm not sure it's really like a juice cleanse but putting that aside, yes you do." Tad holds up his hand and wiggles his fingers. His ring glints. "As your husband, I'd be delighted to accompany you."

Lewis laughs, because obviously Tad is joking. When Tad doesn't laugh back, Lewis's smile fades.

Oh. Tad is serious.

"No," Lewis says. "That's okay. I can't ask you to do that."

"You didn't ask me," Tad says. "I offered."

"Why?"

"Because I don't want to be a widower."

Wow. Okay. Obviously hiking can be dangerous, but Lewis has watched a ton of YouTube videos and read a bunch of blogs. "I'm sure you have, like, a job to get back to. Anyway, aren't you here with your brother?"

With a shrug, Tad says, "I have plenty of time off. And my brother won't even notice I'm not there."

"I'm sure that's not true."

Tad's lips thin as he presses them together. Something sharp and sad ripples over his face. "If you really don't want me to come along, I won't. But you shouldn't backpack by yourself. It's stupid."

Lewis snorts. "Tell me what you really think."

Tad's lips stay thinned. "You know people die when they backpack alone, right? You want me to google it?"

"Please don't." Lewis has googled it, and he's confident he'll be fine. He did his research. He has a first aid kit and knows where to find water.

But. The idea of spending a week with Tad is… really nice.

Impulse control? Don't know her.

"Well…." Lewis looks at Tad's eyes again. And his long, straight nose and his cheekbones and his stubbly jaw. And his damp hair, drying into curls on his neck. "If you want to come, I guess… yeah. That would be…." *Wonderful. A terrible idea. Amazing. Probably more than I can take.* "That would be cool."

"We'll call it our honeymoon," Tad says with a shit-eating grin.

That makes Lewis tense up. "Can you just not? It's not a real marriage."

Chagrin crashes down on Tad's face. "Sorry. I was just—bad joke. Sorry." He twists his wedding ring. "I have to get some stuff. For camping. If you really want me to come."

Oh god, Tad's offering an out, and Lewis is already so all-in on this idea that he's not taking it. "Yeah, of course. Do you want the list I used to pack? I marked off all the stuff I already have. I can text it to you."

"That's okay. What time are you leaving?"

"I'm picking my rental car up at two."

"I'll be in the lobby downstairs at one, then." Tad twists his ring again. "So. Yeah. See you later." He's out the door before Lewis can respond. Why didn't Tad take off his ring?

Lewis touches the matching ring on his hand and thinks about removing it. In the end, he leaves it where it is.

Chapter Four

TAD NEEDS a sleeping bag.

He has a sleeping bag, of course, shoved in a closet in his Inwood apartment—upcycled materials, mummy shape, rated down to fifteen degrees, green lichen colored, AKA green. That one isn't doing him any good right here, now, in Las Vegas, where he's about to leave on a camping trip.

He's eyeing the vaguely rainbow one. The temperature rating is good—Humboldt-Toiyabe can be cold in November—but it's big and rectangular and not great for backpacking. He should get the one he already has, even if it's boring.

The problem is, two people won't fit inside the one he should get.

Tad's head spins. He's still pretty hungover. He shouldn't be thinking about fitting inside a sleeping bag with Lewis, because Lewis made it clear sex, let alone a relationship, is off the table.

It's just. He remembers cuddling last night, Lewis's strong arms around him as they passed out.

Not that a relationship should be on the table for Tad, either. Not when his boyfriend would have to go back into the closet around Tad's family. *I can't live with you constantly saying you'll come out when you're ready*, John said during that last sad, horrible conversation. *You're letting both of us down.*

The band around Tad's head tightens. Note to self: thinking about ex is bad for hangover.

Last night when he left the casino, he sat for a while in the Bellagio's garden, enjoying the peace plants bring him. But a woman started chatting with him, and he couldn't make himself chat back because, well, that's how he is.

As he walked back to his hotel, he saw a man with messy brown hair and a smile like a flower opening to the sun. He saw that man go into a honky-tonk bar with a group of women. And he thought... well, he didn't actually think. He just followed. Drank. Didn't have the guts to talk to Handsome, who was clearly there for a party with his friends. Nothing new there—Tad's pathological shyness is especially bad around men he wants. So he drank some more.

Until he encountered Handsome at the mechanical bull. Like kismet. Thought, fuck it. He had enough liquid courage by that point to slut it up.

Tent. Camping. He needs to buy supplies. And tell Walter he's not flying home in two days, and change his plane ticket, and text his boss. He needs to come up with a reason he's changing his plans that isn't *I'm going on a camping trip with a dude I drunk married last night.*

He needs to buy the sleeping bag that makes sense, but he pulls a card off the shelf for the bigger, rainbow one. Fuck it. He's already used to disappointing everyone, might as well disappoint himself with his own bad choices too.

"YOU'RE WHAT?"

"Staying here for another week," Tad repeats. "I'm going to check out some of the hiking."

His brother looks at him in consternation and confusion. They have the same blue eyes and freckles, but that's where the resemblance ends. Where Tad is tall and lean, Walter is shorter and bulkier. He was a defensive end on their high school's football team, because of course he was. Tad was the tongue-tied freak trying not to get cyberbullied and/or beat up, because… of course he was. Walt's hair is sandier, though it still has that hint of red.

Tad never even wanted to come to Vegas with Walt. But Walt wouldn't let up, bombarding Tad with texts and calls and Facetimes, and finally Tad agreed just to shut him up. But he was actually looking forward to spending time with Walt. He thought… who knows what he thought. That maybe it would be like when they were kids, and they were close. Then Walt invited his friends—his high school friends, a bunch of dudebros who never left Watertown, New York—and the prospect of spending time with them turned Tad's stomach.

Walt's eyes rove over the collection of camping stuff Tad carted up to the room. One bag is still clutched in Tad's left hand to keep the ring hidden. He should have taken it off.

The hotel is right across the street from Lewis's. Tad's mind wanders to Lewis. Is he freaking out? Or is he doing whatever he was supposed to do this morning and not thinking about Tad at all?

"Does this have something to do with where you went last night?" Walt asks.

Tad shrugs. Walt waits. Clearing his throat, Tad says, "I didn't think you noticed I was gone."

"I texted!"

Twice. And the first one barely counts because it was just a meme.

"I guess."

"Is it a plant thing?" Walt says.

Tad hunts for contempt in Walt's voice. He's sure it's there, but Walt's keeping it low-key. It's still annoying to have his passion—and career—referred to as a "plant thing."

Maybe he should go with it. Just agree it's a plant thing so he can ditch his stuff and go across the street to wait for Lewis.

Before he can open his mouth, Walt's eyes widen. "Oh shit. Did you hook up?"

Tad's guts shrivel so fast and hard, his ribs feel bruised from the recoil. Oh god no this wasn't how Tad wanted to come out to his brother, what's he going to do, Tad really needs him to bring his stuff back to New York and if Walt's going to rage at him for being gay—

"You did!"

His mouth bone-dry, Tad rasps, "Walt—look, I don't know what you think you saw—"

Walt's hand comes down on Tad's shoulder, giving it a few bro-y slaps. "Good for you, man. Does she like plants too?"

"Um," Tad says.

Grinning, Walt says, "I was starting to think you were gay! You haven't talked about any girls besides Sydney Clark when you were in—what, tenth grade?"

"Ninth," Tad says. Right, his *maybe if I hook up with a girl, that will prove I'm actually straight* phase. When he made out with Sydney in her bedroom, she stuck her hand down his pants and found him flaccid. Mortified—and freaking out—he ran to the bathroom, only to walk in on her older brother stepping out of the shower.

And, uh, yeah. That did for his teenage dick what no amount of making out with a girl could seem to.

He forces himself to relax. Walt didn't see anything. Walt has no idea Tad spent last night fucking another man.

"Glad you got some action." Walt grins.

"Um, yeah." Tad squirms. "I better go. I'll pick my bag up when I get back, okay?"

Walt's broad grin makes Tad want to flee. "Is she hot?"

An image of how Lewis looked this morning, naked and sex-tousled, sheets tangled around his legs and his lips still swollen from last night, burns through Tad. His gorgeous eyes—calling them brown doesn't do them justice, because they remind him of the inside of a tree, all those rich, earthy umbers fading from one shade to another. That stubble on his face and the dark hair on his chest. Pert little nipples, the V-cut that Tad distinctly remembers licking.

"Um," Tad says.

Which apparently answers Walt's question. Walt claps him on the shoulder again. "The guys are gonna love it. We'll have a drink or five for you."

"Great." Tad gathers his camping supplies and backs out of the room. "And my stuff…?"

"Yeah, I'll bring it back. When you pick it up, you can tell me all about your camping-slash-sex trip."

This is fine. It's fine. Just a little white lie. It's not like Tad hasn't been lying by omission for years.

He gets to the door and thinks he's home free when Walt says, "Hey, Tad—what's her name?"

Tad blanks. "Lew…." He says, because his brain is coming up empty. Wait! Inspiration. "Louise," he says.

Yeah, he's pretty smart. Go him.

On that note, and before Walt asks Tad to describe the super hot, definitely-a-woman-Louise, Tad heaves his stuff out the door. It's just after eleven, which means he's going to be sitting in the hotel lobby for two hours, but he doesn't care. He'd rather do that than spend another second getting interrogated by his brother—who looked heartbreakingly relieved when Tad said he had sex with a woman.

Chapter Five

STACY'S FRIENDS are in various stages of hungover, but a few remember the wedding.

"Think you'll stay married?" asks Ava, sipping Powerade as they stand in the shade outside the hotel. The limo's already here and about three-quarters of the party is inside. Stacy's still in the hotel lobby. Out of everyone there, Ava is an actual *friend* friend. She was Stacy's college roommate, and Lewis was glad she came to Vegas. She's shy in groups, and he knew she was nervous about the trip.

Even though his hands are sweating from the heat, Lewis jams them in his pockets as he shrugs. Then he realizes a shrug wasn't an appropriate response. "No. We're getting a divorce. Obviously."

Behind her giant sunglasses, Ava's eyebrows go up. "Hope you didn't tell Stacy that."

"Yeah, I may have made that mistake."

Ava sighs and shakes her head. "Oh, Lewis. You're supposed to be the one she counts on for the romance in life. Don't be jaded and cynical like me."

What does Ava have to be jaded and cynical about? She's happily married and lives with her wife in a cool brownstone in Bushwick. They have two rescue dogs.

"I'm not the gay best friend in a nineties rom-com," he says. "I can be cynical if I want."

"I think you and Tad make a cute couple."

Lewis doesn't know what to say, so he doesn't say anything. In the limo—which is one of those horrible Hummer limos—there's already some day drinking going on. If Stacy doesn't hurry, they're going to get hangovers from their hangover cure.

Finally, Ava says, "You're all about the meet-cute, right? That was a pretty good meet-cute."

"I'm re-branding." Lewis peers into the lobby through the automatic glass doors. Two of the missing bachelorette party walk outside and make for the limo. Every time those doors open, a blast of arctic air pours out. It's a colossal waste of electricity and makes Lewis, who's a paralegal at an environmental law firm, grit his teeth.

"Because of Diego? Oh, or what was his name? Liam? Wait no, Jayden? Which was the one who stole your shoes?"

"Jonah," Lewis says, wishing Ava couldn't rattle off his last four romantic train wrecks so easily. "And yes."

Ava takes another swig of Powerade. "You haven't had the greatest luck in the romance department. Maybe you should just hang onto this one, since you're already married?"

"I'm going to check on Stacy," Lewis says.

Ava looks embarrassed. "Sorry, bad joke."

At the end of the day, he'll cut her some slack, because this entire weekend has been uncomfortable for her and she's on edge. But for now he walks away, looking for Stacy—who's nowhere to be seen.

Lewis spots her. She's talking to someone sitting behind a palm tree, but Lewis doesn't think it's any of the bachelorette party, because by his count they're all outside.

Lewis rounds the palm, saying, "Stace, you have to get going, you're gonna be la—"

Tad is there. Stacy's talking to *Tad*. Tad, who's surrounded by stuff. A backpack, a sleeping bag, several full plastic bags.

"Lewis, look who's here!" Stacy says, beaming.

"Yeah," Lewis says weakly. He really hopes Tad didn't say anything about the camping trip. "Listen, you really need to go. You don't want to miss your flight."

Stacy's hair is in a messy ponytail and she's wearing a bralette over a waffle crop top with fuchsia leggings, and somehow rocking the whole thing. She looks more fashionable than Lewis does in his jeans and rumpled T-shirt.

Either Tad went back to his hotel to change or he bought clothes wherever he bought the rest of this stuff, because he's not wearing last night's skintight black jeans or shimmery tank. Instead, he's in bootleg-cut jeans and a white tee. There's a blue New York Botanical Garden baseball cap on his head. Cowlicks and curls of hair peek out from beneath it, which is sort of a sucker punch and totally not fair.

"Did you know Tad lives in New York?" Stacy asks accusingly, like Lewis was intentionally and maliciously keeping this information from her.

Like. He *was*. But she still doesn't have to act like she knew it.

Tad's giving him this wide-eyed look that seems legitimately worried. "Yeah, we talked about it," Lewis says.

"I invited him to the wedding!" Stacy says.

Lewis grits his teeth. It's her wedding. It's entirely her prerogative who she wants to invite. Maybe Tad won't go, anyway.

"Thanks for the invite," Tad says softly.

"I mean, you married my best friend, and I was there." She scrunches her face like she always does when she's trying to remember something. "At least, according to my phone I was there. Lew, I didn't show you the pictures!"

"Oh good, you took pictures," Lewis says woodenly.

She's swiping through her photos when Ava yells from the door, "Hey, guys? Driver says we've gotta go now if we don't want to miss our flight?"

Stacy chucks her phone in her bag. "I'll send them to you." She throws her arms around him. "Thank you for the best bachelorette party ever! Have the best time at the chakra cleanse!"

Are you supposed to have a good time at a chakra cleanse? "You're welcome, and I will. My chakras are going to be so clean, you'll be able to lick them."

"I'll leave that to Tad," she chirps, bouncing out of reach when Lewis takes a playful swipe at her.

"You're gross," he informs her. "Have a good flight, I love you, call me when you land." It's been their catch-all farewell for years, flight or not.

"Love you too!" she calls before grabbing her roller bag and dashing for the door.

Which leaves Lewis alone with Tad.

"You said you'd be back at one," Lewis says.

Tad shrugs. "There's a Dick's Sporting Goods on the Strip."

Something clicks. "Wait. You offered to go camping with me, but you had to buy a bunch of camping stuff?"

Tad stands. His height is still a turn-on—at least three inches taller than Lewis, and where the all-black ensemble from last night made him look slender, the white tee and jeans make him look like there's more to him.

That's also a turn-on.

"I didn't come down here to go camping, so yeah, I had to buy new camping stuff," Tad says like it's not a big deal. "I assumed you had a tent. I guess I also assumed it's a tent that will fit more than one person. Or"—mortification flashes over his face—"maybe you weren't planning on sleeping in the same tent."

This is all like, a lot for Lewis. "Why would you...." He trails off. "Yeah, I have a tent. And I'm... pretty sure it fits more than one person? I ordered it from REI...."

He looks hopefully at Tad, as though Tad is A) an expert on camping gear, and B) familiar with every tent REI sells.

"Is it a dome tent? That would be okay, but it's better if you have a backpacking tent."

"Um." These terms seem vaguely familiar, but Lewis can't remember what he ended up buying. "It's lightweight. And it fits in my backpack."

Tad makes a considering noise but seems satisfied. "That's the important thing."

Is Tad an expert on camping gear? Lewis figured he volunteered to come along because he was legitimately—maybe understandably—concerned about Lewis dying. Does Tad actually enjoy camping?

There's still a shadow of stubble on Tad's chin. Lewis's skin tingles with remembered sensation. It takes more effort than it should to not reach up and scrape his palm along Tad's jaw.

"You probably have things to do," Tad says. He waves a hand at his collection of stuff. "I have to pack all this, anyway."

"No, it's cool," Lewis hears himself saying. "I'll help you. Just let me grab my backpack from bell services."

It's cool. I told you I wouldn't fuck you again because we don't know each other, and now I'm doing everything I can to get to know you.

He should've just told the truth, which is that he's not a casual sex guy, and he's not looking for sex that's more than casual. But god, he didn't think they'd see each other more than necessary.

He retrieves his backpack, which feels heavier than when he packed it. When he gets back, Tad has everything out of the bags and arranged around himself. Lewis heaves his backpack to the gleaming tile floor and plops down on the bench. His knee accidentally bumps Tad's shoulder and he jerks back. Tad doesn't seem to notice, which is just as well. Maybe all that awkwardness in the hotel room earlier has evaporated under the unforgiving Vegas sun and the constant blast of air-conditioning. Maybe they can just be whatever two people in a weird situation should be.

What that is, Lewis has no idea. But as he watches Tad efficiently pack all his supplies, he realizes he's glad he's not going on this trip alone.

"Do you like camping?" Lewis asks.

"Yeah. I go a few times a year, usually just for the weekend."

"Alone?"

"Uh-huh." He deftly stashes water bottles throughout the backpack.

"I should carry some of those," Lewis says, watching the water bottles disappear. "That's too heavy for you."

Tad swivels at the waist and plants a hand on the floor. Involuntarily, Lewis's eyes sweep the long line of his body, a graceful curve from his head to his hips. "Be my guest," he says, tossing Lewis the water bottle. Lewis fumbles to catch it but hauls it in. Tad looks charmed.

"I got a water treatment kit in case we need a spare," Tad says.

"Oh! I have one of those." Lewis resists the urge to puff out his chest at this achievement. Yeah, look at him, he may have learned everything he knows from the internet, but he's not a total lost cause.

"I figured you did," Tad says, but Lewis is pretty sure that's bullshit. He's pretty sure Tad bought the water treatment kit because he thought Lewis was totally incompetent. Which should get his hackles up. Lewis hates it when people think he doesn't know what he's doing. It *would* get his hackles up, but there's something about Tad that makes it impossible. Maybe it's his smile.

Packing is clearly A Process for Tad, but he's fast. It's obvious, watching him, that he's done this before and he has a method. When he's done, he looks up at Lewis. Him being on the floor and Lewis sitting above him is reminiscent enough of a position they spent time in last night that Lewis's jeans get a little tight.

He shifts, crosses one leg over the other, and then just stands up. "We can see if my car's ready, if you're finished packing."

"Won't you get charged more if you pick it up early?"

Lewis shrugs. "It's okay." He picks up his backpack. "Ready?"

Tad nods and stands. Well, at least one of them is ready, because it sure as hell isn't Lewis.

Chapter Six

TAD'S GLAD he isn't driving. He hates driving. It sucks in New York, but that's like saying water is wet. It seems to suck here too. Traffic, tourists, and interminable stretches of asphalt. Yuck.

The fact that he's getting outside and camping is salvaging the whole trip. There were three gardens he wanted to see in Vegas, but he only made it to two. One was in the Bellagio, and the other was a cactus garden at a chocolate factory. The only reason he convinced Walt to make the drive was by promising to buy everyone chocolate.

His manager, Callie, texted him back while they were at the Hertz office with enthusiastic support for the unplanned extension of his vacation, informing him that she'd be thrilled to spend an extra week taking care of Hetty (his cat) and all his plants.

They're outside Vegas on 95, all wide-open vistas and asphalt snaking to the horizon. Scrubby bushes and cacti dot the flat, dusty ground. Tad sneaks a look at Lewis. A hot flutter in his stomach makes him look longer than he means to. It's hard not to, because Lewis is really a magnificent specimen. Those shoulders, those *arms*. The soft fall of brown hair over his forehead. That strong jaw, currently covered in stubble.

Lewis laughs out of nowhere, and Tad's first thought is to wonder what dumb thing he did to provoke the amusement. But Lewis says, "I can't believe we're doing this. This is crazy."

He has a really nice laugh. Of course he does. Nice, solid baritone. Tad stretches, not realizing until he does it that he was trying to take up as little space as possible. His shirt rides up and he tugs it down. Lewis's eyes seem magnetically drawn to the exposed skin. Tad's neck heats in self-conscious pleasure.

"Add it to the list of crazy things we've done over the last twenty-four hours, I guess?" Tad says, hoping Lewis isn't going to get weird again. It's strange, because Tad would never ever in a million years think he would be the one who was cool with this situation—he's too shy to use Grindr, for god's sake, and he needs to be four drinks in before he'll flirt with a guy. But he kept waiting for his crushing shyness to reassert itself this morning, and it just... didn't.

"I guess," Lewis snorts. "I'm so not a crazy person. I've never thought about riding a mechanical bull once in my whole life. And suddenly last night I was like, I *have* to."

A smile sneaks onto Tad's face. "You were a natural." Like Tad's ever ridden a mechanical bull.

Tad stares at Lewis's fingers wrapped around the steering wheel. He has nice hands. Kind of knobbly knuckles. They have personality. The bones sketch from wrist to knuckle, veins snaking over the top, and Tad's stomach hurts with a sudden and intense need to kiss them.

"So you're like, a mechanical bull aficionado?" Lewis asks.

"Oh yeah, totally. That's what I do, you know. I go around to all the mechanical bulls in the country and rate them. I have a TikTok—just-the-mechanics-no-bull."

Lewis guffaws. Tad bites the inside of his cheek to keep from laughing. When he stays silent, Lewis looks at him, worry creeping over his face. "Oh, do you... that's your job? Or like... you make money doing that?"

Tad's composure cracks and he laughs. "No. Sorry, I couldn't resist."

"Did you make up that TikTok handle on the spot?"

"Yeah."

The look Lewis darts at him is sort of... enraptured? But he shifts his eyes back to the road quickly. "So you're not a mechanical bull reviewer. What do you do?"

Oh good, they're talking about work now. Tad should've stuck with the mechanical bull TikToker story. "I'm an editor for a botany magazine."

"Really?"

Now he's the gay who cried wolf. "Really. You know in magazines how there are the regular columns before the feature articles?"

"Sure."

"I manage those."

"That's cool," Lewis says. Weirdly, he sounds like he means it. Tad's used to people glazing over when they hear *botany*. "What's it called?"

"You've probably never heard of it."

"Maybe I want to pick up a copy."

Tad has to look out the window at the passing scenery because no one, ever, has said that before. The most common responses he gets are: *Botany, that's plants, right? Are any of the letters to the editor real? And Do you want to write an article about my garden?*

Incidentally, he's never wanted to write an article about anyone's garden.

"Sorry, is that creepy?" Lewis says.

Tad lets out a breath of laughter and turns to look at Lewis again. "No. It's nice."

"Oh." Is Lewis blushing? "I'm just curious."

Okay, now it's moved beyond nice, straight to sweet. "*Hudson Valley Botanists*," Tad says. "Like I said, it's small. We do quarterly publications, three digital, and then one print. We just finished our fourth quarter issue—the holiday one—that's why I could take more time off with no notice."

Lewis's eyes keep darting from the road to Tad. "That's really cool."

The great contradiction of low self-esteem is hungering for compliments, for someone to notice something good about you, and not believing it when one comes your way. "It's a job. It's not really that cool."

"Well, I think it is," Lewis says.

The compliment makes Tad's brain error 404. "What do you do?" he asks.

"I'm a paralegal. I work at an environmental law firm."

"Sounds interesting."

"It can be. Sometimes I feel like I'm doing some good in the world. And it pays the bills."

"And for your burgeoning mechanical bull obsession?" Tad says innocently.

Lewis snorts. "And that."

They pass a mileage sign and Lewis exclaims, "Tonopah! That's where we get off for the park, right?"

Tad unlocks his phone to check the route again. "Yep."

"A hundred and seventy-five miles? So what's that, like…." Lewis's forehead crinkles in thought. "Maybe another two and a half hours?"

With a glance at the clock, which reads 2:32, Tad says, "Sure, but you know the sun sets at like, four-thirty, right?"

Lewis's silence screams *I didn't think about that.*

"And it's a four and a half hour drive total. We're not going to get much hiking done," Tad adds, in case Lewis doesn't get it.

He feels like a dick. Like he's telling a little kid their art project sucks. Or something.

Lewis's shoulders dip. "So... you're telling me it's a bad idea to hike on a mountain in the dark?"

There's a spark of humor in Lewis's eyes, and it makes butterflies flutter in Tad's chest.

Okay. So maybe he didn't only invite himself along on this trip because of altruistic, but entirely legitimate, fear for Lewis's safety. Maybe a teensy tiny part of his motivation also came from the desire to spend more time with Lewis before he walks out of Tad's life. A normal person would be able to turn this situation into friendship. The way Lewis was talking this morning, it was like he was so mortified at getting drunk married that he couldn't stand the idea of continuing any relationship with Tad.

So he'll keep Lewis from walking off a cliff or getting lost and dying of thirst. And maybe at the end of it, they can be friends. Tad isn't going to hope for more, no matter how much of a crush he currently has.

He'll get over it.

"It's only like, mostly a bad idea to hike on a mountain in the dark," Tad says as seriously as possible.

Lewis shoots a grin at him and the butterflies whirl inside Tad's rib cage.

He'll probably get over the crush.

A long drive with someone he hasn't known for even a day is Tad's idea of torture. What does he have to talk about with a near-stranger for four and a half hours? Normally he'd be so stressed about how fast he was going to run out of things to say that he'd choke and not say anything, even the things crowding the back of his throat.

But talking to Lewis is effortless. Talking to him makes Tad feel like they've known each other for longer than twenty-four hours.

No—that's not quite it. The feeling of just meeting is still there, but instead of it being this big, awkward thing, where Tad can't make his words come out and sits there looking like a freak while Lewis regrets spending time with him, it's a vast sense of possibility.

Talking to Lewis is easy. The road and miles fall away until they reach Tonopah, which has a charming Old West main street that looks like it would be fun to explore. Lewis tells him about Tonopah as they drive through—its history as a silver mining town, its current life as the closest town to the Tonopah Test Range, which Tad didn't know existed, and which is apparently called Area 52? Who knew! They drive past a clown motel that claims to be world famous, and Tad says he doesn't want to live in a world where a clown motel can be world famous. Lewis laughs and Tad feels pleased with himself that they've been trapped together in a car this long and Lewis isn't tired of his sense of humor yet.

Soon they're turning off the highway. A cattle stop rattles under the tires as they turn onto a narrow, beat-up road. It's paved, barely. Then the asphalt disappears and the road turns to gravel.

It climbs and turns into more of a track than a road. Tad opens the window and takes a deep breath. The air smells different in places like this. Excitement thrills up his sternum. He may have come along on this trip to keep Lewis alive—and also to keep himself in Lewis's vicinity—but he really does love camping. He loves hiking; he loves the feeling of each step taking you further from your responsibilities and obligations.

They bump along the road, climbing into the mountain range. Tad's sputtering cell signal, down to one weak bar of EDGE, finally dies. There's something he loves about that moment too. That clench of adrenaline when you get cut off from the world. Some people go skydiving; he goes to remote places with no cell signal for the same effect.

Maybe he likes that it's not something in him cutting him off from the world, it's the world cutting him off.

"There should be a parking lot," Tad says, leaning forward in his seat.

Parking lot is giving it more credit than it deserves. There's a gravel area where a person could park a car, which Lewis does. There aren't any others in the lot.

The car shuts off and the quiet is jarring. "Well," Lewis says, "here we are."

Chapter Seven

OKAY, SO… it's embarrassing to admit, but Lewis is intimidated.

Which is why he doesn't. Admit it. He didn't expect Humboldt-Toiyabe to be quite so… wilderness-y. In the street view photo, there are other cars in the parking lot. But it's just them, a quarter of the way up a mountain with no sound except the wind whistling across the slope and the crunch of gravel under his shoes.

The road behind them cuts through a sparsely vegetated, rocky landscape. Ahead are the mountains of the Toiyabe Range. A trail leads from the parking lot into the mountains. A few beleaguered pines stand sentinel over the trailhead.

This isn't the kind of trip Lewis normally takes, and now he's remembering why. He takes trips where he can plan everything: this museum, which opens at this time, lunch at this nearby local favorite, which is within easy walking distance of this other train station, and here's the train schedule by the way, and they'll take the train at this time to their next stop, which is less crowded in the afternoon, and when it closes they'll walk along this picturesque street to a bar that makes the best drinks in the city, before they swing past a park with a historic statue on their way to dinner at a restaurant where he's already made reservations.

Now that he's standing here, he's wondering why he chose a trip where he can't control anything. He can bring the right tools, but beyond that? He's at the mercy of nature and the elements. If Tad weren't here, Lewis would probably get back in the car and drive straight back to Vegas.

Why did he want to do this again?

Jonah's face swims up in his memory, pre-shoe-theft and pre-fucking-the-guy-from-the-gym. When they went away for the weekend to Boston and Lewis had a meticulous plan for their trip, and Jonah rolled his eyes and said, "You're such a control freak, Lewis."

"This is amazing!" Tad says gleefully, breaking Lewis out of his thoughts. "There's *no one* around!"

"Yeah," Lewis says, hoping he doesn't sound as uneasy as he feels.

They're losing the daylight fast. Tad was right about not hiking in the dark, but Lewis doesn't want to camp in the parking lot. Well, he kind of does—his heart is thrumming.

Tad pops the car's trunk. "Let's just go up the trail a little bit so we're not like, literally in the parking lot."

"Okay," Lewis says, relieved he won't have to wander too far into the wilderness tonight.

Tad fits the straps of his backpack over his shoulders, settling them into place. His T-shirt pulls tight across his chest. Lewis has to look somewhere else. They were fucking in his hotel room twelve hours ago, and six hours ago, Lewis made the decision that they wouldn't fuck again. The way Tad's lean body carries the weight of the backpack, the pop of tendon and muscle and sinew, is seriously testing that decision.

"Not very far." Tad's looking at Lewis like he expects an argument. "Just so we can't see the car."

"Yeah, that's fine."

"I know you wanted to go farther."

There's a worried look on Tad's face. Without thinking about what he's doing, Lewis catches his hand. "Tad, seriously. It's good. You were right. Hiking in the dark is stupid."

Tad's eyes are locked on his face, like he's just heard something he can't quite process. Then they flick to their joined hands. Lewis lets go and shoves his hands in his pockets. Stupid. He needs his hands to get his backpack out of the trunk.

While he slips his arms through the straps, he says, "You look like no one's ever told you you're right about something before."

Tad grunts noncommittally. So, shit, maybe Lewis just poked a sore spot. Maybe he should stop talking.

Lewis slams the trunk closed and locks the car. The sound carries in the still, silent air, the beep of the lock feeling too modern for their surroundings. More than too modern, too *human*. It's out of place here.

The pack feels good on his back, though. It gives him a confidence boost. Maybe he's going to turn into a camping guy. That's sexy, right? Guys who camp are sexy.

Tad walks to the trailhead and looks back with a smile that makes Lewis's stomach grow hot. "Your trip, so you get to take the first step," Tad says.

That has the feel of a family tradition, which is adorable.

Jesus, it's going to be a miracle if Lewis can go twelve hours without kissing this guy.

They start up the trail, Lewis in the lead, with the sky fading from denim to indigo overhead. Lewis's wedding ring catches the light. Why didn't he take it off? It doesn't mean anything to him, and it might get in the way.

He leaves it on, though, and they walk up the trail, boots crunching on the rocky ground.

TEN MINUTES later, Lewis has learned that the air is a lot thinner up here, it only takes about five minutes for a backpack to get really heavy, and that the light goes fast in the desert.

They stop at a flattish spot about fifty feet off the trail. Tad scouts for a place to dig a latrine, which is when Lewis faces up to the mortifying prospect of shitting in a hole in the general vicinity of this man.

While Tad takes care of that, Lewis tackles the tent. He practiced at home so he's pretty confident he can do it in a real-world setting. When he gets it set up and staked with minimal struggle, he puts his hands on his hips and surveys his work, feeling pretty damn accomplished.

Tad comes back while Lewis is still congratulating himself, brushing dirt off the folding shovel. "Nice," he says. And then, "Looks cozy."

Oh.

Yeah. Yeah, it does. It does look cozy. If cozy means *uncomfortably small*.

"It sleeps two," Lewis says, like that will magically make it bigger.

Tad looks amused. As he kneels to store the shovel in his pack, he says, "I can show you where I dug the latrine. Want to do that now or after dinner?"

"Dinner?" Lewis looks around. Don't they need a fire to have dinner? And don't they need wood to have a fire? There aren't any trees nearby and Lewis isn't keen on wandering around in the dark to collect firewood.

"I brought a camp stove," Tad says. His voice is kind, but Lewis feels stupid. He just envisioned himself cooking over a campfire. The need for a camp stove never entered his mind, even though it was on every camping supply list he looked at.

So Tad is already saving his ass. If not for him, Lewis would be subsisting on protein bars.

Within fifteen minutes, Tad is heating a couple packets of stew on the stove. Lewis *did* buy those. As the stew heats, they sit next to each other on the ground, which Tad apologizes for, adding, "I actually have some inflatable cushions at home, but I didn't think to get any more."

"Um, you don't need to apologize," Lewis says. He nudges Tad with an elbow. "You bought all new camping gear just to save my ass."

"Think you'd have walked off the side of the mountain yet if I wasn't here?" Tad asks, grinning.

"I'd have found a way."

Tad's grin turns to a softer, contented smile. Lewis can't help sneaking glances at him. They've only hiked ten minutes from the car, but Tad looks different. Looser. Happier. Like he's in his element out here, surrounded by nothing but empty space and loneliness.

His wedding ring is still on his left hand too. What should Lewis make of that? The fact that Tad is into him seems inescapable—why would he volunteer to come on this trip, otherwise?—but Lewis assumed it was all physical. Last night was great. No, last night was spectacular. It was the best sex of Lewis's life, and if it was even half that good for Tad, that still would have made it pretty damn amazing.

But the wedding ring? That makes it seem like it's more.

Lewis should take his off in case Tad gets the idea that this is more than a one-night stand. Which it already is, because they're camping together. They're going to be sleeping in that cozy tent. Together.

He twists it around his finger, then lets go. If he takes it off now, he might drop it, and he doesn't want that, either.

When the stew is hot, Tad serves it in the collapsible bowls Lewis brought. It's not the best stew, but it's not the worst, either. They use one of their water bottles to rinse the bowls and set them on the ground to dry.

That's when the last twenty-four hours catch up with him, hitting him like an Ambien washed down with a glass of whiskey. He's not twenty-two anymore, and honestly it's a miracle he made it this long without crashing. It can't be later than six thirty.

Stifling an enormous yawn, he says, "I'm gonna go to bed."

Tad yawns too, his nose scrunching, which makes Lewis smile sleepily. "Yeah, I'm not going to last much longer either. You need the latrine?"

"I just have to pee."

With a wave of his hand, Tad says, "Well, you can do that anywhere. Go ahead and get settled. I'll be in soon."

Once Lewis empties his bladder, he stumbles back to the tent, dead on his feet. He wrestles his sleeping bag through the tent opening and manages to unroll it without passing out. Getting undressed seems like too much work. He crawls into the sleeping bag fully clothed and zips it up. There's a pillow in his pack, but he forgot that—and it's going to take so much energy to unzip his sleeping bag, crawl out of the tent, and find it.

He will, though. He just needs a minute to find some motivation. Just another minute, and he'll heave himself upright again....

He drops off to sleep, no pillow needed.

Chapter Eight

WHEN LEWIS opens his eyes, there's the faintest suggestion of light on the other side of the tent. He rubs a hand over his face and looks to the side. No Tad, though his sleeping bag is there, flipped open and rumpled, so he slept in it, right next to Lewis.

God, Lewis was out before Tad even came into the tent. He slept like a rock. What time is it?

He rubs a hand over his face again. It's November, so it can't be much before six. The need to know the exact time burns through him, and then—vanishes. There's nowhere to be. He doesn't have to log on for an early meeting; he doesn't have to face the subway to go into the office. There aren't any deadlines. It's either day or it's night.

As he stretches, his hand brushes Tad's sleeping bag. Warmth lingers in the fabric. Lewis arches his back to crack his spine before he crawls out of his own sleeping bag.

When he unzips the tent flap, he doesn't see Tad. His heart speeds up. Tad wouldn't leave him out here, would he?

The thought makes him scramble outside and into his hiking boots, which he doesn't remember taking off last night. It looks like he kicked them off without caring where they landed.

His eyes find Tad standing a little ways from the tent and looking at the sky. Lewis hesitates, then crunches across their campsite to join him.

"Morning," Tad says. His hair is tousled and sticking up in different directions, scruff is growing in along his jaw and on his cheeks, and a bright smile makes his face luminous. "I'd ask how you slept, but I think I already know the answer."

Lewis laughs sheepishly. "I must be getting old."

"Yeah?"

"Thirty-two."

"Cradle-robber," Tad says lightly. "I'm only twenty-nine."

Yesterday, the joke would have made Lewis's chest tighten with anxiety about how soon he can fix the marriage situation. Today, it makes him chuckle. There's a hint of a smile on Tad's face.

Did Lewis really think that Tad looks luminous? He'll unpack that later. Or maybe never, which would be for the best. He's suddenly very glad he was completely unconscious for every moment Tad was next to him in the tent.

The sky is pastel and a few stars are battling the sunrise for the right to be the brightest thing in the sky. Lewis has never been good at knowing what he's looking at. If he hadn't passed out last night, he's sort of confident he could have found the Big Dipper. As for what he's looking at now? No clue.

Would Tad know? He seems so happy out here.

Pink creeps up from the horizon, then red, tendrils of color whispering across the sky. By the time orange appears, brightening until it fades the other hues to nothing, the last of the stars are gone, and Lewis regrets not asking Tad what he was looking at.

Tad lets out a long, relaxed sigh. "I never get tired of this."

"It's beautiful," Lewis says. When he decided to go camping, this was what he envisioned—nature, quiet, sunrise, sunset. Feeling manageably insignificant in the face of the universe, not like, shit-I'm-going-to-get-lost-in-the-wilderness insignificant.

They watch the sun rise. With another happy sigh, Tad says, "I can make coffee, if you want some?"

"Oh, that sounds amazing, but…." Lewis grimaces. "I didn't even think about buying anything to make coffee in."

"I did, though." Tad looks immensely pleased with himself.

It's totally warranted. "You're amazing," Lewis says. "Yes, coffee, please."

Pale, early morning light floods the mountain by the time they're ready to go. Lewis's backpack doesn't feel so heavy this morning. He takes the lead on the trail, feeling confident again about the choice to do this. Amazing what a good night's sleep can do.

The air warms as the sun gets higher. They take regular breaks, which Lewis definitely needs. He's in pretty good shape, but the thinner air is getting to him.

Around midmorning, they stop for a snack, sitting on a boulder next to a dry stream bed. A little brown bird hops around on the ground, studying them. Lewis wonders how many people it sees. It doesn't seem afraid. It also doesn't seem like it wants any food, which is a change from New York wildlife.

"Do you know what kind of bird that is?" Lewis asks.

Tad takes a bite of his protein bar. "Nope. You're either a plant person or a bird person, but you can't be both, and I'm a plant person."

Lewis laughs. "Oh yeah? Is that official?"

"Nerdery's Fourth Law."

The bird hops closer, cocks its head, and scratches the ground. "I guess if we were going to stay together, I'd have to become a bird person," Lewis says. "You know, for balance."

Tad stills mid-chew. He swallows and smiles, though there's something kind of forced about it. "I guess."

Awkwardness alert. In a transparent attempt to distract, Lewis points to a tree nearby. "What's that?"

Tad arches an eyebrow. "A tree."

"Ha ha. What kind of tree, plant guy?"

With a smirk, Tad finishes his protein bar and puts the wrapper in his pack. He approaches the tree while Lewis remains seated, still nibbling the protein bar. He's definitely not admiring the way Tad walks, his smooth, sort of loping swagger. And he's not checking out the way his jeans hug his ass, or how great his legs look, or how the way the morning light hits his white T-shirt makes it a little translucent, so Lewis can see the suggestion of the muscles in his back.

"It's a pinyon pine, but I'm not sure which kind," Tad calls. "Want to eat some nuts?"

Lewis chokes on his protein bar. Even from a distance of twenty feet, he can see how red Tad's face is.

"Um. From the tree. Tree nuts." Tad covers his eyes. "Why is that not making it better?"

Polishing off the bar and stowing his trash, Lewis joins Tad. "I love nuts," he says seriously. "How do I get these? Do I have to tug and squeeze gently?"

Tad's face gets redder. "Not necessary."

"Oh. Okay, well, I like to suck on them—"

"Oh my god." Tad covers his face with both hands, then blindly flails and smacks Lewis in the chest. "Thanks! *Thanks*. I'll remember this moment until the day I die."

Grinning, Lewis grabs Tad's wrists and draws his hands away from his face. "That would be a huge honor. If I'm going to be remembered on anyone's death bed, you can't beat some good old-fashioned sexual innuendo."

His hands are still around Tad's wrists. He can feel bones and tendons and Tad's pulse.

He lets go. Tad plucks a pinecone off the tree. Lewis watches as he sticks a finger between the bristles, until Tad makes a triumphant noise and produces a single seed.

When he drops it in Lewis's open palm, Lewis says, "It looks like a pine nut."

"They're related."

"So I'm not going to die if I eat this?"

Tad gives him a crooked smile. "What would I possibly have to gain by feeding you poison seeds?"

"Well, there's my massive inheritance…." Lewis shrugs. "It's only a couple million though, definitely not worth black widowering me over."

Tad laughs. That sound puts Lewis on very dangerous ground.

YOLO though, right? Ugh, no, he's going to leave that one firmly in 2012 where it belongs. Lewis pops the nut in his mouth, lets the flavor hit his tongue—

And spits it out, gagging. His tongue feels furry. Tad's mouth is twitching in a poor attempt not to laugh. "I could've just *died*," Lewis gripes. "And you're *laughing*."

Tad presses his lips together and shakes his head, but his eyes are dancing. "What did it taste like?"

"*Sap*."

"How do you know what sap tastes like?"

For one wild second, he thinks about kissing Tad, deeply and with plenty of tongue, and informing him, *now you know what it tastes like too.*

Maybe he looks spooked, because Tad's smile fades. "Sorry. It won't hurt you, really. I should've warned you about the taste, though. Sorry."

Lewis doesn't miss how Tad brackets his explanation with apologies. "Hey, it's fine," he says. Tad looks—scared? There's this look in his eyes that makes Lewis want to wrap him up in a tight hug. "I didn't have to put the thing in my mouth."

There's a silence. Tad stares at the ground. Then, he says quietly, "That's what he said."

Lewis snorts with laughter, and Tad's eyes flicker up to meet his. His hair falls in them and Lewis isn't sure he realized until this moment how blue they are. They remind him of Greek islands—bright blue roofs, bright blue ocean, bright blue sky.

Luminous. Like Tad's smile.

Danger danger danger.

Sucking in a breath, Tad asks, "Should we keep going? If we want to get to the campsite, we have to do six miles today."

Six miles seemed totally manageable in the comfort of Lewis's apartment. "How far have we hiked?"

"Um… if I had to guess? A little under a mile."

Oh. Shit. They need to pick up the pace. Lewis really wants to get to this campsite. The pictures make it look really pretty—tall pines, a trickling stream, gorgeous view of Arc Dome and Toiyabe Dome. They can refill their empty water bottles in the stream.

Lewis plotted his route to stay close to water, and the plan is to end the trip at a small mountain lake. He arranged for a camping outfitter to pick him up and drive him back to his car on the last day. That means they have to be at that lake on the last day, or no ride.

"Guess we better get moving," Lewis says.

The day is warm. Lewis works up a sweat as the hours pass. So does Tad, which Lewis surreptitiously admires when they take a break or when Tad is in the lead on the trail. Once, Tad twists up the hem of his shirt to wipe his face, and Lewis gets a view of toned abs, a defined V-cut, and dark hair.

It's nothing he hasn't seen before, but he really wants to see it again—and not in quick flashes. He wants to peel off Tad's sweaty clothes—

He does *not* want to get an obvious boner, so he pulls out the map and calculates how far they've walked.

Maybe it's because he's congratulating himself on not getting a visible hard-on, but as they're traversing a downhill slope, Lewis puts his foot in a bad spot. His heel slips from under him and the weight of his pack throws off his center of gravity.

He tips forward, arms flailing.

Tad is in front of him, so Lewis yells something garbled. It gets the point across—Tad whirls.

Instead of getting out of the way, which is what Lewis wanted him to do, Tad plants himself, opens his arms, and catches Lewis.

Arms wrap around him and Lewis clutches Tad, feet scrabbling for purchase. "I've got you," Tad says, his voice steady and comforting and close to Lewis's ear.

His feet are still slipping. He can't get them back under him. He's just—falling. He's falling and the only reason he isn't rolling down this trail is because Tad's there to hold him up. He needs to get his feet under himself. He needs to get his body under his own control again, gravity be damned.

"Hey," Tad says. "Just—relax. Okay? I promise. I've got you."

Relax? Lewis can't relax. That's the point of this whole trip, to help him relax! Nature already defeated him after sixteen hours and three miles.

The sound of gravel skittering and bouncing down the slope quiets as everything Lewis dislodged reaches the bottom. Birds call, but otherwise, everything is silent. Lewis is breathing hard. His heart pounds.

His feet aren't sliding anymore. Without realizing, he did what Tad said and relaxed.

Tad shifts his grip. Their bodies press together and Lewis is able to get first one foot, then the other, solidly beneath him.

Tad's arms retreat, his hands coming to rest on Lewis's hips. "You okay?"

"Yeah," Lewis says, hating how breathless he sounds. "Thanks."

His own arms are still around Tad's neck. One hand is buried in Tad's hair, silky auburn strands escaping between his fingers. Tad feels warm and vital, chest rising and falling like he knight-in-shining-armors every day, catching dudes in distress in his lean, well-muscled arms. He smells good— like honest sweat and something clean that must be his laundry detergent.

The urge to bury his face in the crook of Tad's neck almost overpowers Lewis. Then the urge to throw himself backward nearly does him in. Just in time, he remembers he almost fell down this hill once already.

Carefully, he steps backward. Tad's hands linger at his hips, a light touch that seems like genuine concern. "Guess my city kid is showing," Lewis says sheepishly.

Tad drops his hands and offers Lewis a lopsided smile. "Don't worry—I fall on my ass at least once every camping trip."

"Well, thanks for the save."

"Any time," Tad says, his voice a little softer.

They stand still, not touching, but eyes locked. Lewis is having a hard time remembering why he can't kiss Tad again. Something something bad at picking boyfriends? Blah blah broken heart? Maybe a broken heart is worth it for another chance to be skin-to-skin with Tad.

He leans forward. Tad's eyelids flutter and lower to half-mast.

Pebbles skitter as Tad turns and continues along the trail. "Six miles!" he calls over his shoulder.

It's teasing, but there's something else, too—something nervy. Something maybe even scared.

Lewis wants to kick himself. He was the one who shut down any more sex or romance between them. He was the one who drew a line in the sand and said they had to be platonic, or maybe even less. And now he's the one who got caught up in the moment and almost kissed Tad.

Idiot. This is why he keeps getting his heart broken.

Good thing one of them remembers the boundaries Lewis set, even if it's not Lewis.

THE VIEW at the campsite is even better than in the pictures.

Lewis spends ages admiring the vista. The sky, the mountains, everything wide open and massive. Dusty green pines against the powder blue dome of the sky and the heathered brown of the mountain.

Tad joins him. They don't speak, partly because Lewis can't figure out how to apologize for what happened earlier, and partly because the silence feels, despite earlier, comfortable.

There's a fire pit at the campsite, ash and charred wood from the last campers still in the center of its soot-blackened ring of stones. They collect enough wood—unlike at their impromptu site last night, this one has trees and plenty of brush—and get a fire going.

Sunset light catches Tad's profile, outlining his high forehead, his slightly-too-long nose, his sharp cheekbones, the elegant line of his throat. Lewis can't decide what colors the sky and the fire are making of Tad's hair and skin; all he knows is he can't look away. They change from one moment to the next, never staying the same, but always, always making Tad more beautiful.

Lewis was wrong earlier when he thought there was only day or night. There's this other thing, this in-between. There's dawn and dusk and the liminal, shifting magic of the light changing, the sky and Tad's eyes refusing to stay one color.

He was wrong earlier when he told Tad there couldn't be anything between them—and now he doesn't know how to take it back.

Chapter Nine

UNLIKE LAST night, Tad isn't tired enough to block out that Lewis is lying next to him in the tent.

Right next to him. Their sleeping bags are touching, which means the two of them are almost touching. That, combined with replaying Lewis's fall, and how good it felt to hold him, is a recipe for sleeplessness.

The fact that Lewis looked like he was going to kiss Tad?

Yeah, Tad's going to be lucky if he sleeps at all tonight.

He just keeps seeing it. Lewis's eyes, big and brown, dropping to his lips, and the way he leaned forward.

Tad panicked. Yesterday, Lewis said they couldn't do this. He didn't say why, but there must be a reason. Lewis was honest and up front, and then—fuck, who knows. It was probably the adrenaline from almost tumbling down the trail, but something made him nearly go back on the line he drew, and Tad isn't going to be responsible for that.

He wants Lewis to like him. He wants that so bad. But he also just, like… he got scared that if Lewis kissed him, Lewis would regret it by the time they made camp.

Is Lewis asleep? His breathing isn't deep and even like it was last night. Fabric hisses as Lewis shifts. His breathing doesn't change. Maybe he moved in his sleep.

"Are you awake?" Lewis whispers.

Or maybe Lewis can't sleep, either.

"Yeah," Tad whispers back.

"Oh." Lewis just breathes for a minute. "Me too."

Outside, embers from the fire crackle softly. The faintest orange glow wavers over the side of the tent. Give it another hour, and the moon will be up, but now it's too dark to see inside the tent, even with the remnants of their fire burning out.

"I didn't wake you up, did I?" Lewis asks.

Tad wants to reach out to him. He clears his throat. "You don't have to whisper."

With an embarrassed laugh, Lewis says, "Oh, yeah, I guess not."

"You didn't wake me up."

"Okay. Good."

Silence again. Then: "I, um. I owe you an apology. For earlier. I didn't mean to be weird."

Tad isn't used to people apologizing to him. "Don't worry about it."

"No, I mean." There's a slither of fabric. "I was the one who made a big deal about... you know. Nothing else happening between us. And I feel like I owe you an explanation."

"You don't." Tad means it. If Lewis doesn't want any relationship at all, not even a friendship, he doesn't need to explain anything. All explanations do is open the way for connection.

"I want to explain," Lewis says quietly. "Is it okay if I do?"

In the darkness, Tad raises his hands to his eyes and digs the heels in. He *should* say no. Nicely, of course. But no.

"Okay," he says, because apparently he likes getting close to guys who seem perfect for him, only to find out he's not enough.

Lewis's breathing seems shallower. God, he's really nervous about this. Even though he can't see shit, Tad tentatively reaches out a hand. His fingers finds Lewis's shoulder.

Bare shoulder. Lewis is sleeping shirtless? Is Lewis sleeping nude?

Tad's cock perks up. Tad's brain tells it to settle down.

"It's fine," Tad says. "Whatever you want to explain? It's okay."

"God, you're being nice," Lewis mutters, sounding despairing. "Um. So, the thing is, I'm on a break from dating. A total break. So it wasn't ever you. I didn't want it to be anything more than a hookup because I'm just...." A sigh. "I'm just really shit at dating."

"Oh," Tad says carefully. "I get that."

"No, but every guy I've dated for the past, like, decade, has turned out to be awful. I fall head over heels and I get my heart broken. Over and over. It's gotta be me. I'm horrible at picking boyfriends. So I'm not dating. Not until I figure it out."

Tad's hand is still on Lewis's shoulder. He's so warm, and his skin is soft, and the ache in his voice makes Tad want to pull him close and hold him. Without the perked-up dick. Which, yeah, his dick is interested in Lewis, but the raw sadness in Lewis's voice scrapes an exposed nerve in Tad's heart. He knows how it feels. He knows exactly how it feels to fall head over heels and be found wanting.

"I guess what I'm saying is, I just have to not fall into all my old patterns." Lewis pauses. "Not that I think you're like all those other guys."

Trying to be fair, Tad says, "I might be."

Another pause, longer this time. "I don't think you are," Lewis says so softly that Tad barely hears him. "That's what makes this hard."

Tad bites his tongue. But then, Lewis snorts. "That's what he said?"

"I kept my mouth shut!" Tad says. "We're having a very serious conversation, and I wasn't going to derail it with childish innuendo!"

"Childish, huh?" Lewis asks. There's a smile in his voice. Tad can picture it perfectly, for all he's only known this man for a sum total of forty-eight hours.

"Well, when you say it, it sounds super sophisticated," Tad says solicitously.

Lewis laughs, his shoulder bouncing under Tad's palm. It's time to move his hand, but it doesn't seem to be bothering Lewis. If anything, after he laughs, Lewis leans into the curve of Tad's fingers. "Thanks. That's me, Mr. Sophisticated."

"Sounds like your stripper name."

The way Lewis laughs makes Tad's entire chest glow. He knows his face is a happy pink. "What happened to you respecting our serious conversation?"

"That was before Mr. Sophisticated came on the scene," Tad says, grinning into the darkness. "Do you have like, a signature move?"

"Yeah," Lewis says, deadpan. "I call it the mechanical bull."

Tad loses it, and after a second, so does Lewis. They're both giggling and snorting in their little tent, wrapped up in their sleeping bags, Tad's fingers still on Lewis's shoulder as he laughs and hurts with how easy this is.

As their laughter dies away, smooth, strong fingers slide over Tad's. "I wish I'd met you when I had my head on straight," Lewis says.

The humor of the previous moment drains away like water through sand. Tad's throat tightens. "Yeah. I do too."

Lewis's fingers curl around Tad's. It's their left hands, and Tad feels Lewis's wedding ring slide over his skin. "Maybe we can be friends, though."

Friends. Sure. Tad doesn't know how he'll be able to be just friends with Lewis, but it's better than nothing, right?

"I'd like that," he says. He doesn't know what else he *can* say.

Lewis's hand remains where it is, his warmth seeping into Tad. His arm is getting stiff, but moving isn't possible.

After a minute, Lewis's breath grows deep and even. The sound is what finally lulls Tad to sleep.

THE NEXT day's hike takes them higher into the mountains. The trail skirts the peak, getting two-thirds of the way to the top. Both of them are breathing heavily by the time they get to the trail's highest point. The treadmill doesn't really prepare you for hiking a mountain.

It's a hell of a lot colder up here. When they stop for a break, Tad puts on a sweatshirt. Lewis doesn't put on anything warmer. "Aren't you cold?" Tad asks.

He's positive he sees Lewis shiver, but Lewis shrugs. "I'm fine."

There's not much Tad can do but take him at his word. Or give Lewis the shirt off his back, which he tries. Lewis won't take it.

The plan is to bypass the campground at the higher elevation in favor of one farther down the slope. The most difficult part of the trail is the final steep stretch that will see them lose a thousand feet of elevation per mile.

And then they get there and Tad stops dead, small rocks skittering over the ledge.

The trail is impassable.

Okay, it's not impassable. But it's in bad shape. Looks like a flash flood, maybe, and a rock fall? Tad's guessing, but the specifics don't matter. They can get down this way, but it's going to take hours. They're quickly losing the light, so they don't have hours.

Lewis is pale and his mouth is set in a thin, determined line. "We have to try it."

"No way."

"We have to!" Lewis repeats. Flinging out an arm to encompass their surroundings, he says, "We can't just stay here."

"No, we can go back to the campsite we passed up the trail," Tad replies. "It was only like forty-five minutes back. We can get there before dark."

Lewis looks like he's going to be sick. It makes Tad want to put his arms around him and soothe him and tell him everything's going to be okay. He'd do just about anything to put some color back in Lewis's face and take away that wan, pinched look.

Well, just about anything, except descend this mountain in the dark.

"I don't want to backtrack," Lewis says. "We'll have to make up the miles if we want to make our pickup."

"We're not going to make our pickup if you break your leg trying to get down this trail in the dark."

"Why do you assume I'd be the one to break my leg?"

"Okay, sure, fine. Maybe I'd break my leg. The point is, we're better off pushing ourselves on a safe part of the trail tomorrow instead of risking dying on this part tonight. I mean, we still have four days. That's plenty of time. Trust me, okay?"

It doesn't strike him as ridiculous until the words are out of his mouth—the *trust me* part. People don't tend to trust Tad with important stuff. He's never been, like, the gay best friend with the platonic soul mate who loves him more than family. And yeah, he knows that's a dumb stereotype from a movie industry that's afraid gay cooties are going to hurt their bottom line, but it's one of the few gay fairytales he's been sold.

Instead, he's got a boss he's close to. He had some friends in college, but they drifted apart, and every time Tad thinks about maybe getting back in touch, his shyness shuts it down, even though he was close with those people once. When he was dating John, he got invited out. Because he was part of a couple, and they could do couple things with all the other couples. Because John had friends. But obviously John's friends chose John in the breakup, not Tad.

Even though Lewis doesn't know any of that stuff—Lewis doesn't know anything about him, really—Tad can't help being afraid it's coming off him. Like pheromones or something. Like he just emanates this overall loser vibe. A this-is-not-a-person-you-want-to-listen-to vibe.

Lewis deflates. "You're right. You're obviously right. Sorry. I just— ugh. Dammit. I just hate when things don't go the way I planned."

"That's camping for you," Tad says.

Now Lewis looks like he's going to cry. "I don't know what made me think this would be a good idea. I'm a control freak. Why would I go on a camping trip when I don't know anything about camping? God, I'm such an idiot. I figured it would be like all the other stuff I've figured out how to do from YouTube videos."

Tad goes to Lewis's side. Without second-guessing himself, he grabs Lewis's hand and twines their fingers together tightly. It seems like Lewis could use the physical comfort, but Tad's also like, mildly concerned Lewis might fling himself over the edge of the trail. "This was a good idea," he says.

"You told me it was a bad idea."

"The going alone part! Not the entire concept of camping." He squeezes Lewis's hand, encouraged that Lewis hasn't tried to pull away. "You've been having fun so far, right?"

Lewis stares into the middle distance. "Yeah. Until this."

Tugging Lewis around until he looks at him, Tad says, "It'll be okay. It really, really will be."

And then—Lewis! Squeezes his hand! Back!

"Okay," he says. A smile tiptoes onto his face. "I trust you."

Those words shouldn't turn Tad's heart into a Catherine wheel, spinning and blazing and crackling in his rib cage.

They shouldn't, but they do.

Tad has to take a deep breath before he trusts his voice to come out normal. "I promise we'll make our pickup. And I promise this is just going to be a little blip. It's not going to ruin anything. It's not even going to ruin the night! I promise."

Lewis looks at Tad like he believes him.

Tad isn't going to let him down.

Chapter Ten

TAD IS totally right about the whole trail-being-destroyed thing not being a big deal.

Okay, well, no. It's totally a big deal. But like, it doesn't have to ruin anything. Tad isn't going to let it ruin anything, and Lewis isn't, either. Tad knows what he's doing. If he says it's not a big deal, it's not a big deal.

Lewis recognizes that he's just shifting the responsibility for control from himself to Tad, but it's better than beating himself up. Maybe? If he can relinquish control, that's progress?

As they head back up the trail, Lewis tries not to agonize over retreading the same ground—and knowing they're going to have to do it again tomorrow. To distract himself, he asks, "Did you ever have any camping disasters?"

"Um." Tad laughs, sounding embarrassed. "Kinda hoped you wouldn't ask? I feel like I have this cool mystique right now. Like, a whole rugged outdoorsman thing going on."

"I promise I'll still think you have a cool outdoorsman mystique if you tell me." Lewis makes his eyes big and bats his eyelashes. "Pleeeeease?"

Tad looks helpless, but he laughs. "Okay! Fine. So my sophomore year, I went camping with this guy I really liked. We weren't, like, official, but we fooled around in his dorm room. I thought I could bring him camping, and it would be super romantic, and he'd ask me to be his boyfriend."

Lewis keeps his mouth clamped shut, because he's pretty sure this story ends with the guy *not* asking to be Tad's boyfriend, and it's sweet that Tad's telling him an embarrassing story to make their current predicament not seem so bad.

"We went to the Catskills to this campground I knew—Sundown Wild Forest, have you heard of it?"

"No, sorry."

Waving a hand, Tad says, "It's gorgeous. I'll bring you someday." His voice stutters and his steps falter. "Um, anyway. So, it was just a three-day weekend thing, and I was super excited to show him the forest, you know? But he mostly seemed to want to, uh, fool around in the tent. Finally I got him on a hike to this waterfall. And we like, started making out, which, you know, I was nineteen, and I was horny all the time, and I liked this guy."

He takes a deep, slow breath in through his nose. "Lewis, you have to understand. I really liked this guy. So, we were like, getting down to things, and we're on the ground, and suddenly this guy lets out this bloodcurdling scream."

Embarrassment and amusement war on Tad's face. "He starts yelling that a snake bit him, he saw the snake, and he's going to die, and we need to get to a hospital. So I."

He takes a fortifying breath. "I said. 'No. It's okay. I'll suck the poison out.'"

"No."

"*Yes*. Yes, I did, Lewis. So there I am, sucking on an alleged snake bite on my not-boyfriend's mossy, dirty ass, when who should come upon us...."

"*No*."

"When who should come upon us," Tad repeats, his tone sepulchral, "but *my advisor*."

Lewis just lets the silence take that and float away with it.

Then, he asks, "Did you at least get the venom out of the guy's ass?"

"There was no snake. He sat on a stick."

Lewis claps a hand over his mouth to muffle his laughter. "I'm sorry."

Tad lets out a snort, then a laugh. "Go ahead, I told you because it's funny. I mean, mortifying, but funny." The sun is slanting low and turning the world gold, while everything in shadow is purple. It catches copper strands in Tad's hair and makes him look haloed. His eyelashes look like they're tipped with gold.

It's the hardest thing not to stare. It's only slightly harder not to tell him how beautiful he is.

Shit.

"I've actually never told anyone that story," Tad says, sounding embarrassed.

"You were a teenager. Teenagers pretty much just lurch from one embarrassing story to the next."

With a laugh, Tad says, "True. I pretty much always felt like I was falling on my face in high school."

"Yeah?" The sun is sinking fast, bringing the red out in Tad's hair. Lewis wants to sink his fingers into it and tease out all the different colors. "You mentioned you have a brother—were you guys close, or was he part of the embarrassing?"

Something unreadable flashes across Tad's face. "He's older, so I was probably the one embarrassing him. But he's…." There's that expression again. Is it sadness? Shame? "He's okay. He mostly looked out for me when we were kids."

"Mostly?"

Tad shrugs. "Do you have siblings? God, I don't know anything about—anything. Where did you grow up? That was your friend— Stacy?—Stacy's bachelorette party you were at the other day, right? How long have you two known each other?"

The barrage of questions makes Lewis laugh. "I have an older sister, her name's Taylor. I'm from Weehawken."

Tad's grin flashes in the rosy light, and he gives Lewis's shoulder a light smack with the back of his hand. "You are *not* from Jersey."

"Guilty," Lewis says with an overblown wince. "Stace and I were neighbors. I've pretty much known her my whole life."

"Neighbors in *Weehawken*. Weehawken. *New Jersey*."

"Okay, okay, Mr. Big Shot New Yorker. We can't all be from the center of the universe."

After a few steps, Tad admits, "I'm not from New York City, either."

"Wow. And you just disrespected Weehawken. Weehawken, Tad! We have the Hamilton Monument!"

"Oh shit, the Hamilton Monument?" Tad gasps, then grins when Lewis pretends to glare. "No, I'm from upstate. Watertown?"

Lewis screws up his face in thought. "Um, sounds familiar?"

"It's close to the Thousand Islands. And only like ten miles from Lake Ontario."

"Oh, so you're from Canada."

Tad sighs. "At least when we put irreconcilable differences as our reason for divorce, we'll mean it."

"I've never been up there," Lewis says. "Do you like it?"

"It's okay, I guess," Tad replies. "It's definitely, like, really beautiful. The lake and the St. Lawrence. I got into camping because we camped on the Thousand Islands every summer when Walt and I were kids."

"But?"

Tad arches an eyebrow. "Did I say 'but?'"

"You heavily implied it."

Tad adjusts the straps of his backpack. "It's upstate New York. You spent much time upstate?"

"No."

"Well." His gaze unfocuses, and Lewis swears he feels him withdraw. After another minute, Tad sighs. "Being a gay boy in Watertown was... not easy. It's the kind of place where you might decide to stay in the closet."

Lewis doesn't know what to say, so he bites back platitudes. *That must have been so hard. It got better, right? Small towns suck.* All of that is true, but c'mon. What gay boy hasn't heard all that? Finally, he says, "Maybe the kind of place you'd leave and not go back to?"

Giving him a sidelong look, Tad says, "Maybe."

He wants to know more—he wants to ask Tad all about everything and learn everything about him, and that's a terrifying feeling. An expansive and out-of-control feeling. It's a good thing they reach the campsite, because making camp gives Lewis an outlet for the energy that's telling him to *ask ask ask get to know him learn everything about him.*

Why is his dumb rom-com heart so set on getting trampled? Tad is an amazing guy, that's increasingly clear, and he's not the kind of guy who'd want to stay with Lewis for the long haul.

Maybe he should stop looking for the long haul?

Maybe if he doesn't look for the long haul, it doesn't count as breaking his Dating Break?

He doesn't realize he's staring into space until Tad comes up beside him and unzips the tent flap to roll out his sleeping bag. "I can do you too," Tad says. His face goes bright red, freckles on his cheekbones like reverse constellations. "Um. Yours. Your. Sleeping bag. I can. Yeah."

Lewis gives Tad his sleeping bag and tries not to think about Tad doing him.

Casual definitely isn't cheating on the Dating Break.

Anyway, it's his Dating Break. He makes the rules! Something casual would be good for him. Because, like, then he wouldn't be tempted to do his whole falling-for-the-first-guy-who-smiled-at-him routine. Stacy says all it usually takes is dimples and he's ready to sign a lease, which is so not fair. He's a hopeless, romantic idiot, but at least he's never moved in with any of the giant mistakes he's dated.

They get a fire going and cook dinner. There are a couple weathered logs around the fire pit for seating. Lewis dithers, trying to decide if it's weirder to sit next to Tad or across from him. Then the smoke blows toward the log across from Tad, so the decision is made for him.

They refill their empty water bottles from a stream nearby. There's a bite in the air, which feels nice after getting roasted by the fire. When they sit again, they're closer than before. Their hips brush.

The fire spits. Sparks scatter at their feet, flaring across Lewis's vision. "I'm kinda surprised you didn't ask what made me stop dating," Lewis says.

Tad glances over. The firelight makes Tad's eyes look deep blue like the ocean, and Lewis could fall into them and drown. "I didn't think it was any of my business," Tad replies.

It's not, but Lewis feels a weird pull to tell him. Maybe it's because Tad told an embarrassing story just to make Lewis feel better.

Looking back to the fire, Lewis says, "I was dating this guy. Jonah. We were together for six months, which—well, for me, that's like, a record. I thought we were actually going to work out."

"And then?" There's a sad smile on Tad's face.

"And then I walked in on him with his face buried in another guy's ass." Lewis tries to say it like the image doesn't still haunt him, but he doesn't think he's fooling Tad. "This dude he met working out. In hindsight, he was probably pumping something other than iron during all those hours at the gym."

Tad grimaces. "God, Lewis. I'm sorry."

"You wanna know the worst part?" Lewis rubs a hand in his hair. It feels greasy. "I refused to talk to him, even though he called me, like, a million times. I texted and told him to leave his key to my apartment on my kitchen counter when I wasn't home because I didn't want to see him. Which he did. But he also helped himself to my favorite pair of shoes."

"Fucker."

"Yeah. They were Pride Chucks. They had this fabulous pink glitter tongue. And the sole was rainbow-y. Ugh, and the *gold eyelets*. I loved those."

"Fucker!" Tad looks infuriated on Lewis's behalf. He puts a hand on Lewis's knee and squeezes. The contact makes Lewis's body tingle. "Seriously. Fuck him. Wanna describe him to me so I can beat him up and steal your shoes back if I ever see him?"

Lewis laughs. "I can't picture you beating anyone up."

"Me either." Righteous anger is still burning in Tad's eyes. "But I'm willing to give it a shot for someone who'd do that to you." The anger dims to something sadder. "I'm really sorry, Lewis. I—"

He presses his lips together and looks like he's trying to choose his words carefully. "I—get why the whole thing with us was just, like, more than you needed to deal with. You're on a totally understandable break, and I was acting like being married was a funny joke."

"It wasn't your fault." Lewis's voice comes out gruffer than he means it to. "You didn't know."

Tad's hand is still on Lewis's knee. He snatches it back and sticks his hands between his thighs, like he has to trap them. "Still feel like a jerk," he mumbles.

Lewis just shakes his head. Damn. Now things feel heavier than they have since the hotel room, when they realized they were married and Lewis freaked out.

He wishes he knew how to fix it. He wishes Tad would put his hand back on his leg. He wishes... he wishes Jonah, and all the guys before him, hadn't broken his heart, because what he really wishes, so much that the longing is a physical ache behind his sternum, is that he wasn't so broken that he had to stop dating.

What he really wishes is that it would be okay to let himself fall for Tad.

Chapter Eleven

THE BITE in the air doesn't feel good once they climb into their sleeping bags. Whether it's the elevation or just a drop in temperature, it's cold. Lewis never planned on being at this elevation overnight.

He doesn't have any pajamas, because he doesn't sleep in pajamas. He has T-shirts and jeans. The T-shirt isn't going to help much, and he can't sleep in jeans.

So he crawls into his sleeping bag in nothing but his boxer briefs. Tad notices him shivering and offers his sweatshirt, which he's sleeping in, but Lewis objects that then he'll be cold. They argue about that for a bit, but Lewis eventually rolls over and refuses to engage anymore. It's not the most mature tactic, but unless Tad's going to wrestle him out of his sleeping bag and force him into the sweatshirt, it wins the argument.

Tad huffs and informs him for the twentieth time, "This is stupid."

"I'm fine," Lewis replies, his teeth chattering.

There's some light in the tent from the moon, but not enough to see Tad's face as he makes another exasperated sound. Whatever. He's not going to make Tad suffer because he was too big of an idiot to pack warmer clothes. He thought about it, but he needed the space in his backpack. And it seemed like overkill when the forecast said it would be warm, and he wasn't planning on camping so high in the mountains. He even congratulated himself on not being so anal, because yeah, of course he's that guy who always overpacks. Not this time!

Which is why he's curled into the fetal position in his sleeping bag, every muscle clenched tight as he quakes with shivers. He just needs to distract himself. Think about something soothing. Like an all-inclusive tropical vacation. A cruise. A Disney cruise! Everything contained right there in your floating hotel, predictable and safe, right down to the music.

This was stupid. This was such a stupid idea. He's so stupid, to think he could pull this off.

"*Oh* my *god*," Tad yells.

Lewis jumps, which makes his entire body spasm, which makes everything hurt, because every single one of his muscles is painfully tight.

Did he say that stuff out loud?

"Lewis. This is stupid. I'm right here, and I'm warm, and it's dumb for you to be cold."

Lewis's teeth chatter. "Wh-Wh-Wh—" They're chattering too hard for him to get a word out, so he settles for, "Huh?"

There's a rustle of fabric, and Lewis sees Tad's silhouette propped up on an elbow. "I'm not trying to start something. I swear. I respect that you don't want to, and I totally get it. You're super not in a place to even consider a relationship, and that makes sense, and I'm not trying to like, seduce you."

"Um—" What the hell is he talking about? "Ok-k-k-kay?"

"I can't listen to you shivering. You'll never be able to sleep."

That doesn't help.

Lewis's silence must communicate his befuddlement, because Tad lets out a loud sigh. "We can share, dummy. Body heat."

Oh. *Oh.* Oh god, that's such a bad idea.

But Lewis is so cold.

And Tad is so… so….

Images flash through Lewis's mind from the past couple days. Tad's shirt pulling taut over his chest and shoulders. Tad's lean muscles bulging and working. Tad's sweat staining his armpits and the center of his back and between his pecs. Tad's laugh and luminous smile.

His shoulders lock up as a convulsive shiver wracks him, and that does it. He's cold, and the idea of pressing up against Tad isn't possible to fight.

"I'm not going to let you get hypothermia," Tad says, sounding fierce. "So—"

Before he can finish, Lewis heaves himself from his side of the tent to Tad's. The air outside his sleeping bag is fucking freezing, and he squeals, "Let me in!" as he paws at Tad's.

Tad laughs and unzips his sleeping bag. Even though it's way too small for both of them to fit, Lewis wriggles in. It's blissfully warm, and when Tad hooks his legs around Lewis's, Lewis's arms go around his neck. The cold on his back makes him shudder into Tad. Tad says into his hair, "You were supposed to bring your sleeping bag with you."

"I'm really bad at camping and I'd probably be dead right now if not for you," Lewis says, which isn't really a reply, but somehow is the only reply that feels right.

"Maybe not dead, but you probably would have climbed down that washed-out part of the trail, and it would've gotten dark, and…." Tad stops talking. "Never mind."

"That's my point," Lewis says. He has his head tucked against Tad's body. It feels really right.

Tad wriggles out of the sleeping bag despite Lewis's attempts to keep him there. The lingering body heat he leaves behind is nothing compared to the heat of his actual body. Lewis shivers again.

In the moonlight's filmy illumination, Tad's crouched form is just a darker shadow. Polyester slithers over the bottom of the tent and Lewis hears a zipper. "What are you doing?" Lewis asks, teeth chattering.

"You'll see," Tad answers. "Well, you won't *see*. It's pretty dark. Unless you want me to get out a flashlight."

"I j-just want you to c-c-come back," Lewis says, feeling thoroughly pitiful.

The black blob of negative space pauses.

Tad comes back, pulling Lewis's sleeping bag with him. "C'mon, roll onto this," Tad urges him. When Lewis just keeps hunching into Tad's sleeping bag, Tad huffs something that might be either a sigh or a laugh, and manhandles Lewis into following his orders.

In a few seconds, they're cuddled up together on Lewis's sleeping bag, with Tad's draped over them. "Bet you didn't know this tent came with a queen-size sleeping bag," Tad says.

Lewis laughs. He'd laugh at anything right now, because he's warm. Tad's body is so warm.

He'd laugh at anything right now, because Tad's arms are around him. They're fitted snug together, chest to chest and hip to hip. The fabric of Tad's pajamas feels soft against Lewis's bare skin. Lewis tells himself not to imagine how soft it would be if it was Tad's skin he could feel.

The body heat gradually unknots Lewis's tense muscles. As he's getting less tense, though, he can feel Tad getting tenser. "You don't like this," Lewis mumbles.

Tad lets out a strangled laugh. "Um, no. I like this too much. Sorry if, um, you know. It becomes… obvious. I meant it, though. I respect your boundaries."

The thought of Tad getting hard, and the possibility that Lewis might be able to feel his erection, makes it suddenly impossible to think of anything else.

And he's the idiot who said no, they can't fool around. He's the idiot who said it wouldn't feel right. Because they don't know each other, and the marriage was a mistake, and Lewis isn't a hookup kind of guy. He's the one who set the boundaries, which Tad is now gallantly respecting.

"Sorry if I smell," Lewis says, because he doesn't know what else to. There's a silence. Then Tad guffaws. "Are we just like, apologizing to each other now?"

"I'm sorry I was a dick the other morning in the hotel too," Lewis says in a rush, which is sort of agreement? But also just sort of something he should have said already.

Tad goes still in his arms. "Oh." It's more of an inhale than a word. Tad gets tenser. "I… don't worry about it. I mean, I get it. You're taking a break. I don't blame you. I get why you reacted the way you did."

A lump rises in Lewis's throat. He has no idea what he wants, no idea how to get what he wants, no idea if Tad would even want the same thing, because Lewis pushed him away. "But I didn't have to be a dick," Lewis says softly. "All my exes called me a control freak. I guess they were right."

Tad's forehead bumps against Lewis's. Warm breath puffs over his face. "You got freaked out over a big thing. That's not being a control freak. I mean, I freak out over little things all the time."

"Yeah, but we could've been in it together, and instead I turned it into like, me against you—" Lewis gulps down a breath and tries to wrestle this moment into something he knows how to handle. But this moment doesn't want to be handled. This moment is Tad's long, lean body pressed against Lewis's, their arms around each other, and Lewis's crumbling certainty that he shouldn't have something with Tad, no matter how short-lived it is.

"Have you been thinking about this for the past few days?" Tad asks.

"Yeah."

Tad is quiet for a second, his breath filling the space between them. "Then I accept your apology," he finally says.

It's that *then* that does it. Lewis giggles. "Wait—if I wasn't thinking about it this whole time, you wouldn't have accepted my apology?"

Seriously, Tad replies, "My minimum apology-accepting threshold is twenty-four hours of brooding, with occasional exceptions for particularly beautiful contrition."

There's another silence. Then Tad snorts and Lewis laughs and everything feels easy and natural between them again. That night in the bar, Lewis thought Tad was so funny—but now he realizes he didn't know the half of it. It's only been two days. Imagine getting to have Tad in your life all the time making you laugh like this?

Tad's arms tighten around Lewis and every single bit of his resolve collapses. How can it not? Tad is funny and warm—literally warm, but also, he exudes a quiet warmth that draws Lewis to him. He's solid and present, like he's not afraid to be who he is. Or maybe more like, it doesn't matter whether he's afraid or not. He refuses to be anyone but who he is.

Lewis likes that. He really, really likes that.

He also really, really likes how Tad's hands feel on his bare back, and how one of his legs has slipped between Tad's without him realizing.

Maybe… maybe they can have something right now. Casual. No strings attached.

"I like you," is how Lewis chooses to articulate any of this, because he's incredibly bad at it. If romance—or even just sex—required a license, he never would have passed the test.

Does Tad's breath catch? It's a second, anyway, before he replies, "I like you too."

"Um." The dark makes this easier. "I know I'm like, on the whole break. Thing. But… I really like you, Tad. And maybe… I mean, I'm just…."

At this point, he half expects Tad to kick him out of the sleeping bag. Instead, fingers brush over Lewis's face. "Yeah?" he asks softly. "Keep going."

Lewis swallows so hard that Tad must hear it. "We're here now. It doesn't have to be forever. It can just be for now."

Tad's palm rests gently against Lewis's cheek. Lewis can feel Tad's heart, hummingbird fast, beating against his chest. He wants to lean into Tad's hand. God, he wants that so badly. But he can't. He can't if Tad isn't into this anymore.

"Just for now," Tad repeats. Huskiness in his voice lights a blazing heat in Lewis's gut. "I… yeah. That would be…." He laughs quietly. "You're not the only one who's bad at this, you know."

"What does that mean?" Lewis asks. He's not assuming the worst, but he's also hardly daring to hope.

"It means…." Tad lets out a breath. "Fuck it."

His lips brush Lewis's. The softest touch. An unspoken question. The feeling Lewis has wanted since the morning they woke up in bed together, but which he's been too scared to admit is completely within his grasp.

Lewis kisses him back, more than a brush, but still light. "Is this okay?" Lewis whispers.

One of Tad's hands settles at the small of Lewis's back, pulling him close. The other wanders up his spine and traces the line of a shoulder blade. "Is it okay with you?" Tad replies.

Lewis feels like he's careening into feelings he can't control, let alone stop. He slips a hand into Tad's silky hair and tugs him closer. This time, when they kiss, Lewis tries to make it clear that this is so much more than okay. His fingers tighten in Tad's hair, his tongue teases Tad's upper lip.

Tad moans and opens.

Their tongues glide against each other's and they're both breathing hard already, kissing like they're never going to get another chance, sucking and biting each other's lips, and every time Tad drags his fingers across Lewis's body, it's like electricity sizzling over his skin.

Tad rolls his hips into Lewis's, and now Lewis can feel his erection. He moans and clutches a fistful of Tad's pajamas, pulling his mouth away from Tad's to scrape his teeth down his jaw. Stubble burns his lips and desire pulses hot in his gut.

He lets out an explosive breath against Tad's neck as he bites his way down to the collarbone he can feel, sharp and defined and skin-hot against Lewis's lips as Tad's shirt rubs the side of his face.

And oh god Tad smells—not good, exactly. Neither of them smells exactly good. But Tad smells like sweat and musk and earthiness, and it's irresistible and Lewis wants to swallow him, all of him, down to the last drop.

He bites and sucks and slides his hands up Tad's shirt, cups the small of his back and feels the muscles working there as Tad moves against him. Tad hauls Lewis's face back up to his for another hard, openmouthed kiss. Their urgency builds, Lewis's tongue fucking into Tad's mouth, both of them groaning as they grind against each other. Tad slips a hand down Lewis's underwear to grab his ass.

"I'm not going to last," Lewis pants. Rubbing against Tad has him so hard and so close to the edge that it's almost embarrassing.

Almost, except Tad's bucking hips are just as uncontrolled. "Fuck," Tad hisses. "I want—can I—?"

"Yes," Lewis says, even though he's not sure what he's agreeing to. It doesn't matter. If Tad wants it, Lewis wants to give it to him. He wishes he could see Tad's face, but he can feel his body. God, he can feel his body, the roll of his hips, the way his muscles bunch and tighten and work under his hands, his hot, hard cock, straining at his pants.

Tad's hand fumbles between their bodies. Elastic snaps and cloth gathers and Lewis gets the idea really quick. He shoves the front of his boxer briefs down and lets out a long moan when their bodies meet again. It's skin against skin, delicious friction, slick hot wetness as their cocks rub and their pre-cum mingles and smears.

They kiss and it's barely a kiss, just mouthing at each other, lips and tongues and teeth and harsh breathing.

"I want to touch you," Tad whispers.

"Yes," Lewis replies, since apparently it's the only word he can say anymore. With effort, he adds, "I want you to do that too. Please do that."

Tad runs a finger up Lewis's cock from root to tip. Lewis shudders and sucks at his jaw, stubble prickling against his lips.

A finger slides over the head of Lewis's cock, delicious, spine-tingling pressure in his slit, and Lewis lets out a helpless, desperate moan against Tad's skin.

"God, you're going to make me come just listening to you," Tad gasps. He glides his thumb across Lewis's cockhead, and Lewis can't help the noise he makes as he feels pre-cum smear.

Tad groans and pulls Lewis tighter against him. At the same time, his hand wraps around both of their cocks, locking them together.

Lewis grinds into him, his hips rocking with need as he chases that incredible friction. Tad pumps his fist and Lewis's mind goes blissfully blank, and there's nothing but them, their bodies pressed tight, cocks rubbing, friction and slick pre-cum and their mouths hungry for each other. Lewis fucks up into Tad's hand and Tad encourages it with a moan.

Tad's body jerks. "Lewis—I'm coming—"

As he shudders and lets go, Lewis puts his hand between their bodies too. Cum shoots from him, onto both their stomachs, all over Lewis's hand, and Tad's movements are jerky, wild, as he moans and moans and—

"Me too," Lewis manages, as his unstoppable orgasm barrels toward him.

The way Tad's moving, and the noises he's making? The feel of his cum slicking both of them? Lewis can't survive that. His muscles screw tight and then it's on him, pleasure exploding like a sunburst through his body, sweet and sharp and piercing.

He buries his face in Tad's neck and breathes him in, lazy, sated, warm… and in so much trouble.

Chapter Twelve

"THAT'S ONE way to stay warm." Lewis sounds well-fucked and sleepy.

Turning his head to nuzzle into Lewis's hair, Tad agrees with an inarticulate hum. "We should clean up, I guess." He kisses Lewis softly on his bristly cheek. "Don't move."

The wet wipes are in his backpack outside. Once he has them, they clean up silently. Tad brushes a wipe over Lewis's stomach, even though Lewis has already done it. Something aches in his chest. It's just... he wants. He wants *something*. He wants to make Lewis feel looked after.

Lewis hasn't said anything except that first blitzed-out *that's one way to stay warm.*

Is he having second thoughts? Is he freaking out?

Under the sleeping bag, Lewis snuggles up to Tad. His arms loop around Tad's neck, and Tad can't stop himself from finding Lewis's lips with his own.

This kiss is slow, banked heat and—maybe, maybe—a promise of more to come. Lewis isn't freaking out, and Tad's body is loose and noodle-limbed, and that's enough for now.

WHEN TAD drifts to consciousness the next morning, he doesn't want to open his eyes, just in case he dreamt everything. Sure, he can feel Lewis's legs tangled with his, the heavy weight of Lewis in his arms, Lewis's arm slung over him, and the tickle of his hair on Tad's face from the way his head is tucked against Tad's shoulder. But you never know.

The slow rise and fall of Lewis's chest and the perfect warmth of his body makes Tad want to stay here forever. He doesn't want to wake Lewis up, but he knows he has to if they're going to make up miles today.

God, it's so tempting to just stay here, cuddled up with Lewis. But he wanted to make Lewis feel looked after last night. He still feels that way. He's kind of felt that way ever since they woke up in the hotel room together and Lewis started freaking out. If he doesn't do everything he can to push them a few extra miles today, then he's not looking after Lewis.

He tries not to think about the fact that maybe when Lewis said they could have something for now, he meant just last night. Gently, he nudges Lewis awake.

Lewis makes a complaining little mewl of protest, which is so adorable that Tad has to close his eyes and breathe deeply. God. He agreed to have something "just for now," but he wants something for way longer than now.

"Lewis," he says. "We better get up."

Instead of progress toward getting up, Lewis tightens his hold on Tad, moving closer and mumbling, "Rather stay here."

"I think you might still be asleep," Tad says. No way Lewis, Dating Break Lewis, We Need A Divorce As Soon As Possible Lewis, is suggesting cuddling over getting an early start.

"I'm not asleep. I'm just comfortable." Lewis's hand slides up Tad's back, and Tad shudders. The hand stops. Lewis pulls back. "Shit. Sorry." He sounds completely awake now. "Should I… was that not okay?"

"It was okay." Tad's face heats. "It was, you know. Really okay."

"*Oh.*" Lewis's hand returns to Tad's waist, slipping under his shirt to continue its slow trajectory up his spine. "Good."

"Mm." Tad leans into Lewis's touch, bending toward it. "Don't think we have time for this, though."

Lewis buries his face in Tad's neck and plants slow, molten kisses there. Tad's half hard and his willpower can only take so much of Lewis's soft, plush lips on his neck and that hand rubbing his back, dipping under his waistband on each trip down.

"Lewis," he groans, rubbing his dick against Lewis.

Lewis makes a satisfied sound. "Yeah, baby?"

They both freeze. Tad doesn't know what to do. His heart wants to soar at the endearment, but he knows Lewis didn't mean to say it.

"Um, sorry." Lewis disentangles himself from the sleeping bag, from Tad, and unzips the tent flap. "Sorry," he repeats, throwing a tortured glance over his shoulder.

Tad can't make his mouth say *It's okay*, or *Please call me that again*. He lets Lewis go and flops onto his back, hand over his face, and the echo of that accidental *baby* ringing in his ears and heart.

After a couple minutes, he joins Lewis outside the tent and gets dressed. The cold is like a slap, so stripping out of his warm pajamas into his cold clothes feels vaguely like torture.

He gives his hair several sprays of dry shampoo and is a little surprised when Lewis clears his throat and asks, "Do you mind if I use that?"

Tad tosses it to him and though Lewis fumbles, he manages to catch it. Why does Tad find that so cute?

As they pack up, they don't talk about what happened last night. They don't talk about that errant *baby.* They don't talk, in fact, at all, and Tad wonders if he traded away all the easy camaraderie and burgeoning friendship for one more fuck.

He knows he should just talk to Lewis, but talking scares the hell out of him. The fact that talking is scary is part of the reason his relationship with John crashed and burned. They never quite got that part down, and then there wasn't anything left to talk about.

If he was too scared to talk to his boyfriend of three years, how the hell is he going to work up the nerve to talk to Lewis?

It seems like it takes forever to get to the washed-out section of trail. They don't speak the entire time. By the time they arrive, Tad is anxious, miserable, and convinced he caused this, even though he's almost positive it's because Lewis accidentally called him *baby.*

Too bad he's never initiated a difficult conversation in his life. Fuck, Lewis is totally right that being married to each other is a horrible idea. Marriage requires communication. Tad doesn't know how to do that.

"Follow my lead, okay?" Tad says. "I've done trails like this before. We'll just take it slow, and tell me if you need me to wait. Sound good?"

He looks at Lewis. Lewis's face is drawn and set, like he's going off to war.

"Lewis?" Tad prompts. Is he freaking out? Like, Freaking Out freaking out?

Lewis's eyes find him. "Tad," he says. Tad waits. Lewis swallows hard. "I might die, and I don't want to die with like, a bunch of stuff unsaid."

"Okay, first of all, you're not going to die," Tad says, even though he'd very much like to talk and he's glad Lewis is initiating. Maybe he should have agreed that death is on the table to inspire more open and honest communication.

For a second, Lewis just stands there, looking at a loss. Finally, he says, "Is there a second of all?"

"Er, no. You, um, wanted to say something?" Tad's pulse picks up. Maybe Lewis is going to rescind the something-just-for-now offer of last night.

Taking a deep breath, Lewis replies, "Yeah. God. I'm—I'm fucking this up. I just—I'm such a mess with dating. Or romance in general. I'm like—you know, I'm a huge rom-com fan? And I think it totally messed with my perception. My expectations are all wrong. Like, I think I'm so smart because I'm not waiting for my prince to come along and sweep me off my feet, you know? Except I'm totally waiting for my Tom Hanks or Hugh Grant or Billy Crystal—"

"Wait, Billy Crystal?" Tad asks.

"Oh my god, haven't you seen *When Harry Met Sally?*"

"Billy Crystal is in that?"

"Yeah, he's Meg Ryan's love interest, he's amazing—okay, look, not the point."

Actually it totally *could* be the point because Tad's kind of hung up on the idea of Lewis having a thing for Billy Crystal. He keeps picturing Miracle Max from *The Princess Bride*.

"The point is," Lewis goes on, "I have all these ideas of what romance is, you know? And it's like… it messed everything up for me. I fall too fast because I keep thinking this is it, this is what leads to that Moment, and this guy's the one. And I just… I'm sorry for freaking out about calling you baby."

Tad isn't quite following the logic, but the important thing is that last bit. "It didn't bother me," he says cautiously.

Raking a hand through his hair, Lewis says, "But I'm not the kind of person who throws terms of endearments around lightly. And I don't want to lead you on or make you think this is something it's not, and I don't even know what this is, and—"

His hair is sticking up adorably. Lewis swallows hard again. "Did it really not bother you?"

Tad offers a tiny smile. "I liked it?"

"Oh." Lewis looks like he doesn't know what to do with that. He rubs his elbow. "I would understand if you want to tell me to take a hike after this morning."

"Pun intended?" Tad's heart still feels like it's going to fling itself out of his rib cage.

A startled laugh fizzes out of Lewis, skipping across the mountainside. The tension between them eases. "Yeah, I definitely thought that one out in advance because I'm really clever."

"And obviously you wouldn't take credit for a pun you didn't intend," Tad says, making his eyes big and innocent.

Lewis laughs again, and this time, when he runs his fingers through his hair, it's a little less frantic and a little more abashed. "I don't know how to do this. I don't even know what this is."

Tad's wedding ring catches his eye. Weirdly, it calms him. He doesn't know what this is either, but they're dealing with it together, and that's something.

"Do you still want…." Tad begins, trailing off when he realizes he doesn't know how to ask what he wants to ask.

Lewis comes closer. "I still want to have—" He hesitates, then smiles. "Something. Last night was…."

"Amazing."

"Yeah. Really amazing."

Tad draws a slow breath. His heart is still pounding, but now giddy euphoria is pinging around his chest. He leans forward, giving Lewis enough time to pull away. But Lewis doesn't, and Tad kisses him chastely.

They smile at each other. Lewis's smile looks goofy. Tad has a feeling his looks the same way.

Tad squeezes Lewis's hand. "Now that you can go to your death with no regrets, want to climb down this trail?"

Lewis laughs, free and relieved. Tad's heart swells at the sound.

This is just for now, he reminds himself.

If he doesn't keep telling himself that, he's going to be in trouble.

WHEN THEY arrive at their planned campsite, Tad takes inventory: two extra miles successfully walked, zero broken bones, nine hours of wonderful, easy conversation, and one sexual fantasy that has him half hard and very glad they talked.

They're like a well-oiled machine while they set up everything. A good team. Like a couple, even if they're only a just-for-now couple.

After dinner, they sit by the fire. It's warmer now that they're off the mountain, so they're still in T-shirts. Their arms keep brushing. Lewis touches Tad's leg once, then again, and the third time, he leaves it there, his thumb rubbing little circles on Tad's thigh.

Tad stands, stretching his arms over his head and letting his shirt ride up. Lewis's eyes go straight to that exposed skin, and his Adam's apple gives a sharp bob.

Tad leaves his arms over his head, hooking one hand around his elbow. "So, I was thinking, considering this is your first camping trip, and you had to do something outside your comfort zone today, you should get a reward."

Lewis's eyes drag up Tad's body. It might just be an effect of the firelight, but his face looks flushed. "What kind of reward?"

With a sly smile, Tad goes to his knees. "The kind that doesn't require pants."

"Fuck," Lewis breathes. His Adam's apple jags again. Tad wants to lick it.

Tad lays his palms on Lewis's thighs and runs them slowly upward. "If you want that kind of reward, I mean."

Hoarsely, Lewis says, "I definitely, very much want that kind of reward."

Tad bypasses Lewis's growing bulge and instead hooks his fingers into his waistband. Lewis groans and his hips twitch up. Tad pops the button on Lewis's jeans and pushes his legs apart so he can shuffle closer.

Slowly, Tad draws down Lewis's zipper. Lewis's cock strains against his briefs, and Tad makes a helpless noise.

Lewis strokes Tad's hair, running his fingers through it, and whispers, "You're so beautiful."

It makes Tad want to die with newness. No one has ever looked at him like that and told him he's beautiful. He's tall and too lean, and his nose is too long, and he has too many freckles.

They gaze at each other, firelight flickering on their skin and clothes. Tad smiles again and tugs on Lewis's waistband. "Off. Help me."

"Bossy." Lewis laughs and lifts his hips. Tad slides his jeans and briefs down to his ankles.

Then Lewis is spread for him, and Tad's between the V of his legs, admiring his cock, jutting upward to Lewis's belly. The thatch of dark hair in his groin, his balls, the fur on his legs. With a hungry noise, Tad touches the tip of his tongue to Lewis's cockhead, running it lightly around the slit.

Lewis gasps and jerks.

Tad smiles. He makes circles with his tongue, varies the pressure, teases Lewis's slit, until Lewis says in a strained voice, "I thought this was supposed to be a reward."

"This is very rewarding for me."

Lewis groans. His fingers tighten in Tad's hair, then loosen, stroking again.

Teasing is fun, but Tad has the taste of Lewis on his tongue—salty pre-cum, which is pulsing out steadily and making Tad ridiculously hard himself. Need throbs low in his gut. With a groan, he takes Lewis in his mouth, swallowing him from tip to root.

The low, guttural noises Lewis makes as Tad sucks him off will live rent-free in his mind for the rest of his life. Before long, Tad's rubbing himself on Lewis's shin, moaning around Lewis's spit-slicked cock and clutching his hips as Lewis grips his hair with one hand and his shoulder with the other.

"Oh fuck—Tad—oh god oh god oh *god* yeah that's it—oh—*there*—"

His hips buck wildly, he lets out a strangled cry, and hot, thick, musky cum shoots down Tad's throat and fills his mouth.

Fuck. Lewis tastes good.

Tad licks Lewis clean as Lewis sags, still groaning. "Holy fuck," Lewis says, then bends over to crush his mouth to Tad's. Their tongues slide together. Lewis tastes like the mac and cheese they had for dinner and woodsmoke and sex as he licks into Tad's mouth.

"Come for me," Lewis breathes into Tad's mouth. Tad nips at his bottom lip and grinds into his leg, and Lewis is stroking his hair and down his neck and whispering, "That's it, baby—I wanna see you come—come for me just like this—"

It's his voice that sends Tad over the edge. It's silk and filth and safety and Tad's helpless against it. His body winds tight and then he's coming, thrusting wildly against Lewis as Lewis swallows his cries.

When he's done, he goes boneless, flopping against Lewis and burying his face in the crease of Lewis's hip. Lewis's fingers are in his hair, stroking his scalp and down his neck to his shoulders. "You're so hot," Lewis says wonderingly.

"Good reward?" Tad asks, his voice muffled by Lewis's skin.

Lewis draws him upright and kisses him slowly. Tad's heart turns to molten gold as Lewis's lips open him up and Lewis's hands cup his jaw, and they kiss and kiss.

Lewis called him *baby* and didn't freak out.

This is the best camping trip Tad's ever been on.

Chapter Thirteen

THE NEXT few days imprint themselves on Tad's memory as too-bright snapshots. A searing red and pink sunset reflecting on a lake with water so still it could be glass. A flock of pinyon jays rising from juniper trees, feathers flashing sapphire under the autumn sun. Pines scraping the blue of the sky, the day so bright, their boughs look black.

Lewis splashing his face with water from a stream, the droplets catching the sun. Lewis scrambling up a boulder and grinning like a goofball. Lewis sitting by the fire, hair falling over his forehead, eyes gold and amber. Lewis stretched out on his side in their tent, smiling at Tad in the morning, sunrise filtering through the canvas to make a fuzzy halo around his head.

Lewis and Lewis and Lewis and Lewis.

The day they get to their pickup spot is the first time they encounter other people. There's a family of five, a lone man with fishing gear, and two women with a lesbian pride bumper sticker on their Subaru.

They're early, so they sit by the lake and dangle their feet in the water. The water feels great on Tad's feet. He never really notices how much they hurt until the end of the trip.

Lewis tosses a couple rocks into the water one after another, ripples spreading across the surface in their wake. When he picks up a flat rock, Tad says, "Hey, that's a great skipping rock." When Lewis looks at it, Tad asks teasingly, "You know how to skip rocks, right?"

Scoffing, Lewis says, "Yeah." Tad raises an eyebrow. Lewis flicks the rock toward water, where it hits the surface with a *plop!* and promptly sinks.

"Best out of three," Lewis says.

Tad laughs and kisses him. Lewis's hand comes up to cup the side of his face. Their tongues brush, and if this was any of the other stops from the past week, Tad would push Lewis down onto the sun-warmed rocks and fuck him. Instead, he reluctantly breaks the kiss and finds another flat stone, putting it in Lewis's hand. "Here, like this. Give your wrist a little flick at the end."

This time when Lewis tries, he gets the rock to skip and crows in victory. The sun catches his eyes and shines on his hair, and he's the most beautiful goddamn thing Tad has ever seen.

Tad's falling for him. Which, like, honestly? Is a realization that's been creeping around the edges of his awareness for days. Maybe all week.

"You're a natural," Tad says, pushing aside his rising sadness at the fact that... this is it. Sure, they'll see each other for divorce stuff. But after they're brought back to Lewis's rental car, this... whatever this is, is over.

"Hey." Tad puts his hand on Lewis's leg. "I never told you that I think it's really cool you did this. Backpacking when you've never even camped before? It's pretty badass."

Lewis gives him a broad grin. "Oh yeah, that's totally me. Badass. That's what they call me at work." His fingertips dance over the back of Tad's hand, and Tad turns his palm up to capture them.

They're quiet for a minute. Tad worries his shift in mood was too obvious, that he killed the easy happiness between them, but Lewis says, "I've been thinking. And I wasn't sure how to ask, because, um. I know we agreed we'd just do *this*"—he gestures between them—"while we were out here. But I'm not flying home until tomorrow, and if you're interested, my hotel has a queen bed." When Tad blinks and opens his mouth wordlessly, Lewis rushes to add, "Never mind, sorry, I was totally overstepping—"

"I'd love that," Tad interrupts, knowing he sounds like a giddy idiot. He's beaming so hard his face hurts.

Lewis relaxes. "Cool."

Tad scoots closer. "I have a condition, though."

"Yeah?"

"We stop at a pharmacy or something." When Lewis furrows his brow, Tad says, "If we can shower, that opens up certain possibilities."

Realization dawns over Lewis's face. "*Oh*. Yeah, we definitely can stop somewhere." He shifts his legs, and Tad glances down. Yep, there's some clear tenting going on in Lewis's lap. With a devilish grin, Tad slips his hand between Lewis's legs and squeezes. Lewis swats his arm and Tad laughs.

Lewis turns red. Looking and sounding flustered, he says, "When do you fly back?"

"Tomorrow."

"Oh yeah? Maybe we're on the same flight!"

Yeah, the idea has occurred to Tad, but he didn't want to find out they *were* and see the look of horror on Lewis's face. "Mine leaves in the morning," Tad says.

Disappointment flashes across Lewis's face. "Damn. I have an afternoon flight." It would be a lie if Tad claimed he wasn't bummed out that they weren't on the same plane—more time together!—but the fact that *Lewis* is bummed is almost as good. "I'll drive you to the airport," Lewis says decisively.

"You don't have to do that."

"I want to." He slips an arm around Tad's back and pulls him close while Tad's chest glows with warmth.

They lapse into silence, listening to birds, the lap of water on the shore, the shouts and laughter of kids running around. The cool water caresses Tad's feet and he moves one. Swirls and eddies whorl around his ankles, then Lewis's. Lewis bumps his foot against Tad's and cuts a smile at him. Tad leans his head against Lewis's and thinks he should take this opportunity to talk to Lewis—about anything—because their time together is running out.

But he can't bring himself to break the silence, not because it's too hard, which is normally how he feels—his shyness creeping up his chest and throat like a tide until it drowns his words—but because it's so easy. Like he could speak at any time, and it would be no effort at all, and he wouldn't have to worry about getting judged or laughed at.

The sound of an approaching engine makes Lewis look over his shoulder. "I think that's our ride." Regret colors his tone, and for a moment, he doesn't move, just pulling Tad tighter against him.

A week ago, Tad would've made a joke about how this turned out to be a great honeymoon. Now? The thought makes his chest hurt, because it would have been a fantastic honeymoon, just the sort of thing Tad would want to do if he ever got married. Er. If he ever got married not on a drunken lark in Vegas.

He and John talked about marriage a couple times. In retrospect, the fact that it was only a couple times in their three-year relationship was a Giant Clue that things wouldn't work out, because one of the things that drew them together was not being into hookup culture and wanting to settle down. *I want to be someone's husband*, Tad remembers saying.

He got his wish? Kinda? In like, a *Twilight Zone* kind of way.

With a sigh, Lewis gets to his feet, offering Tad a hand. Tad takes it, and his heart twists tight with a jumble of emotions. It's on one of those fairground rides in there, spinning fast and throwing everyone around in a laughing, queasy mess.

They hold hands as they retrieve their gear and hold hands as they go to meet the guy who's here to pick them up, and hold hands in the back seat while Tad drops off to sleep.

It's weird getting back in the car that brought them here a week ago. They were strangers, and now they're not. Tad doesn't know what they are, but he knows they aren't that.

The drive back to Vegas feels short. Tad navigates Lewis to the hotel—with a stop at a drug store on the way. Lewis goes inside and comes back with a plastic bag. Face red, he hands it over and asks, "Is this stuff okay with you?"

There's a box of condoms, lube, and—Tad giggles—Vaseline. He holds it up and arches an eyebrow.

Lewis turns redder. "In case the lube isn't any good."

I love you Tad wants to laugh, but he bites his tongue and doesn't. "Smart," he says instead, and Lewis looks pleased with the praise.

At the hotel, Lewis asks if they can get a king bed instead of a queen, and the heated look he shoots Tad makes Tad's belly get tight with desire.

When they get up to the room, they drop their backpacks on the floor. The duvet on the bed is pristine, crisp white, and Tad doesn't want to go near it, worried his week's worth of filth might actually be orbiting him at this point.

Lewis seems to have the same misgivings about his accumulated dust and sweat getting on things from mere proximity. "I'm gonna shower," he says, pointing with a thumb over his shoulder. A smile quirks one corner of his mouth. "Wanna join me?"

"Hm, let me think," Tad says musingly, unbuttoning his jeans.

With a growly chuckle, Lewis pulls him into the bathroom. Once the water is warm enough in the shower, they peel off their clothes and step under the spray. Tad closes his eyes and lets the water run over his hair and face, feeling dirt washing away.

He opens his eyes and his breath catches. Lewis is facing him, wet hair matted against his head, rivulets of water running in glistening tracks down his body, all his naked skin shining and slick.

Tad lowers his head to take a dusky nipple in his mouth, tonguing it slowly. Lewis groans and his hands curl around the back of Tad's neck. Nuzzling into Lewis's pec, Tad works his nipple into a hard nub, then licks in a wider circle around it, catching the fur of Lewis's chest on his tongue.

Lewis groans, "Wait."

When Tad pauses, Lewis picks up the bar of soap. Slowly and deliberately, he washes every inch of Tad, lingering in the most sensitive spots, caressing when Tad shudders, occasionally dropping kisses.

In the end, Tad's shoulders are braced against the wall, his body sparking with need. "Are you going to fuck me now?"

Lewis looks just as worked up. He leans in to give Tad the filthiest kiss he's ever been treated to, and their erections rub together. Pure electric pleasure lightning-bolts up Tad's spine.

"Can I wash your hair?" Lewis asks into Tad's mouth. His hips move against Tad's.

Tad whimpers and clutches a handful of Lewis's ass. "I usually condition too."

Lewis moves away from Tad's lips and licks behind his jaw, down to where Tad's pulse is hammering in his neck. "That's like three to five minutes too long to wait to fuck you, though."

Tad laughs and kisses Lewis hard. "You'll be sorry when you see the frizzy mess I get without conditioner. You'll never want to have sex with me again."

The look in Lewis's eyes makes Tad regret the joke. There's a depth and complexity of feeling there, a mess of lust and regret and happiness and longing and—affection?

Lewis doesn't say anything. He squeezes a pump of shampoo into his hand and lathers it in Tad's hair, massaging Tad's scalp. Tad drops his head to Lewis's shoulder, letting his body go boneless.

What they did the night they met and married wasn't like this. What they did in their tent wasn't either. There's tenderness in the way Lewis is touching him, washing him, taking care of him, and Tad can't stand it for much longer. "Lewis," he murmurs.

Lewis dips Tad's head under the water and rinses his own hair. While he's doing that, Tad gives Lewis's cock a few slow strokes. "If you're going to torture me…," Tad says.

With a moan, Lewis lets his head fall to Tad's shoulder. He bites Tad's collarbone as he grabs Tad's hips. "You win."

Shutting off the shower, Tad replies, "We both win, sweetheart."

Lewis's head pops up at the endearment, eyes wide. Tad holds his breath. Then, Lewis's face breaks into a wide smile as he elbows the shower door open, grabs a couple towels, and tows Tad to bed.

Chapter Fourteen

LEWIS STARES at his fingers on the steering wheel, wedding ring still gleaming on his left hand, when he parks at the departures drop-off at Harry Reid International Airport.

"Well." Next to him, Tad clears his throat. "Um, thanks. For the ride. And... yeah."

"Yeah," Lewis echoes. "I mean, thank *you*. Not for the ride, I guess. But"—he waves a hand vaguely—"coming."

Tad's mouth twitches and Lewis guesses he could have made that less innuendo-y.

Tad swivels, gets caught on the seat belt, and fumbles to unbuckle it. When it rattles back over his shoulder, he sucks in a breath—and holds it, staring at Lewis.

Lewis tells himself not to think. About anything. Especially not about the spangle of freckles across Tad's cheekbones and nose or how the light catches his eyes and turns them aquamarine.

"I guess I'll see you in New York," Tad says. "For the paperwork."

"Yeah."

"Yeah."

They didn't talk about when *just for right now* ended. They made out in bed this morning. And had sex again. How was Lewis supposed to resist sucking Tad's cock one more time?

But now they're on the cusp of this thing between them being over. They had fun. A lot of fun. It just can't continue, because Lewis can't trust himself. And Tad hasn't tried to convince him that actually, he's not like Lewis's exes at all. Lewis is so messed up that he doesn't know if that proves Tad would be good for him or bad.

"So." Tad's fingers fidget. "I should probably get going."

Lewis is tempted to suggest hanging out once he returns the car and gets through security. He's going to have time to kill since his flight isn't until the afternoon.

Except the way Tad keeps fidgeting and chewing on his cheek makes Lewis think he just wants to get this over with. Clean break. Walk away. Meet for coffee at home to go over the paperwork and part ways until the divorce hearing.

Tad probably has the right idea. If Lewis lets himself think, he'll think about how sad he feels right now, and how much he doesn't want a clean break, and how his feelings for Tad aren't just-for-right-now feelings.

"Do you need help with your bag?" Lewis asks like an idiot. Tad's been carrying the backpack around for a week. Of course he doesn't need help. It's just, Lewis doesn't want to stop talking, because when they stop talking, it means Tad's going to leave.

"I'm okay." Tad watches Lewis for a second, then cuts his eyes toward the window. His fingers hook around the door handle. "Well, text me when you want to do the paperwork—"

"Wait!" Lewis's hand closes around Tad's wrist. Tad stops. "Wait," Lewis repeats, and swallows hard. "I just—I had a lot of fun. It was great. I'm not sure I'll ever go camping again because it won't measure up."

The last part makes him turn red. It's true, though.

Tad's face softens, which does something funny to Lewis's chest. "You should go camping again," Tad says.

Maybe we could go together sometime is what Lewis wants to say. The old Lewis would have—the Lewis who cannonballed into every relationship, even when the water was clearly over his head.

"Maybe."

Tad holds his gaze. His eyes look glassy, but he blinks quickly, says, "Bye, Lewis," and gets out of the car. After a second, the trunk slams shut and Tad walks away, backpack slung over his shoulder.

Move, says the part of Lewis's brain that came up with the Dating Break. The smart, logical part. The part that's looking out for him. Keeping him from getting hurt again. *Drive the fuck away*.

Instead, he's still sitting there when Tad stops at the door, his eyes scanning the cars. When he spots Lewis, their gazes meet. Tad blows him a kiss.

Then he's gone.

IT'S BETTER this way.

Lewis returns the car and goes back to the terminal. He checks his bag and goes through security. He tells himself it isn't weird that he scans the Departures board to find Tad's flight, and that just because he knows what gate Tad's at doesn't mean he's going to go find him.

Anyway, as he's standing there trying to figure out which direction Gate D37 is, the status on the flight flips from ON-TIME to BOARDING. So now he can't, even if he wanted to. Which he didn't, because he's letting go.

His flight doesn't leave until two thirty, so he has a few hours to kill. In a gift shop, he picks up a snow globe for Stacy filled with gold glitter dollar signs instead of plastic snow and a sweatshirt for his sister. At one of the probably fifteen Starbucks in the airport, he grabs a Frappuccino and a cake pop for himself, and one of those Been There mugs for his mom. And in a tacky, touristy art store, he finds a hideous mashup of the Vegas Strip and Van Gogh's *Starry Night*, which his dad will love.

His flight still doesn't board for two hours.

Ugh.

He wanders past the Departures board again. Tad's flight is listed as DEPARTED. That's good. It left on time.

Does Tad have someone to pick him up at JFK? Or is he going to get a taxi? He doesn't have family in New York, and he never mentioned any friends. Lewis doesn't like to think of Tad sitting by himself in a taxi, even though thousands of people sit alone in taxis every day. It's just. Tad doing it. That feels bad.

Goddammit, he has to stop thinking about Tad.

To distract himself, he texts his sister to confirm she's still picking him up. She'll complain, but she owes him, because he's been going with her to her IVF appointments.

Then he can't think of anything else to do, so he walks to his gate. He tries to walk slowly, but he's gay, so slow to him is still fast compared to everyone else. At his deserted gate, he flops down in a seat, eats his cake pop, and drinks his Frappuccino.

His phone buzzes. Probably Taylor telling him about her latest D&D campaign.

It's not Taylor.

The text reads: **In the Zone era Britney or Blackout era Britney?**

Lewis looks at the contact again.

"Best Husband Ever 👨‍❤️‍👨 "

It takes him a second to realize the reason his face hurts is because he's grinning so widely.

> *Are you texting from the plane?*
> **Welcome to the future, Lewis**
> **Now answer the question please**
> *Blackout obvs*
> **Correct**
> *But Toxic is her best song*
> **Also correct**

Lewis laughs, still grinning stupidly down at his phone. He sips his Frappuccino, which suddenly tastes much better.

> *1989 era t-swift or folklore era t-swift?*
> **LEWIS**
> **NO**
> **YOU CAN'T**
> **This is like Sophie's choice**
> **Uhhhhhh**
> *This is a timed question*
> **I forfeit**
> *Not allowed*

There's a pause. Then:

> **1989**
> **No**
> **Folklore**
> **AHHHHH IDK**
> **my tears ricochet!**
> **But! All You Had To Do Was Stay!**
> **Whhhyyyy**
> **Ok. Folklore. Final answer**
> *Well we can't all be perfect*
> **A;dfjakdf;dakfj wow Lewis**
> **Park Slope or Williamsburg**
> *Trick question. Neither*

Rofl

They keep texting, the game giving way to talking. Tad makes Lewis giggle with his descriptions of fellow plane passengers; Lewis tells Tad about the presents he got for Stacy and his family. They talk about stuff they have to do once they're home and before heading back to work on Monday. They talk about what that one thing is that you can only get in New York and that you don't think about until you're somewhere else where you can't get it.

"We'd like to welcome aboard our first-class passengers traveling to JFK," rings out, and Lewis's head jerks up. The gate area has filled. People are milling around, and a line is forming at the boarding door. What? Where did the time go?

He glances at his phone. Tad's last message is sitting unanswered: **I'm going to the New York Botanical Garden next weekend so that will be fun. Still bummed I didn't get to visit any of the big gardens in Vegas**

Lewis keeps hesitating, because what he wants to say is, I'll bring you to them someday.

Which is stupid.

Instead, he says, *I've never been to the NY Botanical Garden*

Boring. He rolls his eyes at himself. Then, he types, *Random question, do you have a ride home from the airport?*

There's a lot of typing, but all that comes back is **No**

Lewis has to put his phone away, because his boarding group gets called. He doesn't know why he asked about Tad having a ride. What does it matter? It's not like he's going to give Tad a ride. Like, he *would*. But his flight hasn't even left yet, and Tad will be landing soon. So that's stupid.

When he finds his seat, he gets his phone out again. Tad hasn't said anything else and Lewis feels a curl of anxiety. Shit, he said something wrong. That's why Tad was typing and typing—and obviously deleting— for so long before his one-word answer.

I guess it doesn't really matter but I'd give you a ride if I could

There's no answer, and eventually Lewis has to turn on airplane mode. Once they're airborne and Wi-Fi is available, he thinks about going on it to see if Tad texted back. But what if Tad didn't text back?

If Tad never texted back, then he's doing what they agreed. They're not going to be a thing anymore. It won't work. Tad not texting back is Tad saving Lewis from himself.

He throws his headphones on, puts on his For Planes playlist, and closes his eyes. Apparently he dozes off, because before he knows it, the flight attendants are coming down the aisle cleaning up.

When the plane lands, Lewis turns his phone back on to text Taylor, who assures him she's on her way. They arrive at the gate and start to disembark, and all the notifications, emails, and texts he missed while his phone was off come through.

There's a notification from Tad.

Heart leaping, Lewis opens the text and reads.

Hey sorry we were landing and the wifi cut out
You're sweet about the ride but I'll be ok
Do YOU have a ride?
You must be on the plane
Ok I swear I'm not a stalker but I just checked your flight and yeah you're on the plane
So that's good, I hope you're having a good flight
I'm in my cab now
Omg how weird is this, guess what he's playing
If you said "Britney Spears's magnum opus, Blacklight" you would be correct
Are we in the Matrix?
He's playing the WHOLE album. Amazing
He's starting it over!!!!
I gave him a really good tip
Ok I'm back at my apartment again. My cat says hi. Did I ever even tell you I have a cat? Her name is Hetty Wainthropp
Hey so I didn't have the guts to say this when you dropped me off this morning but I hope we can still be friends
You are a cool guy Lewis Mancini-Sommer
So yeah
Wow sorry for bombarding you with texts. You probably won't want to be friends when you get all these

Lewis can't describe the feeling in his chest. He's not sure he's ever had this before, this ballooning joy and laughter and happiness and giddy bubbles roiling under the surface of his skin.

Just landed at JFK, I just saw your messages
I would love to still be friends
Also send a picture of your cat

Less than a minute goes by. Then, from Tad: a smiling emoji.

Chapter Fifteen

"YOUR ENERGY is fire," Stacy declares over coffee the following week. Lewis is back at work and has only gotten a quarter of the way through his inbox. He definitely needs coffee to keep slogging through, and since he and Stacy coordinate their in-office days, he sent her the super secret bat signal that means *make any excuse you have to and meet me for coffee in fifteen minutes.*

It's just the coffee cup emoji so it's not that super secret.

Lewis sips at his peppermint mocha. "So I have acceptable maid-of-honor energy?"

"You always did, but now you're like, chef's kiss." Stacy squeals. "Oh my god, was it *so* amazing? Don't you just feel totally energized?"

When he first sat down with Stacy and she asked breathlessly, *How was it?* Lewis had to remind himself that he was supposed to have been getting his chakra scrubbed last week, not trekking through the wilderness with a hot man. "My energy has never been more gized," he says.

"Hardy har har," Stacy deadpans. "My dad has better jokes."

"Your dad is hilarious. I *aspire* to be your dad."

"Embarrassing." Stacy gulps her coffee, then fans her open mouth. "Shit, it's hot."

Lewis takes the cup away from her. "Slow down. If you burn your tongue off, you won't be able to say your vows to Alang."

Waving a hand, she says, "I'll hold up cards cue cards, *Love, Actually* style. That's not really the most important thing I use my tongue for in this relationship—"

"Ew." Lewis slides the cup back across the table. "Go ahead, burn your tongue off. I don't want to hear this."

Stacy laughs devilishly. "You're such a prude."

"I'm not a prude, I just don't want to hear your BJ tricks. I have my own. I don't need to know yours."

Laughing again, Stacy takes another gulp of coffee. "Speaking of, did you see Tad again?"

"Maybe," Lewis says cagily.

"You did!" She claps gleefully. "Let me see your hand."

"What?" He balls his hands in his lap. "Why? You can't read my chakra from my hands."

"Gimme," she orders.

Powerless as always to stand against the force of nature that is a caffeinated Stacy, he holds out his hands.

She grabs his left one. "You're still wearing this ring?" Her face gets goopy. It's the same face she makes during their yearly *Sleepless in Seattle-While You Were Sleeping-You've Got Mail* marathon, when each movie gets to its Happily Ever After. It's a face Lewis is well acquainted with, since he always makes it too.

"Yeah, I guess," he says, like he forgot.

Stacy knows him too well. "You're seriously into him. Oh my god, did you bail on the retreat? Don't lie to me, Lewis. Did you bail to spend more time with him?"

"Do you really think I would do that?" Lewis asks, which is a question, not a lie.

"Yes," she informs him. "I 100 percent do, and while I'm totally mad you skipped the retreat, if you did it for true love, that did more for your chakra than the vortex could."

"I never said I skipped it!" Lewis protests. Also not a lie. He didn't say that.

She fixes him with an unblinking stare.

He returns it.

One of her eyebrows slowly creeps upward. She still doesn't blink.

Lewis breaks first, because he always does. "Okay fine, I skipped the retreat and went camping with Tad."

"Ha!" she crows. "I knew it! Also, *lame*, and I'm mad at you for not going, but"—she squeals—"oh my god, *Lew!* Are you two a thing now?"

"No," Lewis says quickly. "No, I'm still on the Break."

She looks exasperated. "But you hooked up while you were camping. Please tell me you made the most of sharing a tent."

He shrugs but smiles. She squeals again. "Have you been seeing him since you got back?" she asks.

It's taken everything Lewis has not to see Tad. They've been texting. Like. Kind of a lot. But Tad hasn't suggested getting together. Maybe when he said he wanted to stay friends, he really meant he just wanted to be friends? But Lewis just… well. He thought maybe Tad was hoping they could be more than friends.

Which is actually really shitty of Lewis, since he's the one who said they couldn't be more than friends. He shouldn't want Tad to have feelings for him, because if Tad does, then it means he's going to feel lonely and sad and full of longing for something he can't have.

Lewis doesn't want Tad to feel the way he feels right now.

"No," he finally answers, knowing it took too long and sounded too fraught.

"Oh, honey."

"It's fine! We had a… an arrangement. He gets it. It was casual, and now we're going to be friends."

His phone, which is on the table, trills with his text tone—which is an orchestral flourish from the scene where Aladdin and Jasmine first kiss. Yes, from the Disney movie, obviously. It's Tad, responding to a text Lewis sent earlier, and he can't keep the smile off his face.

"Is that him?" Stacy asks.

Lewis turns the phone face down. "Hm?"

She looks triumphant. "So you haven't seen him in person, but you're talking."

"Just a little," Lewis hedges. His phone trills again and it takes all his willpower not to look. They texted all weekend. Tad had to drive to Watertown to get the stuff he brought to Vegas from his brother (which made Lewis feel like an asshole; he never even thought about what happened to the suitcase Tad must have packed), and they even texted then. Voice to text, Tad repeatedly assured him.

Now that they're both back at work, Lewis is trying to get used to more than five minutes going by between messages.

Stacy plants her elbows on the table and watches raptly as Lewis stares at his phone. "You can check it," she says. "I love that I'm watching your love story unfold."

"There's no love story," Lewis says. To prove it, he picks up the phone, doesn't even read Tad's latest couple texts, and sends back: *Can we meet tomorrow to go over the divorce papers?*

Putting the phone back on the table, Lewis says, "We're taking care of divorce stuff. That's why we're texting."

Not a lie, since he just sent a text about it. Who cares if it's the first one?

"Lew," she says.

"Stace," he replies.

She huffs. "Why are you fighting this? You two are obviously meant to be."

Meant to be. Right. Lewis used to believe in meant-to-be. He still believes in it—for other people. "I don't think we are," he says.

Not to be deterred, Stacy asks, "Then why did all this stuff happen?"

"Because we were drunk and horny?"

It's like he didn't say a word. "You don't do hookups and you don't wear jewelry."

"That's your incontrovertible proof?" Why *is* he still wearing the ring? He keeps almost taking it off, but as soon as he gets it up over his knuckle, he stops and slides it back down.

His phone trills with Tad's response. **Sure, want to come over to my place? I already printed all the stuff out**

A slow warmth travels from Lewis's chest to his stomach. It's pretty romantic that Tad already got everything ready. He promised they could start this process right away because he saw how freaked Lewis had been by the drunken marriage.

"My incontrovertible proof is the look you have on your face right now," Stacy says. She hates when he uses what she calls "lawyer words," so the fact that she repeats "incontrovertible" without air quotes or an eye-roll is its own kind of proof. She really thinks there's something between Tad and him. Something special.

Something meant-to-be, which Lewis can't let himself believe again. The only thing any of his relationships were ever meant to be was over.

Stacy was right there with him, believing all those guys were the love of his life—until it was obvious they weren't, and then she was there with ice cream cake and Laffy Taffy and her laptop loaded with rom-coms. She's the best cheerleader you could ever ask for. She always has your back. She's the most supportive person Lewis has ever known in his entire life.

But she's not good at spotting a bad relationship. She so desperately wants Lewis to find The One, just like she did. He's just *tired.* He can't keep getting his heart broken.

"I can tell you like this guy," she says gently, because he obviously looks like he's about to have an anxiety attack. God knows she's talked him down from plenty over the years.

"It doesn't matter if I like him," Lewis says. "I'm not dating right now. That's the rule."

She looks sad. "You made that rule."

And if he can't stick to his own rule, how pathetic is that?

He stands up and goes around the table to kiss her cheek. "I better head back. There's a briefing this week on that recycling case and I have a bajillion emails about it to get through."

"Kay." Stacy blows him a kiss. "I love you. Call me when you land."

As he heads back to his office, he texts Tad back: *Your place sounds great. I'll bring dinner*

Chapter Sixteen

TAD'S APARTMENT building is in Inwood, backing on to Broadway and the Seaman-Drake Arch. Lewis has a soft spot for historical preservation, so he maybe gets a bit nerdy about the latter when Tad lets him in.

"It's always killed me that the campaign to get it protected as a landmark failed back in the early 2000s. I mean, how cool is it that a nineteenth-century marble arch is just *there*, and it's part of an auto-body shop? Have you ever been inside? Oh my god, I think this apartment complex is on the site of the mansion!"

His hands are on his face, which he only realizes after he takes note of the expression on Tad's—some combination of amused, impressed, and... fond?

"I don't think I've ever really appreciated it," Tad says. "But yeah, I've been inside it."

"AHHH."

"So you're really a huge dork, huh?" Tad's wearing a soft, faded henley and charcoal sweats that hug his ass, which Lewis is trying hard not to stare at as Tad unpacks the Cuban takeout that Lewis brought.

Lewis runs his fingers through his hair. "I guess camping made me seem more cool and macho than I actually am?"

That makes Tad laugh, which is what Lewis was going for. Before he launched into full-on nerding out, Tad seemed tongue-tied and shy. "I'll neither confirm nor deny," Tad says.

"Great, so I just didn't seem *as* dorky.*"

"How about I give you the tour?" Tad asks, not even trying to seem like he isn't clumsily changing the subject. There's a gleam of mischief and humor in his eyes, and Lewis reminds himself they're here to fill out divorce paperwork, not to flirt.

It's just. Flirting with Tad is so easy.

"Sure," Lewis says. "And I can meet your cat."

"She's shy," Tad says. "I spent the afternoon lavishing her with attention and treats in an attempt—clearly futile—to get her to stick around when she heard the buzzer."

"I would've brought treats for her if I'd known bribery was on the table."

Tad smiles and Lewis mentally congratulates himself on getting in good on the cat front. Though he doesn't really need to ingratiate himself, because if the cat doesn't like him, they can always do friend stuff outside Tad's apartment.

"Next time," Tad says, and looks immediately mortified. "So! Living room, obviously. And kitchen." Tad's face is pink, but he gestures expansively. Light catches on his left hand. He's still wearing his wedding ring.

The apartment isn't a big space, which goes without saying in Manhattan. What it lacks in size, it makes up for in personality. There are plants everywhere: hanging from the ceiling, trailing fronds and leaves, on the windowsills, in big pots on the floor, on 90 percent of the kitchen counter. A mini-greenhouse holds several cactus-y looking things. There's even a vine creeping up the wall by one of the windows.

Lewis knows the names of exactly zero of them. Can't you buy those cactus-y looking things at Target?

"Wow," he says. "Are these all real?"

"Yup." Tad sounds proud.

There's a magnet on the refrigerator that says, *My plants are honors students*. "And you, like… take care of all of these?"

"Yeah. Some are high maintenance. I have an app to help keep track of everything, but honestly, I mostly just remember."

"Wow," Lewis says again, spinning slowly to take everything in. There are shelves all over the apartment at staggered levels, and those have plants on them too, though they're sharing with books.

Tad fingers a leaf of the nearest hanging plant, something with thick, waxy leaves. A sudden image flickers through Lewis's imagination: himself, Tad's app installed on his phone, learning how to take care of all these plants too.

He shakes it away. No. Bad.

Anyway, Tad's leading him through the rest of the small apartment. There's a hallway with one bathroom, a coat closet, and Tad's bedroom.

While Tad flips the light on in the bathroom, he doesn't for his bedroom. "Hetty's in there," he says. "I can get her."

"I don't want to scare her," Lewis says. "If she's shy, she'll be happier hiding."

Tad gives him a funny look. Lewis wonders if he said something wrong, but Tad just leads him back to the main room.

When they're done with dinner, Lewis asks, "You didn't get in trouble for taking extra time off, right?"

That same funny look flashes over Tad's face. "No," he replies. "I meant it about having a ton of unused PTO. My boss actually said she was hoping I'd take another week. She likes hanging out with my plants and my cat."

"Your boss takes care of your cat when you're gone?" The idea of Lewis's boss doing that for him is laughable. Not like his boss is bad or anything, but—he can't imagine having a relationship with her outside of work, let alone one where she has a key to his apartment.

"Er, yeah." Tad flushes and looks down at the remains of his sandwich. "I, um. Don't really have many friends."

Which is honestly baffling. Why wouldn't Tad have many friends? He's amazing! He's so funny and smart, and totally charming, and there are so many endearing little things about him. "Well, I'm your friend," Lewis says.

"I always think it's so sweet when spouses say they're each other's best friends," Tad deadpans.

Lewis laughs. "Yeah, that's me. Keeping the romance alive."

Tad's eyes flick up to meet Lewis's, and Lewis's breath catches. The soft fall of Tad's auburn curls over his forehead makes his eyes look so blue, and so endless. Like you could fall into them and keep falling and falling forever and you wouldn't want anything to ever catch you.

Dating Break. Dating Break Dating Break Dating Break. It doesn't matter that Lewis always *has* been the guy to keep romance alive. Totally the guy swooning over every Taylor Swift song that talks about moving the furniture to dance in the living room. The dork who loves holiday movies, the cheesier the better.

The point is… what was the point, again? He can't remember because he can't stop looking into Tad's eyes.

It's Tad who finally looks away, getting up to clear the table. When he comes back, he has a manila folder. "I wanted to start filling everything out, but I figured you're the paralegal, so I should probably wait to make sure I don't do anything wrong."

"You would've been fine." Lewis flips the folder open and scans the first page. Lots of legalese, which is fine—this stuff is his bread and butter, even if he doesn't do family law.

He shifts on the chair, trying to get comfortable as he loses himself in the text. Or tries to lose himself in the text. He's getting that disconnect-y feeling in his brain that he recognizes all too well as his anxiety ramping up, and before he knows it, he's read half the page and internalized none of it.

With a breath, he goes back to the top and starts over. This isn't hard or scary. He deals with legal documents every single day, and this one's designed for regular people to be able to complete by themselves.

But the disconnect-y feeling gets worse, and suddenly it's hard to get a breath.

"Hey." A hand slides onto his shoulder, warm and grounding. "Are you okay?"

"Um." Lewis feels like he's physically heaving a two-hundred-pound sack—a sack containing his concentration—back into his brain. "Yeah, I…."

Usually it's no problem to handwave his anxiety. He's used to it. He has so many excuses to explain away an anxiety attack that half the time he has himself fooled.

With Tad's hand on his shoulder, the excuses fall away. "Sorry," he says, trying to breathe around the weight on his chest. "I guess I'm still sort of freaked out about this."

Tad squeezes his shoulder. "What would help?"

None of the men Lewis has dated have ever asked that. Then again, Lewis has always taken great pains to hide his anxiety from his boyfriends. He's told himself to get over it and not give away the fire alarm screaming in his head. It's fine. He's fine. He has a place to live, a good job, a good life. What does he have to be anxious about?

Now here's Tad, who understands that what he's seeing is Lewis having an anxiety attack. And he's not minimizing it or rolling his eyes or snapping that there's nothing to worry about, it's just a form, no one's dying. He's not grabbing the folder and taking over, thinking he's removing the source of stress, when that just sets off Lewis's need for control and amps his anxiety up further.

Tad's thumb rubs tiny circles on Lewis's shoulder blade. "What do you need? To like... feel better? Or... sorry, should I not have asked that? You seemed like you were getting anxious, and sometimes people have stuff they do to help them? God, sorry. I should shut up, shouldn't I—"

"No," Lewis says more forcefully than he means to. Tad's hand jerks back. Losing that warm weight on his shoulder seems uniquely terrible, and he reaches up to cover Tad's hand with his and keep it there. "No, no, it's fine. Thank you. For asking. I was just surprised."

"Do people normally not ask?" Tad is quiet.

There can't be a lump in Lewis's throat, because he is definitely *not* close to tears from something so simple and silly.

"Is it okay if we sit on the sofa?" He can't answer Tad's question. Maybe the answer is obvious without him saying anything.

"Of course." Tad squeezes his shoulder again.

There's nothing special about the sofa. It's not like Lewis has a ritual where he has to read forms there. He's read legal forms all sorts of places—in his office, in waiting rooms, on the train. But the moment he sinks into Tad's sofa, his breathing eases. And when he gestures for Tad to sit next to him, the anxiety ebbs away.

"Maybe I *should've* gotten my chakra scrubbed," Lewis says with a wan smile.

Tad smirks. "I've heard chakra enemas are really effective for treating anxiety."

Lewis snorts. "A chakra enema sounds hugely violating."

A crooked smile twitches onto Tad's face. Lewis's heart flutters, and this time it's definitely not anxiety.

Would it be an amazingly bad idea to hold Tad's hand right now?

Before he can argue with himself about it, something lands on the sofa on his other side, accompanied by a querying, "Brrrrp?"

"Hetty!" Tad reaches across Lewis and scoops up the black cat who's now staring at Lewis. Her legs flail as Tad pulls her into his lap and strokes her head. "She never comes out for people she doesn't know!" The smile he aims at Lewis is blinding. "She obviously has a good feeling about you."

"She's so pretty." Lewis holds a hand out for her to sniff, which she does. Tad beams. "Can I pet her?"

"What do you think, Hets?" Tad asks, his voice going sing-songy. Lewis dies a little from how cute it is. Hetty tilts her head back to look at Tad, blinks slowly, and starts to purr. With a soft smile, Tad leans over and touches her nose with his. His hair falls into his eyes as he bobs back up. "Yeah, you can pet her. She's super loving, just shy. But she came out for you, so she'll want you to pet her."

Lewis reaches out, and his intent is totally to pet Hetty. Somehow, he's brushing Tad's hair out of his eyes instead.

They both freeze. Their eyes meet. A hot flush of mortification rises up Lewis's neck to his face. "I… am so sorry," he manages. His hand lands where it was supposed to in the first place, on Hetty's head.

She butts her nose up into his palm and purrs louder. Tad relaxes. "It's okay. I need to get it cut so it's not in my eyes. Then people wouldn't be tempted to do that."

"Do you get a lot of randoms brushing your hair out of your eyes?"

Tad ducks his head in wordless acknowledgment that he doesn't. As he strokes a hand down Hetty's back and lets her tail curl around his wrist, he says, "You're not a random."

They sit in silence, petting Hetty while she soaks up the attention. Lewis has never heard a cat purr so loud, and she keeps rubbing her head against his knuckles when he goes to stroke her.

"I want to get a cat," Lewis says.

"Yeah? How come you haven't?"

He shrugs. "I don't know. I guess I worry it would get lonely, and I'm not supposed to have more than one cat in my apartment."

"Same," Tad says, wrinkling his nose. "I'd love to get another cat to keep Hetty company. It's not as big of a deal since I work from home so much, except now she gets super lonely when I leave." He drops a kiss in the center of her head. "She's been walking around glaring at me since I got home from Nevada."

"I guess she finally forgave you."

"I think she just really likes you." Tad offers him a crooked smile. "Cats know what's up."

Their fingers brush as they both go to scratch behind Hetty's ears at the same time. Electricity fizzes under Lewis's skin.

"So, um." Lewis clears his throat and tries to ignore the way his body is buzzing. "I'm guessing she leaves the plants alone?"

"Yeah." Tad looks at her fondly. "When I got her, I only had a few plants, but she's always been really good about not eating them. I still don't keep anything dangerous where she can get it."

Lewis's gaze travels around the apartment. The plants are calming. It's probably his imagination, but the air feels cleaner and fresher. "Everyone who comes over probably asks this and you're tired of explaining, but how did you get into plants?"

Tad's shoulders hitch and he looks away. "Well, no one really comes over, so, no. Not tired of explaining." Hetty readjusts on his lap. "It's not very exciting. My parents got me this, like, educational book for my eleventh birthday, and it came with a little greenhouse kit where you could grow your own plant. I loved that thing. It was like, my sole purpose in life for months."

Even though Lewis doesn't know what eleven-year-old Tad looked like, he can still picture it. "What kind of plant was it? Not that I know anything about plants at all."

"Want to see it?" Tad asks eagerly.

"Wait, you still have it?"

"Yeah!" He glances down at Hetty in his lap, whose legs are stretched out, paws resting on one knee. "Jail for father for one thousand years," he says, depositing her in Lewis's lap. She looks disgruntled but stays as Tad goes to a table by the window and picks up a pot.

He holds it out for Lewis to see. "It's an African Violet."

It's a small plant with fuzzy green leaves and clusters of purple flowers. Pretty. The pot is painted like a Pride flag.

"You've had this for twenty years?" Lewis asks, unable to wrap his head around that.

"Almost."

"That's so cool."

"Really?" Two splotches of red appear on Tad's cheeks, making his freckles stand out.

"Of course!" Does Tad really not see that? "You started growing this when you were a kid, and now you're almost thirty. This plant has been with you for the majority of your life! I bet it's gone through a bunch of moves, right?"

The red on Tad's cheeks is spreading. His eyes look bright, and he's clearly trying to bite down a huge smile. "Yeah. I was so worried about it when I moved down here for college. I held it in my lap for the entire drive." He cradles the plant against his midsection. "I've repotted it a bunch of times to make sure it stays healthy."

"How long do they live?"

"A long time. As long as I take good care of it, it could outlive me, in theory."

"Whoa! Flowers can live that long?"

Maybe the comparison is too on the nose, but Tad absolutely blooms with Lewis's interest. "They can live that long even outside if you just let them do their thing. There are peonies in the Better Homes and Gardens Test Garden that were planted in the 1950s and are still blooming. And hostas just keep going and going as long as the deer don't eat them. My mom planted a ton of them on this shady bank in our yard when I was little and they're still going strong."

"I don't know what those are," Lewis confesses.

"I can show you?" Tad says without the slightest evidence that he thinks Lewis is dumb for not knowing what he's talking about.

"I'd love that."

Tad reaches over Lewis for an iPad, which is on the other side of the sofa. As he leans close, Lewis gets a lungful of his scent, detergent and a fresh, clean soap smell, and green. It's different than how he smelled in Nevada, but underneath is the smell of his skin, which Lewis feels like he's known all his life.

He snaps himself out of it as Tad pulls up pictures of the flowers he mentioned. The hostas look dainty, with their long stems and fluted, pale purple flowers. The peonies are all loud, brash blooms of violent, vibrant pinks.

"There's this one gardener I follow on insta that has the most gorgeous peonies," Tad says, voice thrumming with excitement. Lewis could listen to him talk about the things he loves all night. The way the passion lights his face makes him even more gorgeous.

There's danger here, sitting next to Tad on his sofa, an iPad and a cat between them, Lewis's body focused on Tad's heat, the lengths of their thighs pressed together, the curve of Tad's shoulder fitted against Lewis's. There's danger in the way the conversation flows effortlessly, never an awkward pause or a fumble for what to say.

An alert pops up on the iPad—11:00, time to go to bed.

"Oh my god! Shit." Tad looks horrified. "I'm so sorry, god you probably wanted to get out of here hours ago, and"—he groans—"we didn't even touch the paperwork. Fuck. I'm so sorry. Fuck, this is exactly what I always do. It drove John crazy, he'd always tell me I needed to talk to other people so it all didn't pour out at home, and wow, I'm doing it again right now...."

"Who's John?" Lewis asks, hating the unknown stranger already.

"My ex."

Now Lewis hates him even more. What kind of guy says something like that to his boyfriend? "Yeah, well, screw him. Tonight was great."

Tad looks flummoxed. "But it's so late, and we didn't get anything done."

"I had fun," Lewis says. "I'm the one who should be apologizing. I took up your whole night."

Shaking his head vigorously, Tad replies, "No. No, this was nice." His hair falls into his eyes again. "I had fun too."

It's true they didn't get the form filled out. Not that they need to fill it out now, since they can't get divorced for another six months. But getting it done will help his anxiety, which is definitely why he says, "I could come back tomorrow if you're not busy, and we could work on the form then? I'll bring dinner again."

"Sure." Tad sounds a little shy.

Hetty grumbles her displeasure with being displaced when Tad gets up to walk Lewis to the door. Lewis slips his backpack on and says, "So."

"Same time tomorrow?"

"Yeah."

Lewis doesn't make any move to go. He can't stop staring into Tad's eyes and breathing him in. He's not close enough to feel Tad's body heat, but he feels it anyway—that, and the ghost of Tad's shoulder fitted against his.

Something gets stuck in his throat. He has to go now, because if he doesn't, he might not leave at all.

"Well, bye," he says.

"Bye," Tad echoes.

When Tad got out of the car at the airport in Vegas, Lewis's chest hurt enough to make him wonder if there was something wrong with him. That pain had nothing on the ache that starts now at the bottom of his rib cage and travels up, crawling along every rib, taking up a grasping presence in his sternum, and pressing down on his lungs and heart.

Lewis ignores the ache in his chest all through the walk down the hall, the elevator, and the ten steps he takes toward the lobby door. But the ache gets worse and worse, and when it's unbearable he can't do anything but stop and think about what's causing it—even though he doesn't actually have to think about what's causing it at all.

When he knocks on Tad's door, it swings open immediately, like Tad hasn't moved. "Oh," Tad breathes. "I was hoping you'd come back."

They reach for each other at the same time, Tad fisting the lapels of Lewis's coat as Lewis wraps his fingers in Tad's curls and tugs his face down.

Their mouths meet as they stand in the doorway, and the minutes stretch out like honey as they kiss.

When they come up for air, Tad pulls Lewis across the threshold and shuts the door. Lewis runs his fingers down Tad's jaw. "You never actually showed me your bedroom when you gave me the tour."

"Well, let's fix that," Tad growls.

They don't talk much after that.

Chapter Seventeen

TAD DOESN'T want to move ever again. His whole body is boneless, sated, wrecked, and he's warm and naked and in the arms of a man he's falling hard for.

It's a disaster. It's a revelation.

Falling for Lewis is an invitation to heartbreak. But he is, and he has to do right by the man, no matter how much he wants to stay exactly where they are, bodies pressed together, arms around each other, legs tangled, the smell of sweat and sex clinging to them.

"Do you need to go?" Tad murmurs.

"Mmph," Lewis replies, nuzzling his face into the crook of Tad's neck.

"Because, like… I know you"—lips find his pulse point—"don't want… to… to date"—and now Lewis is kissing him, and it's hot and slow and wet—"so… um…."

Words fail him and his brain smoothes to white noise and the swell of an endless ocean as Lewis kisses and nuzzles and licks.

"Do you want me to go?" Lewis finally asks, his voice muffled against Tad's skin. His hands are skimming along Tad's body.

Tad makes a noise, which is definitely not a response. He doesn't want to respond because he knows the right thing to say, even if it's the last thing he wants.

"Tad?" Lewis murmurs. "I'll go if you want me to."

"No. Don't." He's a bad person. "Stay. I want you to stay the night."

He Is The Worst.

Rolling away from Lewis and the perfect heat of his body, he says, "But what I want doesn't matter. This isn't what you want."

"What?" The sheets rustle and warmth presses along the length of Tad's body again. "Why do you think what you want doesn't matter? Of course what you want matters."

He hadn't even meant to say that. Obviously he knows what he wants matters. At least, what he wants matters as long as it's not too inconvenient. Like not being able to come out to his family. John would ask, *Don't you* want *to?* And honestly, a lot of days, Tad didn't. His family won't like him being gay, so even if he wanted to come out, what was the point?

Lewis puts a cautious hand to Tad's hip, like he thinks Tad's going to jerk away. Instead, Tad leans into him. What he wants is this. Lewis doesn't. Tad should ask him what it means that they fucked again when they weren't supposed to. The words even form in his throat, but when he opens his mouth, they won't come out.

"You want me to stay?" Lewis asks. He sounds so vulnerable, like Tad could push on his chest and crush his heart.

That's why he has to be careful with Lewis. Maybe Tad isn't Lewis's Happily Ever After, but Tad cares about him. He cares about him way too much. He doesn't want to hurt him, even if not hurting Lewis is going to mean hurting himself down the line.

He turns to face Lewis. The vulnerability in his voice is reflected on his face in worried lines and the turned-down corners of his lips. Tad wants to kiss them to make them curve up again.

Wait—he can. So he does.

With his mouth against the corners of Lewis's lips, he says, "I want you to stay. If you want to."

"I want to," Lewis says in a rush, like he's afraid if he doesn't get the words out fast enough, he'll chicken out.

Tad snuggles closer, wrapping his arms tight around him until he remembers he can't hold on tight to Lewis. "Okay," Tad says. "Yay."

"Yay," Lewis whispers back.

IN THE morning, Tad casually suggests it would be cool if Lewis stayed and worked—only if he wants to! He doesn't expect Lewis to agree.

Lewis does, though! Yay! Now, they're side-by-side on the sofa doing their respective jobs. Work is still slow for Tad, but he's using the time to get things ready for the journal's first quarter issue, which he'll start working on after Thanksgiving.

He's been trying for the last hour not to peek at Lewis's computer, because Lewis's work is probably all private and sensitive and stuff. It's just, he's really curious. He wants to know everything about Lewis, which is—ugh. Stupid. And probably illegal, somehow. At least knowing the work stuff. And Lewis is lawyer-adjacent, so he'd know exactly how Tad's breaking the law.

So, of course, Lewis catches him looking. Tad turns red. "Sorry. I didn't see anything!"

It's like Lewis knows exactly what he's thinking. "It's okay, none of this is sensitive information."

"Oh." Tad lets his eyes rove the screen, though it still feels transgressive. "What are you working on?"

Lewis stretches his arms over his head. His spine cracks. He's wearing one of Tad's T-shirts and it rides up, exposing taut stomach and dark hair and the sharp ledges of his hip bones. Tad's cock stirs.

It's never come up at work—er, not his cock, which probably has— but Tad assumes fucking on company time is frowned upon.

Not that it stops him from wanting to lick a line down Lewis's stomach and rub his face in that body hair, but he can control himself. Probably.

Rubbing a hand over his face, Lewis says, "Still catching up on emails from being out. I'm researching three cases, and it looks like I'm getting another one soon."

Tad watches Lewis fire off a quick email. "Can you tell me about the cases? Or is that like, top secret stuff?"

Giving him a surprised look, Lewis says, "It's not top secret. But it's also not very interesting."

"Try me."

Lewis looks even more surprised. Did his parade of shitty boyfriends never show interest in his work? "Well, I've been working a ton on this recycling case. It's the county versus this waste company because the county says they're not processing what the contract says they will. And another one, it's the Park Board against a landscaper, that one's around the type of fertilizers they're using. And then one involving JFK. The airports are always getting sued for environmental violations. They usually settle." Lewis reads an email, sighs, and flags it. "It's not as interesting as a botany journal."

Tad bumps their shoulders together. "You're literally the first person to tell me that."

Lewis grabs his hand and intertwines their fingers. Tad's stomach flips over. "If your ex made you feel like your job wasn't interesting, that's another reason he sucks."

Compared to John, Tad's job *isn't* interesting. John's a published author now—his debut is the sort of YA novel that gets called Important and Unapologetically Queer and got put on a bunch of Best Of The Year lists before it even came out.

Is Tad allowed to kiss Lewis? They're working, but… if they were a couple, and they were both working from home, no one would expect them not to exchange kisses throughout the day.

He leans over and kisses Lewis on the lips, lingering but keeping it closed-mouth and chaste. "You're really nice," Tad says, which is probably too much.

Lewis's fingers trace little shivering paths on Tad's forearms and he leans his forehead against Tad's. His breath puffs on Tad's face. There's intimacy there that Tad's missed so much since John broke up with him.

It's funny—he doesn't miss John, but he misses all the little comforts of a relationship. He misses being close to someone who gets you.

They stay that way for a while. Lewis is the first to pull back. "You're really distracting."

"I'll take that as a compliment."

"It was." Lewis grabs Tad's hand again and kisses the back. "Thanks for letting me work here today." Hetty saunters by and stops to stare at Lewis. "You too, Hetty," he adds.

Halfway through the day, Tad gets an email from Callie that he's expecting, because they all get it every year, but which still makes him let out a resigned sigh.

"What's up?" Lewis asks.

"Uggghh." Tad's head falls back against the back of the sofa and thunks harder than he means it to. Ow. "My boss just sent her yearly email giving us the entire week of Thanksgiving off."

"That's… good, isn't it? More time off?"

Rubbing the back of his head—his hair's getting long, way too long for his family to see—he says, "My family expects me to have that whole week off now, so they want me to come home for the whole time."

"You don't want to?"

"Not really."

Lewis looks thoughtful. "You could tell them something came up and you can't make it this year?"

"I wish." Tad's shoulders sag. "Even if my mom wouldn't turn it into a whole Thing, I just… well, I spend so much time telling them such a huge lie, it kind of makes me feel like I use up all my white lie credits on that."

Unsurprisingly, Lewis looks confused. And curious. And like, just the tiniest bit wary, but honestly? Not as much as Tad expected. If someone said that to Tad, his mind would jump straight to serial killer.

"So...." Lewis cocks his head. "Probably overstepping, but...."

"You can ask."

With an uncertain smile, Lewis says, "Okay, good, because you really lined that one up. What's the big thing you're lying to your family about?"

It's fine. Telling him isn't a big deal, because they aren't anything serious. Lewis isn't going to backpedal as fast as he can, because this isn't a Relationship. Lewis isn't ever going to be a person Tad should be able to bring home to introduce to his family, to become a fixture at holiday dinners. So him knowing that none of those things are possible isn't going to freak him out.

Still, the wounds John made left deep scars. John talked about how coming out wasn't the safest thing for everyone, and how people should be able to make that decision on their own terms. Turned out that was all well and good for other people, but not for the guy he was dating.

"Um," Tad says. He rubs his hair again. He meant to get it cut before Vegas but never made it to the salon. Every time Walt looked at him, he was sure his brother was going to make some comment about his hair being girly. "I'm not... exactly... really... at all... out to my family. Or anyone in Watertown. I mean, not that there's anyone in Watertown besides my family. I don't have any friends there or anything. I never really had any friends in high school. Well, I had *friends*, but not like, good friends. Not the kind of friends you stay friends with when you all go off to college. I don't even know where any of the people I hung around with are now—"

Great, cool word vomit. He snaps his mouth shut, then bites his lip and chances a look at Lewis.

"That sucks," Lewis says. He looks... sad? "That really sucks you don't feel like you can come out to them."

Relief socks Tad in the solar plexus. Even if Lewis's response is the one that makes the most sense, he was still afraid Lewis would recoil. Like, excuse me, you're setting the cause back; you're not being gay the right way; you're letting the queer community down.

"Yeah, it does," Tad agrees. When Lewis gives him a funny look, he realizes he has a big smile on his face. "Er, sorry. I don't always get much sympathy when people find out I'm twenty-nine and still in the closet around my family."

"What?" Lewis looks incensed. "That's bullshit."

Warmth fizzes in Tad's belly. He is in T-R-O-U-B-L-E.

Lewis locks his computer and slides it onto the coffee table. "You don't have to answer this if you don't want to, but is it a religion thing? Or just like, general homophobia? Are they…?"

This is the worst part—it's kind of neither. And also both. "Gun-toting, Bible-verse spouting, MAGA psychos?" Tad makes a face. "Not that bad, no. But is there a painting in my childhood home of Ronald Reagan riding a horse, with an American flag billowing behind him? Yes, yes there is."

Lewis guffaws, which makes all of this a lot easier to talk about. Tad draws his knees to his chest and loops his arms around them, his heels perching at the edge of the sofa. "It's never been any one thing, you know? It's not like, oh, they're super religious, so they're always talking about how queer people are an abomination in the sight of God or whatever. And it's not an owning-the-libs thing, where you just hate the gays because that's what Your Side does. It's just… I don't know. It's always been a bunch of little things."

Lewis's hand slides over Tad's knee. "It's shitty you can't show them that part of yourself."

"Yeah," Tad says quietly. He turns a memory over in his head, wondering if he wants to share it. It still hurts, even though nothing was directed at him. "There was this one time when I was in high school. We went to a wedding of one of my mom's friend's kids, and the bride's brother was gay. He was there with his boyfriend, and he was wearing a rainbow tie, and I thought he was the bravest person I'd ever seen. I kept trying to work up the nerve to go talk to him."

Tad watches Hetty curl up in a patch of sun on the floor. Sometimes he wishes he had cat problems—wanting food now, wanting attention now, being aggrieved that the sunny spot moves.

"My dad," he continues, "said he didn't understand why the bride's brother had to rub everyone's faces in it. He said he doesn't care what anyone does in their bedroom, but that doesn't mean people should have to see it, especially when there were kids around. And I just…."

He trails off as he registers the look on Lewis's face. Lewis looks *gutted*. Like this tender spot that Tad's tried for years to wall off so it doesn't bother him is the saddest thing Lewis has ever heard. And it's *not*. It's obviously not. They're queer men. Sad stories are part of the experience. It's fucked up, but that's how it is.

"I just thought," Tad goes on, "that coming out was… exhibitionist, somehow? It took me a while to realize no one ever says opposite sex couples are rubbing people's faces in what they do in the bedroom."

Reaching for Tad's hand, Lewis says, "Tad, that's horrible. It's bad enough when strangers act like that. Having it be your family is so much worse."

Lewis's fingers squeeze Tad's, and maybe he shouldn't be so easily comforted by it, but he is. "I'm guessing you don't have issues with your family?"

The feel of Lewis's thumb rubbing circles on Tad's wrist is exactly the kind of intimacy he misses. "No," Lewis says. "My mom works with queer youth groups. My parents have gone to every single New York Pride March, and they brought me and my sister along every year. And when I came out, they started marching in the Jersey City Pride parade."

"Wow," Tad says softly.

"Yeah. They're pretty great. I know how lucky I am." Lewis remains quiet for a moment. "I hate that things are so different for you."

Tad shrugs. Not much anyone can do about it. There's definitely nothing Lewis can do about it. Tad knows he's a coward. He knows there are so many people who have it so much worse. His parents wouldn't have disowned him if he'd come out as a teen, but he couldn't bear the cold silences he knew would descend every time they were all together. He didn't want to deal with his mom looking heartbroken and his dad avoiding the subject altogether. He couldn't handle Walt being weird about bringing his friends around.

It's like Lewis is reading his mind. "Your brother's part of the issue too?" When Tad nods, Lewis says, "Huh. I guess I figured you told him why you went camping."

"Yeah, about that…." Tad grimaces. "I kind of told him I hooked up with a woman named Louise."

He doesn't think Lewis will get mad. He wouldn't have said it if he thought Lewis would get mad. But his shoulders still tighten because he knows the reaction he would've gotten from John.

Lewis laughs so loudly that Hetty jumps up from her sunny spot. He claps a hand over his mouth, which does nothing to muffle the sound. "Louise?" he repeats, giggling.

Tad gives him a light, backhanded little swat on the chest. "I panicked. I'm not good under pressure."

The giggling gives way to a smile, and Lewis leans forward to kiss Tad gently. "That's totally not true. Remember how you rescued me when I almost plummeted to my death?"

"Hm, true. I guess I'm strapping and dashing and heroic?"

"Yes, yes, and yes." Lewis kisses him again. "My brave knight in shining armor."

And oh, that makes Tad ache. He's not brave, and he isn't Lewis's.

Chapter Eighteen

THEY DON'T get the divorce paperwork filled out.

They *do* have sex again.

Lewis is coming over again on Friday. Tad swears to himself that this time, they'll definitely finish the paperwork. Hopefully Lewis won't think he's using the forms as bait to get laid.

In the meantime, he hangs out with Hetty, works, goes to the gym, scrolls mindlessly through social media, and deletes the occasional dick pic from his Grindr DMs. On Friday, they make some progress with the forms. Good thing, because Tad's leaving the next morning for the week in Watertown. There are frequent breaks for kissing. They have to reward themselves, right? And Tad has to stock up on the feeling.

Also, Lewis brings a toy for Hetty—a little shrimp filled with catnip. "She reminds me of a shrimp when she's sort of half curled up on the floor, but her legs are sticking out, you know?" he explain sheepishly, like Tad's going to think he's stupid.

Tad doesn't think he's stupid. Tad has to summon every drop of his willpower to not shove Lewis up against the wall and kiss him to death for being sweet and thoughtful and adorable.

Hetty saunters into the living room during one of their make-out breaks, which they only notice because she leaps onto the back of the sofa and lets out a rusty metal "Mrow!" Even though Tad's used to it, he jumps. His knee comes perilously close to crushing Lewis's balls, permanent sterilization only prevented by the fact that Lewis jumps too, which gets his junk out of kneeing range by a couple inches.

"Hetty-bo-betty," Tad groans.

Lewis looks gleeful. "Oh my god, I *cannot*. You're so cute. Hetty-bo-betty. Jesus, Tad."

Tad flushes. "Sorry, I usually don't call her all my dumb pet names when people are around."

Not that anyone's around anymore. There's his problem. He's out of practice biting down on the more ridiculous nicknames he calls his cat.

God, he's sad, isn't he? No friends, no boyfriend, just a cat and a guy he's hooking up with who explicitly told him he's not looking for a relationship.

Lewis smoothes Tad's hair back from his face. "Sorry? Don't be sorry. I love it."

"Yeah, sure. Sad gay nerd's best friend is his cat—more at eleven."

Lewis laughs and pulls Tad down into a kiss. With a groan, Tad settles between Lewis's legs again. Lewis arches up to meet him and their dicks press together. The first hot, grinding contact makes Lewis gasp. He pulls Tad down on top of him, one arm locked around Tad's back and the other stroking through his hair.

"*Mrow!*"

They break apart. Tad cranes his head over his shoulder to look at Hetty. She grumbles and settles into a loaf, staring meaningfully.

When Tad looks back to Lewis, Lewis is grinning. "Think she knows I brought her a present?"

"Maybe she's trying to keep us on task," Tad sighs.

Hetty's still staring unblinkingly. "I'm gonna get her toy," Lewis announces.

He takes the shrimp toy out of the packaging and holds it out to her, and Tad feels like he's racing down a slope that keeps getting steeper and steeper—and at the bottom is a cliff. He can see it; he knows he's headed over if he can't stop his momentum. The only way to stop is to fling himself on the ground and use the friction of his skin against rock to slow down. He'd scrape himself raw, but maybe, *maybe*, he wouldn't fall.

Lewis lets Hetty sniff the shrimp toy, and Tad knows it's too late to stop the fall.

SINCE TAD couldn't bring himself to lie about having other plans for Thanksgiving, he sets out for Watertown the next morning in a rental car. Mom always wants him to buy a car, because then he could visit more. His excuses about the exorbitant price he'd pay for a parking spot and insurance for a car he'd barely use have the benefit of being true.

The idea of having to visit Watertown even more makes him viscerally ill. Isn't it enough to spend a week there in November and December?

His only lifeline during the upcoming week will be texting Lewis. Tad stumblingly asked him not to send any suggestive texts, especially not dick pics. ("Wait," Lewis said, "should I have been sending you dick pics?") Then he went through the rest of the rules: don't text too much, don't call, don't use pet names, don't say *I miss you*.

Okay, Tad didn't actually manage to get that last one out. It seems super presumptuous.

Not that he doesn't hope Lewis misses him. Because fuck, Tad misses him, and they saw each other this morning. Lewis volunteered—volunteered!—to stay in Tad's apartment to take care of the plants, so he spent the night and they woke up together, kissing and touching languidly.

Now he's driving up 81 with the radio set to scan because his cell signal isn't good enough to stream any of his playlists, and he's a gross mixture of sexually frustrated, anxious, sick to his stomach, and bored.

He pulls into his parents' driveway just after three. Hetty lets out a happy chirp from her kennel in the back seat when he turns off the car.

Tad stretches his arms over his head and cracks his spine. "I'm glad one of us is happy to be here," he says, looking back at Hetty.

She has her sweet little face mashed up against the bars and a paw stretched through them. At his attention, she starts purring. "I know, little girl. It's a long drive. And you're really good. Want a treat?" He keeps them in the front seat so he can feed them to her during gas and bathroom stops, and she takes them delicately from his fingers when he offers them through the bars.

Can he just sit in his rental car and hang out with his cat for the next week?

With a sigh, he checks his phone.

There's a text from Lewis.

Tad's face nearly splits in half, he grins so hard.

Which is exactly the kind of response he can't have to Lewis's texts. Walt will want to know why he's smiling at his phone, and Mom will start asking him if he's seeing someone, and Dad will look quietly relieved, and—

He wants to cry.

The text from Lewis is from ten minutes ago and says: **I haven't killed any plants yet**

The urge to cry recedes a little and Tad lets out a little laugh. *You haven't *watered* any plants yet*, he texts back. *I know the schedule, remember?*

Just thought you deserve an update on the watering situation

The next thing to come through is the water droplet emoji, which Tad has personally used to refer to a couple different bodily fluids, but not actual water.

Um omg I didn't mean to send that!!

Shit

Ignore

Ignore

Omg I swear that was an accident, my phone suggested it and I hit it by accident

Now I'm repeating myself

Wow I am a disaster, I swear I'll do a better job watering your plants than texting you about *water droplet emoji*.

Fuuuuuuuuuuuu

Tad laughs so loudly that a squirrel nosing around the front yard jumps and runs halfway up the big maple. Lewis is totally making his gaffe worse, but he's funny and adorable and fuck, Tad misses him so much. This is so not good.

Snickering, Tad sends back: the peach, eggplant, and water droplet emojis.

There's some typing, then some more typing. Then the three dots disappear. Then they're back. Tad's smile fades. Did he do something wrong?

Did you just break your own rule?

Yup

Ok because it's just... I'm in a tight spot

You have me bent over

A barrel, that is

Things are getting hard here

I guess I asked for it?

That's what he said

Adjadja;dk;ahddfj LEWIS

Ok I'll stop, sorry. Are you taking a break from driving?

I actually just got here
Omfg I'm so sorry
I mean not that you're there!
I'm happy you got there safe!
I'll stop texting you now

A lump lodges in Tad's throat. He almost forgot where he was and that he has to spend the next seven days pretending to be someone he's not.

Thanks for taking care of everything while I'm gone, he texts.

Then—fuck it. He's feeling reckless. Before he thinks better of it, he sends one more message, a red heart.

He puts his phone on silent. The wedding band on his left hand has to go, at least while he's here. Unhappiness spears his chest, but he pulls off the ring and stows it in the glove compartment. He should get used to it being gone.

He gets out of the car. Hetty settles into his arms, purring, when he lifts her from her kennel. Dropping a kiss on her head, he whispers into her fur, "It's okay if you stay in my room the whole time. You don't have to be social if you don't want to be, okay?"

Her purring is so loud that Tad can feel it vibrating in his chest.

He kisses her again, snuggles her closer, and rings the doorbell.

Chapter Nineteen

"TAD! HONEY, you made it, thank goodness! I was so worried. You know I've been hearing on the news about parts being stolen out of rental cars right on the lots and no one realizing it until the car breaks down after it's been rented—"

"I'm fine, Mom," Tad says, getting an arm around her as she throws both of hers around him.

She squeezes him tight and he has to jerk away before she suffocates Hetty, who he can feel trembling in his arms.

"Oh, you brought the cat," Mom says, like she didn't see Hetty when she opened the door. Maybe she didn't. His parents aren't cat people. He always wanted one when he was a kid, but he was told over and over how allergic he was, even though magically he never seemed to be allergic to his friends' cats.

"I didn't want to leave her on her own again," he says, defensive already. He's not even inside. Great start. "I just got back from vacation." She does okay on her own, but she gets lonely. Not that she would have been lonely with Lewis there—but selfishly, Tad wanted her with him. He doesn't want to feel completely alone in his parents' house.

Mom brushes back a few wisps of her red hair. She has it pulled into a severe bun. It's her way of controlling the curls. When he was little, people cooed over Tad's curls, and how he obviously took after his mother, and wasn't his hair beautiful? Then he got older, and one time in the grocery store—he'll always remember this because he was standing next to a teetering pyramid of apples while Mom picked out the brightest red ones, and he kept thinking how good she was at it—anyway, he was standing there, and a grandfatherly man said to Mom, "Your boy looks like a girl with that hair."

After that, Mom always kept his hair short.

"That's right, your vacation." She stands aside to let him in. "Oh Tad, your hair's getting so long."

Instinctively, he raises a hand to the back of his neck, where, yeah, his curls are spilling messily. *I'm growing it out*, is what he should say. What he wants to say.

Hetty digs her claws into his forearm and he hastily tucks his other arm around her again. "Yeah," he says. "It's hard to get an appointment around the holidays."

"I could bring you to the mall? Your father likes that new Sports Clips place next to Penney's."

"Um," Tad replies. "Maybe."

He can't say *No, that sounds horrible—I like it cut a certain way, and I like my hilarious stylist in Chelsea with his stories of throwing bricks at cops at Stonewall and his revolving collection of stilettos, and he gets that I'm quiet, so he's okay just telling me his stories without me making small talk, and the Sports Clips people will expect me to chitchat with them and I'll freeze up and they'll think I'm rude and probably give me a bad haircut on purpose.*

"Thanks," he adds, in case Mom can see through his skull to his Gay Thoughts—and all the other thoughts that are just pathetic.

As he starts down the hallway to his childhood bedroom, Mom calls after him, "I'll go on the phone app and see if I can get you in today. How's that?"

He pretends he doesn't hear her as he walks into his old bedroom.

Every time he comes back, he expects the room to smell the same—like fabric softener and detergent and the soft smell of coffee from his high school job at Dunkin' Donuts, plus Teenage Boy, aka feet, sweat, cum, and Axe body spray. Gross.

It doesn't, of course. It smells like a plug-in air freshener with a name like Turquoise Waters or something. The space is a neutered version of his bedroom. Some of his posters of soccer players are still up (he didn't like soccer, but he did like the players' legs and asses and shoulders and chests, and... well, yeah), and his bed is still there, with a navy blue comforter he picked out when he was fifteen and terrified by the fact that he was getting erections from Rihanna music videos—not because of Rihanna, but because of her male backup dancers. God, that sweaty, cut guy from the Russian Roulette video....

Obviously a navy blue comforter would make him less gay.

"Here you go, Hets," he says, setting her on the bed. She jumps down and slinks underneath it, not that he blames her. He wishes he could do the same.

It takes him longer to bring Hetty's stuff inside than his own. All he has is a duffel bag, but Hetty has her litter box, her food and dishes, a selection of toys, several of her favorite blankets, and a calming diffuser that he replaces the air freshener with.

Once he's washed and filled Hetty's dish with water and given her fresh food—and a few more treats—he closes his bedroom door to give her peace and quiet, then pads out to the kitchen.

He has to pass the horrible Reagan painting on the way. No one can see him, so he flips Reagan the bird. He has fantasies about setting the thing on fire.

Mom's setting food out on the counter. "Are you hungry? I was going to make chili for dinner, but I know you never stop to eat on that drive. I have salami and ham, and some provolone, or I could make you a grilled cheese if you want—"

He's only been a vegetarian since he went to college, but of course, his parents never remember.

"This is fine," Tad says, grabbing the provolone and some wheat bread.

In his pocket, his phone buzzes. If it's Lewis, that was a long delay between the heart and his response. But also, he can't expect Lewis to be tethered to his phone waiting for Tad to text, especially when Tad told him not to text too much.

He realizes he's clenching his jaw and makes a concerted effort to relax. "Is Dad home?"

Mom laughs. "Oh, he's in the basement watching the Ohio State game."

"Still mourning the fact that Walt didn't take the athletic scholarship to play there?" Tad asks, constructing his sandwich.

"Your father has his passions," Mom says, but even she sounds a little exasperated. Tad snickers. "Eat your sandwich, then go say hello to him."

Why can't he come up here and say hello to me?

Tad has whole conversations in his head with his parents—a rich alternative relationship where he says what he means and they respect him for it, even if they don't always agree.

For example, in his head, Mom responds, *He should come up here and say hello to you, but he won't, and it's just one of those things. If you talked to him about it, maybe he'd understand how you feel.*

"How was your drive?" Mom asks.

Tad shrugs. "Uneventful."

"There are so many trucks on the freeway," she says with a shudder. "There never used to be so much traffic. I don't know how you stand living in the city with all those cars."

Does he miss the quiet of Watertown sometimes? Sure. Would he trade that quiet a million times over, again and again, to live in a place where he can be himself, where he can be surrounded by people like him, where he can see men wearing makeup and dresses, where there are gender-neutral bathrooms, where nonbinary isn't a joke, where he can meet the eyes of a person with a purple faux-hawk and the sides of their hair buzzed and exchange a smile because no matter how different they are, they have their queerness in common? Yes, obviously yes.

When he needs quiet, he goes camping.

His phone buzzes once, then again, then a third time. Mom gives him a sly look. "Someone's popular."

He snorts. "Yeah, that would be a first."

"I bet you'd do just fine on those dating apps. Is that what the messages are from?" When he stares at her, wide-eyed and horrified, she scoffs. "Oh, Tad, don't look at me like that. I know about Tinder."

"Um, why would that make me feel better?"

She laughs. "Your brother met a very nice girl on there."

News to Tad, but then again, he and Walt don't talk much. "Walt has a girlfriend he met on Tinder? Interesting."

Maybe it's presumptuous to call the woman a girlfriend, but he's not going to say the phrase "fuck buddy" to his mom, even though, honestly? A fuck buddy is more Walt's speed. Walt's never managed to maintain a romantic relationship for more than a couple months. It's so annoying, because Tad was in one for *three years*, and he can't even rub it in Walt's face, because he'd have to come out.

Then again, *I was in a relationship for three years, until my SO dumped me* isn't really that great of a brag.

"You should download it, honey."

"That's okay. Not really my thing."

She gives him a pleading look. "I know being so shy made you a late bloomer, but you're almost thirty."

It hasn't even been half an hour and she's already giving him sad puppy dog eyes about him Never Finding Anyone. Great.

"I really don't like dating apps," he says, which is 100 percent true.

"But it would make it easier if you could connect with someone online first," Mom says eagerly. "Then you wouldn't get so nervous when you met them in person."

Goddddd he wishes he could tell her that actually, no, it doesn't help, and he knows from experience. But he doesn't want to fudge the truth and say he's tried and failed, because it will bring even more pressure for him to settle down with a Very Nice Girl. Like Walt's apparently doing.

"I'm not sure that would help," he says.

"You never know until you try!" Mom looks like she thinks they're capital C Connecting.

"No, I'm pretty sure—"

His phone buzzes again, and Mom looks smug. "I don't know what else could be making your phone explode like that."

"Blow up," he says absently. There isn't anything on his phone that would send him so many notifications, except texts. And Tad asked Lewis not to text him a lot. It seemed like Lewis would respect that, but maybe he isn't? And now Mom's looking at him like she wants him to whip his phone out and see if any of her imagined Tinder matches for him look like Nice Girls.

He shoves the rest of his sandwich in his mouth, then says around the wad of multigrain bread and provolone, "Gon' g' say 'i t' Da'."

She swats at him lightly. "Don't talk with your mouth full."

Making a zipping motion over his mouth, he heads for the basement stairs. Halfway down, he pulls his phone from his pocket.

The alerts were texts, but they're not from Lewis. Tad pushes down the stupid throb of disappointment at Lewis doing exactly what Tad asked him to do. No, the texts are all from Callie, his boss.

Did you go up to visit your family for Thanksgiving?
You didn't ask if I could take care of the plants?
I didn't kill your plants, did I?
Tad I'm not banned from plantsitting, am I?
You should have said if I killed a plant!

I'm sorry!
But do I need to go over and take care of the plants?

Tad rolls his eyes and smiles. *You didn't kill a plant. I'm visiting my parents but don't worry about going over, someone else volunteered to do it*

Three dots immediately appear, bouncing as Callie types back. Then they disappear. And appear again. And disappear. And now Tad's starting to worry about what she's going to say.

Finally, her message appears. **Someone else?**

There's a lot more typing. Tad can't stand halfway down the stairs forever, so she better hurry up and say what she has to say.

Sweetie, it's not John, is it?
No!!!
GOOD. I would have gone over there and kicked his ass out
No John. You don't have to worry about that
Ok but now you got me curious. Who's there?
This wouldn't have anything to do with you staying in Nevada an extra week, would it?

Tad feels the besotted smile on his face and tries to wipe it away. Mom's already on the prowl to find him a girlfriend; the last thing he needs to do is look like he already maybe has one.

I met a guy in Vegas and he lives in NYC too. He's taking care of my plants
This plant?, followed, mortifyingly, by an eggplant emoji.
OMGGGGGG you're my BOSS
So what happened in Vegas didn't stay in Vegas
O
M
G
Seriously boo I'm happy for you
It's just casual. We're not like seeing each other or anything
Suuuurrre all my hookups definitely offered to stay at my apartment and take care of my dog. That's totally something a fuck buddy does

He just got out of a bad relationship and he's not looking to start another one. And I shouldn't even be telling you this because it's none of your business!

I'll let you get back to the fam. Can't wait to meet your new bf!

He leaves her on read. If he keeps fumbling his replies to her, he'll end up telling her they aren't boyfriends, they're husbands, and then he'll be forced to tell the whole sad story.

Before he continues down the stairs, he pulls up his conversation with Lewis. Just seeing their texts makes him smile.

Doofy, smitten smile. Again. Still Not Pierce Household approved. It probably looks too gay.

Shoving his phone back in his pocket, he makes himself move. As soon as he opens the door to the basement, he can hear the TV blaring commercials. That's football—ten seconds of gameplay, five minutes of ads for fast food, the Toyota-thon sales event of the century, insurance, and that whackadoo pillow guy.

"Hi, Dad!" He has to raise his voice over the TV.

Dad glances over his shoulder. His face lights up. "Tad-o!" Bracing himself on the arms of his favorite recliner, he heaves himself to his feet. "When did you get here?"

The Pierce men don't hug each other, so they just do that manly shoulder-slap/handshake/half-hug thing. "Maybe half an hour ago?" Tad says. Ugh, he has to cut it out with the uptalk. It always comes out more when he's here, like he's constantly asking permission to take up the space he's in.

"Your mom get you something to eat? You're looking scrawny."

Tad folds his arms over his chest. Dad has always been a big man, and Tad's height comes from him—Tad could look him in the eye by the time he was fourteen. But all Dad's broadness went to Walt.

"Yeah, I ate," he says. There's no point in getting into an argument about how he's not scrawny, he's lean, and he'll never be able to bulk up like Walt.

He knows, because there was a period of high school where he spent a truly insane amount of time in the gym and making himself drink protein shakes.

But! He gave his first blowjob because of all that gym time, to a closeted senior boy who fled Watertown the minute he graduated—

which was good, because it meant he wasn't going to let slip what he and Tad did on the shoulder press machine.

"How's the game?" Tad asks.

Dad waves a beefy hand. "Boring. Say, how was Vegas? Walt just said you all got drunk and lost a bunch of money. And you decided to go camping?"

Tad laughs at that summary. "Walt lost a bunch of money. I just got drunk. And uh, yeah, there's some good camping in Nevada, so, you know. When's the next time I'm gonna be down there, I figured."

"That's my boy," Dad says proudly. Tad feels his chest puff out. They're so different, Dad and him, but this is the one thing they've always connected on. Walt liked camping, but Tad was the one who fell in love with it. "Where'd you camp?"

"Humboldt-Toiyabe," Tad says. "Not the part close to Vegas, but the bit closer to California."

Dad whistles. "Pretty remote out there, isn't it?"

"Yeah. It's amazing."

All of a sudden, Dad's expression gets stern. "You know better than to go camping in that kind of place by yourself. You could've broken your leg and died of thirst out there!"

"Oh! Um—" Shit. He should've lied about… something. His brain scrambles for something, anything to get that disapproving, disappointed expression off Dad's face. "Well, I wasn't alone. I went with"—god if he says he went with his "female" hookup "Louise" he'll never hear the end of it from Mom; she'll demand they devote his entire visit to tracking her down—"uhhh, a guy. This uh, dude. That I met in Vegas."

Dad looks surprised. Uh, yeah, no duh. *Tad* made a friend and then they went camping together? Is that more or less plausible than Tad getting married and going camping with his new husband?

God—wait. Did he tell Walt he was going camping with his fictional female hookup? He can't remember. He was so hungover and still kind of wrecked from the sex. Queasiness roils his intestines. He's kept his sexual orientation from his family for fifteen-odd years, but suddenly he feels one slip-up away from outing himself, and this isn't the way he wants to do it.

That's what he always thinks—*this isn't the way I want to do it*. The truth is, he doesn't actually have a "way he wants to do it." He's never been able to envision what it would look like to come out to his family, and he's never really tried. Maybe a little when he was a teenager, a few halting fantasies about everyone hugging him and telling him they'll always love him.

Yeah right.

"Good thing he didn't turn out to be an axe murderer, huh, kiddo?" Dad says. "He didn't go all *Brokeback Mountain* on you up there, did he?"

Tad lets out an awkward laugh that sounds like it should be admissible in a court of law as a confession of guilt. "No."

Dad doesn't seem to notice. Of course he doesn't—it doesn't fit into his worldview that Tad's gay, so his weirdness is just Tad Being Tad. "You wanna watch the game with me and tell me about your trip?"

As much as he'd love to talk about camping with Dad, he can't bear to carve out the beating heart of the week he spent in Humboldt-Toiyabe. How can he talk about the trip without mentioning the furnace warmth of Lewis holding him through the night, or how Lewis kisses so carefully and slowly, like Tad is precious? How can he excise the night they lay outside the tent on their backs as the fire burned down to nothing, and Tad pointed out constellations with one hand while he clasped Lewis's with the other?

How can he pretend he didn't start falling in love?

Bile burns his throat, and he thinks for a second he actually might vomit. "Actually," he chokes out, "I really need to get my hair cut. I think I'm going to go to the mall with Mom to Sports Clips."

Disappointment flashes across Dad's face so fast that Tad's not sure he really saw it. "Good idea," Dad says. "You don't want other guys thinking you're a woman, right?"

"Right," Tad says with a forced laugh. He flees before he can make it even more obvious that he's not the straight bro Dad expects him to be.

Chapter Twenty

THE LAST week with Tad has occupied so much of Lewis's brain that he hasn't even had the chance to get excited about Friendsgiving. It's been an annual tradition since college, when Stacy's roommate, Ava, revealed she wasn't going home for Thanksgiving.

That first year, it was just the three of them—dumb, broke eighteen-year-olds concocting a disaster of a Thanksgiving dinner in the kitchenette of Stacy and Ava's dorm building. They had three Lean Cuisine turkey dinners, Hawaiian Sweet Rolls, a can of Ocean Spray cranberry sauce served on a paper plate, and a pumpkin pie. Ava managed to get some cheap ass wine, and they all got drunk and giddy and had awful hangovers the next morning.

It's way classier now. They host on a rotating basis, usually the Sunday before Thanksgiving, and this year is Stacy's turn. Lewis assures Tad's plants he'll be back later to stick to their watering schedule, laughs at himself, and jumps on the 1 to 14th St, where he can get the PATH over to Hoboken.

The 1 is delayed, so he's the last to arrive. When he walks in, he brandishes a bottle of rosé and says, "Now the festivities can really begin."

Friendsgiving has grown over the years. Stacy's fiancé, Alang, is obviously there now, since they live together. Ava's wife, Elise, has been coming since the two of them got together. Lewis's old roommate Matthew usually makes it, even though he lives in DC now. A couple of Stacy's other friends usually show up—this year it's Ofelia. There's a man Lewis doesn't know sitting next to her, who's introduced as her new boyfriend, Walt.

"Cheap ass wine!" Stacy cheers.

"Now immortalized by T-Swift." Lewis grins and then chants in time with Stacy, "Your roommate's cheap ass screw top rosé!"

Alang pops his head out of the kitchen. "Are we singing Taylor Swift?"

"Not yet babe, you're good," Stacy assures him.

Lewis hugs Matthew, who gives him a kiss on both cheeks and says, "You're *glowing*." To Stacy, he adds, "I thought she wasn't dating anyone."

"I'm *not*," Lewis says, to a chorus of boos.

When Ofelia's boyfriend looks confused, Ofelia says, "Lewis got so drunk when we were in Vegas that he married a guy he'd just met."

The boyfriend laughs as Matthew demands, "What?"

"Holy shit, man," Ofelia's boyfriend—Walt?—says. "I hope you're gay. Or bi, I guess."

"Um, very gay," Lewis says, though he always feels like he needs to step it up when Matthew's around. Matty's dark skin is always flawless, and there's apparently no makeup palette that doesn't look amazing on him. It's especially unfair, since he's the first of them to Settle Down—his husband is back in DC with their two toddlers.

"Why wasn't I informed of this?" Matthew demands.

"If you'd been at my bachelorette party, you could have been Lewis's best man," Stacy says airily. She scrunches up her face. "I think I must've been best man?"

"Maybe *someone* shouldn't have scheduled her bachelorette party for the weekend before election day," Matthew shoots back. "Since I work for, hm, let's see, a senator? Who was up for re-election this year?"

"I forgot it was election day!"

"At least he won the race so you didn't miss the party for nothing!" Alang helpfully adds from the kitchen.

Matthew lets out a theatrical sigh and sits back down. "Only you, Lew. Only you. So are you trying to make it work?"

"Inquiring minds want to know," Elise, Ava's wife, says. Next to her, one of Ava's legs is bouncing—she's probably nervous about Ofelia's boyfriend being here. "We're working on the divorce stuff," Lewis says shortly. He doesn't want to talk about this, especially when Tad isn't here. Maybe if Tad hadn't gone to visit his family, he could have come to Friendsgiving. That might have been fun.

"I still think you're a cute couple," Ava grumbles, like it's a personal affront.

Lewis changes the subject.

At dinner, he ends up seated next to Ava on one side and Matthew on the other. Ava is her usual quiet self. Walt is across the table from Lewis, and he's boisterous and kind of bro-y—but he seems smitten with Ofelia, and he's nice.

Lewis has always brought his current boyfriend to Friendsgiving. The memories make him cringe. They never fit in with his friends—he can't even remember what they talked about with his friends.

It's easy to imagine what Tad would talk about to them. He'd like Ava and Elise—especially Ava, with her sharp cynicism and cutting sarcasm. They'd probably share pictures of their pets and get into some deeply nerdy debate about Captain America versus Iron Man, or something.

The realization hits Lewis like a punch to the gut.

He misses Tad.

For a second, his chest is so tight he can't breathe, and it's partly panic at recognizing how deep he's gotten himself. But it's also partly just the simple ache of wanting to see someone, wanting to be with them, and wanting it so hard that your bones creak with it.

He snags his phone from his pocket. He and Tad haven't communicated at all since yesterday. Lewis waited until late at night, then he sent a heart emoji back to Tad. He didn't get a response, and he's trying to remember that Tad isn't free to text all the time.

But his chest hurts too much now. His heart's too full, and he can't pretend he's cool just not talking to Tad. *Hope you're doing ok,* he texts. Then, *I'm at Friendsgiving with Stacy and her fiancé Alang, and some of the people from the bachelorette party, and my friend Matthew who I think you'd really like. He's fabulous and smart so you two already have a lot in common*

Was that too much? It was probably too much. But he hits Send anyway, because… well, this is how he feels, and Lewis hasn't ever been good at fighting how he feels.

Dating break, some part of him whispers, but he just stares at his phone, hoping Tad texts back.

Then—a miracle! Three dots! Lewis holds his breath.

I'm ok

I was going to ask if you had time to talk later, but if you're busy, nm

Panic seizes Lewis and he frantically types back, *No I'm totally free later*

I'll probably be home around 9? If that's not too late?
Lol I'm 29 not 90

9 is fine
Kk good
It's been weird not talking even though I know it's only been like
36 hours
Yeah
Same
I mean
I wish I was at Friendsgiving even if I'd probably just sit in a
corner like a freak
Sorry that was probably weird
I wish you were here too

Ava glances over at him. "You're into him, aren't you?"

"Huh? What?" Lewis drops his phone and it clatters to the hardwood floor. Everyone looks at him. His face flames, and he ducks under the table to pick it up. There's one more message from Tad: **I can't wait to talk to you later**

Lewis's chest hurts again, winding tighter and tighter until he's afraid it might snap. *Me too*, he types back, wanting to say so much more. He'll save it for their phone conversation.

Next to him, Ava snickers. "You are. God, how disgustingly adorable."

"What if I am?" he asks, trying to sound airy. Judging by the way Ava smirks at him, he doesn't sound any version of cool or smooth.

Sagging in his chair, he says, "He's kind of great. I think he might be different than… you know." *You* know. The asshole parade.

"Do you think he might be different or do you just want him to be different?" Ava asks bluntly.

Lewis winces. Yeah, that's the problem, isn't it? He doesn't trust himself. What he needs is an outside observer—someone to spend some time with Tad and tell Lewis honestly if he's more of the same, or if he's as special as Lewis is starting to think he is.

"I really think he's different," Lewis finally says. Inspiration strikes. "You should hang out with him! I think you two would get along. And like. You could tell me if you think we'll work out."

Ava looks flustered. "Oh, um, I guess… I could? If you set something up…."

"Yeah! I will. I'll talk to him."

She takes a bite of cornbread. "I remember Elise and me were supposed to hang out with you and Jonah, but Jonah ditched you to club with his friends."

Blech. Yeah. Jonah did stuff like that a lot. "I guess he hasn't had much chance to stand me up yet. Not that I think he would. Anyway, we've mostly just been working on the divorce forms."

Her eyebrows go up. "Shouldn't a paralegal be able to wrap those up pretty fast?"

A flush climbs up his neck, and he coughs. "I just want to make sure he understands everything."

"Understands everything about your erogenous zones, more like," Ava says wickedly.

Lewis's face flames and he stuffs sweet potatoes in his mouth. As he's trying not to choke, a snatch of remembered conversation floats through his head. Eventually, he gets the sweet potatoes down, and then he says, "He actually said he doesn't have any friends, so that's probably not a very good standard to judge by."

"Oh, so he's like me." Ava gives him finger guns. "We know how much you love me, so maybe a male version would be great for you?"

"What are you two talking about?" Matthew asks, pivoting away from his conversation with Alang.

"How Lewis can tell if his new guy is trash like all his exes," Ava supplies.

"Has he stolen any of your shoes?" Matthew asks.

Stabbing a piece of turkey with his fork, Lewis aggrievedly asks, "Does *everyone* know that story?"

With a shrug, Matthew says, "It's a cautionary tale, darling."

"Great," Lewis mutters. "So glad I can be of service."

Matthew plants his elbows on the table and fixes Lewis with an unblinking stare. The highlighter on his cheek bones shimmers. "Does he take advantage of you?"

"Oh my *god*," Lewis yelps. "No! My exes were assholes, but they weren't *assaulting* me, Matty—"

"God, calm your tits." Matthew rolls his eyes. "I mean does he take advantage of your endlessly generous nature."

"Oh." Lewis turns red again. Maybe he never went back to his normal color.

"You want to star in your own rom-com *so much*, Lew." Matthew smoothes the front of Lewis's shirt, looking a little sad. "Boys take advantage of that."

Lewis concentrates on his dinner for a second. It hurts to think about this stuff. His brain doesn't want to think about it—he doesn't want to even consider Tad capable of taking advantage of him.

But Tad's been nothing but wonderful. Nothing but generous. Tad upended his plans so he could go camping with Lewis, bought a bunch of camping stuff he already owned, sent his luggage home with his brother, then had to make the four-hour drive to Watertown to retrieve his luggage and drive back to NYC. And they've been at Tad's apartment for the past week. Lewis has been eating his food, taking up his space.

It's nothing like the way Lewis's past relationships have gone.

"He's not taking advantage," Lewis says quietly. "He's... really sweet."

Keeping it casual, Lewis. Keeping it real casual.

Matthew drapes an arm over his shoulders and pulls him into a hug. "Trust your instincts, then."

Trust his instincts. A few weeks ago, Lewis would have scoffed and said his instincts were fucked up at a party somewhere and had lost their phones and keys, and they definitely couldn't be trusted.

Now? Now, he haltingly, hesitantly does.

He checks the time. Only a few hours until he gets to talk to Tad.

Lewis smiles and eats his dinner.

Chapter Twenty-One

LEWIS IS checking the plant app to make sure he isn't mis-watering any of Tad's plants when his phone rings. "Hey!" he says, even though he didn't actually look to see if 'Best Husband Ever' was the one calling.

"Hey." Tad's voice hits Lewis's ears like an embrace. "Can you talk?"

"Yes! Yeah. Definitely. I can talk. I'm home now. I mean, I'm at your apartment. I'm doing the nightly rounds." Lewis is babbling. He's also grinning like an idiot. It's so amazing to hear Tad's voice.

There's a breath of laughter on the phone. "How are the plants?"

"Well, I don't think I've killed any of them yet, so, good?" There's a muffled sound on the phone, like wind, or maybe Tad breathing hard. Lewis tightens his fingers around the phone. "Are you okay? You sound out of breath."

"That's just wind. I'm outside."

"Outside?"

"Don't want my mom listening at the door."

Jesus. "Aren't you cold?"

"I mean, yeah, but it's fine. I go camping in the winter."

"You're crazy," Lewis says, but he's grinning.

It sounds like Tad's smiling too. "You're missing out."

"Well," Lewis says casually, "maybe if you want to take me camping in the winter, it wouldn't be so bad."

There's a pause. Should Lewis not have said that?

"I would, if you really mean that," Tad says. "I love winter camping. It's... magical." He scoffs. "Sorry, that was cheesy. So how was Friendsgiving?"

"Oh, it was good. Matty—I mentioned Matthew, right?—came up from DC, so that was pretty cool. And Ofelia has a new boyfriend, very bro-y, but he seems nice. You might not remember Ofelia from the bachelorette party?"

"I don't remember much," Tad says sheepishly.

"That's okay. She's nice but we're not close. You know what I was thinking, though—you'd probably really like Ava. You might not remember her, either."

"Er...."

Lewis laughs. "Don't worry about it, she's quiet. I feel like I'm talking too much. I'm definitely talking too much. Tell me about what's going on up there? Are you okay? Everything's... okay?"

He's not quite sure what he's asking. His tone kind of says, *you haven't been put in conversion therapy yet, have you?*

Tad makes a noncommittal noise. "We don't have to talk about me."

Lewis's stomach churns. "Okay, but see, that just makes me think we really need to. Seriously. Is everything okay? You're not... I mean, you're... safe, right?"

At the low rumble of Tad's laughter, Lewis flushes, feeling stupid. But Tad says, "God, you're sweet. I'm fine, really. It's just painfully awkward. I'm sorry I've been so horrible about texting, by the way. There was... an incident, and I just—I should've said something, but I wasn't sure how to like, say it in code."

"An incident?" Lewis asks uneasily.

"Ugh. God. Okay. So, you know how you sent me a heart last night?" Tad's voice pinches. "When I got up this morning, I left my phone in my room, and my mom came in to like, tidy up."

"Like a turn down service?" Lewis asks, amused at the idea of his own mother doing something like that.

"Yeah, she's... whatever. Anyway. When I came out to the kitchen she said...." There's another pause, and Lewis has a feeling Tad's drawing a fortifying breath. "She said 'Lewis is an unusual name for a woman.' And I was obviously like, what the fuck are you talking about. I mean, I didn't say 'fuck'—anyway, she said she just happened to glance at my phone and she saw your text. Which is bullshit, she totally looked at my notifications, and it was stupid of me to not clear them before I left the room—"

"Um, hey, Tad, that's like... not normal behavior for a mother towards her adult child?" Mortification sweeps through him. Awesome, he's insulting Tad's mom—that's totally the right move with a guy he really likes. Every son loves hearing his mom get dragged. "I mean—um, shit."

"No, you're right." Tad sounds morose. "But it's how she is. Anyway, I said you were an author I was giving some extra help to at work."

Lewis looks out the window. The Henry Hudson Bridge is lit up, a steady stream of cars crossing. "Sorry. I won't text anymore."

Silence from the other end. Lewis would wonder if Tad hung up, except he can hear the crunch of footsteps. "I don't want you to stop texting," Tad says. "I just have to be more careful."

"I'm sorry if I made things harder for you."

"Stop apologizing, Lewis." Tad sighs. "It feels like I've been here days. And I haven't even talked to my brother yet. He just started dating some woman who lives in the city, apparently, and he's visiting her this weekend. It's practically all I've heard about, by the way. *Tad*"—his voice gets high-pitched—"your brother found a nice girl on Tinder. Why can't you do the same?"

Lewis laughs. "My mom tells me to stay off dating apps. She says Grindr's for fuck boys."

"Oh my god, does she really say fuck boys?"

"She totally does."

Tad cackles. "I want to meet your mom."

"Well, it doesn't take long to get to Weehawken."

"*Jersey*," Tad says, his voice dripping with theatrical disdain.

"Um, hey, I wouldn't talk, Upstate."

Tad laughs again. "You want to know a thing I've done since I got here? It's horrible."

"Go for it."

"I got my hair cut."

That hits like a hammer. Tad got his hair cut? But Lewis really likes Tad's hair. Those curls....

"What's horrible about it?" Lewis asks belatedly.

"Um, well, I let my mom talk me into Sports Clips, for one thing."

"Oh no."

"Unfortunately, oh yes."

"Is that why we're not Facetiming?"

Tad laughs. "I didn't know if you'd want to Facetime. I didn't want to assume."

"I like seeing your face," Lewis says honestly.

There's a garbled noise of frustration. "Okay—fine. Hold on."

The line goes dead, and then an incoming Facetime call lights up the screen. And then—there's Tad. Lewis's chest heats—blazes—and he can't catch his breath.

"Hey," Lewis says.

"Hi." Tad's face is washed out and pale in the glow of his phone screen, but behind him is the orange illumination of streetlights. He's wearing a beanie.

"I can't see your hair," Lewis points out.

Tad makes a face and pulls off his hat. Lewis tries not to look dismayed. "She wouldn't stop cutting," Tad says, so clearly Lewis failed.

"It looks good," Lewis says quickly. It does. It's short on the sides and a bit longer on the top, and Tad looks great. It's not the haircut that's bad, it's the fact that Lewis is too into running his fingers through Tad's hair and feeling it tangle, and those curls against his palms and how it feels when he gets a handful and *pulls—*

"It doesn't." Tad scowls. "You think it looks horrible."

"No!" The idea of Tad thinking that Lewis doesn't like how he looks and going home to his awkward house is kinda sorta intolerable. "I just... your hair is nice."

Your hair. Is nice.

Christ.

Fortunately, Tad looks like he got something out of that. "It is?" he asks. There's hesitant happiness on his face, like light shining through the crack under a door.

"Yeah, like. Your, um." He waves a hand vaguely, which Tad probably can't see. "I just like it. Touching it, and...."

"Pulling it?" Tad asks slyly, his mouth quirking up on one side.

"Maybe."

The quirk at the corner of Tad's mouth gets a little salacious. "So I should let it grow out again."

"Yes." God, has Lewis ever answered a question so fast in his life?

Tad's pupils look wide, which makes Lewis's cock twitch. Then, Tad sighs. "I'm going to get interrogated about why I was gone so long."

"If you need to get back...."

"Yeah, I probably do." Tad sounds miserable. Lewis doesn't want him to be miserable, but the fact that it's because they have to stop talking is a nice feeling.

There's a silence, long enough for Lewis to wonder if they finally ran out of things to talk about. And if they're out of things to talk about, then this will fizzle, or crash and flame out, and Lewis will be left angry and disappointed with himself. Again.

Then Tad says, "Oh my god, I stopped at this gas station on the drive, and they had the *creepiest* hot dog sign!"

Lewis laughs. "Pics or it didn't happen."

"Oh, it happened. I took one to send to you. This thing looks like it's going to crawl out from under your bed at three in the morning and lie next to you until you wake up."

"And then it murders you?"

"I don't know, I think it just wants companionship?"

Lewis laughs again, and the conversation goes on the way it does with people you could talk to forever. Too soon, though, Tad comes to a halt. Lines tighten around his mouth and eyes. A furrow appears between his eyebrows, and his eyes focus somewhere in the distance. "This is my street," he says quietly.

"Okay." The disappointment pooling in Lewis's chest is stupid. "If you need anything or just... I don't know, want to talk... I mean, I'm sure you have other friends, but...."

Tad smiles, but it seems sad. "Thanks, Lewis."

"For what?"

"Just, you know. Talking to me."

"I like talking to you," Lewis says.

They lapse into silence, putting off the inevitable moment when they have to hang up. "Say hi to Hetty for me," Lewis finally says.

"I will. She'd probably like to hear your voice, but...."

"I get it."

Tad looks happy, then sad, then nervous, and Lewis can't parse the progression. With a resigned smile, Tad says, "I could stand outside all night talking to you."

"I know this probably doesn't carry the same weight, since I'm sitting inside in your warm and comfortable apartment, but me too."

If there was a way to bottle laughter, Lewis would bottle Tad's right now. He almost takes a screenshot, because Tad's smile is gorgeous—but it won't capture how Tad really looks, and it certainly won't capture the way he's making Lewis feel.

"See you on Saturday," Tad says. "But hopefully we can talk on the phone again."

"I'd like that."

"Me too. I'll let you know."

Another pause. "Well," Lewis says.

"Yeah." Tad's voice is quiet. "Bye, Lewis."

"Bye, Tad."

They stare at each other through the screen. Tad sighs again, looking heartbreakingly sad. He waves a little, and then the screen goes black.

Chapter Twenty-Two

BEING IN his parents' house is excruciating, but Tad learned how to knuckle through this kind of agony a long time ago. The trick is to become a colorless version of himself. It could be worse—he could have a healthy social life to water down and straight-ify. But there's no social life, so he doesn't have to pretend his circle of gay friends doesn't exist. They don't.

The hard part is biting back the person he's grown into since he moved to NYC. He's less funny, less biting, less smart. He doesn't know how to be less gay, so he just makes himself less of everything.

Imagine if Lewis met him like this. If they'd run into each other in Vegas when Tad was still tagging along with Walt and his friends. Lewis wouldn't have looked twice at him. Even if he had, Tad would have been sober and way too shy to approach him.

Maybe they didn't make great choices while they were drunk, but they're in each other's lives, and… well, Tad hasn't really regretted the drunk marriage this whole time. Now that Lewis and him have whatever they have, he really doesn't regret it. He'll take as much of Lewis as Lewis is willing to give, because it's not going to last forever.

Every time he thinks about how it isn't going to last forever, he wonders why he came up to Watertown for this whole week—which is why he says, "I was thinking I might leave on Friday instead of Saturday."

Mom looks at him like he just introduced her to her grandchild and immediately murdered them in front of her. "But you always stay until Saturday."

"I know, I just…." What? *I just have stuff to do?* Like what? He's made an art of presenting himself to his parents as someone who never does anything.

Obviously he has to do Lewis, but he won't be telling Mom.

"Just thinking about traffic," he finishes lamely.

"If you moved back up here, you wouldn't have to deal with traffic," Mom says, not so much a hint as an anvil landing on his head. "You've been working from home since before the pandemic, haven't you? So there's no reason you can't move back."

Nightmare. Complete and utter nightmare. Move back to Watertown? It sounds like a sentence of life imprisonment. "I like the city," he says.

"To *visit*," Mom says.

"No, to live," he snaps. He bites back on his tone and scratches a fingernail on the counter. "Mom, my life is there. That's where I want to live."

With a defeated sigh, Mom says, "Oh, I know. I just wish there was something that could tempt you to move back."

Unlikely, and growing exponentially more unlikely with every moment he spends with Lewis Mancini-Sommer.

She goes back to her Thanksgiving prep. She does most of it on Wednesday, and ever since he can remember, Tad has helped. Right now she's making dough for the pies, and they'll make the fillings together after that—pumpkin, pecan, and apple. There's nothing in the world like Mom's pecan pie. He has no idea how she does it, but when he's tried to make it at home, it never tastes right, even though he's the one who always makes the filling here.

It doesn't make sense, but Tad just accepts it. He wants pecan pie, he has to come to Watertown.

"Do you remember Nathan Pettis?" Mom says as she kneads the dough.

"Um." Tad scrunches his nose in thought. "From high school?"

"Wasn't he in your first grade class?"

"Oh, maybe." Is this a special parent skill, where they can remember everyone their kids ever came into contact with? "He was kind of a jerk." Yeah, he used to call Tad *fag*. Their lockers were next to each other in high school, so he had lots of opportunities.

"Was he?" Mom asks. "Well, boys will be boys. Anyway, I was talking to Barb Collins and you know what she told me? Nathan moved to the city a few years ago, and the last time he came home, he brought his *boyfriend.* Can you believe it? Apparently now that he moved to the city, he's"—her voice lowers to a near whisper—"*gay.*"

It feels like rainbows are shooting out of Tad's pores. Surely his own gayness is obvious, from the way he's sitting with one leg crossed, to the way one of his wrists is hanging just a bit limply, to the way he's gone completely and utterly still.

"Huh," Tad says, because he has to say something.

"His poor parents," Mom says. "They must have been so shocked."

Tad wants to curl inside a shell like a hermit crab. He wants the tide to come in and wash him away. This isn't the first time he's heard stuff like this. It barely even hurts anymore.

Okay, that's a lie. It hurts. But what is he supposed to do? If he argues, he's afraid the truth will be all over his face, or blaring in a neon sign over his head. Defending the gays is the same as being one of them. And then it'll be *his* poor parents that are so shocked.

What would it be like to have parents like Lewis's? Parents who see their son's queerness as normal?

Tad is so sick of straightness and cis-ness being "normal." But he's not doing everything he can to change it, is he? He's sitting at the counter in his parents' kitchen, twenty-nine years old and in the closet, and he's keeping his mouth shut as his mother dips her toes into some casual homophobia.

He looks at his lap, despising himself. Stupid, hypocritical coward.

Words force their way through his clenched teeth before he can stop them. "It's not like he's doing something wrong."

His stomach rolls sickeningly, and sweat breaks out on his palms. He doesn't look up. That's it. He just exposed his secret. Mom will know he's gay.

"Well, no, of course he's not doing anything *wrong*," Mom says, as though she didn't just dolefully sigh over Nathan Pettis's parents and their tribulations. "But I can't imagine, your son goes away to the city and comes back dating a *man!* I suppose that's normal there, though."

It's normal everywhere, Tad wants to say. Instead, he mumbles, "He was always gay."

"What?"

Tad clears his throat. "The city doesn't make people gay. Maybe it just helped Nathan realize that about himself, when before he didn't?"

"Isn't that the same thing?" Mom says. "He always dated girls, but living in the city made him think he should date men too. Anyway, Tad, I thought you didn't like Nathan?"

"I don't. I didn't. Maybe he's changed."

"Speaking of people who have changed," Mom says, which is such a clumsy segue that Tad is immediately suspicious, "do you remember Jenny Clark?"

No. Then Tad's brain kicks into gear. "Sydney's younger sister?"

"Yes!" Mom beams. "I always thought Sydney and you might date. You were such good friends in middle school."

They were such good friends until it became obvious that Sydney had a huge crush on him, and Tad told himself he had a crush on her too, and they made out because Tad was desperate to be Not Gay. They weren't friends after that. Her younger sister, Jenny, was still in elementary school the last time they hung out.

"We grew apart," Tad says vaguely.

Mom pulls a pie plate closer and drapes the rolled-out dough in it. "I want you to keep an open mind, okay?"

Alarms blare in Tad's head. "About what?"

Mom concentrates on shaping the pie crust. She did something she already knows he's going to hate, and she thinks if she's not looking at him, his hurt or anger won't count.

"I set you up with Jenny. You're having dinner with her tonight at Vescio's."

In the silence, the commercials blasting from the TV downstairs seem extra loud.

"You what?" He heard wrong. He misunderstood. Mom talks about meddling, but she's never actually meddled at this level. She wouldn't do this.

"Jenny got out of a serious relationship, and she's been having trouble meeting people. You just—"

Also got out of a serious relationship, but you don't know that, do you, Mom, because my relationship was with a man.

Mom hesitates. "You have trouble putting yourself out there."

"Mom, I'm fine. I don't need you to set me up!"

"Well, she's expecting you, and you wouldn't want to disappoint her."

Suddenly Tad's on his feet with no memory of standing. "Text her. Or call her. Or however you set this up. I'm not going on a date with a stranger!"

Looking at him like he's dense, Mom says, "Tad, dates are always with strangers at first. They only become not strangers after you go out with them!"

Like the stranger he invited to ride a mechanical bull with him. Like the stranger he slept with. Like the stranger he went camping with. And now Lewis isn't a stranger, and Tad doesn't want anyone else. Even if Mom knew he was gay and set him up with a man, this would be beyond the pale.

Tad doesn't want anyone but Lewis.

He's in love with Lewis.

"I'm not going," Tad says.

Mom gives him that look of complete and utter Mom Disappointment. How Could You. I Didn't Raise You Like This. "You might like her."

"I'm sure she's fine, but I'm not... I'm not looking for a girlfriend."

Beautiful! Not a lie. 100 percent the truth. He is *definitely* not looking for a girlfriend.

"Thaddeus." Mom pauses her crust shaping. "You live so far away. You only visit twice a year. You hardly ever call. Would you do this one thing for me? I'm just asking you to have dinner with a woman. I don't see why it's such an issue."

Because I'm gay. Because I'm seeing a man. Because I'm in love with him.

His mouth is open and the words are *right there*. This is it—he's going to come out.

"It's not" is what comes out instead. Of his mouth. Because he's a coward. A spineless embarrassment. "I'll go," he adds.

This isn't the right time to come out anyway. But... what if he walks into Vescio's, sits down, and tells Jenny Clark he's gay and he's sorry for the misunderstanding? And then what if he comes back to the house and tells his parents? Finally, at last, tells his parents who he really is?

Mom pats his cheek. It's sticky with dough and powdery from flour. It's the childhood he's always prioritized over his true self—baking and hominess and the special bond he has with his mother, which he's always been afraid to destroy by telling her he's gay.

But if she doesn't know who he is, how special is that bond?

Chapter Twenty-Three

VESCIO'S IS a classic Watertown first date spot. It's not too fancy, but it's fancy enough—a couple steps above Olive Garden, at least.

Tad can't get out of the car.

Before he left the house, he lay on his bed, Hetty a cat loaf on his chest, and tried to take deep, centering breaths. He doesn't feel centered. He just wishes he was alone with his cat. He's already five minutes late, though. And he really shouldn't stand Jenny up.

Deep breath in.

You can do this, Tad.

Deep breath out.

Maybe.

When he was a kid, he saw a speech therapist for years. At first it was because he didn't close his teeth right when he made an S sound and it was developing into a lisp. It turned into a kind of therapy for his social anxiety, which everyone said he'd grow out of.

Except he never grew out of it. It stopped being a thing to grow out of right around the time he finished elementary school, and it became something wrong with him.

The E in Vescio's is flickering.

He closes his eyes. Clenches his hands into sweaty fists.

He can do this. Go inside, tell Jenny the truth. Just lay it out there. *Surprise! I'm gay!* Insert jazz hands. *But we can still have dinner if you want? The breadsticks are good.*

God, it's going to be awkward.

A shock of cold air hits his face when he opens the car door. He hurries across the parking lot and into the restaurant before he can think about how fast his heart is beating. The hostess brings him to a table, which Jenny Clark is already occupying.

At least she doesn't look like she made a huge effort. Perfunctory makeup, an outfit that looks like office-casual, and brown hair in a messy bun. Tad's in a button-up, and he bought some styling cream and heinous cologne at CVS, which he sprayed on in the parking lot. He's afraid he'll smell like sweat otherwise.

"Tad?" Jenny gets to her feet. "You look so different!"

His mouth opens, but nothing comes out.

No. Fuck. He has a plan. He's coming out tonight—to her, to his family, and he's going to stop living a lie.

Which sounds so dramatic.

"Uh." Tad clears his throat. Clears his throat again. His face feels hot, and the longer he stays silent, the hotter it gets. His fingers are tingling. That can't be normal.

Jenny leans forward. She looks sad and nervous. Tad wishes he had a straight friend to set her up with.

He clears his throat for a third time. "You," he says.

Cool! Great!

Now Jenny's brow furrows. "Is everything okay?"

"Um. Jenny." He pulls the chair out but doesn't sit.

The expression on her face is halfway between constipation and resignation, like she knew this was a bad idea and had to talk herself into coming anyway. "You remember me, right? Sydney's younger sister? You guys used to be friends."

"Sydney, yeah." Tad's throat is closing up. Is he allergic to something in here? Is he going into anaphylactic shock?

He makes himself shake her hand, but he feels like a robot doing it. She obviously thinks something's wrong with him. Something *is* wrong with him. He needs to act like a human being.

His mouth opens, but no sound comes out. Jenny looks like she's starting to wonder if he's a psycho, like maybe he's going to start flipping tables or screaming at servers.

The words are right there, sitting at the back of his throat, but nothing will push them forward, and so he's just standing here, arms limp at his sides, as he stares and she stares back, her expression growing progressively more confused and troubled.

I'm gay. I'm gay! I'M GAY!

Two words. That's all it will take. If he could just get those two words out, the floodgates would open. He knows they would. And maybe she'll be horrible about it. Maybe she'll be embarrassed. Maybe she'll think it's funny and they'll have dinner together anyway.

All of that is just a pipe dream, though. He has to actually *say the words*.

"Is everything okay?" Jenny asks nervously.

Nothing is okay. He's almost thirty years old and he's so committed to not disappointing his parents that he's on a date with a woman.

"Um, fine," Tad manages to force out.

He hates this. He hates how his stupid brain won't make his stupid mouth just say the words. He doesn't even know what he's afraid of. That she's going to think he's weird? She obviously thinks he's weird! What does he care if this random woman who he'll probably never see again thinks he's weird?

But if he could logic his shyness away, it wouldn't be a problem. It's not about *this* situation. It's something deeper, a fear that he's going to be laughed at or shunned embedded so far inside him that the specifics don't matter.

This was supposed to be a freeing moment. This was supposed to be where he was finally true to himself.

A waitress approaches. "Is everything okay?"

God, he really wishes people would stop asking that.

It's not okay, and he has to get out of here. Jenny will hate him, but whatever. Her sister has hated him since ninth grade so it's not like he's losing some meaningful connection.

"I have to go," he says so quietly that he's not sure she heard him. When her eyebrows go up, he knows she did. "Sorry," he adds, but it's not true. All he wants is to get out of here. The entire restaurant is staring. They might even be recording the freak, but he can't bring himself to look around for the raised phones.

Suddenly he's in his rental car. In the dark. Hands clenched around the steering wheel. Door shut. How did he get here? He has no memory of walking out of the restaurant, or getting the key from his pocket, or opening the car. He's just... here, and he's shaking, and he's choking on a sob that's as trapped as his words were back there.

There's something wrong with him. He's weak, he's a baby, he's incapable of the most basic speaking up for himself that everyone else just *does* without struggle.

Once, he and John got in a huge fight, where John yelled at him that he was so terrified of disappointing someone that he ended up disappointing everyone, and maybe he should care less about the conditional approval of people he lied to so they'd keep loving him.

Later, John apologized, but Tad heard the words thrashing right underneath the surface: you can choose to stay in the closet like a coward, or you can choose us.

In the end, John made the choice for him. Or he thought Tad made the choice and acted accordingly.

Mom's going to be so disappointed with him for fucking up this date. Dad will get that look on his face, like, *what do you expect from Tad.* Tomorrow at Thanksgiving dinner, Mom will tell Walt the whole story like it's a funny anecdote instead of a raw, pulsing wound Tad is trying to staunch.

The sob claws its way out of his throat. Crying is exactly what he needs to add to this tableau: sitting in a rental car in a strip mall parking lot after failing to tell a stranger he's gay and crying about it.

Tears spill out anyway. He dashes them away with the back of his hand. To add insult to injury—or maybe the other way around—he somehow manages to hook a finger into his nostril, and he *yanks*, and it fucking *hurts*, and he cries harder like the baby he is.

His forehead thunks down on the steering wheel and all he wants is to be home. Not his parents' house. His apartment in Manhattan. He wants to cuddle Hetty and listen to her purr and he wants to be surrounded by his plants in his own space where he can be himself, where no one wants anything more of him or to make him into someone he's not capable of being.

The car key jabs his thigh as he shifts his leg. There's nothing actually stopping him from going home, is there? His parents will be upset, but his parents are already going to be upset. Well, Mom will be upset. Dad will get upset because Tad had to go and ruin Thanksgiving.

He almost starts crying again.

The car clock reads 7:09. If he leaves now and only stops to get Hetty and his stuff, he could probably be home by midnight.

The jumping in his throat calms at that thought, and he's able to take a full breath for the first time in ten minutes. He reaches into the glove compartment, gropes for his wedding ring, and slides it back on his finger.

Chapter Twenty-Four

LEWIS IS a few minutes late with his evening watering rounds because he's been texting Taylor about the Mancini-Sommer family Thanksgiving celebration tomorrow. There are always too many relatives, too much noise, too many cousins who Lewis only sees a couple times a year. He kind of loves it. Like, he's happy he doesn't have to deal with it all the time—he's good with their nuclear family—but seeing everyone else once in a while is nice.

Taylor isn't looking forward to it. Her latest IVF treatment was unsuccessful, and everyone in the family knows she's trying to conceive, and on holidays they all air their opinions about her choices.

Sorry but you KNOW Aunt Jean is going to tell me to fInD a MaN and get pregnant the old-fashioned way
Tell her you leave the finding a man stuff to me
She'll think you're vetting potential husbands for me
Oof yeah you don't want that
Poor Lew
Does that mean you're still not dating?

Is he still not dating? Because he's staying in a guy's apartment taking care of his plants, and he's sleeping with that guy, and that guy has pretty much occupied all of his thoughts for the past few weeks.

Also he's still wearing the wedding band.

It's complicated
So you're definitely seeing someone but you don't want to call it what it is because you're afraid you're going to get burned
Shut up
Nailed it
I'm such a smart big sister
Vegas guy?

No comment
Lewiiiiiiiiiiiis

He refuses to tell her anything over text, but she extracts a very serious sibling promise that he'll tell her everything tomorrow.

The thought is actually kind of... exciting? Telling Taylor about Tad makes the whole thing real in a way that's terrifying but also thrilling. He's always told his family about his boyfriends, so keeping Tad a secret was definitely part of the Dating Break.

He yawns and stretches. It's almost midnight, and if he's going to get to his parents' house in Weehawken on time tomorrow and also not be a zombie, he needs to get to bed.

But first, plants. He's pretty sure he's been doing a good job—at least, none of them look dead—and he's determined to keep it up so Tad comes home to an apartment full of healthy greenery. And maybe he'll throw himself into Lewis's arms in gratitude, and Lewis can push him into the bedroom to show him how long the week felt without seeing him.

Smiling at the daydream—which is quickly becoming pornographic—Lewis picks up the spray bottle and starts making the rounds.

There's a noise at the door. A key turns in the lock and he whirls, heart pounding. His brain whirs through possibilities—break-in? Tad's boss, Callie? Maintenance? Landlord?—as he stands there, feet planted, and raises his hands defensively.

Only to realize he's holding the spray bottle.

The door swings open. It's Tad, Hetty cradled in his arms.

Right, yeah, *Tad*. This is Tad's apartment, and Tad has a key. But Tad isn't supposed to be back until Saturday?

"It's Wednesday," Lewis blurts.

Tad eyes the spray bottle. "I can see why you're in law, with that attention to detail."

"What are you doing back?" Lewis asks. That's a little better.

"What are *you* doing with that spray bottle?" Tad shoots back.

Hetty meows and Tad sets her on the floor. She streaks to Tad's bedroom. Lewis puts the spray bottle down. "I was watering. I heard the key in the door." The fact that it's 11:55 at night settles in Lewis's brain as an oddity. Furthermore, Tad's in a button-up, there's a hint of cologne wafting off him, and his hair is sticking up in a way that suggests it was, earlier in the day, heavily tamed by product.

Also, Tad's eyes are red-rimmed and his lips are pressed into a thin line. Dark purple circles shadow his eyes.

"Is everything okay?" Lewis asks.

"Um." Tad lets out a high-pitched, strained laugh, not sounding at all like himself. He shoves a hand into his hair, and Lewis can see exactly how it ended up sticking up. "Um," Tad repeats—then crosses to Lewis, grabs his head, and pulls him into a hard kiss.

It's not exactly Tad throwing himself into Lewis's arms for taking such good care of his plants—Lewis doesn't think Tad even noticed how healthy the plants look—but he's super okay with it.

It's a desperate, grasping kiss, and it's hot until Tad lets out a wounded whimper and fists Lewis's hair hard enough to sting—and Lewis tastes salt and realizes Tad's crying so hard the tears are running into their joined mouths.

Lewis breaks the kiss and puts his hands on both sides of Tad's face. "Baby—baby, don't, it's okay. You're okay, I've got you."

Which is apparently the wrong thing to say, because Tad cries harder. Lewis pulls him into a tight hug and holds him, whispering nonsense and rubbing his back. He's trying to surreptitiously check Tad for injuries or something—god, he's dressed up, could he have been assaulted or something at a club? Are there clubs in Watertown?—but he can't find anything.

When Tad's sobs quiet, he sniffles and wipes his nose with the back of his hand. "Pathetic," he mumbles wetly.

"Tad, you're scaring me," Lewis says, refusing to let go of him. "Are you okay? What happened?"

There's a long silence. Finally, Tad raises puffy, red-rimmed eyes, though he doesn't quite meet Lewis's gaze. He's staring somewhere in the vicinity of that spot between Lewis's nose and upper lip. Does that spot have a name? You never hear anyone call it by its name.

Jesus, not important.

Tad wets his lips and says, "My mom set me up with a woman."

"Like for a date?"

"Like for a date."

"Awkward." Lewis winces.

Tad's jaw tenses and his Adam's apple jags. Lewis pulls him back into his arms, and Tad's body goes soft and pliable. "It was horrible," he whispers. "And that's so *stupid*."

"It's not stupid."

"You don't even know what happened."

Lewis rubs a hand slowly up and down Tad's spine. "I know your feelings matter, and I know it made you feel like this."

With a watery laugh, Tad says, "You must make an incredible boyfriend."

That startles an answering laugh from Lewis. "No one else has ever thought so, but thanks." He tugs Tad toward the sofa and sits him down. Tad curls into him, lanky torso and long legs folding up into a surprisingly small, sniffling, Tad-shaped lump.

Lewis keeps an arm around him. "You bailed on Thanksgiving with your family, I guess?"

"Well, I'm not driving back there tomorrow." Tad laughs humorlessly. "I'm sorry. I should've let you know I was coming back so I didn't freak you out. But I had to turn my phone off so they couldn't call me. I only went back to the house to get stuff. And Hetty, obviously."

"It's okay. Luckily I didn't fire on you with that deadly spray bottle."

There's a little snuffle of genuine laughter against Lewis's neck. Lewis kisses Tad's forehead gently, an ache radiating from his chest, clutching his guts and strangling him. He wants very badly to keep Tad from ever feeling like this, but he also knows he doesn't really understand *why* Tad feels like this. He just—he hates it. He hates feeling so helpless when a person he loves is in pain.

"You wanna talk about it?" Lewis asks quietly, turning his face into Tad's hair. It smells like drug store styling mousse.

Tad worries at the laces of Lewis's hoodie before he starts twisting one around his index finger. "My mom set me up with the sister of a girl I used to be really good friends with. So I—god this sounds stupid—I decided the universe must be giving me a sign. It was a perfect opportunity to come out to my family. I was gonna walk into the restaurant and meet this woman, and I'd sit down and thank her for agreeing to my mom's matchmaking attempt, and then"—he takes a breath—"I was going to tell her I'm gay, so a relationship between us obviously wouldn't work. And then I was going to tell my parents when I got back."

By the end of this, Tad's voice is thick and raspy, and Lewis can tell he's about to cry again. He doesn't push him to go on, just waits.

Every couple seconds there's a tug on the neck of Lewis's hoodie as Tad wraps his finger tighter in the lace. Finally, Tad continues, "But I got in there and she was sitting at the table, and I—"

His shoulders tense. Lewis strokes between his shoulder blades, down the knobs of his spine, and Tad loosens a little. "I couldn't say a word," Tad mumbles. "I stood there and I just stared at her like an idiot. And everything I wanted to say just got stuck in my throat, like it always does."

"It does?" Lewis asks, genuinely confused. The Tad he's gotten to know over the past few weeks hasn't ever seemed shy. Has he? Maybe the first time Lewis came over, but that didn't seem out of the ordinary. A lot of people would be shy in that situation.

Something seems to go out of Tad. Some kind of fight, or maybe a burden he was resigned to carrying. "I'm like. Painfully, pathologically shy," Tad says tonelessly. "I know you haven't noticed. But do you know how drunk I had to get before I could talk to you in Vegas?"

"No," Lewis answers honestly. He's trying to reorient a bunch of assumptions about Tad. None of it is bad, but *pathologically shy* wasn't a phrase he would have used to describe the man who invited Lewis to ride a mechanical bull with him.

Tad lets out a surprised little laugh. "Well," he says. "Really drunk. The only way I can talk to hot guys is by getting drunk."

The fact that Tad just referred to him as a "hot guy" is a high, but it's not the thing to focus on right now. Lewis puts his hands on either side of Tad's face and draws him back so he can look Tad in the eyes. "There's nothing wrong with being shy," he says.

The longing on Tad's face breaks his heart. It doesn't take a mind reader to know Tad's heard this before—probably from everyone he's ever cared about.

"When you freeze up and can't choke out a single word, there is," Tad replies.

Gently, Lewis wipes away a tear track bisecting Tad's cheek. "Does it happen all the time?"

Tad leans into Lewis's touch. His eyes flutter shut, eyelashes fanning against his cheek, and Lewis notices for the first time that they're mostly brown, except at the tips, where they lighten to a light reddish-gold. "Not at work, really. When I was a kid, school was... not awful. I was just quiet. I think it's like, if I have a script, kind of, it's not so bad. That's why I can handle job interviews. It's like playing a part."

His eyes open, and the blue is like a punch to Lewis's chest. "I just realized something," Tad says.

"Yeah?" Lewis runs a thumb over Tad's cheekbone. He wants to feel the fan of Tad's gold eyelashes against his skin. This moment feels as delicate as that sensation would be—gossamer and so easily crushed, and Lewis knows right then that if he ever hurt Tad, he'd never forgive himself.

And *that* is not consistent with keeping it casual. That's not consistent with the Dating Break.

He expects panic, but none comes. He waits for panic. All he feels is Tad's warmth, the sharp jut of his cheekbone, and how right and good this is.

Tad straightens, slipping an arm around Lewis's shoulders. "I got really shy the summer between eighth and ninth grade. That was when I realized the way I was looking at boys was how other boys looked at girls." He falls silent, thinking. "I never knew what to say or how to act when I talked to people. I was always afraid that people could tell. Like, in the locker room, boys were always talking about which girls had big tits who they could tell gave good blowjobs, and I was like, how do I interact with girls when I don't notice that?"

Idly, he smooths Lewis's shirt over his chest. "I was terrified a boy would notice me noticing him. I used to change in the bathroom stall for gym so no one could say I was checking them out. And I almost got suspended because I'd wait till everyone else was done showering before I'd shower, and I was late for the next period."

"Did your parents make the school give you extra time to shower?"

"My dad told me to stop being such a girl and shower faster," Tad says—in a tone that isn't exactly easy but doesn't exactly convey how shitty this actually is. "So I just stopped showering after gym. That didn't make me popular, either."

Lewis holds him tighter. "You didn't have a script for how a gay boy should act."

In his arms, Tad stills. Lewis is afraid he said something wrong until Tad pulls back enough to look Lewis in the eyes. There's a small but genuine smile fighting for purchase on Tad's face. "I've had a lot of therapists over the years and not one of them has ever come up with that."

"Maybe if I get sick of being a paralegal, I can consider a career change."

Tad laughs a little and buries his face in Lewis's chest again. Having him there, snug and encircled in Lewis's arms, feels so right.

"Missed you," comes a mumble from his collarbone.

Lewis's heart jumps, then swells to fill his entire rib cage. "I missed you too. I know it's only been like, five days since we saw each other, but—"

Before he can get another word out, Tad's mouth is on his. Lewis makes a noise and melts into the embrace, into Tad's soft lips and his lean body, all angles and edges that somehow soften into this beautiful man who just trusted him. Trusted him! Lewis is the one who trusts too fast, who throws himself all in, but Tad revealed part of himself tonight.

Lewis wants to make sure he knows he can reveal any part of himself, and he'll never judge him or make him feel bad. Lewis wants to be a place of safety for Tad, just like Tad was safety to him when he was freaking out about the marriage, or when he almost died while they were hiking.

He sinks into the kiss, trying to put everything he's feeling into it—*you can tell me anything. I want to be here for you.*

Tad slides his fingers over the back of Lewis's left hand. They stop on the wedding band Lewis can't take off, which probably should have been a sign he was lying to himself about this all along. "Still wearing it," Tad says quietly.

Catching Tad's hand in his, Lewis interlaces their fingers. "So are you."

Tad pushes up to kiss Lewis. His tongue traces the line of Lewis's bottom lip. "I really missed you." Tad shifts and something hard that definitely isn't an arm or leg presses against Lewis's hip.

"Me too, baby," Lewis says, running a hand over the back of Tad's neck and into his hair. He's been planning on scrubbing Tad's shower walls really well, in fact, because he's *really* missed Tad, and the evidence might still be lurking in the grout. The air plants dotting the walls in the bathroom have seen some things. "But you've had a long day, and I'm going to be a gentleman."

"God, so chivalrous." Tad leans in again, and this time, when he runs his tongue over Lewis's lip, Lewis can't help parting his lips on a breathy groan.

Chapter Twenty-Five

SCREW BEING a gentleman.

Lewis hauls Tad into his lap and Tad comes willingly, tearing at Lewis's sweatshirt as they kiss. His hands run up Lewis's chest and Lewis lets out a filthy moan. Jesus he's already rock hard.

They break apart for Tad to pull Lewis's shirt over his head and Tad lets out a sob of need, grabbing one of Lewis's pecs as he ducks his head to maul Lewis's neck with his lips and tongue and teeth.

Lewis grabs his ass with both hands and pulls him closer, and now Tad's cock is pressed into his stomach. Tad pants against Lewis's neck and rolls his hips. Lewis sees white.

"I'm gonna come before I even get your pants off." Lewis attacks the offending closure of said garment as Tad huffs a sexy laugh and redoubles the movement of his hips. All Lewis can do is moan, but he gets the jeans open, zipper hot as he pulls it down over Tad's dick.

"I might too," Tad growls.

"So hurry up, is what I'm hearing?"

"Definitely hurry up."

Of course, with Tad's thighs bracketing Lewis's, the jeans are going nowhere, and as much as Lewis wants to get Tad naked, this is also really hot. Tad's mouth has moved down Lewis's neck to his collarbone, and then to a nipple, which he's working over with no regard to Lewis's ability to last. Lewis shoves his hands down the back of Tad's jeans, straight into his briefs, and squeezes.

Tad lets out a wanton sound and grinds up on Lewis. He jams his hands between their bodies to yank the waistband of Lewis's sweats lower, and the moment they're under his cock still isn't enough. Lewis needs to feel Tad's skin against his *right now*. All of it, every inch, every sweaty, sexy centimeter of it.

Unfortunately getting Tad's clothes off involves removing his hands from Tad's ass, and Tad's ass is like 75 percent of his world right now. He runs a finger down, from the base of Tad's spine into his cleft, and he spreads Tad one-handed and strokes his hole.

"*Fuck*," Tad hisses, right before his teeth clamp down on Lewis's nipple.

Lewis's hips buck and he clenches every muscle from his ass to his abs to keep from shooting in his boxer briefs. "Oh my god, oh my *god*."

When his vision clears, Tad is unbuttoning his own shirt and wriggling off Lewis's lap. "Fuck me," he orders. He strips his jeans and briefs off in one motion and steps out of them as he tosses his shirt aside.

Then he gets on the floor on his hands and knees. "Fuck me," he repeats, like he's going to die if Lewis doesn't obey. Tad grabs his own cock, breathing hard as he strokes himself slowly.

Lewis gets out of his remaining clothes as fast as he can and practically runs to retrieve the lube from Tad's bedside table. They've both been tested since their last partners, so they haven't been using condoms, and just the thought of another round of barebacking makes Lewis leak.

When he gets back to Tad, he flops on the floor. "C'mere," he murmurs, pulling Tad down on top of him and finding his mouth.

Partly, Lewis just needs a cool down. He'll come the minute he gets inside Tad. But mostly, Lewis wants to lavish Tad with attention and tenderness and care, so he holds him close, kissing and touching him everywhere.

He can feel their pre-cum slicked between them. Tad's back is sweaty. Lewis could lick his whole body, savoring the way each part tastes.

"You're not fucking me," Tad says between kisses.

"Mm, not yet."

Tad grinds his cock into Lewis's, which makes both of them groan. "Guess I have to suck you off to convince you," he says, rolling off Lewis and turning around so his head is at Lewis's hips.

Before Tad can make good on that promise, Lewis hooks a hand around Tad's thigh and pulls him closer, until Tad straddles his chest. Lewis runs his hands up and down Tad's legs and kisses the soft insides of his thighs. He licks the hot, velvet skin. Breathes Tad in. "Sit on my face," he murmurs, nuzzling upward into Tad's musk.

Under his hands, Tad's thighs tremble. "Really?"

With a low growl of a laugh, Lewis says, "Yeah, really." He strokes Tad's flanks. "If you want to, that is. If you're not into it—"

"God, yes I'm into it."

Lewis runs his tongue along Tad's leg again, tugging him closer. He's the luckiest man alive—this view, Tad's balls and cock and the sweet cleft of his ass; the way the muscles in his legs are working; the soft, reddish-gold fur of his leg and pubic hair, which Lewis could bury his face in and just breathe and breathe.

Lewis lets his voice go low and husky. "Let me taste you."

With a moan, Tad lowers his ass. Lewis spreads him and licks. At the first touch of his tongue to Tad's hole, Tad gasps. Lewis feels the muscle flex against the flat of his tongue and he licks more thoroughly, teasing Tad, tasting him, getting him worked up and slick.

Lewis never wants to stop eating Tad out. The noises Tad's making are pure filth, the dirtiest thing Lewis has ever heard in his life, and he keeps letting out strings of just-coherent praise and begging.

When Lewis shoves his tongue inside Tad's ass, Tad sobs, "Oh fuck oh Lewis god that's good, god you're amazing, oh *fuck yeah* that's it, just like that, right there—"

He's circling his hips on Lewis's face as Lewis holds him there, licking and eating his fill and getting closer and closer to coming. He's pretty sure he rimmed Tad that night in Vegas, but the memories are too hazy. This is bright and searing and burning itself into his body and brain.

Lewis's breakpoint rushes him, liquid ecstasy pooling in his gut, and he has to push Tad away a little to stop himself from coming. Tad's taste lingers on his tongue.

Above him, Tad shifts clumsily, like his limbs won't work in concert anymore. Now he's the one who flops on the floor, stretched out against Lewis. "Are you going to fuck me now?" Tad asks. His words are hazy and careful, like he can't remember exactly how to talk.

Lewis takes him in—pupils blown wide, hairline damp and dark, lips swollen and red. Sweat running down his body. Wordlessly, he pulls Tad in with a hand cupped around the back of his neck. As they kiss, mouths open, tongues fucking into each other's mouths, Lewis rolls them over so he's on top, Tad's lean body under his.

He tears himself from Tad's mouth and kisses down his neck. "You still want it on all fours?" he manages to ask. Words are hard. Thinking is hard. The only thing driving him is the absolute necessity of fucking Tad. Nothing else matters.

Tad groans and grabs for the lube. "Just—please—anywhere. Now. I just want you." His hips arch and his cock pushes into Lewis's hip. It's wet and sticky and Lewis would totally go in for a taste if he didn't think putting Tad's dick in his mouth would make him come.

They both take a second, breathing hard, before Tad squeezes lube into his palm. As he slicks Lewis up, then himself, he whimpers and says hoarsely, "You're so fucking hot."

"Unng," Lewis manages.

Tad spreads his legs, locking them around Lewis's back. Lewis grabs one behind the knee and pushes it up as he guides himself in.

And oh. *Oh.* This is still new, but Lewis can't imagine ever getting used to this feeling. Tad is so tight, so hot, but there's hardly any resistance as Lewis slides inside. He has to stop—they both have to stop, because Tad's breathing sounds labored. Lewis's hand slips in the sweat behind Tad's knee, so he leans his forehead against Tad's calf before he licks a long line down his leg.

Then he moves. *They* move. It's not Lewis fucking Tad, it's the two of them fucking each other, Tad meeting Lewis thrust for thrust. Tad's heat is unbearable, and Lewis just—he needs it, needs more, needs to be as deep as he can get so he can bury himself in that heat and burn up. It's all he wants.

Tad has a hand buried in Lewis's hair and when Lewis finds the right spot inside him, he arches and lets out a strangled, "*Lewis*, that's—oh god."

"Is that good, baby?" Lewis pants.

"Oh *fuck*."

He'll take that as a yes.

Lewis makes sure he hits that spot on each thrust. Tad's eyes roll into the back of his head; his mouth hangs open. Every inch of Lewis's body is sparking with pleasure that's about to explode. He reaches for Tad's cock and jerks it, snapping his hips at the same time to get in deeper, to pound that spot in Tad that's making him look like he's seeing god.

Tad winds tight, yells, and comes all over Lewis's hand, pulsing out thick, hot ropes that smear over both of them. His hips buck wildly, and he clenches so tight around Lewis, so so tight, and they're both slicked in sweat and there's cum smeared on their stomachs, and—

And yeah, Lewis comes so hard that he maybe blacks out for a second.

He collapses on Tad, who's breathing like he just finished a 100 meter dash.

"Holy shit," Tad slurs.

"Mm." Lewis can do better than that. "Yeah."

Apparently not much better.

They lie there catching their breath for a few minutes. Or maybe an hour. Lewis's concept of time is hazy. There's a vague awareness on the fringes of his brain that they should get cleaned up, but that seems like a lot of effort when he feels so good.

They might have fallen asleep there, except Hetty plants herself next to Tad and glares at Lewis.

"Oh no," Lewis says. "Does Hetty know about the facts of life?"

"Hetty is an innocent, Lewis. What are you letting her see?" Tad pulls Lewis in for a long, slow kiss. "Stay the night?"

"Yes," Lewis says. "Yes, definitely."

EVEN THOUGH Lewis has only been part of Tad's nightly routine a few times, he loves the domesticity of it. It cracks him up how Hetty runs around Tad in circles in the kitchen while he gets her canned food ready, and how she weaves between his legs while he sighs exasperatedly, "You know what, if I die, I can't feed you, so this is really self-defeating behavior." There's zero real irritation in his voice, and it's super sweet.

After Tad puts her food on the floor, he and Lewis brush their teeth in the cramped bathroom. It shouldn't be nice to be in each other's way, but Lewis likes it. Their shoulders press together and Tad gives him a shy smile.

In bed, Tad wraps himself around Lewis and lets out a contented sigh. Lewis strokes his back and holds him close. "Are you okay?"

Tad buries his face in the crook of Lewis's neck and plants a gentle kiss there. "Yes. No? Being with you makes things better."

Those words do something to Lewis. Molten gold lights him up inside, from the pit of his stomach, up through his rib cage, to his heart, and he feels... well, he feels the way he's felt before, which he knows should scare the shit out of him, because that was the whole point of the Dating Break.

But maybe he just had to kiss a lot of frogs before he found his prince. Lewis may have fallen for Tad fast and hard, just like he always does, but Tad isn't like the other men Lewis has been with.

Lewis takes a deep breath. "I think we should stop pretending we're not dating."

Saying that, it's like something out of alignment finally slots back to place inside him.

There's a hiccup of a breath from Tad, who shifts like he's going to move away—then settles back into place. His embrace feels tighter. "What about your Dating Break?"

"Well, I mean." Lewis presses his lips to the top of Tad's head. Tad's curls tickle his face. "I think when you're spending several nights a week with the same guy, and you're thinking about him all the time, and you miss him like crazy when you aren't with him… yeah. If you still don't want to say we're dating, we don't have to."

"I want to," Tad says so fast that it's clear it's what he wanted all along.

Lewis hugs him tight. "Sorry it took me so long to figure out."

Tad shakes his head. "Don't apologize. I didn't want to push and scare you off. I wanted… I wanted you to want it, I guess. If I made you feel pressured and then I just ended up being another guy who disappoints you…."

"Tad," Lewis breathes, and kisses him, all soft heat and banked urgency. "Never. You couldn't."

It's such a beginning-of-a-relationship thing to say, and maybe Tad won't believe him. After all, Lewis has been pretty clear about his abysmal luck in the dating department.

They break the kiss slowly. "I hope I don't," Tad whispers.

Little claws tick on the floor, and a weight thumps onto the foot of the bed. Hetty purrs loudly on her way to her favorite spot—curled up next to Tad's head. She detours to sniff Lewis's face and he feels like a rare honor was just bestowed on him.

They never finished talking about what happened with Tad's family, but that's okay. Another time.

Chapter Twenty-Six

IT'S OBVIOUS from the moment Lewis comes groggily awake with his hand wrapped around Tad's very erect cock and Tad sleepily thrusting into his fist that getting to Weehawken by ten is way too ambitious. Tad's half-asleep moans and whimpers are worth all the disapproval his family can throw at him.

They thrust and rub against each other slowly, then with increasing urgency, and since it's a day for giving thanks, Lewis gives thanks for how fucking hot Tad is when he comes, and the fact that Lewis is the one that got to make it happen.

The lazy making out afterward can't be interrupted either, so when Lewis finally checks the time, he grimaces. It's after ten, and he has so many texts from Mom that his phone is asking him if he wants to temporarily mute notifications.

Tad kisses the back of his neck and runs a hand over Lewis's shoulder before leaning against him, chest to back, and propping his chin on Lewis. "Do you have to go?" he asks.

Lewis weighs whether he can mitigate the damage by texting Mom back right now—but no, he's in for it no matter what. Rolling onto his back so he can loop his arms around Tad, he asks, "My mom's not texting you too, is she?"

Tad snorts with laughter. "Would she do that if she had my number?"

"Um, yes. She'd be telling you to get your boyfriend's ass over to his parents' house so he can help with the yams."

Tad's face lights up. "Boyfriend," he repeats softly. "I like that."

Lewis bites his lip against the huge smile fighting to split his face. "Me too."

They lose themselves in another languid kiss, but then Lewis's phone, no longer on Do Not Disturb, buzzes. With a sigh, Lewis says, "I have to go. I was supposed to be at my parents' like fifteen minutes ago."

"Oh!" Tad looks guilty. "Shit. Sorry."

"You don't need to apologize. I had a *very* good reason to be late." Lewis takes him in. Tad Pierce, his boyfriend. He's giddy. The constellations of freckles sprayed across Tad's chest and shoulders are like a mirror of the constellations wheeling inside Lewis right now.

Mom texts again: *Taylor says you have a new boyfriend—bring him too if that's why you're late!*

He groans. Taylor and her inability to mind her own business. No way is he inviting Tad over for a Pierce Thanksgiving, especially now that he knows Tad's shy. Talk about traumatic.

His phone buzzes again, and Tad laughs. "You better go."

With a louder groan, Lewis climbs out of bed. Before he heads to the bathroom to take a much needed shower, he stops to admire Tad one more time. Weak November sunlight filters through the room and gilds him. "When can I see you again?" he asks.

The question looks like it takes Tad by surprise, but then a smile creeps across his face—radiant and shy and gorgeous.

"I'M HERE!" Lewis shouts as he opens the door to his parents' house in Weehawken. It's the house he grew up in, a brick multi-family home that his parents have long since bought in its entirety. They rent out the upper apartment on Airbnb. His mother is very proud of their impeccable reviews.

"LEWIS, I NEED YOU TO BRING ME THE CRANBERRIES FROM THE BASEMENT FRIDGE!" Mom yells from the kitchen.

Dad comes thundering down the stairs with an armful of linens. "Oh, Lewis, you're here! Did you bring your boyfriend?"

"We're barely even official, so no, I definitely did not." Lewis takes some of the linens before Dad drops them. "I guess I have to have the boundaries talk with Taylor again?"

"Oh, umm, I don't think it was Taylor who said anything." Dad looks guilty, which is an automatic giveaway that he's lying, and also there's literally no one but Taylor who could have told him.

"Yeah right." Lewis gives Dad the best hug he can with both of them holding a bunch of towels, cloth napkins, and at least three table runners. Mom can never choose which one she wants to use until the last second, which always makes Lewis roll his eyes and smile. It's not like any of them are even nice—they're all homemade by Lewis and Taylor.

One of them is this macaroni and macrame monstrosity that he made in sixth grade when it was absolutely Not Cool to make runners for your mom. Every year they lose some of the macaroni, but the next time it comes out, the holes have been patched.

Lewis kisses Dad's cheek. "I gotta get the cranberries."

"Downstairs fridge," Dad says. "Happy Thanksgiving, Lew!"

Once he's retrieved the cranberries—and Christ, every year there are more, are they really going to eat ten bags of cranberries?—he goes to the kitchen, where his family is congregated. Mom squeals and rushes him, throwing her arms around him. Lewis grins and hugs her back tightly, though no one gives tighter hugs than his mom.

"You didn't bring your boyfriend!" Mom admonishes. She looks fierce, but it's hard to be too scared of her when she's got her thick mane of dark hair tied back in a high ponytail and a sweatband in the trans pride colors around her forehead. Mom isn't trans, but one of Lewis's cousins is, and Lewis's parents are nothing if not allies.

"Why does everyone know about my boyfriend?" Lewis asks.

From the counter where she's eating a waffle, Taylor throws her hand in the air. "Figured if you didn't get your shit together with him, we could pressure you into it."

Lewis rolls his eyes. "Boundaries."

Dad adjusts his glasses. "Boundaries? Never heard of them."

Mom elbows him, even though she's just as bad as Taylor. "Tell us everything."

"Mom," Lewis groans, but he's secretly thrilled. Maybe not-so-secretly. He's grinning. He thinks he might actually be glowing.

Taylor pops the rest of her waffle in her mouth and wanders over to give Lewis a hug. When she lets him go, her eyes drop to his hand, and she laughs, "Are you wearing a wedding ring?"

"Um."

With that one syllable, he unleashes chaos. Taylor cackles, Mom shrieks, Dad hollers, "Lewis Stephen Mancini-Sommer, we are *not* an elopement family!" and though it actually has nothing to do with him opening his mouth, the stock pot on the stove boils over right at that moment, which makes Mom shriek again.

Lewis dives for the stove to turn the burner down. When he turns around, his family is staring. "If I find out you robbed me of planning a ridiculously over-the-top wedding with too many rainbows, it's not too late to write you out of the will," Mom says, a hand on her heart.

"Too many rainbows by whose standards, yours or mine?" Lewis checks once more that the potatoes are at a reasonable boil. "Long story short, I met him in Vegas at Stace's bachelorette party. We, uh, overindulged and got married."

"And they say romance is dead," Taylor says.

The playfulness has fallen off his parents' faces. Lewis feels like a shithead. "You really got married?" Mom asks in the same tone you'd say, *How many months do you have left?*

"No. I mean, yeah, technically. But we're getting divorced."

"I need some chocolate for this conversation," Dad says. "I think we all need some chocolate for this conversation." No one disagrees, and Dad duly doles out leftover Reese's from Halloween. As he hands one to Lewis, he says, "I thought you weren't dating for a while, Lew?"

Hm, maybe if Lewis wants boundaries, he shouldn't tell his family everything. Now that he's thinking about it, they probably didn't need to be in on the particulars of the Dating Break. "Well, I wasn't." He looks down at the wedding ring, which makes him think of Tad, which makes him smile softly. His chest feels warm.

Mom takes a deep breath and checks the stove, the oven, and something in the refrigerator. She glances at the pile of cranberries on the counter and waves dismissively before taking Lewis's hand and leading him into the living room.

Lewis loves his parents' living room. It's an insane riot of color—band posters from the 70s and 80s, paintings they've picked up on their travels or at art festivals, old art projects of Lewis's and Taylor's, pins and buttons from all the activism his parents have been involved in. One of Lewis's favorite things is an old flyer for an ACT UP! die-in. Mom and Dad participated in a lot of them in the 80s and 90s and helped organize some. Mom always says she's white and straight and she's going to use her powers for good.

It was funny, though, when he came out to them, he was still nervous. And then he was nervous because he thought they'd make fun of him for being nervous. After coming out went predictably well and he confessed to the nerves, Mom hugged him tight and said they would never *ever* laugh at him for being himself.

Yeah, his parents are pretty cool. Even if they don't have good boundaries.

Which is why it feels so shitty that—yeah, he *did* get married, and they weren't there, and they're only finding out about it now. Plus he's doing a horrible job of explaining everything.

Lewis flops down on the sofa and Mom does the same, slouching into the worn cushions. "What's his name?" Mom asks in the kind of voice that says *I already love him.*

"Tad." There's a stupid smile on Lewis's face. "He came camping with me. We were just going to be friends, not anything more, because...." Because why? It's hard to remember because from where he's standing, his feelings for Tad have always been obvious, even if they weren't smart. "Anyway, I guess we became official last night? Because the whole just-being-friends thing didn't really take."

"That's amazing," Mom says, wrapping him up in another hug. "You look happy, and I've really missed you looking happy."

Dad has a goofy smile on his face too. His parents are nothing if not romantics. "I second that."

"So what's with the divorce?" Taylor asks.

"Well...." *Well*, he shouldn't really talk about this with his family, because he hasn't talked to Tad about how their official coupledom changes or doesn't change their plan. "TBD. We haven't exactly talked logistics. We were, um, celebrating."

"When was the last time you were tested?" Mom asks.

"After Jonah, don't worry. More than once. And Tad's been tested too."

"Good kid," Dad says. "Both of you. So since we get to skip the safer sex reminders—are you going to tell us about him or what?"

His phone buzzes and Lewis slips it out of his pocket to glance at it.

Hey boyfriend, hope you got to your parents' ok

The smile on Lewis's face has reached new heights of stupidity as he texts back, *Hey boyfriend, I'm in picturesque Weehawken. Hope you and Hetty are having a good day*

He sticks his phone back in his pocket and looks up to see his parents beaming at him. Is he going to tell them about Tad?

Yes. He totally is.

So he does.

Chapter Twenty-Seven

"THIS IS crazy," Tad mutters, glancing up to make sure no one's close enough to hear him talking to himself. He shoves his hands in his pockets and hunches his shoulders against the cold wind cutting through him. West 43rd is like a fucking wind tunnel tonight, and it's cold as balls.

Ugh, December. It snuck up on him, because Thanksgiving was so late, and now everything is CHRISTMAS! And it's not that Tad doesn't like Christmas, he actually loves it, but now all the cheeriness and lights and evergreen boughs and garland everywhere just reminds him that he's going to have to face his parents after the trash fire of last week's Almost-Thanksgiving, and that, *that*, is not something he loves.

He bounces in place, shivering. He's early for the blind-friend-date Lewis set up between him and his friend Ava, because of course he is. Meeting new people shouldn't be this scary.

Tad tugs at the collar of his coat with one hand and rubs the spot on his neck Lewis was sucking twenty minutes ago while they made out on his sofa. It's tender. The whole side of his neck is tender, actually, but it's stubble-burn everywhere else, whereas this is definitely a hickey.

"Tad?"

He whirls. A short, chubby woman is approaching. In the dark, it's hard to see details, but she's maybe the woman he vaguely remembers from Stacy's bachelorette party?

Nerves are written all over her round face. "Um, hi, you're Tad, right?"

You're meeting your boyfriend's friend. This is not a threat on your life. You can do this.

With a deep breath, he answers, "Yeah. I'm Tad. Ava?"

"Yeah!" A huge breath gusts from her. "I've been hovering across the street trying to figure out if you looked enough like the picture Lewis showed me to come over here and introduce myself. And I shouldn't have even told you that. Ugh, I'm so awkward around new people."

Tad laughs, surprising himself. "I am too." His brain catches up to his mouth and he realizes he spoke to a stranger without picking it to death first. He's not even drunk!

Ever since Lewis pointed out that Tad didn't have a script for how a gay boy talked to girls, it's been a revelation. He reminded himself all day that there's no expectation for him to make a pass at Ava, and it's... actually helping?

Weird.

They bundle themselves into the Japanese restaurant they're eating at and are shown to their table. It's a nice place but not too nice, one of those restaurants that has private tea rooms but tables in the main dining area.

The menu gives them both something to concentrate on for like, a solid three minutes. But. The whole point of this is to make a friend. So once they order—including hot sake to warm up—Tad asks, "So, um, you're married, right?"

"Yup. The wife's name is Elise."

"Oh. Cool." Yeah, cool. God. He clears his throat. "How'd you guys meet?"

"College." She seems to realize he's making an effort to start a conversation. "We met in an Akkadian class."

"Akkadian...?"

"Ancient language. Like, you know the Sumerians and Babylonians?"

"Like the Hanging Gardens of Babylon Babylonians?"

She cocks a finger gun at him. "Exactly! The Akkadians were another Mesopotamian culture. They came after the Babylonians. Anyway, we both took Akkadian—the language—as one of the language courses for our Ancient Civilizations major."

"Oh, that's cool." Tad fiddles with the cloth napkin in his lap. "I think Lewis said you're in grad school?"

"Yeah, ABD." She glugs down some water. "All but dissertation. Sorry."

"I knew that, believe it or not. The journal I work for publishes a lot of ABD grad students."

"Oh, you work for a journal? That's cool. I don't suppose you're looking for articles on mikva'ot in the mid-first century BCE?"

Tad shakes his head. "It's a botany and gardening journal. The religious stuff has to be garden related."

"Hm, yeah, not a lot of magnificent Jewish gardens. It's kinda hard to garden in the ghetto."

Oh no. Oh *no*. She sounds angry. Tad wants to crawl under the table. Words ricochet around his brain and crawl toward his mouth, climbing over each other, but his throat won't open to let the air through, and his jaw feels wired shut. How did he manage to offend her already? Is his upbringing rearing its ugly head? Anyone who's not a cis, straight, white, Christian person is outside his immediate experience, so he doesn't even think about their existence as he's bumbling through his cis white man world?

"You're Jewish!" he manages to force out, which just makes him sound shocked, like he's never met a Jewish person before.

"Yes?" She looks wary. "Is that noteworthy?"

"No—I mean, I—I said—but I didn't mean—"

Her forehead wrinkles, and then her eyes widen. "Oh wait! Did you—you don't think you offended me, do you?"

His legs feel trembly, like they might give out. But then maybe he'd just slither under the table, so that wouldn't be so bad? "I think I did."

She snorts. "You didn't. Jews don't have gardens. Well like, Jews have *gardens*, but not that like, English formal garden shit. I have a garden, actually. Er, I have a planter with some herbs. I'll write a paper about it and submit it to your journal."

Relief makes him say, "We don't really publish articles about people's hobby gardens."

"Okay, well, I'll write a paper called 'Reclaiming the ghetto: the Jewish garden as worship.'"

A startled laugh hiccups out of Tad. The title is spot-on to all the capital A Academic stuff they get. "Did you just come up with that?"

"Elise and me like to play a game we call Put On Your Academia Glasses. It's when you view everything through the lens of an academic trying to get a paper published."

Tad snorts with laughter again. Ava looks more relaxed, which makes Tad feel more relaxed too. Maybe he's not fucking this up too much. "I do that sometimes with my friend. Well, my boss. But she's my friend too."

"Lewis said I'd like you." Ava grins, then looks horrified. "Oh god, I said that out loud, didn't I? Should I have pretended like Lewis didn't talk to me about you?"

"Wait, stop, go back. Lewis talked about me to you?" Tad's heart flutters.

Ava looks more appalled. "I'm not supposed to answer that question."

The fluttering gets leaden. "Was it bad? Did he warn you about me?"

Their food and sake arrive, so Tad's left to spiral about the possibility that Lewis said something bad about him, even though he can't imagine why Ava would have agreed to meet him if Lewis was talking shit about him. Luckily, as soon as the waiter leaves, Ava says, "I can't even imagine Lewis saying anything bad about you. That's not a thing."

A smile blooms across Tad's face. "So he said good things?"

She pointedly tears her chopsticks open and shoves a piece of sushi in her mouth.

"He said good things," Tad repeats, feeling like he might float away.

Ava looks nonplussed. When she swallows her sushi, she says, "I'm so glad I'm married to a woman. Men are so"—she waves a hand vaguely—"*this*. I can sit here and think the cluelessness is cute because I'll never have to deal with it again."

"Ouch."

"Are you going to argue?"

"Well. No." He pauses. "But for the record, my cluelessness is very cute."

She laughs. And—it's not like he's magically not anxious about being at a table alone with someone he doesn't know, but minute by minute it recedes, like the tide going out, and it sneaks up on him while they're eating—he's having fun. He likes Ava a lot, finds her easy to talk to and funny.

Before he knows it, the meal is over. They split the check and hang out talking awhile, until Ava says with what sounds like real regret that she has to get home. "I always walk the dog at night," she says. "And okay, legit I'm going to say this to you because you're cool and I think you'll get it, but I swore to Elise I'd do it tonight in case I needed a reason to get out of here if this wasn't going well."

Tad laughs. "That's fair. Pet schedules are important. And so are excuses to flee awkward social situations."

"Right?"

They grin at each other and Tad says, "I'm going to run to the bathroom before we go, but if you want to head out—"

"I'll stay. Want to walk to the train together?"

"Sure!"

Tad's beaming as he heads to the bathrooms. Does he now have *two* whole friends to his name? That is, objectively, pretty sad, but considering he's only had one friends for years, he'll take the W.

The bathrooms are down the hall past all the tea rooms. He's still smiling about the fact that he and Ava hit it off when a flash of glitter and color on the floor catches his eye. Outside the last tea room are a pair of rainbow Chucks.

Tad stops dead and stares. Could they be—? Lewis lost his Pride Chucks....

No. Come on. There have to be a million pairs of rainbow Chuck Taylors in the world.

Tad's eyes dart to the doorway. There's a low murmur of conversation, punctuated by laughter, from the room. The curtain is closed. Tad tiptoes closer and silently picks up a rainbow shoe.

It's the way Lewis described them—the block colors of the Pride flag on the canvas and the bottom sole. The pink glitter on the tongue. Gold eyelets.

Holy shit, is Lewis's scummy ex on the other side of this curtain?

Tad stands there, frozen with indecision as he holds a stranger's shoe. Or possibly not a stranger's shoe. Possibly his boyfriend's shoe? He really needs to find out if the ex is in there. What's the ex's name?

From the other side of the curtain, a man cackles, "Ewww, *no*, that's Jonah's!"

Jonah. That's the guy.

Sidebar, hopefully they're talking about food in there and not... honestly, anything else of Jonah's that's gross.

Tad looks at the shoe in his hand.

He snatches the other off the ground, clutches them to his chest, and strides back the way he came.

"We gotta go," he says to Ava. "Like, now. Right now."

Ava looks up from her phone. "We have time to make our trains—" Her eyes fall on the shoes he's hugging to his midsection. "Oh my god, are those—?"

"Yes!"

"Holy shit, did you…." She glances toward the tea rooms and grins wickedly. "Oh, you *did*. Oh man, I *like* you, Tad."

She doesn't need to be told a second time to get out of there. Just as they get to the door, someone asks loudly, "Where are my shoes?"

"Run!" he hisses.

They shove through the door and out onto the sidewalk, then run like hell. They race three blocks down W 43rd, taking their lives in their hands at a crosswalk with a Don't Walk signal, and skid to a stop outside a mini-storage place.

Ava puts her hands on her knees, winded. Hell, Tad's breathing heavier too, and he's in pretty good shape.

Then, he realizes Ava isn't gasping for breath because she's winded—well, that's part of it, but mostly she's laughing. "I can't believe that just happened!" she finally gets out gleefully. "Damn, Tad, you know Lewis has always wanted a prince, but this is some straight-up fairy-tale shit!"

Tad blinks, then has to snort. "Oh no, that's really on the nose."

"If the shoe fits," she cackles.

"Dad jokes! Okay, friends forever?"

Normally he'd be mortified by saying something like that. But he just stole a stranger's shoes from a Japanese restaurant with this woman. They have a bond now.

"Definitely friends forever."

Chapter Twenty-Eight

LEWIS IS settling in for a few episodes of whatever Netflix is recommending him when his phone dings at him. It's Tad, and he's—downstairs? Tad wasn't supposed to come over after dinner with Ava. Oh no. Lewis's heart and gut clench into a tight ball of anxiety. Did it go badly? Did Lewis severely misjudge their friend potential?

He'll never forget how Tad looked the night before Thanksgiving—his tear-stained face and his hopelessness, the crushing defeat slung over his shoulders. If Lewis put him in a situation that made him feel like that again, he'll never forgive himself.

He buzzes Tad in, his heart rate ratcheting up with every minute it takes Tad to get from the front door to Lewis's apartment. Did be betray his boyfriend barely a week after they went official?

When Tad knocks on the door, Lewis flings it open. His mind can't make sense of what it's seeing. He's done such a good job of convincing himself that Tad's distraught that the beaming man bouncing happily in place in the hall makes him feel like his brain is glitching.

Tad thrusts a pair of shoes into his hands, then snatches them back before Lewis has processed that he's seeing pink glitter and rainbows. "Wait, I wanted to do like a whole Cinderella thing to see if they fit! Dammit!"

Lewis stares. "Are those my custom Pride Chucks?"

His voice comes out in a whisper. How is this possible? They're definitely his Chucks, not just a pair that looks like them. There's the pink glitter/gold eyelet combo he picked out. There's the rainbow sole. There's the scuffing on the right toe that he always gets because his right foot turns in a little.

"How did... what?" He shakes his head like there's something to clear, but he's pretty sure he's not hallucinating. "What about dinner with Ava?"

"Dinner was great. The shoes are spoils of war." Dramatically, Tad hands the shoes to Lewis, who hugs them to his chest. Ew, wait, they smell. Instead, lovingly, Lewis sets them down, pulling Tad inside.

"How did you get them?" Lewis looks at them again, dazzled by their sparkliness.

Rather than answering, Tad kisses him fiercely. He tastes like seaweed and sake. "Does it count as stealing if you're taking back something that was stolen in the first place?"

"Oh my god. You committed a crime for me." Is this what 'be gay, do crimes' refers to?

"Yes!" Tad looks thrilled. His smile is so bright that Lewis can't keep his own off his face. "Your scummy, cheating ex was in one of the tea rooms, so I took the shoes and ran."

Lewis laughs. All these months later, and he still remembers himself walking in on Jonah like it's a scene from a movie, with a tragic zoom-in on his stricken, heartbroken face. Now it has an epilogue— Jonah finding the shoes gone and having to walk around Manhattan in just his socks. He had to get on the *train* in his *socks*. Ha! Lewis isn't a vindictive man, but he's not going to feel one speck of bad about Jonah getting his comeuppance.

The fact that Tad gave him this closure makes Lewis's body hurt with tenderness from his head to his toes. Fiercely, he wraps his arms around Tad, hands wandering and grasping, not able to touch enough. What good are hands and arms if they aren't full of Tad?

LEWIS IS thinking about his exes, which, given the way his shoes were serendipitously returned to him, isn't surprising. Really, he's thinking about how different Tad is. It's the week following Lewis's personal Cinderella moment, and the two of them are snuggled under a blanket on Tad's sofa watching a cheesy Christmas movie. It goes without saying that most of his exes hated cheesy Christmas movies. Most of them didn't like rom-coms, either. When he tried to watch *Love, Actually* with Liam, Liam said the plot confused him.

Liam doesn't like to overthink things he remembers telling Matthew.

Honey, Liam doesn't like to regular-*think things,* Matty said. Stacy told him to be nice and Ava exchanged a significant look with Matty.

In the movie, the guy is getting the guy, and they're doing one of those Hallmark closed-mouth kisses in a white-picket-fence neighborhood while children play in fake snow in the background. It's saccharine and gag-worthy.

Lewis is totally sniffling.

Tad kisses the side of his head. "You're so cute. I love that you get into these dumb movies even more than I do."

Grabbing for a tissue to blow his nose, Lewis says, "I love that you get into them at all."

Tad runs his fingers through Lewis's hair. "So, um, awkward segue, but I think we need to talk? Not in a bad way! Don't freak out."

Lewis's reptile brain *is* freaking out, because "we need to talk" is never not meant in a bad way. But Tad's fingers are still in his hair, and he looks earnest and worried. "Okay," Lewis says. "About what?"

"Um." Tad seems like he's fighting some kind of internal battle. "About the, um, divorce?" He stands up. "Wait here."

His chest tightens as anxiety washes over him. Sure, Tad told him not to freak out, but that's easier said than done.

When Tad returns, he's holding the manila folder containing the divorce papers. "I finished filling these out. All you need to do is sign your part. I just, I didn't know if… I mean, things are different. Between us. Than they were? And um." Tad bites his lip and takes a deep breath. "I didn't want you to like, think we had to stay married, because I know you really didn't want to. And just because we're dating now doesn't mean we should stay married. Right? So in case you're worried about hurting my feelings by not pushing the issue. I know we can't file these until May, but… yeah. Maybe we should talk about it now."

Lewis takes the folder. All he can think to do is tell the truth. "I actually haven't thought about it since we started officially dating."

"Oh." Surprise flits across Tad's face. "Really?"

"Yeah." Lewis flips the folder open, scanning the forms. They look right. All Lewis has to do is sign, and in May—six months after their drunken Vegas marriage—they can file them. The divorce will probably be finalized by Pride.

The thought doesn't make him happy.

He closes the folder. "You're going to think I'm crazy, but what if I hold off on signing for now? We can't file for another five months, so no rush, right? I mean, unless you want me to sign them now? If you want me to, I will."

"Wait a second, are you saying you want to stay married to me?"

"I… don't know? It doesn't seem like there's a right answer to that question."

Tad hums. "Probably not." He flops down on the sofa and Lewis pulls Tad's legs up so they're in his lap.

If the relationship is working and they're serious about each other, it makes sense to not divorce. It costs money, it takes time, and what if… well, what if they decide they want to get married in the future? How stupid would that look, to get divorced and then get engaged again?

Sure, neither of them remembers their wedding, and it's questionable how much their guests remember. And yeah, his family wasn't there. But if they wanted to, they could have a ceremony down the road. Big deal if the legalities are over and done with.

And big deal if that was never what he pictured when he imagined his wedding—which he did, often and early. He staged his wedding so many times with his My Little Ponies that those things probably could have opened their own wedding planning business by his tenth birthday.

"I'm not trying to rush us into anything," Lewis says, rubbing Tad's ankles, then his calves. Tad's eyes narrow to contented slits, and his head tilts back.

"I know." Tad wriggles. "Me either."

"You're not trying to break up with me?" Lewis teases.

Tad pushes himself up on an elbow and grabs for Lewis's hand. "No," he says fiercely. "No, I'm not, I—if either of us is going to break up with the other, it's going to be you dumping me."

"I definitely don't want to do that."

Tad looks doubtful, so Lewis squeezes his hand. "Hey, I kinda get the sense that maybe you have some baggage from your ex?"

With a snort, Tad asks, "Who doesn't?"

Rubbing his thumb over Tad's knuckles, Lewis says, "Well, I mean, yeah. True." *Control freak*, Jonah's voice whispers. *Hot mess*, hisses Liam. *Basket case*, adds Jayden, just in case Lewis hasn't gotten the point yet. He shoves those voices away. He's with Tad now, and Tad saw him at his worst right away—but here he is anyway. "You were with him for a long time, right?"

"Three years." Tad looks down at their joined hands. "We met at a writing workshop—"

"You write?"

Tad turns faintly red. "I don't… I mean… I used to, a little."

Every time Lewis discovers something new about Tad, it's like Christmas morning. "That's really cool. But okay, sorry, I interrupted. You met him at a writing workshop?"

"Yeah. He came up to me and started talking to me and I—okay, I know you were surprised that I'm so shy, but I swear I am, and I'm really not great in social situations. And like, good-looking men coming up to me and flirting? Not something I handle well. Like, at all. But with John, it seemed really easy. And I don't know, for a long time, I thought he was the one. Or more like, he had to be the one, because who else was going to put up with me?"

Oh, Tad. Lewis wants to pull him into his lap and hold him. "People aren't 'putting up with you' when they love you." Lewis skims a hand over the short sides of Tad's hair. Tad's been trimming the sides but letting the top grow longer, so his auburn curls flop all over the place. It looks hella gay, not to mention hot as fuck. "If anyone ever makes you feel like they're just putting up with you, that's not love."

Tad's throat jumps as he meets Lewis's eyes, and Lewis feels a real *oh shit* pit in his stomach. He's going, going, gone for Tad—he's in love and falling harder every day. It slipped in through the cracks, filling the fractured spaces inside him that he thought were just part of his foundation.

No matter how sure he is, though, it's too early to say it. Historically, he's dropped the L word the minute he thought he was falling; this time, he'll control himself.

"I know it's not," Tad finally says. "I just… when I was a kid, I used to stress out about falling in love. I didn't understand how I could have a crush on someone, and out of everyone in the world, they'd have a crush on me back? It just seemed so unlikely."

"And then the whole being gay thing."

"And then the whole being gay thing. And I think, like, that fear never really went away? When I saw you, I thought, god, wouldn't it be amazing if by some miracle he liked me too. It wasn't like, oh I'll flirt with him and I bet he'll flirt back, and maybe we'll fuck. Well." Tad wrinkles his nose. "I did think that after I got drunk."

"In all fairness, the drunk thoughts were right." Oh, what the hell—Lewis wraps his arms around Tad and hauls him into his lap. Tad squeals, then laughs, then straddles Lewis, facing him, with his forearms resting on Lewis's shoulders and his fingertips brushing the back of Lewis's neck. "I'm glad it all happened."

"Even though you didn't want to date anyone?" Tad asks shyly.

Lewis pulls him in for a gentle kiss. "You're not anyone."

Tad makes a tiny noise and kisses Lewis again, harder and more urgently. Lewis clutches Tad's back, one palm slipping inside his joggers, the other going under his shirt to feel bare skin, and Tad rocks on his lap, cock pressing into Lewis's stomach—

Dolly Parton's voice blares from Tad's phone (Lewis has been informed it's "Coat of Many Colors" in a tone of horrified disbelief that it needed to be said). They both jump, and Tad cranes his head to glance at the screen. "Ugh, that can go to voicemail," he says, which Lewis is very happy about, since Tad's hand is pressing against his dick.

They're just getting into the make-out session when Tad's phone rings again. And *again.*

"Um," Lewis says around Tad's tongue. He pulls back. "Seems like they really want to talk to you."

"It's my brother," Tad says flatly.

Oh.

Tad hasn't talked to his family since the fiasco at Thanksgiving. "Maybe you should just see what he wants?"

"Not compatible with what I want," Tad says. He squeezes Lewis's cock, and Lewis groans.

"When you put it like that."

Several texts come through on Tad's phone and Tad makes a frustrated sound, grabbing it. "I'm putting it on Do Not Distu—"

His eyes widen. "Shit," he says. "My brother's outside. He wants to come up."

Chapter Twenty-Nine

I'M OUTSIDE your building and I know you're home bc I can see your light on

Walt's text narrows Tad's vision to a stifling, claustrophobic tunnel and for a second he feels like he's breathing through a straw. The words swim on his phone screen.

A sound penetrates the walls of the tunnel. Lewis's voice. Lewis is saying something.

"What?" His voice comes out too loud.

His vision snaps into focus. Lewis is staring at him, concerned. "Are you okay, baby?"

"I—" Deep breath. Lewis's hands are tight on his waist. He knows how to play this. When it happened with John, he had more warning, but he can get rid of Walt pretty fast. He's probably here to talk about what Tad did at Thanksgiving. "Yeah. Yeah, I'm fine." He's totally not fine. "I should let him in."

When he climbs off Lewis's lap, he sends a text to Walt to let him know he can come up soon. To stall for time, he uses the first lie that comes into his head—he's cleaning cat vomit right now. *Sorry, Hetty.*

Lewis hasn't moved from the sofa, though he adjusted his erection so it's not as obvious. Tad knows he's an asshole for what he's about to say, but it doesn't stop the words from coming out of his mouth. "I need you to hide."

The uncomprehending expression on Lewis's face is like a knife straight to the heart.

It's all well and good for Lewis to talk about wanting to be together, but this is the reality of being with him. Lewis probably thinks he's seen Tad at his worst after the night he came home a blubbering, snotty mess.

This is Tad at his worst. Pretending his boyfriend doesn't exist and forcing his boyfriend to take an active role in erasing his own presence.

"Please," Tad says.

"I could pretend to be a friend," Lewis says, then shakes his head. "No, sorry. I'll hide. Where?"

"Um." Tad can't look at him, so he drops his eyes to the ground. "My closet. He definitely won't go in there."

There's a silence. Tad can't bring himself to look up. "Okay," Lewis says. It's impossible to tell how mad he is. He sounds totally reasonable and not pissed, but Tad knows that can't be true. John was always pissed, and he had a right to be. This is pathetic.

"There's space in there," Tad adds, cringing at the easy metaphor.

"Okay." Lewis strokes a thumb over Tad's cheekbone. "Tell me when I can come out."

Tad wants to laugh. That's exactly what he's been waiting for too—someone to tell him it's safe to come out.

He waits until Lewis is in the closet and goes to stroke Hetty, who's sleeping—was sleeping—in her cat tree. The fact that Walt knows which windows are his is a new piece of information, and frankly a chilling one. Thank god he and Lewis were on the sofa and not making out in front of the window. The thought makes Tad sick to his stomach, and his skin gets clammy, even though he knows they weren't in front of the window, and he knows Walt didn't see them.

He squints down at the street. He can't see Walt.

One more deep breath, then he lets Walt know he's ready, buzzes him in, and waits. And tries not to hyperventilate.

The knock on the door sends Hetty streaking for the bedroom. Tad tries not to feel abandoned and opens the door.

"Hey," Walt says.

"Hi."

"Are you busy?"

"No, I—"

Oh shit. The divorce papers. They're still out, the manila folder laying open on the sofa.

Shit shit shit fuck fuckity fucking *fuck*.

Okay. It's fine. Tad turns and does his best to walk casually back to the sofa. "Just doing some work," he says.

"I thought you were cleaning up cat vomit?" Walt says like he's making a hilarious joke. There's a bro-y smile on his face as he steps inside Tad's apartment. Every single muscle in Tad's body winds tighter.

"That's more of a five-minute interruption than a hobby," Tad says shortly. "What's up? Why are you showing up at my apartment on Sunday night totally unannounced?"

He flips the manila folder containing the divorce paperwork shut, which is also the moment he realizes the TV is still on, and the gay Christmas movie they just watched is selected on the Netflix home screen. The tendons in his neck lock.

Walt perches on the back of the sofa, glances at the TV, and looks back to Tad. He has to have clocked what he's seeing—it's two men gazing into each other's eyes under mistletoe—but he doesn't react. "I was wondering if we could talk."

"This could've been a phone call."

"I wanted to talk in person." Walt sounds uncomfortable now, and that sure as hell doesn't make Tad *less* uncomfortable. "About—well. You haven't called Mom."

"How do you know?" Tad asks stiffly.

"Uh, because she told me."

Well, yeah. That makes sense. Tad looks at the floor. "So she sent you to talk to me?"

With an exasperated sound, Walt says, "No. Jesus. I was in the city with my girlfriend this weekend. I wanted to talk to you about what happened when you were home."

"If Mom tells you so much, then she probably told you what happened," Tad says, more poison in his tone than he really means to let out.

There's a look in Walt's eyes that says he's Trying Really Hard, and it gets Tad's hackles up. "Yeah, she told me what happened," Walt says. "She's freaking upset, Tad. She thinks you hate her because of the way you ran out of there. You're not returning her calls or texts. Do you have any idea how much it sucks to be the kid who stuck around, having to constantly reassure our parents you don't hate them?"

The comment lands like a sucker punch. What the actual fuck. Does *Walt* realize how much it sucks to get driven away from home because Tad can never be himself there?

Tad clenches his fists. "I don't hate her, I'm just pissed! Why would I be happy she set me up on a blind date?"

"Didn't you say you'd go?"

It doesn't feel like it. It feels like he got strong-armed into it, because if he didn't agree, then everyone would get suspicious and start probing, and they'd find out he has rainbows shooting out his ass every moment he's not in Watertown.

Walt won't get it, though. The strong-arming part. Obviously he won't get the gay part. Walt doesn't know what it's like to constantly disappoint their parents, to constantly not be the son they want, and to force yourself to do things you hate to try to make up for it. He has no fucking idea.

"I didn't really have much of a choice," Tad grinds out. "She already set the whole thing up."

Walt shakes his head. It's so goddamn patronizing. "So instead you went to the restaurant, then ran out of the place like you were on fire?"

Tad's pretty sure that's not what he looked like. Psychotic episode, maybe.

"I thought it would be fine." God, he sounds whiny.

There's a brief silence. Walt looks like he's gathering himself, or regrouping to not make this conversation even more of a train wreck. "She's not mad. She's—" He stops and shakes his head. "Dude. I know you're shy."

"Gold star," Tad mutters.

It looks like it takes some effort, but Walt ignores the barb. "You should've just said you weren't comfortable going, you know? Mom's embarrassed, and she feels bad about the whole thing. Can you please just talk to her? It's not like you're going to get grounded."

"Did you seriously just come here to scold me?" Tad snaps.

Walt's nostrils flare. "I don't want Christmas to be a complete shitshow, which it's going to be if you don't grow up and apologize to Mom!"

Grow up. Apologize. Be someone you aren't to make other people happy. Tad tilts his chin up, defiance coursing through him. "Maybe I'm not coming back for Christmas."

Walt scoffs. When Tad clenches his fists and glares, his brother shakes his head, blue eyes flashing. "Seriously? You're going to throw a tantrum and stay here for Christmas? And do what? Sit here by yourself with your cat and your plants? *That's* not lame."

"Fuck off," Tad spits. "Just—fuck off!"

Rubbing a hand over his hair, Walt says, "Okay, you know what? Fine. Act like a spoiled little kid. Mom was just trying to do something nice for you since you have such a hard time meeting people. You're acting like she murdered someone."

"Maybe I just want to live my life the way I want to live it!" Tad yells. It's perilously close to the truth he's never been able to say to his family.

"No one's stopping you." Walt shakes his head again and goes to the door. "I'm not telling Mom and Dad you don't want to come for Christmas. If you're going to break Mom's heart, you can fucking do it yourself."

He slams the door behind him. Tad picks up a coaster and flings it at the door. It bounces off in the most unsatisfactory way imaginable. Then he buries his face in his hands and tries not to cry. *Grow up*, Walt said, and here he is, fighting the sting in his eyes.

Pathetic.

Now he has to spend Christmas by himself too.

With a deep breath, he drops his hands away from his face, pushes his shoulders back, and goes to his bedroom to retrieve Lewis from the closet. When he opens it, he mumbles, "How much of that did you hear?"

Lewis pockets his phone. He was definitely texting someone. Probably Stacy or Matthew or Ava. Or his sister. Or maybe his parents. Probably telling them his boyfriend made him literally hide in a closet rather than come out of his own.

As he steps over Tad's dumbbells, Lewis says, "Mostly just you yelling some stuff at the end. And the door. Wasn't sure if you slammed it or your brother did."

"He did," Tad mutters.

Lewis hesitates, then reaches for Tad. His fingers trace the bones of Tad's wrist, and he takes his hand. Tad hooks his fingers over Lewis's, and Lewis looks relieved. *Tad* is the one who should be relieved Lewis wants to hold his hand, not the other way around.

"You wanna talk about it?" Lewis asks.

Tad shakes his head and slumps to a seat at the foot of his bed. Lewis sits next to him. He rubs his thumb over the back of Tad's hand and Tad stares at the floor, digging his toes into the thick cerulean rug. The fibers spring back when he lifts his toe, so he mashes them down again.

A black paw sneaks out from under the bed and bats his toe. Lewis stifles laughter. Tad lets his head fall against Lewis's shoulder while Lewis's arm goes around Tad, holding him tight and safe.

"I told my brother I'm not going back for Christmas," Tad says.

"Oh," Lewis says. "Wow."

"Yeah." One thing Walt was right about is that Tad can't ghost his parents for Christmas—he'll have to tell them he's not coming.

"He pretty much said I'm pathetic." Tad moves his foot back and forth for Hetty to pounce on, but she's lost interest.

"What?" Lewis's voice sounds dangerous.

"Because I have no friends, and I'm just going to sit here alone for Christmas. Which is true. So I guess I *am* pretty pathetic."

"You have friends," Lewis says fiercely. "Your boss is your friend."

"She's also my boss."

"Ava's your friend."

Tad opens his mouth to tell Lewis why she isn't, really, but their dinner flashes through his mind, and their shoe heist, and the fun he's had texting her since then. They've been playing Words With Friends, and she's really good. He's never had a friend to play Words With Friends with. John thought it was pedestrian.

"She was your friend first," he settles on.

Lewis makes a noise and hugs Tad. "You're not pathetic. You're amazing. If your family doesn't get that, screw them." He kisses Tad's temple. "You want to come to game night? Meet some more people who are going to love you for exactly who you are?"

Startled, Tad turns his head, which makes their noses bump together. "Game night?"

"Yeah, we try to do them regularly."

The idea is terrifying—but Tad also wants it with corrosive need. He doesn't know why Lewis's response to being hidden away is to welcome Tad further into his life, but it... is?

"I'd love if you were there," Lewis adds. "We're doing it at my place. Everyone's nice. It'll be Ava and her wife Elise, and Stacy and Alang. A bunch of queers and our token straight."

"Stacy's queer?"

"Alang. He's bi."

Hetty emerges from under the bed and situates herself right in front of them to wash herself. It pisses Tad off that Walt called him pathetic because he likes being around his cat. It's just another thing his family doesn't get about him. Hetty is part of his family.

"Okay." Tad buries his face in Lewis's shoulder. Lewis smells like sandalwood and cedar and something fresh and clean. "Yeah. I want to come."

"Really?" The excited happiness in Lewis's voice makes that painful need flare in Tad's chest again. Need shaded with hope and want, like the petals of a flower getting more saturated in color toward their center.

Chapter Thirty

EVEN THOUGH it's been years since Tad played Settlers of Catan, he does pretty well. He beats Ava (competitive, but made enemies with the robber), Alang (who Stacy boxes in early with road-building), and Stacy (who Alang systematically victimizes for the rest of the game in retribution while Stacy flails dramatically and laments, "I let him pick the DJ and this is the thanks I get").

Elise wins and Lewis ekes out second place over Tad. "You're ruthless!" Lewis laughs when they total their points at the end. "Why didn't you mention you've played?"

"I was hoping we were playing for money," Tad says, smiling shyly.

"Lewis, your boyfriend came in here thinking he could hustle us?" Alang puts a mock-affronted hand to his chest.

"I like him already," Elise says, shuffling the deck. "Go again?"

"I don't think my impending marriage can take it," Stacy says, sticking her tongue out at Alang.

He lays his head in her lap, the sweep of his dark hair falling across her jeans. "Forgive me, fair lady?"

"Mm, maybe. Get me another wine box?"

Ava knocks back the rest of her wine, packaged like a juice box. "These things are like peak bougie millennial culture."

"Oh my god babe, we live in Bushwick. *We* are peak bougie millennial culture," Elise says, fiddling with the barbell in her eyebrow.

Brandishing her empty wine box at Elise, Ava says, "But now we're reconstructing our lost youth through the nostalgic reclamation of the juice box beverage format, and that's even more bougie."

"Yeah, well," Elise says, "we're also calcifying a toxic lionization of the past as… ah, fuck, I've had too much of this juice box wine."

Everyone cracks up. It was nerve-wracking coming here and meeting Alang and Elise, and having to be in a Social Situation. But they're all really nice, just like Lewis said, and—maybe Tad's beating this metaphor into the ground, but he has a script for this event, because they're his boyfriend's friends, and one of Tad's friends is here, and it just—it didn't seem as hard as he was afraid of.

Alang gets to his feet. "More wine all around?"

When everyone answers in the affirmative, Tad decides to be brave and gets up too, offering, "I'll help."

The way Alang looks so genuinely pleased to have his help is a foreign feeling. Nice, though. Definitely nice.

In the kitchen, Alang pulls wine boxes out of the refrigerator. "Thanks for coming tonight. Lewis is obviously so happy. It's awesome."

Warmth spreads through Tad's chest. "I... yeah. I mean, you're welcome. Or thanks?" He laughs at himself, but it's not as self-conscious as he would normally be. "Have you known Lewis a long time?"

"Just since Stacy and me got serious. A few years. Well, okay. Funny story, but we actually matched on Grindr before I met Stacy."

Tad chokes. "*Um?*"

Laughing, Alang says, "Yeah, we messaged a bit but never could make anything work. And then I deleted all my dating apps because I was so tired of people asking for dick pics."

"Yeah, everyone wants to see your dick." Tad turns red. "Not your dick! I mean, maybe your dick. I guess your dick, since that's why you deleted the apps? But like, the general you. The general you's dick. Wow. I'm going to stop saying dick now." Taking a deep breath, Tad says, "Anyway, it's cool that you and Lewis are friends."

Once Alang stops laughing, he says, "When I met Stacy it was like I got this whole family. Like I just fit, you know? My actual family is kinda...." He makes a face. "*Traditional.* So, yeah, how did I get on this? Weren't we talking about dicks?"

"Uh, let's have more wine," Tad says, still beet red. Then he feels stupid. Alang just told him something personal and Tad acted like he was horrified to hear it.

So, being himself, he makes it ten times more awkward by blurting, "My family too! I mean." He wishes his hands weren't full of boxes of wine, because he really wants to cover his face. "My family's traditional. Or, I guess more conservative than traditional. But. Yeah."

"People like us have to make our own family," Alang says sagely.

"You make it sound easy."

"Well, that's because I've had like three of these." Alang holds up a box and Tad laughs. "Anyway, you ever want to talk about not living up to your family's expectations, hit me up."

"Okay," Tad says, surprising himself by meaning it. Alang grins and they go back to the living room, where the others are setting up a different game.

Plopping down on the floor next to Lewis, Tad asks, "What's this?"

Lewis wraps an arm around Tad and pulls him close to kiss his cheek. "Never Have I Ever."

"Queer edition," Elise specifies.

"They make a queer edition?" Alang sounds surprised.

"No, it was a Kickstarter for an indie version of it."

Tad can feel his face getting hot. Lewis glances at him and his forehead crinkles. "Are you okay playing this?"

"Um." Tad stabs the straw into his wine box. "I'm… yeah? I just, you'll all want the raunchy questions and I'll be like, never have I ever eaten cold pizza."

"Wait, you haven't had cold pizza?"

"No, but did you hear the rest of it?"

Lewis makes an intensely thoughtful face. "Something something you've never eaten cold pizza."

Ava smiles reassuringly. "You can just watch the rest of us embarrass ourselves if you don't want to play."

The idea of the game *does* freak him out. But also, Lewis's hand is absently rubbing his knee, and that makes him feel like maybe it doesn't need to be such a big deal? The two things aren't even connected, but he's having fun, and he's happy, and being around Lewis's friends is nice.

"I'll play," he says decisively.

Stacy cheers, then finishes shuffling the deck and deals ten cards to each of them. "Okay, so we're playing with the we're-all-slightly-drunk rules tonight, which is: someone reads a card, and then we go around and say if we've done it or not. First person who admits to it gets the card, and first person to ten cards wins."

"So whoever makes the poorest life decisions wins the game?" Ava asks. "Got it."

"I'll go first," Lewis volunteers, squeezing Tad's knee. Tad leans in to him to show his gratitude. Since Lewis is to his left, that means if they go clockwise, Tad will be the last person to answer.

A minute goes by while they study their cards. Tad's aren't horrible. Mostly. There are a few he really hopes he doesn't have to read, though.

Finally, Lewis says, "Stace, did you rig this deck so I'd get the most embarrassing ones?"

"Mwa ha ha," Stacy says. "I wish. Let's hear it!"

"Okay, um, Jesus, these are…."

"Bawdy," Ava says gleefully.

Lewis makes an apologetic face at Tad and reads, "Never have I ever been to a sex party."

Next to Lewis, Stacy shakes her head. Alang does the same, as does Ava. Elise, however, sighs loudly. "Point to me?"

"WHAT?" Stacy shrieks.

Elise snatches the card from Lewis. "I went out with this girl who was really into kink. I was trying to support her interests."

Stacy goes next. She picks her card out of her hand with a flourish and says, "Never have I ever gotten a blowjob at a glory hole. No, I can't say that I have."

Neither has anyone else, it turns out, so into the discard pile it goes. Alang and Ava both choose tame cards—*never have I ever marched in a Pride parade* (Ava has, so she gets the point) and *never have I ever watched a movie just because it was gay* (Elise gets that one, which everyone boos at because they've *all* done that).

When Tad's turn comes around, he reads, "Never have I ever been to a gay bar."

Lewis takes the card from him. "Thanks, babe, don't mind if I do."

They keep playing, their hands dwindling. Tad's losing, but he doesn't mind, because as their hands get smaller, the questions get way more embarrassing. There's one in his hand that he really doesn't want to have to say, because he's done it. Surely someone will accumulate ten gay things before he'll have to read this?

Nope. Lewis and Elise are tied at nine cards each, and Tad's holding the last card.

He stares at it, throat working. "Never have I ever"—he chokes a little—"bleached my asshole."

Lewis shakes his head, Stacy giggles and does the same. Alang: no. Ava: "Do queer ladies do that?"

Elise: "I mean, I'm sure some do. I never have."

Which means they're back at Tad, and he has to lay the card down in front of himself.

"Ha! Nice!" Ava holds up her hand for Tad to high five, which he does, because what else are you supposed to do when you announce to a group of brand-new friends that you bleached your asshole once?

"We won't ask for details," Stacy assures him. Lewis doesn't look so sure about that.

They decide they need a tiebreaker to determine whether Lewis or Elise wins, and the winner is Lewis, on *never have I ever sucked off an uncut penis.* He gives Tad a sidelong look as he claims his victory, and Tad feels hot for an entirely different reason than embarrassment. Tad trails his fingers lightly up Lewis's spine. It rewards him with the most delicious shiver, and suddenly Tad just wants everyone else to leave.

Not that he's not having fun and enjoying their company. He is. But. He has an uncut penis in need of sucking off.

Luckily for his libido—and his pants, which are too tight to hide the boner he's trying really hard not to get—game night wraps up soon. Everyone finishes their wine, and they chat about Stacy and Alang's quickly approaching wedding as they pack up the games. Catan is Lewis's, but Never Have I Ever is Stacy and Alang's.

Stacy rattles the box before tossing it into her metallic hobo bag. "We're definitely playing this again. There are so many things I don't know about you hos!"

"Which is arguably a good thing?" Ava snorts. She hugs everyone and murmurs to Tad, "You're totally telling me what possessed you to bleach your asshole, by the way."

"Never," Tad murmurs back, but he shoots her a smile to show her he's kidding. Kind of. If she buys him a few margaritas, he might spill.

Elise and Ava leave, calling their goodbyes, and Alang and Stacy follow them out the door. Before Stacy walks away, she hugs Tad again and kisses his cheek. "You make Lewis so happy. Thank you."

If he was the tiniest bit cool, he would be smooth about this. But Tad isn't cool, so a smile spreads across his face, so wide it's painful. He just got the seal of approval from Lewis's best friend. That's… huge. That's amazing.

"He makes me happy too," Tad says. Stacy squeezes his arm and follows Alang.

The two of them clean up, talking and laughing, exchanging mindless little touches whenever they're within reach of each other. Except the touches get less mindless and less little as the minutes go by, until they wash and dry the last of the dishes and Lewis flings the towel across the room. The hungry look in his eyes makes Tad's stomach swoop.

Before he can return it, Lewis backs him up against the refrigerator. He braces his hands on either side of Tad and presses against him. His body is hot and hard and solid, and Tad moans as Lewis pushes up to kiss him.

Tad grabs Lewis's ass and squeezes, opening his mouth so Lewis can slide his tongue in. Lewis hooks a hand under Tad's thigh and pulls his leg up and Tad's happy to oblige the new position, wrapping his leg around Lewis. Lewis's cock pushes into Tad's balls, the pressure and friction making his head spin.

"Totally sucking that uncut dick of yours tonight," Lewis growls.

Tad laughs. Sort of. It's more like a breathless moan. "Good."

Lewis leaves Tad's mouth to kiss a line down his neck. His stubble scrapes Tad's skin as he sucks hard, then licks. Tad pants and arches into him, clutching his shoulder with one hand and his ass with the other.

"That was such a good night, baby," Lewis murmurs into Tad's skin. "Oh my god, you were the best, and they all loved you. I knew they would—"

He breaks off as he mauls Tad's neck again, and Tad laughs and wonders if they should just fuck against the refrigerator. "Me getting along with your friends turns you on?"

Against Tad's neck, Lewis chuckles, low and hoarse. "You fitting in perfectly turns me on." There's a joke to be made there, but Lewis makes a tortured sound and leans back to look Tad in the eyes. His hand slides down Tad's still-raised leg to the underside of his thigh. As he rubs up and down, he says, "Hey, so. I've been trying to work up the nerve to ask you something. You're probably going to tell me it's way too soon and you're totally right, but I just can't stop thinking how amazing it would be, even if it *is* too soon—"

Tad's starting to get nervous. "Lewis, what is it?"

"I was wondering if you figured out what you're doing for Christmas yet?" Lewis asks. "Since it's only a week away?"

"Nothing."

"Do you want to have Christmas with me? And my family?" Lewis stays very still after he asks this question, like he's afraid moving will spook Tad.

Tad's never met a boyfriend's family. John's parents kicked him out when he told them he was gay. If Tad's honest, he's never thought he deserved to meet a boyfriend's family, because he can't ever introduce a boyfriend to his own. John having no relationship with his parents made it easier.

It would've been nice if John could have been a little more understanding about Tad not being out to his family considering his own, but, you know. He wasn't.

"Is your family okay with me being there?" Tad bites his lip. "I'm… I mean… they don't know if I'm… long-term?"

"They're dying to meet you," Lewis says.

"Really?"

"Really."

"You told them about me?"

Lewis nuzzles behind Tad's jaw. "Of course."

Like there's no question. You tell your family when you're seeing someone you really like.

He wishes he was brave. He wants to tell his family about Lewis. Would they like him? The thought makes him anxious. They probably wouldn't. Lewis is definitely the kind of New York City reprobate who turns your son gay.

"How much did you tell them?" Tad asks.

"Broad strokes," Lewis replies. "Taylor—my sister—was the one who spilled to my parents, actually. They know we got married in Vegas."

"And that we're getting divorced," Tad supplies.

There's a tiny pause. "Yeah, I mentioned we were working on divorce stuff."

Tad's stomach twists a little at that. The same thing happened when Lewis first said he was going to hold off on signing the papers over the weekend. The really WTF thing about it is that the very first time Lewis brought up divorce—back in Vegas—Tad was hurt. Like, this guy wanted to leave him already and wasn't even going to give him a chance. But now they're together officially, not just legally, and Lewis is giving every indication that he's all in, and maybe he wants to stay married, and… it's freaking Tad out?

No. No, it's not *freaking him out*. That's too strong. He just….

What if he's not good enough for Lewis? What happens when Lewis *realizes* Tad isn't good enough for him? When he realizes he was telling his family about Tad right away, folding him into his friend group, so willing to let Tad into every part of his life, and meanwhile, Tad was thinking, *well, it would be nice if I could tell my family about us, but I can't, oh well?*

"Are you sure your family would really want me there?" Tad asks. "Did you ask them?"

"Yes and yes."

"Oh." Tad figured Lewis was inviting first and telling his family later.

"You don't have to if you don't want to. My family is kind of a lot. Like, we can all get super involved in each other's lives. It's the Italian from my mom. And my dad's along for the ride. But they want to meet you. They expected you to come with me to Thanksgiving dinner."

Tad's eyes widen. "You didn't tell me that."

Huffing a laugh, Lewis rubs a palm over the short hair on the side of Tad's head. "Thought it might freak you out."

"It does a little," Tad admits. "But if you really want me there, I want to come."

Lewis's thumb traces along Tad's cheekbone to his lips, a smile dawning across his face. "Of course I want you there. You're sure? You really want to come?"

Tad sticks his tongue out and licks Lewis's finger, which makes Lewis laugh and push his hips into Tad's. "Yeah. I want to. I'll probably be weird and awkward but I want to."

With a happy noise, Lewis closes the distance between them and kisses Tad hard. He pushes Tad's arms up over his head and holds them there, pinning Tad as his hips rock. Tad uses the leg still wrapped around Lewis to pull their bodies closer together.

"I'm gonna suck your cock now," Lewis growls into Tad's mouth.

It takes much less thinking to agree to that.

WALT WAS right about one thing—Tad has to call his parents to let them know he's not spending Christmas with them. He puts it off and puts it off some more. He ignores his phone when his mom calls him and deletes her voicemail without listening, not because he doesn't want to hear it but because thinking about listening gives him an anxiety attack that has him repotting a parlor palm that doesn't need it. Instead of calling back, he texts an apology that he missed her call.

With Christmas less than a week away, he forces himself to make the call, one hand white-knuckling the phone while the other is curled in Hetty's fur. Mom answers after the first ring.

"Tad!"

"Hi, Mom." He digs his fingers deeper into Hetty's fur. She curls into a tighter circle in his lap. "How are you?"

"Sweetheart, I'm so sorry about setting you up with Jenny," Mom says in a rush instead of answering. "I thought because you knew her, it would be fine."

Of course she wants to talk about this. Tad's still distantly upset about the blind date fiasco, and part of him wants to point out that when you haven't seen someone since they were ten years old, saying you know them is a stretch. But if he doesn't tell her he's not coming for Christmas right now, he might never get the words out.

"I can't make it back this week," he says quickly. It's like they're having two separate conversations.

There's a silence. In the background, Tad can hear music and road noise. She must be driving. "You mean you won't be able to make it up by Christmas? That's okay. We can celebrate on a different day."

Great, the torture is prolonging itself and he has to say it again. "I can't come at all." His brain scrambles for all the excuses he workshopped with Lewis, but he's forgotten all of them. "I'm—um. Busy."

"Busy on Christmas?" They should give awards for the ability to sound suspicious and heartbroken all at once. His mom would sweep. "If this is about the date—"

"It's not. Really, it's not." Tad's hand is shaking so much that Hetty raises her head, sniffs his fingers, and gives them a little lick. His pulse eases a tiny bit. "Something came up and I just. I have to stay."

"But it's Christmas. What could be so important that you can't spend Christmas with your family?"

In an alternate universe, another version of Tad takes a deep breath and says, *Spending it with my boyfriend and his family, that's what.* In this universe, a perfectly timed call from Callie coming in on his work computer saves him from having to answer. "I have to take a work call, Mom—love you, talk to you later!"

He hangs up before she can respond and lets Callie's call go to his work voicemail too. Heart still hammering, he scoops up Hetty into his arms and buries his face in her fur. She squirms but also purrs immediately. After a second, she settles, nuzzling her face against his cheek. Her whiskers tickle and he cuddles her tighter, glad she doesn't mind that he's getting her fur all wet with the tears leaking from his eyes.

Chapter Thirty-One

ITALIAN FAMILIES are more about Christmas Eve than Christmas, so Lewis's family does the giant holiday gathering on the 24th. Mom's side of the family, that is—Dad's an only child and his parents passed away when Lewis was in high school. The location of the Mancini Christmas Eve Spectacular is determined on a rotating basis, but whoever did Thanksgiving doesn't get stuck with Christmas too.

Lewis takes a commuter train to the Jersey suburbs to his aunt's house. One of his aunts—his mom has three sisters and a brother, plus a bunch of cousins that Lewis and Taylor have always called aunt or uncle.

After the Giant Italian Dinner (Feast of the Seven Fishes FTW), Lewis and Taylor always pile into the back seat of their parents' Volvo and head back to Weehawken, where they spend the night and have Christmas Day at home.

This year, Lewis is standing at the corner of Park and Clifton Terrace, hands shoved in his pockets as he waits for the 89 from the Hoboken PATH station. He gave Tad his parents' address, so he doesn't need to stand in the cold, but he got antsy. He wants to meet Tad at the bus stop in case he gets anxious about meeting Lewis's family.

Well, he *will* get nervous—Lewis knows Tad is already anxious about this. He's asked a million times if it's really okay for him to crash their Christmas, and a million more times if Lewis is really really sure he wants Tad there overnight, and furthermore if it's actually all right for Tad to sleep in Lewis's bedroom.

The wind cuts through his denim jacket. He stamps his feet to warm his toes in his rescued Pride Chucks. His hair is still damp from his shower—he smelled like fried seafood, which was gross, but he should have dried his hair before rushing into the cold.

The scent of impending snow is in the air. Lewis doesn't want to jinx it by checking the chance of precipitation on his phone. Checking it again, that is. He refreshed the app obsessively this morning, watching the chance of snow creep up, as though by keeping an eye on it, he could make a white Christmas happen.

It's just, how perfect would it be if it snowed tonight? It's snowed a few times, but it hasn't stuck, and everything is ugly and brown and dead. Lewis wants this Christmas to be the most romantic ever.

A bus goes by, but it's not the 89. Thick, low scud chokes the sky, reflecting the dull orange light pollution of Manhattan and the unbroken urban sprawl of Union City/Weehawken/Hoboken/Jersey City. If they get a white Christmas, it might be the right time to tell Tad he loves him.

Another bus slows as it approaches. It's the 89. Lewis takes his hands out of his pockets and tries to look cool and casual. What a weird headspace to be in love but keep it to yourself. He knows that every smile he shoots Tad's way, every time he touches Tad, screams it. Does Tad know? How can he not?

The bus stops and with a pneumatic hiss, the door opens. Tad steps off holding a green Fjällräven Känken backpack by its rainbow straps. Lewis's heart skips a beat. It's totally cliché, and it's totally true. It's a thing. The dull orange streetlights make his hair look copper. His curls bounce and lift off his head, clearly styled for lift. He's clean-shaven and wearing a blue and brown plaid jacket over black skinny jeans, and even in the dark, his eyes light up when they find Lewis.

"You didn't have to meet me!" Tad says, but he sounds so joyful that Lewis knows it was exactly the right thing to do.

Lewis pulls him into a hug. "I thought about meeting you at the PATH station but I didn't want to seem too desperate."

Tad kisses him lingeringly. He tastes like tea and something Lewis can't quite name, except that it's *Tad*. Something that reminds him of the sharp green of a forest. He smells like oak and amber, and a little bit like sweat. That's probably the nerves. It's not bad. Lewis could, quite honestly, breathe in the smell of Tad's sweat all the time.

"Are you freaking out a little?" Lewis asks, interlacing their fingers.

"Um, I'm freaking out a lot, actually." Tad's throat jags. "I've never met a boyfriend's family. What if I freeze up and can't get a single word out?"

"Then you freeze up and can't get a single word out," Lewis says, squeezing his hand.

Tad laughs nervously and lifts his free hand to his hair, like he's going to run his fingers through it. He stops at the last second and instead pats it into place. "Your parents will think I'm a lunatic. Or maybe they're already expecting me to be weird? Did you tell them I'm weird?"

"I definitely didn't tell them you're weird, because you're not weird." Lewis brings Tad's hand to his mouth and kisses the back of it. "I said you're shy. They get it. Taylor was so shy when we were kids, she didn't say a word all through first grade." He doesn't remember that because he was too young, but it's family lore.

"Taylor," Tad repeats. "Taylor's your sister."

"Yep. My mom's name is Lisa and my dad is Robin."

Tad mutters the names under his breath and squeezes Lewis's hand back. "Okay. I'm sorry in advance for acting like I'm an alien whose spaceship just dropped him off a couple hours ago."

"It's going to be fine. And if you're uncomfortable, we'll just go to my room. No big deal. Okay? They're excited to have you, because they can see how—"

Wait. Should he say this?

But Tad is looking at him expectantly, so Lewis finishes, "—how happy you make me."

Tad looks a little flustered and a lot happy. "Merry Christmas to me," he says, hugging Lewis's arm to his body. "Can we go inside? It's fucking freezing. And somebody had a window open on the bus. Did you see it's supposed to snow?"

"Shh!" Lewis slings an arm around Tad's waist as they walk down the sidewalk. "I don't want to jinx anything."

"You're such a romantic," Tad teases. "I love it."

Which is close enough to *I love you* that Lewis buzzes for the entire walk. And yeah, it's Too Soon for I love yous. At least for Dating Break Lewis, who was going to be more circumspect about his love life. Maybe it's time to just let Dating Break Lewis die. Poor kid never really had a chance.

"Oh. Wow." Tad jerks to a halt when Lewis turns onto the walkway for his house. "This is… wow."

The small front yard is festooned with inflatable Santas, reindeer, snowmen, and a massive dragon, which isn't Christmassy, but Mom bought it for Halloween and thinks it's too cool to only have its time in October. There are Christmas lights and garland on it to make it more seasonally appropriate.

The entire front of the house is covered in Christmas lights too—with no attempt to stick to a color scheme. There's white, green, red, multi, blue, and some purple that are probably from Halloween, but Mom has never cared about stuff like that. See: the dragon.

Lewis barely even notices it anymore but... yeah. "This is a pretty good introduction to my parents."

A slow smile creeps across Tad's face. "I think I like them already."

Tad grins, kisses Tad's smile quickly, and leads him up the walkway. When he opens the door, he yells, "I'm back!"

From the living room, Mom squeals, but thankfully doesn't come galloping to the door. Lewis repeated a few times that Tad's shy and to please not overwhelm him, and she promised she'd be calm. Of course, Mom's definition of calm is skewed several degrees toward hyper compared to most people.

Dad's and Taylor's hushed voices come from the living room, too, so his family is hanging out around the Christmas tree exactly where he left them. Lewis takes Tad's jacket, noticing Tad's leg bouncing nervously. After he hangs the jacket in the closet, he returns to Tad and rubs his hand up and down Tad's spine. Under his palm, the tense muscles in Tad's shoulders relax a tiny bit.

"I'm here," Lewis says. He spent a lot of time thinking about the best way to help Tad through his shyness and nervousness about meeting new people, and he decided he wouldn't say things like, *It will be fine* or *They'll love you* or *Don't be nervous*. Lewis understands anxiety. You can't just turn it off. Maybe Lewis doesn't have the same kind as Tad, but he knows what it's like to have your brain doing its best, constantly, to doubt everything good about yourself.

Holding Tad's eyes, Lewis repeats, "I'm here. And I'm really, really glad you came."

Tad's shoulders jerk as he takes a quick sip of air. The flutter of his heart is visible at his throat, and Lewis wants to put his lips over it.

With another breath, Tad says, "Okay. Introduce me to your family."

Lewis takes Tad's hand again. Their wedding rings click together.

From the living room, Taylor hisses, "They're coming!" which is followed by the sound of her racing from one end of the room to the other and the creak of the sofa as she launches herself onto it. Subtle. Really subtle.

The lights are dimmed and the tree is lit in the living room. Everyone has glasses of wine, and there are two empty glasses sitting on the coffee table. The gesture makes Lewis love his parents even more. If they want to join the rest of his family, the invitation is there, but the wine hasn't been poured to make them feel like they have to stay.

"This is Tad," he says, hearing the warmth and affection in his voice. Hopefully Tad hears it too. "Tad, this is my mom and dad, Lisa and Robin, and my sister, Taylor."

They all get up. Tad holds out a hand to Mom, clears his throat, and says in a small voice, "Um, hi—um. It's"—a breath he struggles with—"it's nice to meet you."

Mom's eyes are warm. "I'd love to hug you. Can I hug you?"

"Oh! Um." Tad's eyes are wide. "Yes? I mean. Yes. Yeah, that's fine. That would be nice."

The hug Mom enfolds Tad in is careful and kind. She's worked at LGBTQ+ youth centers for most of Lewis's life, and her gentleness with Tad reminds Lewis why she's good at it. She just makes people trust her. She's like the Every-Mom.

It would be great if Tad loosened up after Mom's hug, but he doesn't. But—he doesn't run away, either. He sticks it out, and Lewis stands at his side, touching him frequently to try to pass his love and pride to Tad through his fingertips. They all stand there making small talk for a few minutes—typical get-to-know-you stuff, like where are you from, what do you do for a living, and Taylor's contribution: "When I picked Lewis up from the airport after he got back from Vegas, I *knew* he met someone there."

Tad flushes and glances at Lewis, who feels his face get hot. Yeah, when he was supposed to be holding Tad at let's-just-be-friends arm's length, he was so bad at it that his sister immediately guessed what was up. She said it to him in the car when she picked him up, too, so he knows she's not retconning.

"Do you two want a drink?" Dad asks, gesturing to the empty glasses.

Lewis feels Tad tense, so he says, "I'm going to get Tad settled upstairs. Maybe we'll come down later, though."

For some reason, Tad tenses even more at that. Shit, did Lewis misread him? Did Tad want to stay and have a drink?

"The wine needs to breathe anyway," Mom says brightly. "Go on upstairs. I guess I can't make you keep the door open?"

"Oh my god, Mom," Lewis groans as Mom laughs gleefully.

The exchange makes Tad relax, though, so the parental humiliation is worth it.

On the way to the stairs, Lewis grabs Tad's backpack, which he left by the door. "Once I hit puberty, my parents wouldn't let me have the door closed when I had friends over."

"Did they know you were gay?" Tad asks.

The stairs creak underfoot as they climb them. They're narrow and definitely not to code, but his parents say they have character. "I asked them that when I came out. They said they were just trying to break down outmoded sexual and gender stereotypes."

They reach the landing upstairs. "Your parents are cool," Tad says.

"Yeah, they are," Lewis says proudly. He leads Tad to his bedroom, pushing the door open and walking inside with only a tiny bit of trepidation. His exes, those who came here, always laughed at his childhood room. Which honestly, Lewis probably deserves, because this room is ridiculous.

Tad's mouth drops open. "Oh my god."

He turns slowly, taking everything in, from the twinkling dew lights to the animal posters to the fake plastic vines hanging from the ceiling. There are posters of glistening, mostly naked men. There's a rainbow mobile he got at NYC Pride when he was ten. There's a small collection of his old plushies on his bed.

Actually he meant to move those.

"Um." Lewis hurries across the room and sweeps the plushies up in his arms. "Sorry, I forgot to put these in a tote."

The dolphin he got at the Bronx Zoo when he was in first grade flops back to the bed. Before Lewis can grab it, Tad picks it up. It's well-loved, the fuzzy gray fabric of its skin less gray and more dishwater. Lewis brought it with him everywhere when he was a kid. He brought it to school and got teased mercilessly when all the other kids had stopped doing stuff like that—but there he was, Lewis Mancini-Sommer, toting around his dolphin stuffy while everyone else was transitioning to tween-dom.

Having it with him just made everything seem more manageable. And his parents never made him feel stupid or childish for needing it. Once, a teacher suggested he stop bringing it to school, and Mom drew herself up to her full height (an unimpressive 5'3") and said, "When Lewis is ready to stop bringing Ocean to school, he'll stop bringing her."

Tad turns the dolphin over in his hands, then rubs its nose. "Does she have a name?"

Lewis knows he's bright red. "Uh, yeah. Ocean." A smile creeps slowly across Tad's face and Lewis fights the urge not to bury his own in the armful of plushies in his arms. "I was six."

Tad's smile doesn't look mocking. It looks... soft? "May I please snuggle Ocean?"

"You... um... yes? What's happening? Are you making fun of me?"

Hugging the plushie to himself, Tad shakes his head. "No! You're adorable. I love—" His face goes scarlet. "—er, this. I love this. Your crazy, gay room, and the fact you still have your plushies, and that your favorite was named Ocean. Also." He points to a poster of pre-*Magic Mike* Channing Tatum. "I *really* like that."

He cocks his head as his eyes track over Channing Tatum's assets, lingering at the prominent bulge in his Abercrombie & Fitch briefs, which had been a major draw for teenage Lewis too. "Your parents let you have this?" he asks, sounding surprised and like he doesn't want to sound surprised, but can't help it.

Lewis deposits his plushies on the dresser (which is bedazzled thanks to a burst of creative energy during the summer between seventh and eighth grades). "My mom bought it for me when she found a stack of Taylor's Abercrombie catalogs under my bed. She said she didn't want me to be ashamed about masturbating, but she was getting tired of Taylor having ten fits about the catalogs always disappearing."

"Wow."

"Yeah." Lewis laughs and rakes a hand through his hair. "I know my parents weren't exactly typical. I mean, especially with...."

One of Tad's eyebrows quirks up. "Especially with my parents being small town, heteronormative-loving, homophobe-lite killjoys?" He hugs Ocean again and looks sad.

Lewis pulls him onto the bed and rolls on top of him, which gets him a smile and laugh. "There he is," Lewis murmurs, kissing Tad lightly, then a little harder, slipping his tongue between Tad's lips.

"I can't believe your parents are so cool with me sleeping in here." Tad wraps his arms around Lewis and kisses back. "They are, right?"

"Of course they are." Lewis nestles his face in the crook of Tad's neck, letting Tad take the full weight of his body. He can feel Tad's heartbeat reverberating through both of their rib cages.

For a few minutes that feel liquid and endless, the two of them lie there, breathing together. Finally, Tad murmurs, "We can go back downstairs with your family."

"I want to stay right here," Lewis murmurs back, the salt of Tad's skin on his lips.

"No you don't." Tad plays with the hair at the nape of Lewis's neck. "Seriously, you don't have to humor me. I can handle spending time with them." He pauses, then adds, "That sounded wrong. What I mean is, they're nice. It's stupid of me to be nervous about having a glass of wine with them."

He starts to shift, like he's going to get up, but Lewis makes himself dead weight, pinning Tad to the mattress. "I'm not humoring you. It's not stupid you're shy. And I don't want to go anywhere." For good measure, he kisses Tad's neck. "I just want you to feel comfortable here."

Tad wriggles. "Yeah, well, *I* want your parents to like me. And I want to be able to sit in a room with them and talk without fighting down an anxiety attack. Like exposure therapy. Wait. No. Not like exposure therapy. That sounds bad."

Lewis smiles and kisses Tad's neck again. "You want my parents to like you? How come?"

Making a protesting noise, Tad says, "*Lewis*. Come on. Why does anyone want their boyfriend's parents to like them?"

Lewis props himself up on an elbow and looks down at Tad's face. Since they got back from Nevada, Tad has gotten paler. His freckles have faded too, but the ones that are there stand out starker against his skin. With a thumb, Lewis traces the scatter of them from one cheekbone, over the bridge of Tad's nose, and across to his other cheek. "I don't know," Lewis says. "Tell me."

Tad shifts a leg and gets it out from under Lewis, then promptly hooks it around Lewis's leg, locking them together. "Because."

"Because?"

"Because maybe I kind of want to be around for a while." Tad looks like he wants to hide his face, but there's nowhere for him to go.

The words are making it hard for Lewis to respond, anyway. His rib cage, already full of the beat of Tad's heart as well as his own, and the tide of their breath, fills up with this too. It's heat and light and gold edging along all his bones from the center and outward.

But Tad will worry if Lewis doesn't say anything, so he makes himself breathe, and he says, "Maybe I kind of want you to be around for a while too."

They gaze at each other before Lewis brushes a stray curl off Tad's forehead. "You really want to go back downstairs?"

"Yeah." Tad's smile is a little crooked. "I'm facing my fears for you. Total character growth moment."

Lewis slides off the bed and offers Tad a hand. "Okay. Let's go hang out with my family."

And it strikes him, as they head back downstairs, that not one of his exes ever wanted to spend time with his family. None of them ever bothered to appreciate Lewis's closeness with them. Yet here's Tad, with his own family he can't be honest with, wanting to embrace Lewis's.

That gold filigreeing Lewis's bones feels like it's shining.

Chapter Thirty-Two

WHEN THEY wake up on Christmas morning, they have sex. So that's a good start to the day. At least until the shower turns on down the hall, and Tad kinda sorta remembers Lewis's entire family is probably only feet away. "I can't believe we just had sex in your parents' house," he mumbles into Lewis's neck.

Sex, which Lewis smells like, which honestly kind of makes Tad want to have it again. Which is bad. *Bad.*

Lewis settles an arm around Tad's back. "It's not like the house has never seen sex. I'm pretty sure my parents have sex here."

"Is that the point though, really?" Tad asks, his voice muffled by Lewis's skin. Mm, he tastes salty and sweaty.

Bad. Bad, Thaddeus.

"I think the point is that Christmas is off to a great start." Lewis drops a kiss on Tad's head. "You know what would make it even better?"

As Lewis slides out of bed, Tad stretches out, enjoying the way Lewis's eyes track the motion and how he bites his lip. Since Lewis's question doesn't seem rhetorical, Tad offers, "Blow jobs?"

Lewis's eyes get positively hot at that, but he shakes it off. "I mean, yes, obviously, but I was thinking about snow. We were supposed to have a white Christmas."

He crosses the room to the window and raises a hand to the curtains but hesitates before pulling them aside. Tad gets out of bed to join him, pressing the length of his body up against Lewis's and slipping his arms around him. Lewis makes the smallest sound of contentment and leans back, pressing them tighter together.

Contentment isn't exactly the right word. It's contentment mixed with yearning—the contentment at the end of an eternity of yearning, and it makes something ache right at Tad's center. Lewis doesn't even need to say a word. Tad knows that sound and everything it implies.

He never thought he'd be the contentment at the end of all the endless wanting, the amorphous bellyache of need and missing something you can't even name.

Tad closes his eyes. Squeezes them tight. He doesn't know if he can be that.

But it's Christmas, and he'd like to be.

"Let's look," Tad says, reaching out to flutter the curtains without opening them. The honor should be Lewis's.

"Okay, moment of truth." Lewis nudges the curtain aside, letting bright white light flood the room. Tad squints and can't see anything, snow or otherwise. But Lewis makes a happy squealing sound and bounces. "It snowed!"

Gleefully, he spins in Tad's arms, puts his hands on Tad's face, and pulls him into a kiss. Only his grin is so wide that it's more like bumping their teeth together—and that's okay, because Tad's laughing and happy because Lewis is happy, and—and—he's so in love. He's so, so in love, and it's terrifying and wonderful and he doesn't know what to do with it.

Tad's heart skips and his stomach swoops, and he decides the only thing to do with it right now is kiss Lewis hard and enjoy this day.

When they stop kissing, Tad asks, "So what's the Christmas routine? I hope it's okay to shower before going downstairs for presents, because, um—" He makes a vague downward gesture, meant to encompass their chests and stomachs, which have managed to become both sticky *and* crusty.

Lewis grins wolfishly. "If I said no, would you let me clean you off?"

Tad groans, "Oh my god, that's filthy and really hot. Yes."

There's a fleeting look of temptation on Lewis's face but he says, "No, we get ready first. Not like when we were kids. Taylor and I used to get up at like five in the morning."

They decide Tad can shower first, so he pulls on the pajamas he didn't sleep in last night and heads to the bathroom. When he's done, they trade, leaving Tad alone in Lewis's room to get dressed.

Once he's done, he stands in the middle of the room, wondering if he should wait for Lewis or go downstairs by himself. Lisa and Robin are incredibly kind, and Taylor seems really cool. The worst that can happen is… okay, no, bad strategy. He can imagine a lot of really horrible situations. Better to just not think about it and go downstairs.

He pulls the cards he got for Lewis's family from his backpack, then Lewis's Christmas present, careful not to tear the shiny paper he painstakingly, and badly, wrapped it in. It sounds like everyone's in the kitchen, so with a deep breath, Tad heads there. When he pokes his head in, Lisa and Robin are sitting at the counter having coffee.

Lisa spots him first. "Tad! Merry Christmas!"

"Merry Christmas," he says shyly. He wants to give himself a high five for not stumbling over that. He holds out the gift and cards and says, "I wasn't sure if it's okay to put this stuff under the tree."

"Oh! You're so considerate. There's no special rules," Lisa assures him.

"Anymore," Robin supplies before taking the most well-timed sip of coffee ever.

Lisa laughs. She has the same laugh lines in her face as Lewis. Or—he guesses Lewis has her laugh lines. Either way, it makes something warm and gooey happen to Tad's insides. "Yeah, we had to resort to police tape that one year, didn't we?"

"And threatened to dust for fingerprints if anything looked out of place." Robin clears his throat and raises his eyebrows as Taylor comes into the kitchen, wearing an ugly Christmas sweater with cats and Christmas trees all over it.

"That was totally Lewis leading me into sin," Taylor says. "Hi Tad, Merry Christmas."

"You're the oldest," Robin replies. "And we know it was you."

She bats her eyelashes and gives him a hug, then does the same for Lisa. "Okay, fine, but in my defense, he was really easy to lead astray. And kind of an enabler."

"Are you talking about the Christmas Mom and Dad threatened to dust for fingerprints?" Lewis asks, popping his head into the kitchen.

"Lewis! Close your eyes. Tad needs to make a stop at the tree!" Lisa orders. Wow, Tad's boyfriend's family who he met twelve hours ago has his back better than his own does.

Lewis claps a hand over his eyes and Lisa gives Tad a thumbs-up, which he returns before creeping past Lewis.

The Mancini-Sommer Christmas tree isn't pretty. Tad loves it. All the ornaments clearly mean something. Half look homemade and the other half look like they're decades old. The lights are a mishmash of multicolored and white and some of them are showing their age, the colors dulled with years of use.

He tucks Lewis's gift among the other presents and props the cards up, staying to admire the tree for another second. His parents' Christmas tree is his and Mom's project. Every year, they go to HomeGoods and get decorations that fit the year's color scheme. They never had too many ornaments, because from year to year, most didn't fit with subsequent themes, and Mom has always been ruthless about culling clutter. Choosing the colors and the ornaments with her is fun, though.

He feels bad for abandoning her to do the tree by herself this year. Especially since when he finally found the balls to call and say he wasn't going back for Christmas, he lied about a special project at work that was taking up all his time. He promised to call today.

The thought makes his stomach twist, and he returns to the kitchen before he can dwell on it.

The radio's on when he gets back—WQXR, New York Public Radio's classical station. Lewis puts his arm around Tad and pulls him close, murmuring, "We never said we were doing presents for each other."

"Did you get me one?"

"Yeah."

Tad smirks and Lewis wipes it off his face with a kiss.

And it's just.

He never thought he'd have this.

He never thought he'd be able to casually kiss the man he's with in front of family. It never mattered that he knew people whose families were totally accepting. That was for other people, not him. That was his punishment for being a coward about his own family.

"I made you tea," Lewis says.

"You," Tad says stupidly.

"It's 'holiday blend,' whatever that is," Lisa chimes in. "That's all we have—clearly we're not tea drinkers here."

For emphasis, she swigs a mouthful of coffee. Wait, they're making a second pot, aren't they? They already drank an entire pot of coffee? What?

"You guys have a problem," Taylor says.

"It will only be a problem when we have to use the IV drips every day," Robin says, deadpan.

There's laughter and Lewis brings Tad his tea. Robin thumps his coffee mug on the counter to get everyone's attention. "Let's move this into the living room."

As the two of them settle on the sofa, Lewis leans in and asks Tad quietly, "Are you doing okay? I know they—we—are a lot. Just tell me if you need a break to recharge."

Tad takes Lewis's hand. "I'm okay."

Taylor distributes gifts with great ceremony. When gifts, as in, plural, multiple gifts, find their way to Tad's collection, his mouth drops open and he looks at Lisa and Robin in shock. They're already opening presents, so he can't even say anything, like, *Hey, you definitely made a mistake because these are to me? From you? And you don't even know me?*

Instead, he turns to Lewis, who's opening a box from Taylor. Wordlessly, he points to the fact that Lewis's family appears to have made a mistake and accidentally purchased gifts for him. Lewis smiles and shakes his head fondly. "Duh. Open them."

Tad does. From Taylor, there's a card with a cat knocking stuff off a table on the outside, and a gift card to his favorite queer-owned bookstore in New York. The note says, *Sorry, I know gift cards are kind of lame, but this way you can get the exact right book that you've had your eye on!*

Lisa and Robin have gotten him several gorgeous planters with glaze that looks like galaxies and nebulas. They're exactly the right size for the spider plants that are getting pot bound and that he's been planning on repotting soon.

"I may have mentioned you were in the market for some new pots," Lewis says. He sounds anxious. Like Tad is going to do anything but cry at the kindness of these strangers.

He has to wipe his eyes. "These are beautiful." And all he got them were cards. Is he a complete asshole? He wrote nice things in them, but like. No comparison.

Now he's terrified his gift to Lewis is going to look like shit. He was definitely trying to be thoughtful, but what if Lewis doesn't see it that way? Lewis is such a romantic, and even though he hasn't made Tad feel like he's expecting a Big Gesture, he'd probably love one. This gift isn't a gesture. It's just a gift.

He's just about made up his mind to snatch it back and say...
something (he wrapped the wrong thing?), but Lewis is already opening
it. Tad steels himself for disappointment on Lewis's face.

Lewis pulls the wrapping paper off and breaks into a huge grin.
"*Forgotten Manhattan: Fifty Weird, Wild, and Wonderful Slices of
History in the Big Apple.* Oh my god, I see what the author did there."
With a gasp, he exclaims, "It's the Seaman-Drake Arch! On the cover!
The arch by your building!"

Tension unwinds from Tad's shoulders as pleasure unspools in his
chest. He didn't fuck up. "Look inside," he says.

With a mystified expression, Lewis flips the book open. On the
front page is a short message and the author's signature in black Sharpie.
Lewis's mouth drops open. "You got this signed for me?"

"The author lives in my building."

Tad is just going to leave it at that, because it was, of course, A
Whole Thing. He found the book first, but something kept niggling at
him about the author's name. He was sure he'd seen it somewhere.

Finally, he figured it out as he was getting his mail and saw the
name on the mailbox above his. The author lived in his building! He
lived *down the hall!* After that it was a simple matter of knocking on his
door and politely requesting an autograph.

Haha, yeah right. He paced his apartment, took one of his dwindling
supply of propranolol pills (he needs to get that prescription refilled),
paced some more, made Hetty so nervous she hid from him and wouldn't
come out, and then he got teary and spent a bunch of time trying to lure
her out with treats, which she refused to be lured by. *Then* he forced
himself to confront the fact that he was stalling, and he needed to just
walk down the hall, knock on the door, and say, *Hi, sorry to bother you,
but my boyfriend is interested in local history and I bought your book for
him, and it would mean a lot if you could sign it for him?* Only with no
uptalk.

When he finally worked himself up to it, he talked so fast that he
had to repeat himself. Twice. But once his neighbor could understand
him, he was thrilled. They actually got chatting, and eventually Mr. Ortiz
invited Tad in for a cup of cafe con leche. When Tad went back to his
apartment an hour later, Hetty had forgiven him.

It was all totally worth it, because Lewis looks thrilled. "This is so
cool," he says. "Taylor! Look!"

He shows her the book and she says, "Cool! You're such a nerd, though."

With a laugh, he says, "Says the person unwrapping her new DND dice."

She rattles them gleefully in the tube. "I totally want to do my hair this color, then I'll match! Tad, what do you think?"

The dice are purple and sparkly. "I think that would be amazing," he says honestly.

His attention returns to Lewis, who slides his gift into Tad's lap. It's thin and rectangular. "That's mine," he says, picking at a hangnail and jiggling a leg. Wait, is Lewis nervous about his present to Tad?

"Oh my god." Tad holds up a framed photo of—them. Tad in his shimmery black tank and black skinny jeans and Lewis in an orange and white western shirt with classic pearl buttons. They're in what is pretty clearly the Vegas wedding chapel where they got married, their arms around each other while they gaze into each other's eyes.

Lewis leans over so he can speak softly into Tad's ear. "I hit up the group chat to see if anyone had any pictures of us and got a bunch back. This was my favorite."

"We look like a real married couple," Tad says, still reeling. Whatever emotion just dropkicked him isn't doing the decent thing and making itself easily identified. Tad is overwhelmed. Overwhelmed by the sight of them back when they didn't even know each other, but it looks like they did.

God, it looks like they did.

There weren't any photos of Tad and John like this. They never *gazed* at each other the way Tad and Lewis are gazing at each other in this picture.

"Do you like it?" Lewis asks hesitantly.

"I love it." Tad looks at him. "This is—I love it. I love it."

If he doesn't stop repeating that, he's going to slip and say *I love you*, which is what he really means.

"Okay." Lewis's voice is soft. "Good. I'm really glad."

His fingertips graze the back of Tad's hand, and Tad turns his hand over so they're touching his palm instead. It's a ghost of a touch, but it makes Tad's heart flutter.

They all spend the next hour thanking each other and showing off what they got. Then it's time for breakfast, after which they go for a walk around the neighborhood before getting ready for the main meal of the day. Taylor and Lisa make a pot of red sauce from scratch, the kitchen filling with the scent of olive oil, garlic, and herbs, while Lewis makes pasta. Homemade pasta. From scratch. With his hands.

What. *What*.

After the dough is rolled out, he gets a bowl of something goopy and green out of the refrigerator, which he says is spinach and ricotta filling for the pasta. He spreads filling on the pasta dough and rolls them to make manicotti. As Lewis works, he explains that it was his maternal grandmother's recipe.

"I didn't know you could make *pasta*," Tad says, still floored.

"I have a lot of tricks up my sleeve, baby." Lewis wiggles his eyebrows and Tad, perched on a stool at the counter where Lewis is working, snorts.

"Okay well, I'm interested in any and all tricks, but like. Pasta. Homemade pasta. Marry me."

"That's easy, we're already married," Lewis says, squinting at a tube before he removes a little of the filling.

Tad smirks and Lewis glances up, a goofy smile on his face.

This is the best Christmas Tad can remember. The warmth of the kitchen and the delicious smell of the red sauce cooking gently on the stove, the steady rhythm of Lewis making manicotti, the sounds of conversation and laughter from the living room, and the way every few minutes, a member of Lewis's family wanders in to check on the sauce and chat. After the first few times they stop in, Tad realizes he's barely nervous anymore, and soon, the nerves are gone entirely.

He's sure that next time he sees Lewis's parents and sister, the social anxiety will knock down whatever flimsy confidence he's gained today, because that's how it always is. He'll get comfortable with people, and then the next time he's seen them it's almost like he's meeting them for the first time all over again.

It was never that way with Lewis, though. And all this time, he just sort of figured it was because of the way they met. It feels like something more than that, now.

Chapter Thirty-Three

CHRISTMAS DAY passes in a haze of delicious food, good wine, and the feeling of what family seems like it should mean. After everyone stuffs themselves on manicotti, they let the food settle, then go back for dessert, which is a huge assortment of Italian cookies (not homemade, Lewis confesses). They take another walk around the neighborhood after that. A few families are outside, the kids running around and playing with new Christmas gifts.

As the day creeps to a close and thick midwinter darkness falls, Tad knows he's going to have to go outside this idyllic little bubble and back to the real world. His plants need him, and he misses Hetty. It will be lonely taking the train home by himself.

He's surprised when Lewis asks, "Should we leave soon? I'm not sure what time you wanted to be home by."

"We?" Tad repeats like he's never encountered the word before.

"Yeah," Lewis says. "Of course. I wouldn't send you back to Manhattan alone."

Right. Of course. Unthinkable. Is this what a good relationship feels like?

"Unless," Lewis says, sounding like he's afraid he said something wrong, "you want some time by yourself. Shit. You probably do. Sorry. Jesus. I'm not trying to make decisions for you or be a control freak—"

Tad grabs a fistful of Lewis's shirt and hauls him in for a kiss, not caring one bit that anyone could walk into the room and see them.

Lewis relaxes into it. "I wanna spend the night with you again," he murmurs into Tad's mouth, "but it's super rude to just invite myself over, right?"

"Invite yourself over," Tad replies and kisses Lewis again.

That's how they find themselves back at Tad's apartment after a long, loud, joyful goodbye with Lisa and Robin. They make Tad promise to come again and Lewis promise to bring Tad again. Taylor drove to

Weehawken, so she drops Lewis and Tad at the Hoboken PATH Station. With Lewis at his side, Tad feels like he could sit on the train forever.

When they get back to Tad's place, Tad scoops Hetty up and hugs her, which she tolerates for a while before squirming to get down. Lewis plays with her and plies her with treats while Tad takes care of the plants, trimming, cutting back, watering, and moving them around as needed.

Once that's done, Tad says, "I want to show you something." Of course, Lewis gives him a wolfish grin, which makes Tad laugh. "Not that. I mean, not yet. We have to go back outside for this. Get your coat."

"I love bossy Tad." Lewis shrugs his coat back on and gives Hetty a little scratch behind her ears. "Like when you told me to ride the mechanical bull with you."

"I'm pretty sure I politely invited you to ride the mechanical bull with me," Tad shoots back playfully.

Christmas night isn't an ideal time to stand on a roof in Manhattan, but the roof of Tad's building is one of his favorite places in the whole world—a place where he can stand, surrounded by the life of Manhattan, but in his own island of peace and solitude. It makes him feel like a prince, like it's all out there waiting for him. The meek shall inherit the Earth, or something.

"Whoa," Lewis says when Tad leads him to the edge of the roof. The city spreads out in all directions—Manhattan to the south, George Washington Bridge and Jersey to the west, the Bronx to the east and north. Manhattan's skyscrapers twinkle in the clear, frigid air, the Empire State Building lit up green and red and drawing attention like a crown jewel in a collection of royal treasures.

Ordinarily street noise would drift up between buildings—trucks, car horns, traffic whooshing by, the beat of reggaeton and hip-hop floating up between brick and glass. Tonight, it's quiet. There's a stillness that feels like the indrawn breath before you step up to a mic and sing, or take that final leap off a diving board, or before the gun goes off at the starting line of a race. It feels like that moment when it's all possible.

"Like it?" Tad asks.

Soft city light shines on Lewis's face. "I love it. This is—wow."

He shivers, and Tad puts an arm around him. "Cold?"

"Cold, but totally worth it." Lewis snuggles into Tad, shifting so he's standing with his back to Tad's front. Tad loops his arms around

Lewis's midsection and Lewis leans back. "You want to hear something really stupid?" Lewis asks.

"Sure."

"You're supposed to say you're sure it's not stupid."

"Yeah, but it might be stupid," Tad says innocently.

Lewis makes an affronted noise. "Anyway," he says, sounding amused and teasing, "the stupid thing I was going to say is—I feel like I'm living a rom-com right now. Like, everything I always dreamed about... it's coming true."

Wind gusts, and it feels like it takes Tad's breath away with it. "With me?" he finally manages.

"No, with my other husband who I drunk married."

"How do you keep us straight?"

"Easy. You're the handsomest."

Tad shakes his head, realizes Lewis can't see that, and says, "Guys don't think I'm handsome."

"Bet they do. I do."

"I have too many freckles."

"I love your freckles."

"I have a pointy nose."

"I love your nose."

"I don't have a body that fits into any of Grindr's boxes."

"Tad." There's such warmth in Lewis's voice. "You're perfect."

Tad wraps his arms tighter around Lewis, pulling his warmth close. It feels like... home. That's how Lewis feels to Tad—like home. Like the home his parents' house hasn't been in so long. Like the home he's wanted New York City to be, and which it's been in so many ways. But Lewis makes it complete. Lewis is the final piece that holds it all together.

That feeling washes over and through him. Overcome, he buries his face in Lewis's hair.

"What are you thinking about?" Lewis asks. "Hopefully not more ways you're not perfect, because I can definitely counter every single one of them."

Tad opens his mouth to answer, but he doesn't actually know what to say. Should he say what he's thinking? Is it too much? It's way too much, right? Yeah. It's totally too much. This is new, and Lewis probably doesn't want to get in too deep so fast.

So now he's just not saying anything. Lewis tilts his head back and nuzzles along the side of Tad's face. "Getting shy on me?"

Burying his face in Lewis's hair more fully, Tad mumbles around a smile, "No."

"It's okay if you are."

"No, I'm not." Lewis turns in his arms so they're facing each other and Tad says, "I was just thinking about homes. And families. And how your family is just… amazing. Thank you for letting me be part of today." The way Lewis's face gets so soft does something irreparable to Tad. He can't stop the next words that come out of his mouth. "You're amazing."

A glow starts at one corner of Lewis's mouth as it lifts into a smile, and it slowly suffuses his entire face. Eyes alight with joy, Lewis cradles Tad's face in both hands and breathes, "Oh—baby, you are too. You really are too."

Tad could tell Lewis he loves him right now. Maybe he should—but maybe not. No, definitely not. It's too much. And it's cheesy, anyway, telling his boyfriend he loves him on Christmas Day.

So he brushes his lips over Lewis's. He tastes like the pignoli cookies he was mainlining at dessert and underneath that, himself—something Tad doesn't know how to describe except that it's *Lewis*, and it's the sweetest thing Tad can imagine having on his tongue.

They kiss on the roof of Tad's building on Christmas night with the wind swirling around them and the city alight as far as the eye can see, and it's like Tad's soul spread out: lights and lights and lights.

Chapter Thirty-Four

THREE WEEKS after Christmas is Stacy's wedding. Lewis gets crazy busy with his maid-of-honor responsibilities on January 2nd, throwing the bridal shower, keeping track of arriving gifts, making sure dresses and his tux are going to be ready for final fittings, helping Stacy and Alang with last minute RSVPs, coaching Stacy through a centerpiece disaster that ends with them DIYing the whole thing in one night and which results in him taking the subway home at five in the morning covered in glitter, glue, and several stray fake flowers.

After the penultimate dress-and-tux fitting, which runs late because Stacy is adamant that her dress absolutely cannot be taken out anymore because she needs to be a certain size for her wedding, Lewis takes a Lyft to Tad's. He's texted multiple apologies to Tad for being late, but he couldn't leave his ride-or-die in the state she worked herself into, which involved tears, a vow to take laxatives between now and the wedding, insisting the dress can stay the way it is because she won't eat anything except celery and wheat grass powder during all that time, and locking herself in the boutique's office while she wailed that she was ruining the wedding with this.

Once he talked her down from that, he had to talk her down from her horror over the fact that she was buying into fat-shaming culture and that the whole wedding-industrial complex was based on harmful beauty standards and patriarchal, heteronormative gender nonsense from a less enlightened era.

"But I still want my wedding to be perfect," she sniffled with his arm around her, mascara so smeared around her eyes that it was almost impossible not to tell her she looked like the Hamburglar.

He kissed her forehead, assured her that the wedding would be perfect because he'd make sure it was, and *then* told her she looked like the Hamburglar.

Lewis lets himself into Tad's apartment and sprawls on the sofa. The shower is running. When Tad emerges from the bathroom, his face lights up. "Hey! Sorry, I hung out at the gym longer when you said you were going to be late." He comes over to the sofa—nothing on except a pair of blue briefs that are doing delicious things to his anatomy—and straddles Lewis's thighs. "You look tired."

"I'm so glad this is all going to be over in a week and a half. I don't know if I could handle any more than that."

"You could," Tad says fondly. "You love it. You're like, totally in your element. Stacy got super lucky that her best friend happened to be incredibly organized and good at telling people what to do and when to get it done."

"Yeah, my control freak abilities are really coming through."

Tad's face falls. "I didn't mean—"

Lewis grabs his hands. "I know you didn't. Sorry. Old baggage. When Stace asked me to be her maid of honor, Jonah said—" He pauses. What Jonah said was that it was perfect for him—he was going to get a chance to be a control freak bridezilla before his own wedding. But why would he want to repeat that? Jonah was a cheating asshole. "You know what? It doesn't matter what Jonah said."

Tad's watching him, looking worried, and Lewis wants to smooth away the grooves between his eyebrows. "I didn't mean that," Tad murmurs. Practically whispers. "I don't think you're a control freak."

Now Lewis feels like a jerk for making such an unfunny joke. Obviously if he'd realized Tad would be so hard on himself, he wouldn't have said it. "It's okay, babe," he says, squeezing Tad's hands. "Hey, so—how do you feel about coming to the wedding?"

"What?" Surprise ripples over Tad's face. "I'm invited?"

"Well, yeah. Of course." Lewis drops Tad's hands to wrap his arms around his back instead. He's still all warm and soft from the shower, his skin a little pink from the hot water, and as Lewis pulls him closer he breathes in the clean, sharp scent of soap and the bright, citrusy shampoo Tad uses. The whole thing is so distracting that he forgets what he was saying and has to find the thread of conversation again. "Stacy was serious about the verbal invitation, but anyway, you're my plus one."

Tad wriggles closer and Lewis's dick perks up. "Mm," Tad says noncommittally.

"It's going to be a big wedding," Lewis admits. "So I'd understand if you didn't want to come."

"Do you want me there?" Tad asks. There's something on his face Lewis can't totally read that appeared when Lewis called himself a control freak and hasn't gone away.

"Of course I do," Lewis says. He presses a soft kiss to Tad's shoulder, where the freckles spray and scatter over his skin. Tad's sharp little intake of breath is like candy, or like a drug, and Lewis needs more of it. Slowly, he moves his lips along Tad's collarbone until he gets to the hollow of Tad's throat. Tad's pulse throbs under Lewis's mouth, and Lewis swirls his tongue there, licking into that warm dip of skin in a way that feels filthier than he intended it to be.

Tad's hands come up to clutch at Lewis's hair, and he makes this tiny groany sound that goes straight to Lewis's dick. Really, he shouldn't have tried to have any kind of mildly serious conversation when Tad was in nothing but briefs.

Now, in addition to the clean smell of freshly washed skin, there's the distinct tang of arousal. Lewis drifts one hand from Tad's back to his crotch, where he's hot and hard and wet.

His brain goes straight to static. With a moan, Lewis rocks his hips up, wanting friction, dimly aware the angle isn't right at all, and trusting that his body is going to figure it out without much input from his brain.

Tad tugs his hair and Lewis raises his face, where he's immediately met with a hard, openmouthed kiss. Tad fucks his tongue into Lewis's mouth and Lewis sucks at it. There's something in the back of his mind poking him to actually *talk* about whether Tad's going to come with him to the wedding or not, that they actually haven't had many serious conversations about... well, anything, and that maybe they're due to start. And that sex—fucking hot sex—is amazing, but can't stand in for all the other stuff that a relationship needs to continue past the infatuation stage.

And Lewis knows this is more than infatuation.

So he really should pause the sex to talk about the wedding, which isn't even that big of a conversation, but, guhhh Tad is grinding into him and pushing his shirt up and the skin-to-skin fuzzes out whatever remaining brain cells Lewis can devote to non-fucking related thoughts.

Tad's phone jangles with an incoming call.

Tad tears himself away from Lewis's mouth with a groan of the distinctly un-sexy variety. "Let it go to voicemail," Lewis whines, sticking his hand down the back of Tad's briefs to follow the curve of his ass.

"I have a needy author for our first quarter issue," Tad says, not sounding happy about it. "She requires a lot of handholding."

"Isn't that what texting is for?"

Tad makes a noise that Lewis is pretty confident in identifying as *I tried and it didn't take*, and even though Tad is grabbing his phone, Lewis leaves his hand exactly where it is. He should've said he requires a lot of dick-holding.

When Tad picks up the phone, he says, "What the fuck does he want?"

Lewis catches a glimpse of the name on the screen as Tad answers: Walt.

The way Tad tenses is utterly mood-killing. Completely boner-deflating. It would be nice if Tad stayed where he was on Lewis's lap, but he slides off and hunches on the sofa, a thin strip of empty air between them. It's like his brother's in the room with them instead of a couple hundred miles away.

His fingers are white as they clutch the sides of the phone and he's pressing it to his ear so hard that Lewis isn't sure how he can actually hear his brother talking. Sound needs air to travel through, right? It looks like Tad's creating a vacuum between the phone and his ear drum.

"Yeah," Tad says, his other hand on his leg, fingers worrying at some small, otherwise invisible blemish on his skin. He keeps picking at it, and Lewis wants to tell him to stop, that he's going to make himself bleed—but he doesn't want the brother to hear him. Not that he thinks Tad's brother would think anything of a man being in Tad's apartment, but Tad would freak out.

"Um," Tad says. He's pulling on his leg hair now, and Lewis can't stand it. Silently, he puts his hand over Tad's. Tad stills but doesn't look at Lewis. But he stops picking at himself. Lewis will take it. "When?... I actually... no, I'm busy that weekend. I'm going to a wedding too, actually.... Yeah."

There's a pause and Tad's jaw clenches. "Why is that so hard to believe?"

Now a muscle is twitching just below Tad's temple. "Well, I do. Do you really think I'd make up that I'm going to a wedding just to get out of seeing you?" Another pause. Anger, then panic, then guilt flash across Tad's face in succession. "I did not! I couldn't leave New York for Christmas! I told Mom—*yes*, work! I know it's shocking to you, but I actually really *care* about my job, and—"

Lewis can hear a tinny voice on the phone, but he's only catching a word here and there—something something don't want something something home, just grow something something tell the truth—

"Did you just call to tell me what a horrible son I am? I'm pretty sure we covered that last time I saw you," Tad snaps.

The voice on the phone goes silent. Tad doesn't speak. Lewis just… sits there, arm outstretched, hand resting on top of Tad's, which is now fisted on his thigh. The skin of Tad's hand feels stretched thin enough over his knuckles to break.

Tad must shift the phone a little, because Lewis hears his brother's voice as he says, *"I just wanted to see if you wanted to hang out when I'm down there in a few weeks. If you think I just call you to fight, that's your problem."*

"Yeah well, like I said," Tad replies tightly, "I have a wedding to go to. So I probably won't have time to see you."

"Yeah. Okay. Maybe another time. Bye."

Even though Tad's brother hung up, Tad keeps holding the phone to his ear for another half a minute, staring into space. Lewis bites his lip and squeezes Tad's hand, trying to draw him back to the moment gently, without making him feel like he's doing something wrong.

"Babe?" he asks softly.

Finally, Tad drops the phone away from his ear, tossing it to the side. It bounces off the sofa and to the floor, but Tad makes no effort to retrieve it. Instead, he climbs back into Lewis's lap, shoves him back against the sofa, and kisses him bruisingly.

It's hot, no doubt about it—Tad wearing nearly nothing, grinding against him, kissing hard and demandingly, his mouth scorching and his tongue slick and wet as it opens Lewis's lips.

It's also not about him. Not after that call. And maybe they started in a place where they had sex to forget something shitty. For Lewis, it was his loneliness and his humiliation, and for Tad, it was his shyness and the way he didn't fit in with his brother and his brother's friends.

But that's not what they are anymore, at least Lewis doesn't think so, and he doesn't think it's his sappy, romantic heart lying to him about the fact that Tad doesn't think that's what they are, either. They aren't just a fling or convenient sex or a rebound. They're special. They have something. Lewis wants to be there for Tad, but he wants to make sure Tad knows he can be there in ways other than sex.

"Hey, hey, babe, slow down," Lewis murmurs, drawing back from Tad's urgent kiss. Tad's face is pale and he's breathing hard. Lewis smoothes a thumb over his collarbone and traces the line of his pec. "Hey," he says softly, cradling the back of Tad's head with his other hand.

"Your family is so perfect, and mine sucks so much," Tad finally says. Where Lewis expected anger, all he hears is weariness. "You're probably already tired of dealing with it."

Stroking the back of Tad's head, Lewis says, "I don't like how they make you feel. What it does to you when you talk to them." He wants to kiss away the tightness in Tad's jaw, in the tendons of his neck, which are taut, practically vibrating with stress. He wants to kiss all along Tad's freckly shoulders and rub away all his tension and worries and everything bad he's feeling.

He also kind of wants to hit Tad's brother, but that's probably a less healthy impulse. Not just because violence isn't the answer, blah blah blah, but also because Lewis is pretty sure he wouldn't come out ahead in a fight. The one time he tried to throw a punch (in high school, at some guys who were being dicks to his friend Lee, who was campy and refused to be any other way), it hurt so much he was convinced his hand was broken.

The tightness locking Tad up goes nowhere. If anything, it gets worse. Lewis massages his shoulders. "What do you need from me right now?"

"Your dick up my ass," Tad says bluntly.

Lewis remembers the night Tad drove back from Watertown, a crying mess who walked in the door and threw himself on Lewis. And he remembers the way they fucked, and this is definitely a pattern now, isn't it? Tad wants to fuck away his feelings. Lewis, though, Lewis likes to talk. He needs to talk things out. It drove his exes crazy. It will probably drive Tad crazy, too.

"You don't want to talk about it?" Lewis asks. When Tad just stares, Lewis adds, "I mean… maybe it would help to get it off your chest?"

"Talking about it is the last thing I want to do." Tad blows a hard breath out through his nose. "I just want to—I don't want to think about it." He puts his hand on Lewis's chest and rubs a slow circle around a nipple.

Lewis wants to do what will help Tad the most. But maybe Tad isn't right that this will help him? If he never talks about it, then none of it will ever get better. You can't just keep pushing everything down forever.

Also, he's like, really not turned on right now.

The hesitation doesn't go unnoticed. Tad's face shutters and he slides off Lewis's lap. "Okay, so, what do you want to do."

It's not even a question. Tad's voice has gone flat and it makes Lewis's stomach sink. He hates fighting, and he especially hates fighting with boyfriends. This isn't a fight yet, but it sure feels like it's headed that way. "It's not about what I want to do." Lewis tries to make his voice soothing. "It's about what you want to do. Whatever would make you feel better."

Tad folds his arms over his chest. "I told you want would make me feel better. You obviously don't want to."

"I didn't say I didn't want to."

"You didn't have to. I can take a hint." Tad disappears into the bedroom and when he returns, he's dressed in a sweatshirt and flannel pants. He flops down on the sofa, a good foot of empty space between them, and turns the TV on.

They've been watching one of those gay K-dramas and the next episode starts playing, but Lewis can't concentrate on it. Every ounce of his attention is fixated on the space between Tad and him. It feels like a physical presence, a yawning gulf that keeps getting wider. It feels like Tad's on the other side of the room, like there's a chasm growing between them and soon Tad will be unreachable.

And now Lewis's chest is tight, and he shoves his hands under his legs and tries to breathe mindfully. It doesn't help. His chest gets tighter. He can't breathe.

He forces himself to take deep breaths. In through the nose, hold for a few seconds, out through the mouth. Again. And again. His heart is jackhammering at his rib cage, the skin and bone and muscle feeling too flimsy to keep it where it's supposed to be. It doesn't matter how many anxiety attacks he has, he always thinks, *this is it. This is the time my heart explodes out of my chest.* Every time he holds his breath, his heart strains harder to break free.

The world narrows and blackens around him, so there's only the space he's occupying, and way over there, far away, on the other side of the gulf he just created, is Tad, who's unreachable. Lewis can feel the distance like a physical thing, and even though intellectually he knows Tad is close enough to touch, he also knows that if he reached out, his arm couldn't possibly stretch across the empty space.

Something warm touches his hand. "Lewis?"

Lewis opens his eyes—he didn't even realize they were closed—and can't make sense of what he's seeing. Tad is leaning close to him, his hand resting on Lewis's, and his lip is caught between his teeth so hard that the skin looks broken. "Lewis, hey. It's fine. It's okay."

There's a vise around Lewis's throat, but he tries to speak anyway. "No—it's not—I'm sorry. Making this about me."

"Oh Lew," Tad whispers, and he wraps his arms around Lewis, pulling their bodies together. "Breathe, sweetheart. Breathe."

This isn't right, this isn't right at *all*. Tad's the one who's in a bad place; he's not the one who should be comforting Lewis. It should be the other way around. But Tad *is* comforting him, and it's working, because gradually, breathing gets easier, and Lewis's heart doesn't feel like it's going to burst out of his chest like the xenomorph in *Alien*, and his brain's off-kilter perception of distance fades away until the room is normal-sized and Tad is holding him and the idea that there was any kind of insurmountable space between them seems like a hallucination.

Lewis buries his face in Tad's sweatshirt, breathing in the scent of laundry detergent and soap. "Fuck," he mumbles. "I'm so sorry. This is backwards."

Rubbing Lewis's back slowly, Tad says, "It's not backwards to help your boyfriend when he's having a panic attack."

"I shouldn't have a panic attack when you're the one who had something to deal with. *Fuck*." Lewis wants to cry, but that would make this even *more* about him, so he bites down on the inside of his cheek to stop the urge. "I fucked this up, and—Jesus. I'm sorry. Do you want me to go home and leave you alone?"

Tad presses a gentle kiss to Lewis's forehead. "No."

"Are you sure?"

Tad holds him tighter, his fingers combing through Lewis's hair. "Of course I'm sure."

"I'm sorry," Lewis mumbles, his mouth full of sweatshirt.

Fingers rub slow circles on the back of his neck. "You can stop saying you're sorry." Tad lets out a little laugh. "I like taking care of you, anyway. I don't usually feel like I'm very good at taking care of people."

There's something about Tad saying this that makes Lewis look up at him. "But that's not true. You've taken care of me since we met."

Tad's mouth twitches. "I definitely took care of you the night we met."

Despite the tightness in his chest, Lewis laughs. "You know what I mean."

Shaking his head, Tad says, "Not really. I don't take care of people. People take care of me." His smile gets bitter. "John said that was one of the reasons I wouldn't come out to my family. He said I couldn't stand the thought of them not taking care of me anymore."

"Fuck him," Lewis says.

Tad blinks.

So Lewis says it again. "Fuck him. Fuck your ex. John? What's his last name?"

"Um, Cooper?"

"Fuck John Cooper," Lewis says. Then, he leans back and yells at the top of his lungs, "FUCK JOHN COOPER!"

There's a banging from the ceiling, and someone shouts from the apartment above Tad's, "Fuck him yourself!"

Lewis and Tad meet each other's eyes and burst into undignified snorts and giggles. When they quiet, Tad says, "I have some baggage, if you haven't noticed."

"Same."

Is this the moment to tell Tad he loves him? Staring into his eyes that are the same blue as the water and the sky at Humboldt-Toiyabe, clear and bright, beautiful and endless?

Something loud and clearly climactic happens in the K-drama, which is still playing, and they both turn to look at the screen. "I have no idea what's happening," Lewis admits.

"Yeah, me either. We might need to start the episode over."

Lewis snuggles closer while Tad restarts the episode. Now isn't the right moment to say those three words to Tad. "I love yous" aren't for post-panic attack snuggling or nights where your family calls and makes you feel like shit. They aren't for starting episodes over because you were freaking out the first time it played. When Lewis tells Tad he loves him, it's going to be the right time. He's going to make his Grand Gesture, and it's going to be perfect.

Chapter Thirty-Five

ON THE morning of Stacy and Alang's wedding, Lewis's alarm goes off at 5:00 a.m.

He jolts halfway out of bed before he's fully awake, not remembering he's at Tad's apartment until he slams his foot into the radiator that's not near his bed at home, but is very much within toe-stubbing distance of Tad's if you leap out of bed like the smoke alarm just went off.

"*Fuck!* Shit shit goddammit ahhhhh oh my *god*," Lewis hisses, falling back on the bed. His elbow smacks something warm but hard, and there's a yelp of pain.

Fumbling for his phone to turn off his jangling alarm and turn on the flashlight, Lewis says, "Shit—sorry baby—did I just hit you?"

"Mmph," Tad replies. When Lewis swings the light toward him, Tad throws up a hand in front of his face. The other is clapped over his mouth.

"Oh my god, what did I do? Stacy's going to kill me if you have a split lip. Or OH GOD I didn't break a tooth, did I? Okay, it's fine, it's *fine*, totally fine, we'll just find an emergency dentist, they can put a cap on it, shit okay let me google it. This is New York! There's definitely probably like, hundreds of emergency dentists open on Saturday—"

Tad, his face scrunched into a half-awake squint, pushes Lewis's phone so the flashlight isn't shining directly into his eyes. Lowering his other hand from his mouth, he says, "I think it's fine."

He's poking at his lip and his teeth experimentally with his tongue, so Lewis scoots closer and holds the flashlight up to inspect the damage. Tad bats at him. "I'm fine! God, do you seriously think Stacy would care?"

Given the way Stacy has become increasingly reliant on iced coffee with ever-more-numerous extra shots of espresso in recent days, with the corresponding altered mood that comes with caffeine overdose and lack of sleep, Lewis is not at all confident that she wouldn't freak out about her maid-of-honor's plus one having a chipped tooth. He got up in the middle of the night to make sure some kind of freak cartoon violence accident hadn't befallen his tux and that it was still safely in its plastic sheath and hanging from the shower rod in the bathroom.

Lewis flexes his toe. If it's broken, he'll tape it. Hell, if the whole foot is broken, he'll tape it.

Rubbing his face, Tad says, "I can't believe y-y-you"—a huge yawn overtakes him—"managed to convince the NYBG to let you in this early to set up."

"I deal with lawyers all day. This was easy." He pulls on a pair of jeans and a sweatshirt. "Get some more sleep. Remember, don't leave Hetty alone in the same room as my tux, and if you have to use the bathroom—"

"I'm going to have to use the bathroom."

"Okay, right, if you *absolutely* have to, put my tux in a different room first."

"I will not splatter toothpaste or pee on your tux."

"Or anything else," Lewis says, hunting for socks.

"You realize I'm not looking for loopholes in a legally binding clause, right? Like I'm not going to spill bleach on it just because you didn't specify that I shouldn't."

Lewis freezes in horror. "Okay, that joke didn't land," Tad mutters. "I'll take good care of your tux. See you in a few hours."

By the time he arrives at the New York Botanical Garden, Lewis's anxiety has done all the prep and setup for the Myers-Tran wedding in his head about three dozen times. He readies Stacy's dressing room, directs the placement of the seating and the decorations for the ceremony (lots of red and gold to honor Alang's Vietnamese heritage, plus candles and incense placed in artful and non-fire-hazard spots around the room), and makes sure there's space for the musicians. Stacy forwards him an email from the lion dancers—all she wrote was I CAN'T HANDLE THIS PLEASE HELP. He breaks into a cold sweat but texts her, *I'll deal with it. Don't stress. Send me anything that comes up. This is your day!!!!*

She sends him back a string of heart emojis. Even if she wasn't up early to get ready for the tea and candle ceremony this morning, Lewis knows she'd be up. This is it—this is The Day. The Day they've both been dreaming of since they were little kids, raised on Disney movies and rom-coms. Every time the two of them staged their future wedding (if it was Lewis's wedding, he made Stacy pretend to be a boy), this was what they were preparing for.

Lewis deals with the lion dancers and the rest of his list of pre-wedding tasks, until it abruptly runs out. Work continues around him, but he's exhausted his usefulness for the moment.

His mind goes back to all those play weddings. When they were really young, they swore they'd have a double wedding. When they got a little older, when Lewis realized he was gay, Stacy swore she wouldn't get married until he could get married too. Through it all, there's been this... assumption? Feeling? That they'd get married around the same time, even if it wasn't a joint ceremony. Neither of them ever questioned that when one of them found love, the other would too.

And it kind of worked out that way. So, yeah. Just like they talked about.

It would be nice if Lewis could remember his own wedding.

He pushes that thought away. Today is about Stacy and Alang. His friends making it *official* official, standing up in front of their family and friends and swearing to love and take care of each other forever.

Did he swear that to Tad in Vegas?

Lewis tries to remember. Just like all the other times he's tried, it's a blank spot in his memory. He remembers bars, he remembers karaoke, he remembers sex. He can't remember the wedding.

Melancholy washes through him. His wedding was supposed to be the ultimate romantic moment. The final Grand Gesture. And it's just... gone.

The alarm he set for himself to wrap up his prep work goes off. Time to head back to Tad's place.

TAD LOOKS amazing in a suit.

It's three piece, dark green, and fits him perfectly, cut to accentuate those legs for days and his tight ass. The waistcoat hugs his slim torso and the jacket hangs perfectly, skimming along his ribs to his hips. The shirt he paired with it is white and the tie is brown and subtly patterned.

When Lewis tells him he looks amazing, Tad blushes and says, "There's cat hair on it."

"I had a bulk pack of lint rollers shipped to the venue," Lewis says. "It doesn't matter, though; you still look amazing." He crosses the room to hug Tad, burying his face in Tad's neck to inhale his cologne—spicy and masculine without being heavy, a hint of something floral brightening it.

Tad's warmth and scent and nearness is an oasis. "This is nice," Lewis mumbles. "I could stay like this for the rest of the day."

"C'mon, today's your big day."

"It's not, though," comes out of Lewis's mouth before he can stop it.

Tad gives Lewis a puzzled look. Yeah, that probably sounded mildly insane, considering the time he's been devoting to Stacy's wedding.

"Never mind," Lewis says. "I'm just…." Dozens of adjectives volunteer themselves to complete the sentence, but none are right.

Tad grabs his hands. "What's wrong?"

Lewis shakes his head. "I can't say it. I'm the worst best friend ever for even thinking it."

Tad's lips thin as he presses them together. "That's not possible. You're basically Stacy's wedding planner at this point. You got up at five in the morning and went to the Bronx to get stuff ready for the actual wedding planner!"

"That was just my job. That's what we promised we'd do for each other." He lets out a gusty sigh. "Which is exactly the problem."

The notch appears between Tad's eyebrows. "You don't think she'd do the same for you?"

"She'll never have the chance to," Lewis wills his voice to come out less miserably than it sounds in his head. "I already got married."

Horrifyingly, now that he started talking, he can't stop. "It's just, you know, I always dreamed about my wedding day. I have, like, thirty inspo boards on Pinterest for what my wedding could look like. It was supposed to be the most important day of my life. We can't even remember it. And even if we could, it's not much of a memory, probably. It definitely wasn't my dream to get married at a twenty-four-hour wedding chapel on the Vegas Strip."

When the word vomit stops, Lewis squeezes his eyes shut. He'd cover his face with his hands, but Tad is still holding them. "See? That's horrible. I'm jealous of Stacy, when I shouldn't be anything but overjoyed and supportive."

There's a silence. Tad's opinion of him probably just nosedived.

But Tad squeezes Lewis's hands. "You'd never act on any of that."

"No! God, no. Of course I wouldn't."

"Okay, so." Tad presses down on Lewis's knuckles and it's more steadying than it has any right to be. "All Stacy's going to see is everything you've done for her and what an amazing friend and maid of honor you've been." He pauses. "Why didn't she just call you man of honor?"

"Oh, that was a joke that we leaned into a little too hard." Lewis lets out a shaky laugh and meets Tad's eyes. "How do you do that?"

"Do what?"

"Calm me down. It's like you always know exactly what to say."

"I'm not doing anything special. I'm just... I don't know. Saying what seems right. It's... yeah. Not special."

God, he's so wrong. Tad is one in eight billion, and Lewis wishes so badly he could understand that.

With a self-effacing snort, Tad says, "You don't even need to be sad about not remembering your wedding. We're getting a divorce, so you can have the big wedding you want to have."

Something heavy rolls into the pit of Lewis's stomach and he says the first thing that comes into his head: "I was kind of thinking we wouldn't bother getting divorced."

It's definitely the wrong time to float this half-baked idea. But it's out there now, hanging between them. Tad's fingers seem to shrivel.

"Oh," Tad says. His Adam's apple jags. "Oh," he repeats. "So you just... I mean... you think... this is, like...."

This is excruciating. "We don't have to talk about this now!" Shit, too loud. Lewis takes a breath. "Sorry, I'm all over the place, I'm just saying stuff. I mean, I *have* been thinking it might be better to not get divorced, but—I shouldn't have brought it up now. I should stop talking about it. I *am* stopping. We can talk about it later. Not like, today later. But just sometime. Later."

Color has drained from Tad's face. His freckles are standing out starker against his skin. Lewis has a sick, crawling feeling about what that might mean, so he forces a too-hearty smile onto his face. "Anyway, we should probably get going."

"Right! Right, I just need to make sure Hetty has enough food and water."

Tad hurries from the room and Lewis tries not to read into it. It could be for anything, right? Sure, Hetty has plenty of food and water because Lewis refilled both when he got back earlier, but maybe Tad doesn't realize that. Or maybe it's just an outlet for what is surely a lot of seething social anxiety.

Yeah. It's probably one of those things.

His chest tightens. He fucked up and he's going to spiral, because of course he is.

Tad calls, "Do you want me to get a Lyft?"

"Yeah, thanks!" Lewis's voice comes out tight, so he closes his eyes and breathes deep. Tad's voice sounds normal. There's nothing to have an anxiety attack over. Tad knows Lewis is in a weird headspace right now, and he'll brush off what Lewis said.

This will be like the other week, when Lewis had a panic attack and Tad was steady and strong and pulled him out of it. Everything's fine.

Tad pokes his head back into the room. "The Lyft will be here in four minutes. You ready?"

He still seems spooked, but nowhere near the way he looked when Lewis said… what he said. "Yeah, I'm ready." Lewis glances at himself in the mirror one more time. He was so caught up in how fuckable Tad looks that he barely registered his own appearance. His three-piece tux is a smoky black paired with a dusty pink button-down. It's making his eyes pop, which isn't something he's used to thinking about his eyes. Brown eyes don't pop. And his hair looks like something richer than "brown"—mahogany or chestnut or something.

It's a good effect, all in all. He and Tad are going to make a striking couple.

A smile breaks out over his face and his jangling anxiety recedes. So does his ugly jealousy and bitterness about Stacy having what he never will. This is a great day. He's going to his best friend's wedding with his gorgeous boyfriend. It's a *happy* day. And dammit, Lewis is going to be happy.

Chapter Thirty-Six

TAD'S HANDS are sweating in the back of the Lyft. Three major things are competing to be Tad's Big Fear right now. His pulse keeps yo-yoing as he talks himself down and then remembers the other stuff waiting to duke it out in the Anxiety Thunderdome.

"Are you okay?" Lewis asks.

"Um." Tad isn't sure which thing he should choose. Big Scary Wedding? Maybe-We-Shouldn't-Get-Divorced? He lands on the one that's been giving him flop sweat and digestive issues since that phone call a few weeks ago. "I'm worried the wedding my brother's going to is at NYBG today."

Lewis looks relieved. "There are two other weddings going on at NYBG today, and the bigger one is out at the Stone Mill."

It's like golden light spills out of some non-denominational but benevolent heaven, accompanied by choirs of angels. "That's all the way on the other side of the gardens," Tad says.

Lewis nods. "And the wedding in the conservatory is super small *and* super gay. They were setting up as I was leaving. Your brother probably isn't one of five people invited to the wedding of two drag queens."

"Wait oh my god, which two drag queens?"

The relief on Lewis's face tips over into affection. "Is that the only thing that's bothering you?"

"Now I'm also bothered by the fact you're not telling me which two drag queens are getting married."

With a grin, Lewis says, "I don't know. The wedding planner just mentioned they met at Diva Royale while they were performing."

"Oh my goddddd," Tad groans. "Okay, you have very effectively distracted me from my anxiety, so well played."

It's not true, but Tad slaps an easy smile on his face and pretends like everything is okay. He's been pretending so much of his life—it's second nature.

It just sucks he has to pretend for Lewis. He hasn't ever had to do that before, and it feels like something rotting inside him.

This is the part of Tad that Lewis doesn't understand. The hiding. The pretending. This is the part of Tad that will inevitably disappoint Lewis, and Tad will just be another in a long line of men to let him down.

A hand squeezes Tad's heart; then hooks its claws into his lungs and crushes those too. Something that's half sob and half laugh crawls up his throat and lodges there, because that's where he keeps every choked-off word, every muffled sob, every stifled outburst, every smothered scream.

On that morning they woke up together in Vegas, Tad was already half in love with Lewis, and he wanted more than anything to be with him. Now that they're together, he's just waiting for it to slip away.

Tad thanks their driver when they get to the NYBG, and he smiles and tries not to freak out, and smiles some more. He'll just keep smiling and get through this day, and maybe everything will be better tomorrow when there aren't a million things going on and his brain isn't spinning out of control and telling him he's garbage at everything.

Since they're early, Tad finds a corner of the Garden Terrace Room where he won't be in the way. Lewis disappears to do his wedding duties. The room is already decorated—swags of organza drape from the ceiling in swoops of dusty rose and warm gray. Scattered unlit tea lights dot the room.

At the front of the room, where the officiant will stand with the bride, groom, and wedding party, there's a podium draped with red and gold, which doesn't go with the color scheme at all—but Lewis mentioned how red and gold are traditional colors in Vietnamese weddings.

When guests start arriving, Tad finds an unobtrusive seat off to the side. His stomach can't decide if it has butterflies or acid reflux when he thinks about Lewis in that tux. It's a fantasy to think Lewis will want to stay with him forever, but god, it's such a *nice* fantasy.

And then he feels ill, because Lewis will probably dump him, and they'll get divorced and be strangers again instead of husbands, and Lewis will meet a guy somewhere who won't let him down and or be a giant disappointment, and they'll get married and Lewis will have his gorgeous wedding and look absolutely beautiful in a tux and some other man will be kissing him and getting to wear his ring, and—

"Hey!"

Tad jumps as Lewis lands heavily in the chair next to him. He looks flushed and flustered and slightly at the end of his rope. Seeing that tugs something embedded deeply in Tad's center, and he smoothes Lewis's hair back.

"Here." He offers Lewis his pocket square. "Your tux doesn't have one."

"Thanks." Lewis dabs his forehead. "I shouldn't have gotten dressed until the wedding was about to start. I feel sweaty. I probably look sweaty—oh god do I smell?"

Obligingly, Tad takes a deep breath through his nose. He loves sweaty Lewis. It's one of his favorite smells in the world, the sharp, masculine scent of sweat. But yeah, probably not great for a wedding.

"You're clear," Tad says. "All I smell is your cologne." Which is sexy too.

That alleviates a little of the stress on Lewis's face, but not all of it. He probably won't be totally calm until they get home.

Not *home*. It's not like they live together.

"Ofelia was late," Lewis grates out. "Something about waiting for her boyfriend because he had to drive in from upstate. I finally got on the phone with her and told her to get her ass down here and that her boyfriend could get a cab."

Tad snorts. A third sexy thing—Lewis getting bossy. "Is the ceremony going to start late?" he asks.

"I think I instilled a sense of urgency in her," Lewis says aggrievedly. "So we should start on time. I just wanted to say hi."

"Hi," Tad says, smiling.

Lewis's eyes sweep over his face and linger on his mouth, and he smiles too. "Hi," he says softly before he leans forward and brushes his lips over Tad's. "Save a dance for me later?"

"I'll need a lot of alcohol to dance."

"That can be arranged." Lewis kisses him again just as gently. "Hey, listen—sorry for being so weird earlier. I've just been like, super stressed, and my filter is pretty much gone."

"It's okay. Don't worry about it."

Lewis looks relieved, like he wants to believe this and is going to grab at the chance to. Tad wants to believe it too.

"Okay." With one more kiss, Lewis says, "I better go make sure Ofelia's ready. Had to wait for her boyfriend! Seriously!"

With that, he rushes off again. His seat and the one next to it are taken by a young Asian couple. Tad shrinks into himself and hopes no one will want to talk to him.

No one does. He's pretty good at giving off *don't approach the weirdo* vibes.

The ceremony finally begins. Several older couples process down the aisle to a Sigur Rós song and take their seats at the front of the room. Next comes Alang, alone, and then the wedding party. Alang's groomspeople (there's a woman and a nonbinary person) walk slowly down the aisle with Stacy's bridesmaids. Tad only knows Ava.

Then comes the part Tad is secretly most looking forward to—Lewis walks down the aisle arm in arm with Alang's best man, a handsome Sikh man who's wearing a rose quartz turban.

Lewis looks… oh. Lewis. He's beaming. He looks so proud, and so happy, and so beautiful. He looks like he was born to walk down the aisle at a wedding.

The Sigur Rós song ends and Canon in D begins, played by a string quintet that includes a đàn nguyệt. Everyone stands with a scrape of chairs and cranes their heads to see Stacy walk down the aisle.

Her arm is looped through her father's, and she looks radiant. It's totally a cliché, but it's true. She's glowing. Her blond hair is in a messy updo and topped with several sparkling hairpins. The dress—ugh, chef's kiss. It's ivory, the gown layers of tulle and lace, off-the-shoulder sleeves draped over her upper arms, and a fitted bodice with delicate boning. Beads and pearls sparkle in the gown and the bodice. She looks like the fairy-tale princess that, by Lewis's account, she's always dreamed of being.

Tad's gaze drifts to Lewis. That huge, beaming smile is still on Lewis's face as he watches Stacy come down the aisle. As though he feels Tad watching him, his eyes find Tad's.

His smile changes. It gets—not wider, but *more*. Softer, and more intimate, more loving. That smile says a million things Lewis hasn't actually said, and it fills Tad with euphoria and terror. Imagine if he could be the guy worthy of walking down the aisle with Lewis, instead of the guy who drunkenly married him under fluorescent lights in some corny, run-down Las Vegas wedding chapel?

But he holds Lewis's gaze, because he has this for now, and he might as well take all the perfect moments and tuck them away for a time when he doesn't.

The ceremony is inclusive, nice, and short. At the end, Stacy and Alang kiss, and everyone stands and applauds as they process back up the aisle hand in hand.

Tad knows he should go through the receiving line, but every time he joins it, he has trouble getting a breath. After getting out of line three times, he gives up and drifts to the reception ballroom. Servers circulate with trays of hors d'oeuvres and the string quintet is playing instrumental arrangements of pop songs. "Blank Space" wafts through the room.

A head of brown hair makes its way through the crowd. Tad's heart lurches in happiness. Lewis. He reaches Tad's side and grabs his hand. "It was good, right? The ceremony? It was perfect?"

"Completely perfect." Tad squeezes Lewis's hand. "I could *not* keep my eyes off the maid of honor. What a hottie. Do you think he's single?"

Lewis slips a hand onto Tad's hip. "He's actually not single at all. He happens to have a boyfriend who's super incredible and super gorgeous. The whole package."

Tad squirms at the praise, his face getting warm, and pulls Lewis into a quick hug. He lets go before it can turn into more than a fleeting embrace but keeps his hand in Lewis's. "Sure, the whole package, who's currently worrying about what table he's at for the reception."

"Oh, you're with all the other plus ones of the wedding party!" Lewis gives his hand a reassuring squeeze. "You and Elise can commiserate about how this is the last place you want to be."

"It's not the last place…." Tad trails off at Lewis's knowing smile. Clearing his throat, he says, "Do you know the other people?"

"Not really. I met Ofelia's boyfriend once. But who knows if he ever made it."

Lewis snags a peanut satay from a passing server and offers Tad a bite. Tad leans forward, but then he hears an incredulous, "Tad?!"

Every muscle in Tad's body locks. That was—that sounded like— but it can't be. Walt can't be here—

Everything Lewis said in the Lyft about how unlikely it is for Tad and Walt to run into each other today floods his mind. And Lewis was right. Whatever wedding Walt is at today can't possibly intersect with this one.

He misheard. Obviously! That wasn't his brother's voice calling his name.

"Tad! Yo! Thaddeus Pierce!"

"Oh," Lewis says flatly. "It's Ofelia's late boyfriend." Confusion flashes over his face. "Wait. You know Ofelia's boyfriend?"

Oh god. Oh god oh god oh god this cannot be happening.

A hand slaps down on his shoulder and spins him. Tad drops Lewis's hand like it's one of those poisonous frogs that lives in the Amazon.

Walt's face a mixture of surprise, befuddlement, and happiness. A petite Latinx woman is at his side.

"Hey Ofelia," Lewis says. "Hey—Walt, right? Glad you made it."

"He missed the ceremony," Ofelia says.

Walt's hand is still on Tad's shoulder. It weighs a thousand pounds. "Yeah, traffic—I don't know how you stand living here—"

"Um, it's called leaving enough time," Ofelia shoots back. She doesn't sound playful. Tad hopes maybe he'll disappear if they keep talking.

But no—no. Obviously not, because Walt, *his brother, Walt,* is here.

"You didn't mention you were going to be at *this* wedding," Tad manages without sounding too strangled.

"Well, I don't think you know everyone in New York," Walt says. "Small world, though! Are you friends with Alang?"

Tad makes a gurgling sound.

"Oh my god, Walt!" Ofelia beams. "Tad's the guy Lewis married in Vegas!"

Walt looks even more confused. Tad considers running out the door and disappearing into the NYBG, possibly never to be seen again. Once in a while school groups will catch sight of a feral queer running through the gardens. He'll be a homegrown cryptid.

Even though there's no saving this, Tad looks to Lewis—who looks even more confused than Walt—until realization clicks on his face.

He gets it.

Dimly, Tad registers that Lewis has met Walt. If Tad had shown Lewis a photo, *one photo* of his brother, this situation could have been avoided.

"I think Stacy needs me!" Lewis practically yells, reaching for Tad.

Ofelia looks crestfallen. "Okay—but you have to tell Walt later about how you and Tad were grinding on the mechanical bull! It's adorable you're still together. What happened to the divorce stuff? Oh my god, are you going to stay married? That's so cute!"

Tad knows he's just one small, insignificant person at this wedding. No one is paying attention to this conversation, and no one sees how all the air leaves Tad's lungs. No one feels how the Earth stops spinning in just this one pocket of space.

It would actually be funny if it wasn't such a complete fucking disaster. Walt looks so flummoxed. Like he knows he's missing something, and he's putting the pieces together, but they don't fit. Of course they don't fit, because he's putting the wrong ends together. If he'd look at things the way they are instead of the way he thinks they should be, he could snap everything into place.

Walt's eyes are locked on Tad. His confusion dribbles away. "Stacy's bachelorette party was the same weekend I was in Vegas," he says, but he's not looking at Ofelia. "With Tad."

Now Ofelia looks like she's putting puzzle pieces together. Her mouth drops open, but she looks delighted. She's completely unaware she's lobbed a grenade into the middle of Tad's family. "This is your brother?"

She sounds thrilled. How can she sound thrilled? How can she be so bad at reading the room?

"Tad, come with me." Lewis's voice is pleading.

"Tad?" Walt sounds unsure. "What the hell is going on? What does Lia mean about you gr—about a mechanical bull?"

Finally, Ofelia realizes something is amiss. "Did… I say something wrong?"

The idea of sticking around for the answer is enough to rot a hole through Tad's stomach. There's nothing he can do but turn away from Ofelia and Walt, from Lewis, and beeline for the door.

He thinks he bumps into a few people. He thinks he hears someone call his name.

He doesn't stop running.

Chapter Thirty-Seven

"TAD!" LEWIS yells. Tad doesn't turn around, disappearing through a doorway. Lewis takes a couple steps in that direction before he whirls to face Ofelia and Walt.

"What the fuck, Ofelia?" he bites out, remembering to keep his voice low at the last minute. It's his job to make sure nothing goes wrong at this wedding—he can't *be* the thing going wrong.

"I don't even know what's happening!"

"You—" Lewis stops and breathes. Tries to breathe. His chest is getting tight, and this is not the time to have a panic attack.

"Tad's *gay?*" Walt asks.

Oh right. Walt's still here.

"That's really not something for me to share," Lewis says, grasping for politeness.

Walt gives him an incredulous look. "Lia just said you're married. And all that stuff about... um, the mechanical bull. Oh my god. Is that a euphemism?"

Yeeeeah, cat might be out of the bag re: Tad's sexual orientation. "No, it was an actual mechanical bull," Lewis says, passing straight through mortification into some kind of post-embarrassment state.

"Gay," Walt says like it's the most insane thing he's ever heard. Lewis gets ready to stand up to a homophobe. Well, if he's going to make a scene at Stacy's wedding, at least she'll approve.

"Wait, you didn't know?" Ofelia asks. She sounds horrified. "Oh. Oh no. Oh my god. I didn't—I had no idea. Oh my god. Why didn't you tell me your brother was going to be here, Walt?"

Slowly, Walt shakes his head. It's like he didn't hear a word Ofelia said. Lewis opens his mouth to tell him where to stick his fragile masculinity if the idea of two men having sex is going to make him swoon in horror, but then Walt says, "Why wouldn't he tell me he's gay?"

There's no horror or disgust in his voice. He sounds... hurt?

"I think that's something you should talk to Tad about," Lewis says.

"Did he think I wouldn't accept him?"

Ofelia's hands are over her mouth. "I didn't mean...." But she trails off and instead asks Walt again, "Why didn't you say he'd be here?"

"I didn't *know!*" Walt sounds frantic. "We don't... talk much. He.... Tad, he's...."

Whatever he's going to say dies. Yeah. They don't talk much. Because Tad never felt like he could tell his family he's gay. Because he thinks their love is conditional on him being someone he's not.

Now Tad is freaking out and he's *alone*. Walt can deal with the shit he clearly needs to deal with. Ofelia can process that she just walked into a minefield. The two of them can figure out what that means for their relationship on their own.

Lewis needs to find his husband.

THE WEDDING planner points Lewis in the right direction, because she saw Tad rush outside. Lewis stumbles out into a bright, cold winter day. Where could he have gone? Parking lot? Main gate?

Lewis calls Tad and paces, shivering, as it rings and rings. Nothing. He takes off for the Haupt Conservatory. Tad talked about how much he loves it when they went camping, which—god, seems forever ago. It seems like a different life, a Tad-less life, and Lewis doesn't want to return to that.

Despite the cold, he works up a sweat by the time he gets to the conservatory. A blast of warm, humid air hits him first, and then a riot of color, lush greens and bright, tropical flowers. Visitors mill around, but Lewis's eyes are drawn straight to a lone figure on a bench.

Breathing heavily, Lewis approaches Tad and sits beside him. Their legs touch and Tad startles, his head whipping up to stare at Lewis with wide eyes. "It's just me," Lewis says, trying to sound soothing.

Tad's shoulders heave. His eyes are wet and his eyelashes are dark with tears, sticking together in clumps. His nose is red, and tears have left tracks down his cheeks. Lewis reaches for him but Tad scoots away.

"Did he come too?" Tad asks hoarsely.

"Walt? No. I left him and Ofelia."

A piece of Tad's hair has come loose and is falling into his eyes. He brushes it back with a badly shaking hand, and Lewis's stomach hurts with the desperate need to make this better.

"Hey—baby—" Lewis puts a hand on Tad's shoulder, only for Tad to jerk away again. "Baby, it's gonna be okay."

"You don't know that." Tad's voice hitches in a sob.

"I don't think your brother—I mean, I got the impression that mostly Walt's sad you never told him, but you being gay—that doesn't bother him." When Tad shuts his eyes tightly, Lewis adds, "Not that he has any right to be sad you never told him."

Tad sniffles. Tears leak from his closed eyes. "I can't do this."

The ache in Lewis's chest makes him reach for Tad's hand again before he remembers Tad doesn't want to be touched. "I'll be with you. However you need me, I'm going to be with you. We're in this together."

Tad's eyes are still closed, and he shakes his head hard. "No. I m-mean—I can't—I'm bad, and I can't—I can't. I can't be someone who just ends up d-disappointing you."

"You've never disappointed me," Lewis says fervently. His whole body hurts. He wants to make this better. "I can't even imagine you disappointing me—"

"Of course I'll disappoint you!" Several people look their way and Tad shrivels, hunching his shoulders and hugging his arms around himself. Tears slide down his face. "I'm n-not some perfect rom-com guy. I'm a complete shitshow, and—and all this shit, me not being out to my family, you having to pretend to just be my friend, you say it doesn't matter to you—"

"It doesn't!"

"It doesn't now." The words sound like they're being pried from Tad. He finally opens his eyes. They're agonized. "But it will, and then I'm just going to be another disappointing guy! And you want to just stay married, but you barely know me! You don't know how much I'm— I'm—just *poison.* I'm poison, and you should be with someone good, someone who's not going to let you down, and—"

The hiccuping sobs fall away. Tad sounds empty. "I can't, Lewis. I can't."

"Tad—"

"I'm too much of a mess." He doesn't bother to wipe his tears away. "You'll hate me in the end."

He could never hate Tad. The stuff with his family isn't ideal, but it's not insurmountable. They'll figure it out together. That's what couples do.

Before Lewis can say any of that, Tad's on his feet. The sun behind his head, shining through the glass ceiling of the conservatory, makes a copper halo of his hair. "I can't, Lewis," he says again. Its finality jolts Lewis to his core.

His chest tightens. Instinctively, he looks to Tad for stability, because Tad's been there for him since they met. When anxiety takes hold of Lewis, Tad's there to lean on, to steady him, to help him breathe.

But the way Tad can't look at him, the way he's crying, it's making it so much harder for Lewis to breathe. Tad backs away, and Lewis's throat feels like it might close up. He can't get a breath, and cold sweat suddenly coats his back. His stomach plummets, a dank, sick, leaden weight.

"I think—maybe we shouldn't—" Tad stops and swallows several times. "I think maybe you should just sign the divorce paperwork and send it in. And I'll—I'll see you at the divorce hearing."

"You're breaking up with me," Lewis says, the effort leaving him breathless.

"I have to," Tad whispers.

Lewis knows what to do. He knows how to fix it. If he'd already done this, Tad wouldn't even be saying these things, because he'd understand how Lewis feels and how he's at the center of everything now. How he made Lewis believe in love again. How special he is, and how Lewis wants to be with him forever.

"I love you," Lewis says.

Tad doesn't say anything. That's good, isn't it? That has to be good.

"Don't," Tad says.

And he walks away.

Chapter Thirty-Eight

TAD KNOWS he should turn off his phone.

He's glued to it, though—watching texts and calls roll in. Lewis. Walt. Ava. Lewis. Even Alang and Stacy.

Lewis.

Lewis's texts continue past midnight. Tad doesn't read them, exactly, but it's also hard not to read them when he looks at his lit-up phone screen. *Please can we talk* Lewis keeps begging. *Please.*

The word starts to look weird to him. Plllease. Puh-lease.

At 1:07, he goes to bed. Hetty settles on his stomach, a warm, furry weight. He pets her and she's the only thing that keeps him from sobbing.

What if he ruined Stacy and Alang's wedding?

His stomach churns, bile climbing his throat. Maybe he should apologize. But fuck, no, it's their wedding night, and if he ruined the wedding, they don't need to deal with him begging for forgiveness and being a needy asshole.

Plus, if he looks at his phone, he'll see Lewis's messages. He'll listen to the voicemails. There are at least five.

His throat aches and his back gets tight, a spot dead center between his shoulder blades, and he really needs to roll over onto his side but he can't because Hetty is still sitting on him, but if he could just move at least he could make his back stop hurting.

"Sorry, Hets," he whispers, gently pulling her off him so he can roll onto his side. Maybe she'll let him cuddle her.

She remains in the circle of his arms and he hugs her, burying his face in her soft fur. After a minute, she stands up, sniffs his face, and wanders across the bed. She sniffs Lewis's pillow and looks at Tad.

Oh god. His cat is mad at him because his boyfriend isn't here. Ex-boyfriend. Because Tad is the worst.

Nervous energy thrums through him. He's not even tired. Why is he in bed?

He paces back to the living room. Turns on Netflix. The show he and Lewis were watching pops up with Netflix's cheery offer to keep watching, so he turns off Netflix. Refills Hetty's food dish, which confuses her. Checks his plants. Finds some brown tips on the leaves of his newest spider plant.

With the kind of zeal only sleeplessness brings, he trims the brown tips off. Then he pokes the soil. Could it be pot bound? Should he repot it?

Yes! Yes, he should definitely do that.

He covers the table with the old sheet he uses for repotting and transplanting, hauls out a bag of potting soil, finds a good-sized pot, and gets to work.

The spider plant isn't actually pot bound, but the familiar rhythm of repotting soothes him. When it's newly homed and back in its spot, Tad cleans up meticulously.

Now it's 2:23. Tad goes back to the sofa and looks at the notifications on his phone. The most recent is a text from Lewis from seventeen minutes ago.

Madonna or kylie?

Tad's stomach clenches and he sinks to the sofa. Oh god. Oh fuck. Oh, he messed up, didn't he? He replaced one horrible thing with another, but it doesn't mean the first horrible thing is going to go away. He panicked. All he saw was a repeat of John, who loved him and grew increasingly disappointed. And he loves Lewis so much, he can't bear for Lewis to ever look at him the way John did at the end.

But, his brain offers tentatively, *is it worth throwing everything away because of something that* might *happen?*

Tad doesn't have a good answer to that.

No, he does. It's not worth throwing away what he has with Lewis because his last relationship crumbled under the inexorable weight of two people who weren't right for each other. Lewis isn't John.

Fuck. Fuck fuck fuck he fucked up so badly. Oh god. What was he thinking?

He forces himself to confront what happened at the wedding and it's like something he watched instead of experienced. He knows Walt was there, and he knows Ofelia outed him. He knows he bolted, but he can't really remember doing it?

And then—Lewis was there, but Tad's brain was air raid sirens and jackhammers on concrete, screaming at him like he was prey on the savanna and the lions were closing in. His instinct when confronted with danger has always been to run and hide, to shut himself off in the most extreme way he can because that way the scary thing can't get him.

Lewis wasn't the scary thing. Tad just panicked. He panicked and ran from the man he loves, who loves him back.

Maybe Lewis doesn't love him anymore.

His phone buzzes with a notification from one of his games, but the lit screen draws his eye to Lewis's text. **Madonna or kylie?**

Slowly, Tad picks up the phone. His notifications are a mess. He's never had this many texts in his entire life. The thought of reading them is overwhelming. What if they're bad? What if everyone is telling him how horrible he is?

Hetty jumps up next to him and rubs her face against the corner of his phone. It yanks him out of his spiral, and he strokes her head. "Hi, honey," he murmurs. "I know this isn't normal. Sorry, sweetie."

She blinks slowly and he almost starts crying. Even if no one in the world loves him, Hetty does. Maybe that's stupid to a lot of people, but it means everything right now.

Tad's finger hovers over his messages. He breaks out in a cold sweat. He can't read them. They'll be horrible. Why wouldn't Lewis take back his *I love you*?

Except his finger slips, and Lewis's texts fill the screen.

His stomach lurches sickeningly. God he's going to vomit. Except... he can be brave, right? He wasn't brave earlier, but he could be. Walt found out he's gay, and the world didn't end, even though it felt like it at the time.

The first text from Lewis must have been sent immediately after Tad ran away: **Please call me back, I didn't mean to freak you out**

Which isn't so bad. Tad keeps reading.

Please can we talk
Please Tad, I really want to talk to you. Please can we not leave stuff this way
I'm so sorry
Tried calling you again but it went to voicemail
Please Tad can we just talk

I've been thinking about it and I've been an ass about the divorce stuff and not sticking to our original plan. We agreed on something and instead of talking to you about doing something different I just kind of did what I wanted to do. You're right that maybe I got in my head that we had this like, perfect fairy-tale romance, and that's a lot for someone to live up to. And that wasn't fqir of me

*Fair

Maybe we can talk tomorrow

On the phone

You don;t have to see me if you don't want to

Bt I really wANt tp see u

Srry I am drink

I am drink

Drunk

I miss you

Like a lot

The dj is playing I wanna dance with somebody and I want to dance with you

Remeber when I almost fell down the mountain when we were camping and you saved me? Thats how you and me are. Like I was all noooo I'm going to be alone forever and love is dead but then I met you and you cuaght me so ii didn't falll

But actually I did fall so yeah

*In love

Blahhhh sorry fr spamming you

Hey now the dj is playing love at first sight. Kylie!! Brings me back

Now express yourself. Madonna

Madonna or kylie?

Something tickles Tad's face and he puts his fingers to his cheek. They come away wet. He's crying.

How could he be so stupid? How could he walk away from Lewis? How can he make this better? Once Lewis sobers up, will he want to talk to Tad? Maybe he'll see these texts in the cold, hungover light of day and regret sending every single one. Maybe he won't even remember sending them.

But maybe he *will* remember—and maybe he won't regret.

Before he chickens out, Tad sends one text. If Lewis regrets all his messages, he'll either tell Tad to fuck off or just never respond.

Can't choose between Madonna and Kylie. I would have danced to both with you

TAD WAKES up when Hetty yowls in his face. He starts violently and topples off the sofa, where he apparently passed out.

Hetty stares down at him from her perch on the sofa, clearly wondering what he's doing on the floor along with when the hell he's going to feed her.

His stomach feels like battery acid has spent the last six hours eating a hole through it. His mouth is cottony and foul-tasting. He rubs his face and pushes himself up with his other hand, looking for his phone to check the time. Based on the way he feels, it's five in the morning, but based on the way light is slanting through the windows, it's definitely later.

His phone is MIA and Hetty is now swiping at his face with a paw. "Okay," he groans, his entire body protesting as he climbs agonizingly to his feet. Note to self: don't fall asleep slumped against the arm of the sofa.

Hetty trots after him as he trudges into the kitchen, twining around his ankles like she's trying to murder him and collect on the life insurance. "Except I don't have any, so joke's on you," he informs her.

"Mrow," she replies, and he pets her.

The microwave clock says it's 7:35. As he prepares Hetty's canned food, he tries to math how many hours of sleep he got, until he realizes he doesn't know what time he passed out.

Has Lewis seen his text? If he drank a lot, he'll probably sleep in.

For a minute, Tad just stands in the kitchen staring vacantly. Caffeine. That's what he needs. That will help, because it helps everything. While the water boils for tea, he conducts a more thorough search for his phone and finds it between the sofa cushions. A quick scan of his notifications shows nothing from Lewis, but he does have one text.

It's from Walt. **Are you around today? I really need to talk to you. Let me know pls**

Tad feels too wrung out and sick for the panic attack that text would usually cause. A flare of fear and anxiety cramps his stomach, but more than anything, there's an overriding sense of *fuck it*.

Fuck it, Walt already knows. Fuck it, let him say what he's going to say. Fuck it, let his family disown him. He feels like complete and utter garbage right now, a human pile of rotting trash, and Walt can't make it worse. Does throwing more trash in the landfill make the landfill worse? No. It's already full of trash.

I'm home, he sends back. *Text when you get here. Or just come up. Whatever*

Tad is halfway through his second mug of Lady Grey when Walt texts that he's outside. He must have jumped in his car the second Tad said to come over.

The knock on the door sounds more like a jail cell clanging shut. Hetty slinks away. Normally Tad's okay with her shyness, but right now he wishes she'd stick around, because he could use the moral support.

Feeling like he's walking to his doom, Tad opens the door.

His brother is twisting his hands together in front of his hips. Swallowing hard, Tad backs up, then curses himself for acting cornered in his own home.

Walt carefully shuts the door behind himself. He looks like he didn't sleep much last night, either. Dark purple bags shadow his eyes. His red hair is messy and greasy, the way Tad's gets when he can't stop nervously running his hands through it.

But he doesn't speak. The silence gets thicker and heavier until Tad feels like he's suffocating. "Now that you're in the same room as me, you can't pick the perfect homophobic slur?" Tad asks, his voice shards of glass. "FYI, we reclaimed queer and faggot."

The exhaustion lines in Walt's face deepen. He takes a step forward, then back. He bends to remove his shoes and lines them up with Tad's—and fuck, Lewis's Pride Chucks. Tad's chest aches.

Walt takes a couple more steps into the room, still maintaining a healthy distance from Tad. Probably doesn't want gay cooties.

Walt blinks quickly, like he's trying to stop himself from crying. Which can't be right, because Tad hasn't ever seen his brother cry. Slowly, deliberately, Walt says, "I'm sorry I made you feel like you couldn't tell me."

Tad stares.

It doesn't seem like Walt expected him to say anything, because he keeps going. "I'm sorry I didn't make you feel safe enough to tell me." He closes his eyes and when he opens them, there are tears.

That's the moment Tad realizes maybe he was really wrong about how this is going to go.

"I'm sorry I made you feel *un*safe," Walt says. "Fuck. Tad. I'm just—I know I can stand here and say I don't have a problem with gay people, and I have friends who are gay—"

Okay, that's news to Tad.

"—or I can say when I've said stuff it wasn't because I was homophobic, it's just because I was stupid—" Walt fists his hands. "But I know... I *know*... it doesn't really matter. Because I said it. And I can't unsay all that stuff. But I'm so sorry. I'm just—I'm so fucking sorry, Tad. I'm sorry for being stupid and for being a shitty brother."

Tad has to sit down.

A minute goes by while the two of them stare at each other. Walt stays where he is, standing a few paces in front of the door in his socks and knockoff North Face puffer vest. His hands are still fisted, his knuckles are white, and if this was twenty-four hours ago, Tad would assume Walt wanted to punch something. Probably him, for being gay.

The weight of how badly he misjudged Walt crushes all the air from his lungs for a good ninety seconds. He stands up. His legs are shaking, though, so he has to sit back down.

Finally, he says, "I thought you'd beat me up."

Which is totally not even true, not anymore. When he was a kid, sure. Thirteen years old and panicking over the fact he got a boner when Daniel Craig walked out of the water all shirtless and dripping in *Casino Royale*? No doubt in his mind that Walt would beat the shit out of him if he found out.

Walt looks at the floor. His shoulders rise and fall with several deep breaths before he says in an agonized voice, "I can't say that's never been true."

The honesty is what finally cracks the sick layer of ice slicked over this conversation. Tad pulls his knees up and hugs his legs to his chest. "You want to sit down?"

Walt nods and crosses the room to sit next to Tad. His eyes roam the apartment like he's seeing it for the first time. He's hardly spent any time here, and Tad's collection of plants is always growing.

"I remember coming here once and you only had about a third the number of plants. This is"—Tad braces for Walt to say something insulting—"kind of incredible. Is it hard to take care of all of them?"

Tad tries to decide if he should call out the subject change. Maybe this conversation needs to be approached in manageable chunks, though. "It's a lot of work, but once you know what you're doing, it's not hard."

Walt nods slowly. "I suck at taking care of stuff, so it would probably be hard for me. I'd kill a plant if I had any."

"Walt." Tad turns faces his brother, keeping his knees hugged to his chest. The movement looks stupid, but he doesn't care. He's in his pajamas and his hair hasn't been washed since yesterday. He already looks stupid. "You really don't care that I'm gay?"

"No," Walt answers so reflexively that Tad knows it's true. Then, he grimaces. "I mean—sorry. Shit. I—last night—fuck, I'm screwing this up. I knew I would." He scrubs at his face with a hand. "It's not a thing for me to care about. You know? You're my brother. The only thing I care about is that you're okay."

A lump rises in Tad's throat and his eyes sting. "I just… I thought you'd care," he whispers.

Tentatively, Walt squeezes Tad's shoulder. "I was a stupid asshole in high school. Well, I'm still a stupid asshole. But I don't care who you sleep with or who you're attracted to or whatever."

Tad feels some of his tension dribble away. A lifetime's worth of tension, of thinking his brother would hate him if he knew who Tad really is. One conversation can't wipe all of it out. But there's pain in Walt's eyes that can't be anything but genuine.

So yeah, it's going to take more than one conversation. But it sure as hell is a start.

"Are you going to tell Mom and Dad?" Tad asks.

"No!" Walt says vehemently.

The tension creeps back. "Because you think they won't take it well."

"Because it's not my place to tell them," Walt says, his tone edged with the tiniest suggestion that Tad's very stupid for not grasping this. He hesitates. "But. I don't know. They might not be great."

"Thanks for the vote of confidence." Tad shifts, sitting cross-legged instead of his knees-to-the-chest, functional-fetal-position pose. With his shoulders straightened, he can breathe better.

Walt smiles hesitantly. "Was that some Tad sarcasm? Are we good?"

"Did you just imply sarcasm is my love language?"

"Isn't it?"

With a hand to his forehead, Tad laughs, and it's not even that hysterical. "God. I've spent so much time dreading this moment."

"Yeah." Walt looks pained. "I… yeah."

Super articulate. But maybe that's something they both have in common—they can't spit out what they mean when they get nervous. It's been a pretty long time since Tad looked for things he has in common with his brother.

"We're good," he says. "Even if, you know. It takes me a while to be totally good."

"I get it."

Tad flops back, letting out an explosive breath. "So how the hell did you end up dating Ofelia?"

Walt laughs, loud and startled. "It started in Vegas, weirdly. We matched on Tinder a couple days before the trip, and she DMed me to say hi. She was visiting her family, that's the only reason we matched— she's from Carthage, did you know that?"

"I don't know her, really." Tad rubs at the knobby part of his wrist. "I mean, I guess I technically met her in, um, Vegas. But I don't really remember."

There's a look on Walt's face that clearly says *we're coming back to this*, but he goes on, "Anyway, we were chatting, mostly about home. I just started naming stuff from the area and she got a kick out of it, I don't know. I liked talking to her, but she lived so far away. Then we went to Vegas and I figured that would be it, but she messaged me and it said she was only like half a mile away."

"Wow," Tad says. Lewis would love this story. This is exactly the kind of fairy-tale stuff he goes nuts for. His stomach hurts when he realizes he might never be able to tell Lewis about it.

"Yeah, right?" Walt shakes his head. "We figured it was so crazy that we should at least go on one date."

"People use Tinder to date?"

Walt snorts. "Okay, yeah, I know I talk a big game, but I'm not really a hookup guy. So… yeah. I do, at least." He faces Tad. "Tell me about Lewis."

Maybe it would have been better if Walt was uncomfortable with Tad being gay so he wouldn't have to talk about Lewis. The idea of talking about him is physically painful. He looks at his hand, where his wedding ring gleams in the early morning light. At this point, it would feel wrong to not wear it.

"Well," Tad starts, "I broke up with him."

"Yeah, he kind of said something about that." Walt holds up his hands when Tad glares. "It was a lot for me, okay? I found out that not only is my little brother gay, but he's also married—"

"Basically a technicality," Tad mutters.

"You wouldn't be with him if it was just a technicality," Walt says.

"I'm not with him. I dumped him." Like an idiot.

Walt clears his throat. "It was a lot. And I met Lewis at Stacy and Alang's Friendsgiving thing, so he was the only person I felt like I could talk to, I guess. He was *pissed* at me. Asked me if I have any idea how shitty I make you feel." He hesitates. "We talked for a long time. Not about you, really"—good, because Tad was about to get indignant—"but just about, like... how I can be a better brother. And support you. And stuff."

Tad can't help a tiny snicker. "So when's the PFLAG presentation?"

"Ha, ha. Asshole." Walt punches Tad lightly on the shoulder and Tad sticks his tongue out. "He told me some websites that might help. I guess his mom works at a LGBT youth center? So he knows a lot about this stuff."

"He does," Tad says proudly, even though maybe he doesn't have a right to be proud of Lewis anymore.

Walt gives him a serious look. "Tad, that guy's crazy about you. You know that, right?"

All the light seems to flee the room and Tad's stomach twists. "Maybe he was before I freaked out and broke up with him."

"You should talk to him, I think," Walt says gently. "I'm pretty sure he's still crazy about you."

"Are you the expert on gay relationships now?"

"I thought love was love?"

"Ugh, *yeah*, fine."

Looking thoughtful, Walt asks, "Or maybe you wanted to break up with him anyway?"

"No," Tad mumbles. "No, I... that was stupid. I shouldn't have done that." He covers his face with his hands. "Oh my god, is this what siblings do? Do siblings normally talk about their relationships with each other?"

"Probably depends on the siblings." There's a pause. "Do you want to be?"

"Do *you?*"

"Well, it would be kind of nice to be part of your life again. Like when we were kids. I miss that."

Tad drops his hands to his lap. Walt is squirming and turning red. This is surreal. Tad's spent the last fifteen years hiding his sexuality and here his brother is, saying he wants to talk boys?

Tad takes a deep breath. "I need to apologize to him. I really… I mean… oh my god, this is awkward."

Okay, and now Walt looks like he's enjoying this. "Do you loooove him, Tad?" When Tad flushes, the grin drops off Walt's face. "Oh shit. You do. Oh. Hey, Tad. It's okay."

Which is when Tad realizes he's gone from embarrassment to crying in the space of thirty seconds. "I really, really fucked up, Walt," he sniffles. "I got all in my own stupid head, and I thought it would be like John again—um, John's my ex who I dated for like three years"—Walt looks flummoxed and sad—"and I just freaked out and thought you'd hate me for being gay, and you'd tell Mom and Dad and they'd hate me too, and Lewis would have to deal with me being a huge mess and he'd hate me eventually because he's like this huge romantic and I'm like the furthest thing from a fairy-tale prince but oh my god I was *so happy* with him—"

"Whoa, whoa, okay, slow down!" Walt puts his hands on Tad's shoulders. It forces Tad to find some ground that isn't spinning out of control. "So we'll get you back together with him. That's what you want?"

"Yeah," Tad whispers. Then, louder, "Wait, what do you mean, we?"

Walt pats Tad's shoulder. "I was there at the beginning of this relationship, so I feel like it's only right I help you get the guy. Again."

"Um, you were very explicitly *not* there at the beginning. I purposefully ditched you and your bro friends."

Walt guffaws. "Okay, but I'm still taking some credit. I drove you into his arms. Now that I'm thinking about it, I probably should've guessed you're not straight when you put that shimmery thing on that night. Wasn't it see-through?"

"That probably shouldn't have been your first clue." If you'd told Tad twenty-four hours ago he was going to be joking about his queerness and plotting to get his boyfriend back with his brother, he would have thought he was having a psychotic break.

The amused expression on Walt's face turns to scheming. "Did you say he's romantic?" Tad nods, and Walt says, "So he'd definitely appreciate a Grand Gesture."

The surprises keep coming today. Who knew Walt had any awareness of romance tropes? "Yeah," Tad says. "Probably."

There's a gleam in Walt's eyes. "Does he like rom-coms?"

A spark catches in Tad's heart. "Like? Try *love*."

Walt grins. And even though Tad torpedoed his own heart last night, things somehow look brighter.

Chapter Thirty-Nine

THIS DAY could be worse. Sure, Lewis watched his boyfriend get forcibly outed last night. And sure, it was at Lewis's best friend's wedding, in which he had a major role. Yeah, he left the wedding to take care of his boyfriend, who, in the grips of a panic attack, broke up with him. After Lewis dropped the first *I love you*. And yep, then Lewis got real drunk. Drunk and emotional and extremely verbose in Tad's DMs.

Now he's hungover. And sad.

No, sad doesn't do it justice. He's used to sad. Sad was how he felt when he walked in on Jonah with his tongue up Mr. Gym Bod's asshole. Sad was how he felt when Liam and Jayden and the rest of the dickhead parade dumped him.

When Tad walked away last night, Lewis felt his ribs splinter as they crushed his heart to dust. He had to pretend everything was fine because he didn't want to ruin Stacy's big day, but he was empty. Stacy knew something was wrong immediately. He set a timer on his phone and said she could comfort him until it hit zero, and then she had to enjoy her wedding. So she hugged him tight and rocked him until the timer chimed.

But. *But.*

Tad texted him back.

It's right there, timestamp next to it. 2:31. **Can't choose between Madonna and Kylie. I would have danced to both with you**

Maybe there's still time to fix this. Maybe Lewis can convince Tad that he's realistic and he wants to make this work for real, and that starts with sticking to their original agreement.

The divorce papers are in his custody. When he woke up, he signed them. It's a pretty shit grand gesture, but life doesn't need to be a rom-com. Maybe Lewis should stop looking for the happily ever after, the end of the story, and start looking for the beginning.

Maybe this marriage with Tad needs to end before they can have their beginning.

His moment of character growth doesn't stop him from wanting the universe to reward him, though—and from being subsequently disappointed when Tad doesn't text him upon completion of the forms.

He reads Tad's text from last night again. It helps. He's trying not to have an anxiety attack, but it's hard. You'd think he'd be used to having his heart broken by now, but it hurts the same every time.

Midmorning, the texts start rolling in from his friends. Ava and Matty want to know if he's heard from Tad. Ofelia apologizes for the millionth time. Lewis doesn't have the energy to tell her he's not the one she needs to apologize to.

Even Stace texts. Lewis tells her he's fine and to stop worrying about him and enjoy her first full day as a married woman. She responds that of course she's worried about him, he shoots back that he already feels like a dick for causing a scene at her wedding, to which she responds that Alang's family is very dramatic and it wouldn't have been right if there hadn't been any drama.

Which gets his first smile of the day. He sends back, *I love you so much Stace*

How much time should he let go by before he texts Tad back? What's the etiquette when your boyfriend dumps you after you tell him you love him, and then you send him increasingly pathetic texts while you get no response, but then… you do? And it seems like he still wants you?

Ugh. Lewis's head hurts. How long ago did he take that ibuprofen? Can he take some more? Is he going to die if he does? Would dying be worse than the way his head hurts right now?

He takes the ibuprofen and chases it with an energy drink that's past its expiration date. Hell yeah, he's living on the edge today.

A shower makes him feel less like re-heated death. He stays in there longer than he normally would, letting the hot water sluice over him, mentally apologizing to the water table.

No text or call from Tad when he's out of the shower. Maybe Lewis should call?

No. He should give Tad space. Right?

Definitely. Yeah. He'll let Tad decide when he wants to initiate communication. He won't fixate on the time and how long it's been since Tad texted and he definitely won't keep his phone from locking so he can watch his conversation with Tad for the three dots of incoming communication. He for sure isn't going to check his phone every thirty seconds as he gets to all the cleaning he's been putting off which suddenly seems like a brilliant way to spend his Sunday morning.

So yeah, by noon, smelling like bleach and sneezing from all the dust he's kicked up, he texts Tad: *Hope you're ok today. I spent some time talking to Walt last night and he seemed accepting. Actually he was kind of distraught over everything and wanted to make sure he said the right things when he talked to you. I showed him some sites my mom recommends to people. So yeah, I hope if you talked to him, he wasn't a dick or anything*

Send.

He reads back what he wrote. Should he leave it at that?

Lol. No. He's not going to leave it at that.

I really want to talk to you/see you. But also I get if you don't want to talk today. I know you ended things and I know why but I just hope that maybe we can talk and idk. Maybe work it out.

Then, *I want to work it out. I shouldn't have said it then but I meant it when I told you I love you*

Maybe I shouldn't have said it again now

Anyway let me know

Jesus.

He locks his phone and buries his face in his hands, wishing he could cry, because at least it would be an outlet for this horrible, grinding pain behind his sternum. The tears won't come, though.

Okay. He's going to do something. He's going to… go to the gym. Yeah. Take out his feelings with some weights. And then he'll go grocery shopping. Maybe he'll go for a walk. Maybe he'll go out to dinner! By himself! Because that's a thing he's capable of doing!

His phone buzzes and Lewis dives for it.

His lungs stop working. It's Tad. **Are you at home today?**

Yes, Lewis texts back immediately, all thoughts of the gym and grocery shopping and eating alone like a sad, recently dumped loser forgotten.

Like, all day?

Yeah no plans

Ok

Lewis waits, but that's it. Tad doesn't text again.

What's happening? Is Tad coming here? Should Lewis clean up?

He spins eagerly, happy for A Task to occupy him—and he realizes he's already gone through his entire apartment in an anxiety-fueled haze this morning, tidying and scrubbing. At least the place looks immaculate.

Lewis frowns. He's never thought much about it, but it's not very interesting in here. Not like Tad's place, which is tranquil and green and riotous with life, or even like Lewis's childhood bedroom. He tries not to buy a lot of plastic for the environment's sake, so he doesn't have many knickknacks, but the stuff he *does* have is boring. His sofa is cream-colored, the armchair is statement-piece peacock blue, but the effect is more Williams-Sonoma catalog than any kind of statement.

Even the few pieces of art on the walls are things he got from chain stores. There were a few he kept seeing everywhere—that origami-style art, photos of European cities—so he eventually figured he might as well get a few, because everyone liked them.

It dawns on him. He got them because everyone liked them. Because he wasn't good enough for people on his own, so he unwittingly made his apartment the home equivalent of a dentist's waiting room.

It's like he spent so much time projecting onto the rom-com leads he's always worshipped that he made himself into a rom-com character his boyfriends could project a Happily Ever After onto.

That's so pathetic that it makes him want to rush out to the quirkiest possible neighborhood in New York and buy a bunch of really crazy stuff to showcase his personality, which… is really not crazy. Oh god, is he the *human* equivalent of a dentist's waiting room? Is that why Jonah wasn't satisfied with his asshole and went looking for it elsewhere?

Okay. Wow. *Okay.* He's totally spiraling because Tad's on his way.

But seriously. He should have a plant or something. *Not* one of those potted palms you always see in dentist's offices, god.

He sucks in a deep breath and tells himself to calm down. Then he says it out loud: "Calm down."

The buzzer shrills like a reply. Lewis jumps and hurries over to it, his heart in his throat and his palms sweaty. "Hello?"

A tinny voice comes out of the speaker. "Hi, Lewis? I mean, oh my god, hi. Lewis. It's Tad."

Lewis buzzed him in within two syllables, but he has to remember to say, "Yep! Yes! Come in!"

Tad's voice gets muffled. "No, just—yeah, can you get it? Thanks." Lewis furrows his brow, and Tad's voice comes back louder. "Okay, be up in a minute!"

Sweat prickles under Lewis's arms and on his back and shit it's too late to change, isn't it?

There's a knock on the door. When he reaches for the doorknob, his hand feels like it isn't attached to his body.

The door swings open. Tad's standing there, holding a boombox on one shoulder and a stack of card stock under the other arm.

Tad fumbles with the boombox and Peter Gabriel's "In Your Eyes" starts. He shakily holds it up over his head with one hand, where it teeters. Before it topples, Tad catches it, which sends the stack of card stock tumbling to the floor.

"This was so much smoother in my head," Tad groans.

"Here, give me that!" someone else says. Walt darts forward and takes the boombox, sidles behind Tad, and lifts it above his head. Tad scoops up the cards and holds them so Lewis can read them.

"I hate the way you talk to me and how you make me so aware," Lewis reads. Tad flips to the next card. "I hate the way you drive rental cars, I hate it when you stare." Next card. "I hate your big gay Pride sneakers and the way you read my mind. I hate you so much it makes me sick, it even makes me rhyme. I hate the way you're always right, I hate it when you lie. I hate it when you make me laugh, even worse when you make me cry—oh my god! *Ten Things I Hate About You!* And *Say Anything* and *Love, Actually!*"

With a huge whoosh, Tad drops the cue cards. "I'm just a boy, standing in front of a boy, asking him to love him."

There's this feeling in Lewis's chest, like the way flocks of birds swell and contract in fluid murmurations of air and wings and connection that doesn't make any sense from the outside. "You did a FrankenGesture for me," he says, his heart thrumming.

Tad's fingers twist together. "I'm so sorry for yesterday. I got scared about my issues. And baggage. I got scared it would be too much for you, maybe not now, but later, when you realize I'm not Heath Ledger or Tom Hanks or something."

"You're way better looking than Heath Ledger or Tom—not the point, right."

Walt adjusts the volume on the boombox and Peter Gabriel fades to a soft serenade. There's a nervous look on Tad's face. "I'm not the perfect guy from a rom-com. But god, Lewis, I love you so much, and if you can forgive me for being a complete asshole yesterday, then—"

Lewis steps forward, puts his hands on Tad's face, and kisses him.

Tad makes a noise and his mouth opens, and Lewis sinks into it, the brush of tongue on tongue and the taste of Tad—tea and mint and home.

"I signed the divorce papers," Lewis says.

"This is the weirdest apology ever," Walt opines from the peanut gallery.

Before Tad can respond, Lewis kisses him again. "I'm sorry. I'm sorry I made you feel like I was pushing you into something. I'm sorry I went back on what we agreed. I'm sorry for treating you like a character in a rom-com and not a real person with flaws and issues, who I'm definitely going to have fights with because real people in real relationships fight, even when they love each other more than they thought was possible. Which, just, you know. Is how I feel about you, so."

For good measure, Lewis kisses Tad again, and this time, Tad fists the front of his shirt and hauls him closer. There are definitely some conversations to have but. *This.* Tad and him.

This is right. This is perfect. Not rom-com perfect, but perfect in a real-life way that matters, that works, that Lewis knows he'll fight for and protect forever. He knows what special looks like, because he's been searching for it for so long.

"In Your Eyes" ends and starts over. Tad buries his face in Lewis's neck and murmurs, "Love you."

So really, what is Lewis supposed to do but press his face to the side of Tad's, breathe in his scent, and murmur back, "Love you too."

Walt clears his throat. "Soooo hey, it seems like you've got this, bro. I can get going and leave you guys to it." Walt's beaming. Lewis is so fucking happy that whatever happens with Tad's parents, his brother is in his corner. There's someone in Tad's family who loves him for who he is. "You want me to drop the boombox at your apartment before I get on the road?"

It occurs to Lewis that he's never seen a boombox in Tad's apartment. "Wait, did you buy a boombox just for this?"

"And a CD!" Tad's face is flushed with happiness and Lewis could spend his life mapping the constellations of his freckles and how joy dawns like sunrise in his eyes. "I love New York. You can find anything. Also, Lewis! Did you know there's a movie about two people who get drunk married in Vegas?"

Lewis laughs and pulls Tad to him again.

Chapter Forty

TAD SHUTS off the car. Bitter cold immediately seeps in from outside. It's unseasonably frigid for the end of February, and Mom reminded him multiple times to make sure he had blankets in the car in case he stalled along the freeway and enough hand and foot warmers so he didn't get frostbite in his extremities—and was his coat warm enough? Did he have a hat and scarf?

The back seat is piled high with blankets. A single duffel bag packed with clothes for one night is beneath them. Maybe it's dumb, but Tad likes doing these little things for his mother.

"You doing okay?" Lewis asks, sliding a hand onto Tad's thigh.

"Um, no?" Why did that come out in a vocal register he hasn't hit since he was pre-pubescent? Tad concentrates on his breathing, because if he isn't careful, he's going to spiral into a panic attack. That's why he drove. Lewis offered, but Tad said he needed something to focus on for the hours between Manhattan and Watertown.

"No," he tries again—as a declarative, just to prove he can.

Lewis squeezes his leg. "What do you need from me right now? What's the best way for me to be there for you?"

Tad doesn't say, *wrestle me into the passenger seat and drive us out of here before my parents realize we're sitting in the driveway.* He counts seconds as he takes deep, grounding breaths, holds them, and lets the air out slowly. "Just be ready for me to be a complete mess."

There's such love in Lewis's eyes that Tad's heart slows. His lungs open and make it easier to breathe. "I'll be right here," Lewis says.

Giving him an appalled look, Tad says, "What? Right *here*? No— it's freezing!" He sounds like his mom. "Come in with me."

"You want me to? You're not just worried about me getting cold?"

"I want you to." Tad kisses the back of Lewis's hand. "Don't hate me, but I'll have to introduce you as my friend. Until I. You know. Tell them."

"I could never hate you, baby." Lewis's voice is fierce. "Never. If you need to tell them I'm your friend, that's what you need. I'll do anything you need."

Tad squeezes his hand—maybe too hard, because Lewis's smile gets a little fixed. "Thank you for coming with me," Tad says.

The front door is unlocked. When they step inside, Tad calls, "It's me!"

"Oh!" comes Mom's exclamation from upstairs. The TV is blaring in the basement as usual. What sport is even on in February?

The stairs creak as Mom descends. Her arms are already open to hug him before she gets to the bottom, but when she spots Lewis, she stutters to a stop and says "Oh!" again.

"Mom, this is Lewis." Tad does his best to keep his voice from shaking. His stomach is in knots, his heart is racing, and there are damp patches under his arms.

"Well, we're happy to have you, Lewis." Mom gives Tad a questioning look that she probably thinks is subtle.

He hugs her. "He's my...."

Friend? Is Tad really going to say that? Lewis may be okay with it, but that doesn't mean Tad is. "He's... er, Lewis," is what comes out of his mouth, like that's any better.

Lewis holds out a hand. "Nice to meet you, Mrs. Pierce."

"Kathleen, please," Mom says, shaking his hand. "How nice of you to drive up with Tad to keep him company! Do you need a place to stay? We could make up an extra bed."

"We're actually staying at a hotel, Mom," Tad cuts in. "Both of us. I didn't want to put you out."

She looks confused. "We have the space—Lewis can stay in Walt's room. I'm sure you can cancel your hotel rooms."

Sweat sticks his shirt to his back. Maybe he should let this go.

Except if he can't hold the line on not spending the night here, how is he going to hold the line on anything that matters? It's time to start asserting himself with his family. It's time to stick up for himself and to stop worrying they won't love him if he makes them unhappy. If the cost of their happiness is his unhappiness, their love isn't worth having.

"Thanks, but we're going to stay at the hotel," Tad says.

Mom looks disappointed. "Is it one of those places that won't give you the deposit back if you cancel with less than twenty-four hours? Which hotel is it?"

"It's not about the money. It's just…." Tad's brain spins uselessly. Now he knows how his work computer feels when he loads too many flat plans and pages in his magazine editing software. "That's just what we're doing," he finishes. When he takes a chance and darts a look toward Lewis, the pride on Lewis's face bolsters him.

Before Mom can object about the hotel again, Tad says, "I actually wanted to talk to you and Dad about something."

"That sounds serious," Mom jokes. When Tad swallows hard, her smile fades to concern. "Oh, honey, is it—what's wrong? Is everything okay?"

"Everything's fine," he says firmly. Tries to say firmly. "Just want to talk."

"I'll get Dad," Mom says. She looks scared. This is going *great*. "We can talk in the living room."

Tad leads Lewis to the living room and almost motions for him to take a chair while Tad sits on the sofa out of stupid, self-hating habit. Instead, he forces himself to sit on the floral-patterned loveseat, holding out a hand for Lewis to sit next to him.

Leaning close, Lewis says close to his ear, "You're doing great."

With a breath of only mildly hysterical laughter, Tad replies, "I'm not, but thanks for saying it."

When Dad appears in the living room with Mom, Tad feels faint. There's still time to back out, but Tad stands and says hi to Dad. Handshake, back slap, et cetera. Lewis's presence seems to confuse Dad but all he does is eye him.

Mom and Dad sit on the sofa and Mom asks worriedly, "What's wrong, Tad?"

"Nothing's wrong!" Tad wipes his palms on his jeans. "It's not a bad thing. It's…."

His parents stare. Helplessly, Tad's eyes find Lewis's. He centers himself in their whiskey and sunlight brown, the little crinkles at the corners that are going to turn to fuller and deeper laugh lines as he gets older.

And oh, how Tad wants to be around for that. This, right now, is something that has to happen, or he doesn't think he'll get that chance. Lewis deserves someone brave.

Tad takes a deep breath. "I'm gay."

A second ticks by, then another. Mom has a weird, fixed smile on her face. Dad looks… still kind of confused. Tad might as well burn everything down.

He grabs Lewis's hand tight and holds it up for his parents to see. "Lewis is my boyfriend."

Mom jerks her head to look at Dad like she thinks he's going to be able to explain. Like maybe she thinks this is a joke he and Tad are in on together.

Dad's the first to break the horrible silence. "Are you being funny?"

"Um." Tad's hairline is damp, his skin icy. When Lewis squeezes his hand, he manages to answer. "No. I'm, um. Very gay. I like men."

Dad glances at Mom for guidance. It's impossible to tell if she even notices—she's staring at her lap, fingers clasped together and knuckles white and bloodless.

The helpless look on Dad's face reminds Tad of himself one of the times they camped in the Thousand Islands. As they rowed to Canoe-Picnic Point, Tad and Walt in one canoe and Dad in another, Tad fumbled his paddle and couldn't grab it in time before it splashed into the water. That hapless moment where he just sat, gaping at his paddle floating on the surface, sunshine yellow against the greeny-brown-blue of the water, as Walt's paddling in the front of the canoe carried them farther away.

Of course, Dad always kept his eye on them, so when he saw what happened, he swung around and retrieved the paddle. Problem solved, paddle rescued!

Now Dad's the one looking for help, but this is a lot bigger than a wayward paddle.

"Like those Schitt's Creek kids?" Dad asks.

It's not the time to correct him that David is actually pan, so Tad nods, his mouth dry.

"Well." Dad clears his throat. "Well, if that's what makes you happy."

The words hit Tad like a punch to the chest. His next breath is more of a gasp, like he forgot how to breathe. There's a temptation to take this faint… praise? and consider it support, because it could be worse. Dad could have shouted slurs and told him never to set foot in this house again.

He makes himself wait until his breath is back—sort of back—before saying, "It's not really about whether it makes me happy or not.

It's just who I am." The pressure from Lewis's hand increases. "But," he adds, and now he *does* look at Lewis, "I am happy."

Pride doesn't really describe the expression on Lewis's face. He looks fierce and adoring, and god, Tad is so happy he made a stupid, horny decision that night in Vegas. Lewis has changed his life.

Dad looks at Tad, then at Lewis, then back at Tad. He nods. "Okay." There's a gruff note to his voice. "Lewis? Lewis. Never thought I was going to meet my kid's boyfriend, but I guess that's life." Even though they already met, he pushes himself off the sofa and holds his hand out. "Bill. Don't know if I said that before. You treating my kid right?"

Gamely, Lewis shakes Dad's hand. "Nice to meet you, Bill. I hope so, but you probably should ask Tad."

That seems unspeakably awkward for some reason, so Tad just volunteers, "Yes! Yeah. You are. I mean, he is." When Lewis looks at him again, Tad wishes he could pull him into a hard kiss. Baby steps, though. First, it would be nice if both of his parents would say something.

"Mom?" Tad asks hesitantly. "You, um… you haven't said anything."

The skin over her knuckles is stretched tight. Dad says, "Kathleen."

"What? Oh!" She looks up, and though her gaze lands in the vicinity of Tad, she doesn't quite meet his eyes. "What your father said. If that's what makes you happy."

Tad doesn't realize his heart had lifted with Dad's reaction until it plummets again with Mom's.

"I mean, yeah, I'm really happy right now," he says.

She nods.

Then she nods again.

Then she says, "I just don't understand how you could be gay all of a sudden?"

Somewhere in his digestive tract, his small intestine knots itself around his large intestine. "I've always been gay."

"But you've never—" Her lip trembles. "What about Sydney Clark?"

The one girl he kissed in high school to try to turn himself straight? "Mom, that's ancient history. And we were just friends. I was gay then too. I've always been gay."

"But if you only found a boyfriend now, maybe you'll change your mind." She sounds hopeful.

There's a buzzing at the edge of Tad's awareness and he finds himself concocting an elaborate fantasy where a giant swarm of bees is approaching and he's very allergic so he has to get out of here *right now.* "I've had boyfriends before," Tad says, which is better than *I've had sex with six men in my life and even when it hasn't been great it's never made me want to try sex with women.* "I just never told you."

He's not going to ask if she's upset. He's not. It's her problem if she is, and it's definitely not his responsibility to coddle and comfort her through his coming out.

"Are you upset?" he asks.

"No!" Mom objects. Tad really wants to be imagining her defensiveness. "You know how much I love you. How could you think I'm upset?"

"You seem sort of upset." Tad's voice shakes. Maybe this is good enough. He told them, and nothing really horrible happened.

But then Lewis squeezes Tad's hand hard enough that his bones creak. It's probably driving Lewis crazy to sit here silently. He said on the drive that he'd do whatever Tad wanted him to—either speak up or keep his mouth shut. Tad said he needed to do this on his own.

What he didn't say was that he had to do it on his own because he wants Lewis to be proud of him. He wants Lewis to see that he's the kind of man who will stand up for himself—and stand up for them.

"I don't really get why you'd be upset, Mom." Tad straightens his shoulders and looks her in the eye, even though he feels like he's going to throw up.

"I told you, I'm *not.* It's just a lot to take in! And you brought your—" Her eyes skitter to Lewis. "Don't you think this should have been a family conversation? The three of us could have worked through this."

Tad tastes bile and metal. "Worked through what?"

Mom's mouth opens and closes a few times, and finally she says, "This is just a shock. I wish we were talking alone."

"Hon, I don't think talking just the three of us is going to change his mind. It's like he said, he's always been gay," Dad—Dad!—says.

"No, I—of course I don't think that, I just"—Mom's talking fast now—"this is so much all at once… I always imagined a normal life for you, Tad, and you have to understand what it's like to suddenly have that taken away—"

Finally, something snaps inside Tad.

"I didn't *take anything away* from you!" Tad stands and immediately regrets it, because his knees wobble and almost give out. But Lewis is there, standing next to him and holding him up. "And I'm not going to apologize to you for being gay! I'm not going to apologize for bringing my boyfriend here! I've been forcing myself back into the closet every time I've visited or talked to you. I've been fucking apologizing for my existence for the past twenty years and I am *done*. I didn't do anything wrong. This is who I am, and how dare you say I'm not normal when I have someone who makes me happier than I've ever been in my entire life? How can you sit there and say you love me and then tell me I'm not normal because the person I love is another man?"

His voice gives out on a crack. He feels light-headed. When was the last time he took a breath? He's having trouble getting one now, and he realizes he's headed straight to panic attack city.

He starts hyperventilating and turns away from his parents, pulling Lewis with him. "Let's go," he manages to choke out.

Dad follows them. As Tad pulls the door open to a blast of arctic air, Dad says, "Give her some time, Taddy. Of course she loves you."

Tad makes a noise that isn't words. Awkwardly, Dad pats him on the shoulder.

Then, even though the door is wide open and flooding the house with cold, he wraps his arms around Tad in a real hug. Tad can't remember the last time Dad hugged him. "I love you, kiddo," he says gruffly. "Mom does too. It'll all be fine."

"Love you too," Tad manages. "And um. Sorry for swearing."

He doesn't believe it will be fine, but he can't make the words come out.

Chapter Forty-One

TAD HAS no memory of the drive to the hotel. One moment he's battling to stay upright between the front door of his parents' house and the rental car, and the next, they're in a parking lot with the car shut off. They sit there until their breath starts fogging.

"Hey," Lewis says softly. He's in the driver's seat. "Let's go inside, okay?"

"Okay."

As they get their bags from the trunk, Lewis leans in to kiss Tad on the cheek—which is the first time a man has ever openly shown affection to Tad in his hometown.

Their room is standard hotel-chain modern. Clean lines, mostly soulless, but comfortable. Tad flings himself on the bed and puts a pillow over his face. He can hear Lewis puttering around the room, unzipping bags, getting toiletries out. "You can scream if it'll help," Lewis says.

"Urrrrrgghhhh," Tad responds, his voice muffled by the pillow.

"Or make that noise." The bed depresses and Tad feels Lewis's warmth at his side, then Lewis's hand on his stomach. "I'm sorry that didn't go better, babe."

The haze in Tad's mind is clearing like fog burning off with the sunrise. Groping for Lewis's hand, he says into the pillow, "Yeah, well."

There's more to be said, but for once, it's not that words are crowding into his throat while his mouth refuses to let them out—he can't think of a single thing to say. He grips Lewis's hand tighter and shoves the pillow off his face. "Thank you for being with me for that train wreck."

Lewis lies down and puts his arms around Tad. "I'll always be there for anything you want me for." Lewis holds him tight and strokes his hair. "I'm so fucking proud of you, you know that?"

Tad's eyes sting. "Why?"

Somehow, Lewis hugs him harder. "Because you were so brave. You did something incredibly scary and—Jesus, Tad. You're so fucking brave."

Tad starts crying.

Lewis holds him through it, stroking his hair and kissing his forehead, his temples, the top of his head, murmuring nonsense until eventually, Tad's sobs subside to sniffles. When he raises his face from Lewis's—now soaking wet—sweater, Lewis gently wipes his cheeks. "I look disgusting," Tad says snottily.

"You look like the most fucking courageous person I know." Lewis tips Tad's chin up and kisses him softly. "I love you so much."

Tad makes a noise and wraps his arms around Lewis. "I love you too," he whispers.

They stay that way awhile, hearts beating together. The only reason Tad moves is because he promised Walt to let him know how it went, and he can tell from the frequency of the texts he's receiving that Walt's getting concerned.

It's not just Walt texting, though. He has texts from... everyone. All his friends. Ava, Stacy, Alang. Callie sent a gif, and even Matthew, who Tad barely knows, wished him luck.

He almost starts crying again, but he gets it together enough to text Walt back.

> *Didn't go well*
> **FUCK. Dude I'm so sorry. I'll talk some sense into them**
> *Dad wasn't too bad actually. He gave me a hug at the end. But Mom was, idk. Not happy*
> *You don't have to talk to them*
> **Whatever you want bro. You need to talk or anything rn?**
> *No that's ok. Lewis is here. I'll call you tomorrow*
> **K. Love you**
> *You too*

The fact that his brother has now become a confidante is one of the best things to happen to Tad in... ever? Closeness is regrowing between them, like a plant you think has withered and died, until you give it the care it needs—and then it surprises you by coming back just as strong as before. Maybe stronger.

That's the thing—even though coming out to his parents didn't go the way he wanted it to, Tad feels so much green growing into all the cracks and crevices in his life. All the empty places he thought were dead and lifeless were waiting all this time to be nourished, and now he has....

Tad puts his phone on the desk and looks at Lewis, who's still spread out on the bed. Something catches in his chest, and he crawls onto the bed next to Lewis. Nose to nose, Tad says, "Hi."

"Hey." Lewis rubs circles into Tad's back. "You don't have any responsibility to do anything else with your mom."

"I know," Tad says, and he even almost means it. "But I still kind of want to drive back and tell her—I don't know what, exactly. That she's wrong? Or that, I don't know. I won't flaunt it around her. I'll act so not gay that she can pretend I'm not." At the heartbroken expression on Lewis's face, Tad fists a hand in his sweater. "But I don't want to say that, not really. I just... I knew this was a possibility. But it still really fucking sucks to have it happen."

He squeezes the wool of Lewis's sweater in his hand. "I guess I had this fantasy that I was wrong all these years. Like maybe my family could be like yours."

Lewis's arms slide around him. One of his hands strokes up and down Tad's spine.

"What if you don't want to be with a guy whose family isn't accepting like yours is?" Tad asks quietly.

Both of Lewis's hands come to rest on Tad's face and Lewis kisses him softly. "I want to be with you, Tad. I'll help you with your family however you want me to. I'll support you no matter what you decide to do after today, whether you figure it out tomorrow or in a year, whether it's what I personally would do or not."

Wait. A year? Sparks crackle in Tad's chest.

After another soft kiss, Lewis says, "I'm with you for you. I just want to be with you."

Tad remains silent. Then, with a smile so bright he can practically see the glow reflected in Lewis's eyes, he asks, "A year?"

With a sheepish laugh, Lewis replies, "I mean. Yeah. Or like. Five. Or ten. And I'm doing the thing where I throw everything I have into a relationship even though it's still pretty early—"

Tad cuts him off with a hard kiss, so much heat in it that clothes come off within minutes. If Tad had his way they'd be fucking within minutes, too. But Lewis wraps him up in his arms and kisses him, and kisses him, and kisses him, hands stroking through his hair and down his neck, over Tad's shoulders that are still tight with tension, down his back to his ass.

Hot, heavy pleasure unspools low in Tad's stomach, in his cock and balls, and the more Lewis touches him, the further it spreads across his skin. Hot, prickly need coils in his thighs and throbs deep inside him.

"Lew," he groans. "Please."

Lewis kisses and licks down his neck slowly as his hands push Tad's legs open. Everything is hot and sticky and some kind of liquid gold—honey or syrup or caramel, molten and just this side of scorching.

Lewis teases Tad's opening with a wet finger. Pressure gives way to the feel of Lewis's finger breaching him, and *oh* oh god it feels good. Tad bucks his hips, demanding more, and a second finger curls inside him and—*there*—oh—oh he's just crackling nerve endings, he can't take it, he's raw and scraped so close to the bone that the pleasure teeters on the knife's edge of pain.

When Lewis withdraws his fingers, Tad makes a noise that leaves him hoarse. Then Lewis's lips are on his again, and soon they're positioning Tad's legs against Lewis's shoulders. It's such an exposed position, and Tad loves it, loves how Lewis grips his legs hard enough to bruise as he lines himself up, loves how Lewis looks down and watches himself slide inside.

When Lewis is buried tip to root, he pauses, shoulders heaving, sweat shining across his chest and matting his chest hair to his pecs. His eyes flutter shut and he rolls his hips, slow and shallow, which makes Tad fist the sheets and grunt.

"Fuck, Tad. You feel so good."

All Tad's nerves spark like live wires, his skin scorching and damp with sweat and screaming for more. The hot, swirling pleasure in his gut reaches out greedily.

Tad arches, burying Lewis's cock deeper and sliding it against his prostate. Heat floods him and—that. He needs more of *that.* "Fuck me," he says hoarsely.

Lewis draws out and *oh* that drag, the sweet burn of friction and piercing ache of emptiness. And then he snaps his hips, and his cock hits Tad in the exact right spot, leaving him seeing stars and white-knuckling the sheets.

If Lewis was all slow tenderness before, need has burned it off. He fucks Tad hard. Tad's heels dig into Lewis's back as he hoists himself higher, always trying for a deeper angle, wanting Lewis closer, inside him further. Just—more. His toes curl and he's spiraling closer and closer to the edge with each hard thrust. The muscles in his back and legs tense; everything tightens, throwing off sharp heat.

Lewis is panting and god he looks so hot, hips pistoning, sweat sheening his skin, his face contorted in concentration and agonized pleasure. "Oh Tad—baby—fuck, I'm gonna—"

"Fucking *yes*," Tad manages.

It's only another few seconds, and Lewis is crying out, his thrusts sloppy and fast, as he clutches at Tad's legs and bites the meat of one calf. Searing pleasure crystallizes deep inside Tad, teetering on a cliff, before it explodes, thundering through his body until he's coming in thick, hot pulses, one after another across his stomach and chest.

Gradually, Tad realizes the vision whiteout he's experiencing is actually because he's staring at the ceiling. "Fuck," he says.

Lewis groans his agreement.

Woozily, Tad unsticks his eyeballs to look at Lewis, who looks pretty dazed himself. "You," Lewis says, then gives his head a shake. "You shouldn't be allowed to be so sexy."

"I'm banned in three states," Tad says.

Lewis laughs and kisses Tad's leg, then the other. "Stay here." Slowly, he pulls out, which is when the soreness twinges. Good soreness. Tad loves the feeling of being well-fucked, of being able to feel Lewis still inside him.

Lewis returns with a wet washcloth and gently cleans first Tad, then himself. Tad probably needs to do some more thorough cleanup, especially before they go out for dinner, but all he wants to do now is lie in the circle of Lewis's arms, skin to skin all down the lengths of their bodies.

When they eventually rouse themselves, Tad checks his phone. There's a text from Mom: **I love you so much**, it says.

He almost taps into it to see if there's more, or maybe to respond. Why, though? Why, when he's let fear of his parents' approval shadow most of his life? So his mom loves him. Great. Is it conditional on him still pretending not to be gay around her? Does she want to discuss how Lewis maybe shouldn't come with Tad when he visits? Instead of assuming, Tad will ask. Tomorrow, though. He'll deal with it tomorrow.

Hands slip over his shoulders and rub gently. "You okay, babe?" Lewis asks.

Tad puts his phone aside to sink into the circle of Lewis's arms. Lewis's embrace feels like home. "Yeah," Tad says, hugging him back. "Yeah, I'm fine."

This time, he believes it.

Chapter Forty-Two

June

HOT SUN beats on Lewis's head as he descends the stairs of the New York County Supreme Court building. His shoulder bumps Tad's and the backs of their hands brush.

"That woman next to me wanted to take me out for a drink when I told her it's my birthday," Tad says, hooking his pinkie around Lewis's.

Lewis curls his pinkie so it's securely intertwined with Tad's. "Was she buying? Maybe you should've gone."

"Nah. She said ex-husbands weren't allowed, and who else would I want to spend my birthday with than my ex-husband?"

They reach the bottom of the stone steps. Lewis takes the opportunity to tug Tad into a kiss. "You sure? You're finally free."

Tad barks a laugh. "Oh, am I?"

Lewis grins. "I mean, legally. Best birthday present ever, right? Our divorce hearing?"

"Can we have divorce-slash-birthday sex later?"

"Obviously."

"Then yes," Tad agrees. "Best birthday present ever."

They filed the paperwork for the uncontested divorce the minute they hit the six-month mark. The summons was for June 17th—Tad's thirtieth birthday. At the small party they had last weekend, Matthew joked he didn't get his starter marriage over with before he turned thirty. Walt, visiting from Watertown, laughed harder than the joke deserved, which he does a lot around Matty. Lewis wonders if Walt maybe has a crush on Matty. Maybe Tad's straight brother isn't as straight as everyone thinks?

Lewis's anxiety ticks down the checklist of things to fixate on today: getting to the courthouse on time. Not fucking up the divorce proceedings. Not saying something stupid that would make Tad realize he doesn't want to be with this loser after all.

Now, he touches a hand to his jacket, making sure the little box is still safe inside the pocket. There's a whole possibility tree of anxieties tied to that little box, but weirdly, they're not freaking him out as much as he expected. Maybe it's the beautiful day, maybe it's because it's Tad's birthday, maybe it's the fact that they got here together, helping each other through the hard parts. Or maybe it's because of the way Tad looked at him when Lewis let slip those months ago in Watertown that he wanted to be with Tad in a year, or five, or ten.

Lewis has been in a lot of bad relationships. But he's never had anyone look at him like that—like he hung not only the moon, but also the planets and stars around it.

Tad's spinning his wedding ring around his finger right now, chewing on the inside of his cheek. "I guess we should take them off," he says. "Maybe it was weird to wear them all this time."

"It's romantic," Lewis tells him with a wink. Tad rolls his eyes but leans into Lewis, bringing a whiff of gin and rose and spice and the barest hint of sweat, and it feels like it's all just for Lewis. He has to be embarrassing for a second and bury his face in Tad's neck, breathing deep and mumbling, "You smell good."

Tad shivers with pleasure and rumbles inarticulately. "I brought one of those tiny bottles of cologne in case my flop sweat got overwhelming."

"Mm, well, I love your flop sweat."

"Gross."

"Is it gross, or is it just really gay?"

"It can be really gay and still be gross."

Laughing, Lewis kisses Tad's neck and straightens. "I do need your wedding ring, actually." Tad blinks, his mouth opening in an unverbalized question. "Just trust me," Lewis adds.

One of Tad's eyebrows quirks up. "If you're quoting *Aladdin*, I believe the line is, 'Do you trust me?'"

"*Wow*, coming for me where it hurts, huh?" Lewis laughs.

Tad shrugs, grinning. "Guess I'm one of those catty ex-husbands." But he twists his ring off his finger and places it in Lewis's palm, where it's joined by Lewis's. An adorable furrow appears between Tad's eyebrows as Lewis pockets the rings, which he has big plans for.

Lewis takes Tad's hand, lacing their fingers together. "Now that we're divorced, let me take you on a first date. We never got to have one of those."

As long as he lives, Lewis will never get tired of the pleased pink flush that rises into Tad's cheeks at times like this. Sometimes, it's really easy to see why Tad is so shy—his face hides absolutely nothing. If you're looking, you always know what he's feeling.

They walk away from the courthouse, hand in hand, Tad's face still pink with happiness. "Did you do something?"

"Maaaaybe," Lewis says innocently. The Lyft he called on the way out of the courthouse pulls up on the corner. "Your carriage awaits, my prince."

The pink on Tad's face deepens to red. "You're the fairy-tale guy, not me."

"Mm hm." That may be true, but it hasn't escaped Lewis's notice that Tad seems to enjoy rom-coms, cheesy romances, and Disney movies almost as much as Lewis does. Plus—somehow it took Lewis months to discover this—Tad is a total sucker for queer Regency romance novels. "Sorry—do you prefer 'my lord, the Viscount of Mimblemumbleshire, who was honorably discharged from His Majesty's Army due to an injury received at Waterloo?'"

"Oh my god," Tad says, now full-on red. "I'm never letting you read my books ever again."

"I think he's quite dashing." Lewis sighs. "And yet I'm a commoner just trying to scrape by in a legally questionable way, and even though circumstances keep throwing the two of us together, I can't imagine a way we'd ever fall in love."

"Oh my *god*." Tad's laughing now. "You know what, those poor Regency gays didn't have it easy. There were way fewer tropes for them to work with!"

They hop in the Lyft, trying to think of what tropes the Regency gays had access to and holding hands across the seat. "I do, by the way," Tad says. At Lewis's questioning look, he adds, "Trust you. Obviously I trust you."

Lewis squeezes his hand. The box in his jacket pocket feels like it's glowing and like Tad's definitely going to ask about it, but Lewis is apparently acting normal. So go him! It's not like this is one of the biggest days of his life or anything, nothing to be absolutely losing his shit over.

With traffic, the drive to their destination takes about an hour. When they cross into the Bronx and get on the Bronx River Parkway,

Tad's face lights up. He doesn't seem surprised when they're dropped off at the main gate for the New York Botanical Garden.

As they scan their tickets at the entrance, Tad bounces on the balls of his feet. "Did you remember that I said the roses are at peak right now?"

"Yep."

"And the perennial garden?"

God, it's hard not to grab him and kiss his brains out right here, but there's a line behind them, so Lewis restrains himself. Barely. "You said most people come for the roses, but you love the perennials because they're not as showy, but you like how they're survivors." The adoring expression in Tad's eyes destroys Lewis's willpower and he pulls him in for a quick kiss. "I love listening to you talk about the things you love. And I love going places with you that make you smile like this."

"I'm smiling like this because you make me happy." Tad closes his eyes and turns his face up to the sun. "I never said stuff like that out loud before you."

And that. Well, that takes any lingering doubts in Lewis's mind about that little box in his pocket and blows them away like dandelion seeds.

They walk through the gardens as the golden sun angles lower, admiring the roses with the crowds first. Lewis can't get over how many different shades of pink and red there are. Some of them make him want to sink into the color and swim in it, and the smell curls around them, reminding Lewis of Tad's cologne.

Then they get to the Perennial Garden. It's a riot of different colors and textures. There are flowers, plants, shrubs, trees, and the Haupt Conservatory rises behind the landscape in Victorian domed stateliness.

Tad points out phlox, thick purple clusters of flowers mobbed with butterflies, and tiny white Bowman's root. Searing orange and red daylilies crowd each other for sun and Monk's hood sways in the light breeze, its violet flowers fluttering their hoods.

Lewis really likes the balloon-flowers. "They really look like little balloons!" he says gleefully. Tad reels him in by his belt and puts an arm around him.

Eventually, they stroll into a shady section of the Perennial Garden and sit on a bench under the spreading branches of a leafy tree. Lewis puts an arm around Tad's shoulders and Tad leans into him with a soft sigh of contentment. Above them, birds flit from branch to branch, singing. Lewis points. "Look. Cardinals." Red feathers flash and Lewis tries not to be too proud of himself for knowing the duller, brown bird with the pink beak next to the bright scarlet one is the female. Maybe they're a pair.

Tad smirks at him. "Are you turning into a bird person?"

"Well, I mean, one of us should be. If you're the plant person, guess it has to be me."

"For balance," Tad says, echoing words Lewis said a lifetime ago, when the idea of being married to Tad was scary and they were two strangers-turned-husbands.

Lewis takes his hand and a calm certainty settles over him. He expected his heart to beat hard enough that nearby wildlife would hear it and flee, but if anything, it's the opposite. His pulse slows and steadies. It's time.

"Tad," he says. Tad looks at him and Lewis reaches into his jacket pocket, closing his fingers around the box. It's warm from his body heat. Its contents probably will be too. "Tad Pierce. You make me stupidly happy. Will you marry me?"

The box in his hand pops open with a creak. There's an engagement ring inside, gleaming gold even in the shade.

A long silence goes by as Tad stares at the ring. It doesn't faze Lewis. He's probably the most confident new divorcé ever. There's hardly anything in his life that he's completely certain of. His feelings for Tad, though? Wanting to spend the rest of his life with this funny, smart, shy man who made Lewis re-fall in love with love?

Yeah. No question. He's never been more sure of anything.

Finally, Tad raises his eyes. They're wide, and the light catches and glints on the bright blue of his irises. Lewis could stare at them forever counting all the different colors in Tad's eyes—cerulean and cornflower, sapphire and sea glass. He's beautiful, and Lewis wants to spend forever giving him everything.

"But," Tad says. He blinks, golden hour sunlight making the tips of his eyelashes glow rose gold. "But," he tries again, "we just got divorced."

"I know," Lewis says. His chest is so full. "But I love you, and I want to spend my life with you. And you deserve to remember your wedding. You deserve to have all of it—the tux, the champagne, the cake. The vows. Whether it's us and a few other people or a huge crowd—"

"Oh god no, I don't want a huge crowd," Tad says with a shudder.

The feeling in Lewis's chest gets fuller and lighter, more shot through with gold. He takes Tad's other hand. Tad slides his palm over Lewis's. "You deserve to have a real wedding," Lewis says. "And I do too. So what do you say? Will you marry me... again?"

Tad laughs helplessly and brings both of Lewis's hands to his mouth, kissing one, then the other. His eyes squeeze shut and he holds Lewis's fingers against his lips. "Yes," he mumbles against Lewis's skin. "Yes, of course, *of course*. A million people aren't looking at us, are they?"

Lewis wants to jump up on the bench. He wants to dance and spin around and yell TAD JUST SAID HE'LL MARRY ME! But Tad, his lovely Tad, would hate being the center of attention like that, would hate all the eyes and phone cameras on him. That means Lewis would hate it too, because he'll spend his whole goddamn life making sure Tad feels safe and comfortable.

"No one's looking," he assures Tad.

Tad grins wickedly and swings a leg over Lewis's lap so he can straddle him, knees jammed into the back of the bench. "I can't believe you proposed on my birthday. You've seen too many rom-coms."

He leans down and kisses Lewis. The kiss tastes like green plants and fresh air and bright sun. It tastes like the beginning of an adventure. It tastes like home, and it tastes like forever.

They break apart slowly. Tad leans his forehead against Lewis's and Lewis tips his face up. All he can see is blue eyes and a blur of freckles. "We'll have a long engagement," Lewis says.

Tad laughs and kisses him again.

Acknowledgements

THIS WAS the second book everyone tells you to write while you're querying (and getting rejections on) your first book, so all my thanks and gratitude to Dreamspinner Press for giving Tad and Lewis's story a home. The entire team is wonderful to work with, from editing to artwork to marketing and all the other behind-the-scenes work.

Thank you to my beta readers Mary, Anke, and Mark. Anke, time vindicated you on the shoe heist aftermath. Mark, sorry for scandalizing you with the sex scenes.

Thank you to the local booksellers who have been so supportive, especially Cream & Amber in Hopkins.

Thank you to my cat, Isabella, who provided most of the inspiration for Hetty.

Finally, thank you to my wife, Laura, who is my first and best reader. Thank you for reading every unedited word, for cheering me on, and for your support and love.

Keep reading for an exclusive excerpt from
Six Places to Fall In Love
by Lee Pini!

Coming in 2025

June

THE RED of the sand against the blue of the reflected sky is so stark and bright it sears Percy's eyes. His camera shutter snaps as he takes a picture. It won't sell—who wants a picture of a puddle?—but it captures something about this place. The sky, the earth, the colors—maybe it's because he's from here, but there's nothing like an African sky to make him feel connected to everything. Everything that matters, at least.

The hum of an engine drifts in on the cool breeze. Percy's knees pop as he stands from his crouch in front of the puddle. He's feeling every one of his thirty-two years lately. It's going to be hell when he's actually old, but he'll keep coming to the bush until he literally can't. They'll have to drag him away.

No, scratch that—just let the hyenas and the jackals have him. Back to the land, or something. When he tells his friends he'd rather be eaten by scavengers, they either laugh like he's joking or look horrified. But if he says he wants to be part of the landscape he loves, that lives inside his soul, for eternity, then they look at him like he's mad. Maybe a bit happy clappy.

A Land Cruiser comes into view, bumping along the rutted road. Less road, more track. This is the part of the reserve set aside for conservation, so the roads are nearly nonexistent.

Percy shifts his camera and his rifle on his shoulder and watches the vehicle's approach. Its occupants resolve into two figures, driver and passenger. He hooks his fingers into his water bottle and pulls it out of his backpack, twisting the cap off to take a long drink.

The Land Cruiser pulls up in a cloud of dust and a man jumps out. It's one of those quintessential safari moments. Percy thinks about snapping a photo but doesn't. The man lifts out a pack and swings it onto his back, thumps the side of the Land Cruiser, and heads Percy's way. Percy lifts his hand in a wave to the driver—it's Rhys, who cheerfully offers to sleep with Percy every time Percy's here (and just as cheerfully accepts the rejection)—then turns it to a thumbs-up. The Land Cruiser reverses, turns around, and is gone, leaving dust and the growl of its engine behind. Both settle to nothing as the man jogs across a gully with a trickle of water at the bottom.

Percy shoves his water bottle back into its pocket, considers smiling, and decides against it. Smiling doesn't come easily these days, and he's awkward enough without his weird hostage-situation rictus.

Midday sun glints off the silver in the man's hair. The contrast between the silver and the black of the rest of it is as stark as the sky against the ground. It would make a nice photo. The silver is premature— this man is surely around Percy's own age, maybe even a year or two younger. It's odd having seen someone's CV and knowing when they finished university, and by extension how old they are, but not having met the person yet.

As the man gets close, he extends a hand. "Hey there. I'm Rob. You must be Percy de Villiers."

Rob Hale's—he pronounces it Ha-lay, which is something Percy is determined to get right—easy grin makes it difficult not to like him immediately. The grin, plus the shadow of stubble on his jaw, plus his golden skin and the beachy wave to his salt and pepper hair, also makes it difficult not to find him attractive, which is sort of the last thing Percy needs.

"Yeah," Percy says, shaking Rob's hand. He watches for the flicker of reaction at his limp handshake. The bush is for the man's man, and Percy has been around enough men overflowing with misplaced machismo to last a lifetime.

Rob doesn't react. "It's great to finally meet you," he says in an indeterminate American drawl that might be southern. There's a little gravel to his voice. He's shorter than Percy, but most people are. Some sort of Dutch gene for height was hiding in his mixed-up family tree and came out of hiding when he hit puberty. Rob is solid, too, almost stocky. Muscular. With a beard, he'd make a great bear. He's dressed appropriately for South Africa in late fall: brown khakis, gray t-shirt, green hoodie tied around his waist.

Percy casts a critical eye over Rob's pack, but it looks good. Compact, with the bedroll secured at the bottom. Percy has the tent— only one—strapped on his own pack. For safety's sake, he wanted them sleeping in the same tent, because that way Percy will wake up if Rob decides he wants to go on a late night bush walk.

Hint: this is a bad idea.

"Listen," Rob says, "I want to start out by thanking you for letting me come with you. I know you had a lot of journalists submit applications, so it's really an honor to be selected."

God, Percy *hates* this sort of fawning. But Rob is right that a load of journos wanted this tag-along. What Rob doesn't know is that he only got the gig by the skin of his teeth. Percy's agent, Eunice, lobbied hard for a big-shot French nature writer, but Percy dug his heels in. He wanted Rob, and he's not sure he could even tell you why. His credentials aren't anything special and he's never had a piece blow up. His blog does middling numbers. On the surface of things, he's an entirely average travel writer.

"Thank you for accepting the offer," Percy says. Can't go wrong with platitudes, yeah? "How was the trip in?"

"We had to stop and wait for elephants to cross the road!" The pure glee in Rob's voice makes Percy smile.

"Ellies are still hanging round the main fence then, yeah?" The camera bumps against Percy's hip. "They were there when I drove up the other day, too."

Percy could never be in the hospitality industry—and safari camps are a whole other level of hospitality. But the wonder on Rob's face gives Percy an inkling of why people do it. And he can tell that Rob is the kind of person who makes it worth it.

Something eases in his chest. This whole thing has been so stressful, even though it was his idea in the first place. The endless second-guessing about his choice has plagued Percy ever since Rob signed the contract. He hasn't had a solid six hours of sleep in months. Then again, he's got plenty to lose sleep over, so.

"I love it here already," Rob says.

"Your first time in Africa?"

"I went to Morocco once to write a piece on Moroccan leather work," he offers. "But sub-Saharan Africa, yeah. First time."

"You like it so far?"

Rob rakes his fingers through his shaggy black hair. "Honestly, I went straight from the airport to my hotel, and my transfer picked me up this morning and drove me up here. So I kind of feel like I've barely seen any of it so far."

Yeah, Americans don't tend to stop and play tourist in Joburg. Percy's usually torn between pride in his country and complete and total agreement on that score.

"Well," Percy says, "hopefully you got to stop at the lodge for some lunch before Rhys brought you out here."

Rob's eyes light up again—and again, Percy is struck by how good-looking he is. Obviously, Percy did some light online stalking of all the serious candidates, but he doesn't remember thinking Rob was anything special. Turns out, he was very, very wrong about that, because Rob is dead fit.

"Yeah!" Rob replies. "Wow. It's gorgeous, isn't it? Have you stayed there?"

Percy nods. "The camp manager is a friend." Sort of an understatement. Katlego is the reason Percy made it out of childhood with his sanity intact. Intact-ish. She was his governess's daughter, and they were basically raised together. Katli is more like a sister than a friend. "You're staying a few nights after we're back from the bush, right?"

There's that easy grin again. "Are you kidding? That's definitely not the kind of place I can afford normally. I'm taking the chance to stay in the lap of luxury."

Percy's bankrolling this whole thing. He sees it as an excellent use of family funds. Doubtless his father would disagree, but his father has rather worn through his credibility where it comes to the proper use of money.

"Good," Percy says. He's itching to get out into the bush. His camera is loaded up with two blank memory cards, he has his other lenses snugged in the custom pocket in his pack, and he can tell the light's going to get better and better as the day goes on.

He clears his throat."So. I know you signed all the waivers and release forms—"

"Yeah, if a lion eats me, my family won't sue."

With a snort, Percy goes on, "We have to go over some rules, though. Mainly one, really—the rest are all sub-rules of that." He pauses to make sure he has Rob's attention. "You must, at all times, do what I say. If I say stop, you stop. If I say go, you go. If I say climb that tree, you climb the tree. If I say run—and you better hope I don't say 'run'—then you run. Also, my rifle is off-limits."

Rob nods. "Understood. You're the expert."

Sometimes people say that, and they're patronizing him. It doesn't matter how many awards he's won, how many back country or bush or mountain treks he goes on. Some people hear de Villiers, and all they can see is a pampered, rich Cape Coloured kid. Never mind that he's got an Apprentice Field Guide qualification, and that includes the four hundred required hours. To plenty of South Africans, Percy is always going to be rooftop infinity pools, manicured gardens, eight beds/eight baths, and so far removed from the way most South Africans live that it's a joke.

Not that having the NQF2 is exactly a window into how most South Africans live, but, well—he did that on his own, and no amount of money or family connections could buy it. It's one of his proudest achievements.

It's also the only reason he can be out here in the bush with, as far as insurance is concerned, a tourist.

"My job isn't just taking nature photos this week." Percy gives Rob a serious look. "It's keeping you safe. Just because your family won't sue me if a lion eats you doesn't mean it's a good look."

Rob holds his hands up. "Sure. You have a reputation to consider. I get it."

Percy's shoulders tighten and he can't help the twitch of tension. 'Yeah, right. My reputation. That's the idea behind all of this—get the focus back on my work, instead of"—he grimaces—"my personal life."

There's a sympathetic light in Rob's eyes, but Percy seriously doubts he has any real idea of what Percy's gone through the past few months. Which—ugh—sounds so whinging, so poor little rich boy. Other people have it worse. Obviously. So much worse. In fact, Percy feels responsible for a lot of that so-much-worse.

"I'm here to focus on your work," Rob says, before adding with a half smile, "And to not get eaten by a lion."

Oh *no*. He's this good-looking and he has a sense of humor?

Percy shifts his pack on his shoulders and steadies his camera and rifle. "Any questions before we start? Concerns I can alleviate?"

"Isn't bringing a healthy level of concern into the bush the right way to approach this?" That half smile flits across Rob's face again, a flash of crooked front teeth that Percy didn't think Americans were allowed to have.

It's impossible—literally impossible—not to return the smile. And that's red flags across the board, alarms and red alerts, all hands on deck level, *do not get this way with the journo you handpicked for this excursion.*

"I think we're going to get along," Percy says. He swigs from his water bottle and offers it to Rob, who takes it without any hesitation and drinks. "We walk single file. Keep your voice down and stay close to me so we don't look like something big and easy to pounce on."

Rob nods. Percy surveys their surroundings once more. There's nothing but birdsong and the occasional buzz of the insects that survive South Africa's fall and winter.

With a quick hand signal to indicate the direction they'll start off in, Percy takes the first long stride that will take them into the bush.

This had better all be worth it.

LEE PINI is a queer author who has been writing since they could pick up a pencil. They have lived in England, Northern Ireland, and Florida, and currently live in their home state of Minnesota with their wife and cat. Lee studied archaeology at the graduate level but currently uses their degree primarily to chuckle knowingly at classics memes. When they aren't at their day job or writing, they're reading vociferously, listening to music, enjoying nature, or nerding out. Their dream is for someone to one day write fanfiction about their characters.

The Boyfriend Fix

LEE PINI

Renowned surgeon Ben McNatt is up for the job of his dreams, and when he gets it, he'll be the youngest chief of neurosurgery in his hospital's history. His success rate is flawless, but his perceived lack of compassion is hurting his chances. He's always viewed relationships as a distraction, but a loving partner might change his colleagues' ideas about his heartlessness. He'll do whatever it takes for this promotion—even pretend to date. The natural choice for his fake boyfriend is the cute guy at the coffee shop.

Jamie Anderson is in student loan debt up to his eyeballs. He has three roommates, and not in a quirky found-family way. He works sixty hours a week as a barista, and his boss won't stop hitting on him. He's even given up on love. He makes do with fantasies about the hot doctor that comes in for coffee every day like clockwork.

A fake relationship might solve Jamie's handsy boss problem too. And there's no way it will lead to real feelings when that's the last thing either of them wants.

So why are they having so much trouble convincing themselves they aren't falling for each other?

Scan the QR code below to order

In a last-ditch effort to finish a manuscript, Thomas Kovacs packs up his teenage daughter, Alexis, and relocates to a small town in northern England. Things have been strained between them for months, but the closer Thomas gets to the end of his book, the more distant Alexis becomes.

Krishna Singh came to Corbridge to open a bookstore and start a family. After two years, his business is thriving. His family? Well, he hasn't gotten around to that yet. Actually, he hasn't even dated. The closest he gets is bonding over books and music with an American teenager who comes into his shop.

When it turns out the teenager's dad is none other than Krishna's favorite author, he wastes no time in getting to know Thomas. But attempts at something more go about as well as Thomas's writing, or his relationship with Alexis. Can Krishna convince Thomas that they all deserve a happy-ever-after?

Scan the QR code below to order

When We
Finally Kiss
Good Night

LEE PINI

Jake lost his Christmas spirit when his husband left him on December 26. This year, when a friend offers him her reservation at a resort in Florida, he jumps at the chance to get away. No snow, no Christmas trees, no problems.

Except the resort does a Christmas Golf Cart parade every year, and Alex, the man in the neighboring cabin, wants Jake's help with his.

Jake just wants to be left alone... until he spies Alex's design. Maybe working together won't be so bad. Can an unexpected friendship reawaken more than Jake's holiday spirit?

Scan the QR code below to order